MW00462863

EUROPA DEEP

GARY GIBSON

Brain in a Jar
BOOKS

First Published by Brain in a Jar Books 2023

First Edition.

ISBN 978-986-06770-4-1   (Paperback)

ISBN 978-986-06770-5-8   (Hardback)

Illustration © Tom Edwards

TomEdwardsDesign.com

This book primarily uses English (UK) spelling.

❀ Created with Vellum

CHAPTER 1
SUBSTITUTES

Once she felt Earth's gravity loosen its grip on her bones and muscles, the thunderous roar of lift-off dropping to a steady bass rumble, Sally Braemar glanced out of the suborbital's tiny window to see a broad arc of greens and blues spread out beneath a dome of perfect black.

They were still only a few minutes out from Seoul, and already she could make out the coast of Japan through the cloud cover, nearly a hundred kilometres beneath her feet.

Rare moments like this—when Earth's grip on her body dropped away to almost nothing—were always to be savoured. All Sally wanted to do was stretch her legs and stare out the window at the curve of the planet below her, knowing it would feel like no time had passed before they began their descent into hot and humid Florida half a world away.

Jeff Holland, unfortunately, had other ideas. The moment the seat-belt sign changed, he unbuckled and reached for his flimsy.

"This might be our last chance to talk in private for a while," he said, unrolling the flexible plastic and giving it a brief shake so that it snapped into rigidity. Lines of text and images appeared on its screen as he laid it across his lap. "The latest intel shows significant developments in just the last couple of hours."

"Look at that view," said Sally, her gaze still fixed on the world turning beneath them. She always took a window seat on suborbital flights. "Isn't it a marvel?"

Holland responded with only a slight twist of his lips. He always seemed happiest with an aisle seat. Apart from the flight crew, they were the only passengers.

"Sure," he said, "but this is important too." Tables of information scrolled across the screen when he tapped an icon.

"What is that?" Reaching over, Sally turned the device towards her, so she could get a better view. "And all of this is up-to-date information?"

Holland nodded. "News of another launch came in just before we took off. That's six unmanned cargo resupply drones taken off from Hainan in the last few days, all headed for the New Chinese Republic's Von Karman base." He paused for effect. "No mention of why they need extra supply runs."

"Okay," she said. "So, do we have any idea what the shipments might really be for?"

He raised one shoulder in a shrug. "Donaldson's our embassy contact. Do you know if he's heard anything out of the Summer Palace?"

Sally glanced up front to where a flight attendant, wearing a dark blue uniform, had emerged from the pilot's cabin. The woman overshot the galley, only managing to stop her wayward flight by quickly reaching out and grabbing hold of a bulkhead.

This naturally drew Sally's attention. By now, she'd flown suborbital enough times that she'd come to know a few of the attendants by name. Most were seconded to the agency from the military and, in some cases, could take over from the pilot in an emergency. Few had less than a hundred hours of experience in LEO. But if she hadn't known better, she'd have thought this attendant was entirely new to suborbital flight.

Or perhaps they were having a bad day or suffering a hangover following a layover. Hardly professional, thought Sally. But not unprecedented.

A childhood memory came to her just then, of her mother gripping the armrests aboard a commercial jet en route from Fort Worth to San Francisco to visit Uncle Dan. Right from the moment the plane lifted off the tarmac, to the moment it taxied to a halt at SF International, Frances Braemar had maintained a death grip on the armrests of her seat, as if by doing so she could keep the jet and everyone on board from falling out the sky.

After their visit was over, and even though it meant she wouldn't get a refund on their return flight, her mother had loaded Sally and her brother into a rented car before driving back home cross-country, seemingly not caring that the trip took so long she missed a deadline in her freelance video editing work.

And yet, Sally had loved that first experience of flying. For the longest time, suborbital flights had been the closest she got to orbit, and she'd loved every one of them.

What would Holland have thought of her, she wondered, if he'd known that on the rare occasions Sally flew alone, she'd release her seat belt to float down the length of the cabin?

Maybe he'd approve, given their upcoming assignment. So far, she'd logged thirty hours aboard the agency's LEO training facility, and a three-month security shift at the tiny US research outpost at Mare Imbrium—

"Sally?"

Sally blinked and shifted her attention back to Holland, who was still waiting for an answer.

"Sorry," she said, a touch sheepishly. "Nothing but rumours out of the Summer Palace. No sign of any official announcements coming down the pipeline either." She shrugged. "That could be a sign in itself. Whenever the Summer Palace locks down tight like this, it's usually right before something big."

Holland nodded, finally letting his gaze slide past her to focus on the black expanse of space outside the window. "So all we can do is wait and see what they do next."

"Except," Sally pointed out, "everything we *do* know indicates that the Summer Palace is strongly focused on Jupiter. And where else would the Tianjin be going, if not there?"

"But we still don't have solid evidence of the Palace's intentions," Holland reminded her. "And this administration doesn't like uncertainties. Uncertainties lead to budgetary questions, and budgetary questions lead to oversight committees demanding information the agency can't supply without risking operational security. Such as, why it's inserting government agents into a commercial deep space operation."

"Just the kind of thing to get those old-time Republicans *really* riled up, huh?" Cassie offered.

Holland smiled, a little more genuinely this time. "I reminded them we're just a backup plan," said Holland. "Someone to keep an eye on the Tianjin in case we're right about the NCR's intentions."

"I still think the crew should have been told about us," she said. Glancing out the window, she saw stripes of white cloud high above the Pacific. "Imagine waking up a couple of billion kilometres from home and finding two strangers had come along for the ride." She glanced sideways at Holland. "We'll need them to trust us."

"We'll work on that when we get there," Holland said gruffly. He glanced back down at his flimsy. "Says here the Tianjin's fitted with a next generation nuclear thermal propulsion system. If that's true, they might get to Jupiter before us."

Sally, however, wasn't giving him her full attention. The flight attendant had reappeared from inside the galley and was now manoeuvring her way down the length of the cabin towards them. Only at the last second, as the woman came abreast of Holland, did Sally see she was holding something in one palm.

Before she could react, the attendant had pressed the object against Holland's chest, her knuckles whitening as she squeezed.

Sally heard a muffled thump, like a hammer wrapped in cloth hitting an anvil.

Holland, who had just looked around at the attendant that moment, jerked spasmodically. He looked surprised, as if he'd only then remembered something important, his mouth opening and closing and his hands grasping at his armrests like he meant to push himself out of his seat.

Then his eyes rolled up, his arms swinging loose in the zero gravity.

The attendant had meanwhile failed to compensate for the kick from her weapon: the shot that killed Sally's boss sent the other woman careening backwards across the cabin. The attendant flailed wildly, then got hold of the back of a seat to reorient herself.

By then, Sally was already in motion. The suborbital had dipped back down towards the atmosphere, and she knew she had perhaps seconds before gravity reasserted itself.

In the meantime, she had something the other woman clearly didn't have—hours of combat training in zero gravity.

Pushing up with her heels, Sally flew up and out of her seat, stopping herself against the cabin roof with both hands. Then, bracing her feet against the back of her seat, she prepared to launch herself towards the attendant.

She'd studied a dozen different ways she could kill an armed combatant in zero-gravity.

Before she could do that, however, a thousand tiny knives pierced her chest and lungs.

The cabin spun around Sally, and she glimpsed a second

figure, close to the open door of the cockpit: the pilot. He held a second gun in a two-handed grip, his back pressed against the compartment wall to keep from being thrown back by the recoil.

For one fleeting moment, Sally was back in her weapons instructor's class, listening as he detailed the carnage that could be wreaked by smart bullets armed with lead azide cores. Illegal as hell, given their ability to seek out and shred a target's internal organs, but a guaranteed kill at any range.

And she'd just been shot with one.

Sally opened her mouth to say something, but could draw no air from her lacerated lungs. The sun flashed through a window across the cabin, and as her body turned in a slow somersault, her vision filled with a black deeper than any she had seen through a suborbital window.

———

"YOU WAITED TOO LONG," the pilot groused as he helped pull the dead woman's body down onto the floor of the cabin. "You should have killed them as soon as we lifted off, not mid-fucking-flight."

The pilot was about the same height and build as the man his partner had killed. An operation had altered the pigmentation of his hair follicles to more closely match that of Jeff Holland.

"Stop complaining," the attendant snapped. "And check what's in his briefcase. You remember your name?"

"Jeff Holland," he said, looking almost hurt. "I'm insulted at the implication I'd forget."

Working with practiced speed, they zipped the dead woman's body inside one of a pair of lightweight waterproof sacks the pilot had brought out of the cockpit, then did the same for her boss.

Finally, they strapped the bagged bodies back into their

seats. The man who would take Holland's identity returned to the cockpit and requested an emergency landing at Anchorage due to suspected engine failure.

The attendant, meanwhile, strapped herself into a cabin seat and quickly ran through a mental checklist of everything she knew about Sally Braemar. The suborbital's nose dipped further, slicing through the troposphere on a silent, battery-powered descent.

————

As soon as they taxied to a halt on a private airstrip near Anchorage, the waiting cleanup crew boarded the jet and got to work, cramming the bodies inside a single, oversized flight case.

Unfortunately, the two bodies didn't quite fit, and so they were forced to waste extra time removing the bodies from their bags so that their arms and legs could be broken.

This done, both bodies finally fit inside the flight case.

Even taking that snafu into account, thought the attendant, things had gone smoothly; the original attendant had been given emergency leave to attend to a sick and dying relative in Maine, while her accomplice—who, from now on, would be known to her only as Jeff Holland—had his own cover story.

Most of a decade from now, when they returned home to Earth, she might resume her former identity. Or she might find another: she would have to see. Either way, she'd be compensated well enough to buy her own private island if she wanted.

And she'd never have to take on another assignment ever again.

The woman who now called herself Sally Braemar watched as they wheeled the flight case into a waiting truck. Two of the cleanup crew, a man and a woman, remained behind, changing into the attendant and pilot's uniforms. Sally Braemar and Jeff Holland, as they were now known, changed into dark suits more or less identical to those worn by the two dead agents.

Less than an hour later, they touched down again, this time at Valkaria Airport on Florida's east coast.

As they disembarked, the new Sally Braemar saw a car parked close by the runway. Its dark paint job and tinted windows made it a dead giveaway for an agency ride. Next to it stood a young-looking agent with a round face and dark, close-cut hair, and as they disembarked, he walked across the tarmac to greet them.

The attendant stiffened, thinking of the many, many things that could still go wrong. What if this man had known the real Sally Braemar and Jeff Holland?

A quick glance around revealed no witnesses—none she could see, at least. But if they were forced to kill the agent, there was a risk they might have no choice but to abort.

The young agent took off his sunglasses and squinted at each of them. "Agents Holland and Braemar?" He extended a friendly hand. "Art Ramirez. I'm your liaison here. I heard you had a problem. Nothing bad, I hope?"

The attendant took his hand first, shaking it. "False alarm," she said. "But they still made us stop over all the way up in Alaska."

"Alaska! Jesus." He shook his head, nothing in his gaze suggesting he thought they were anything other than the people he had been sent to meet. "Of all the things. Anyway, I'm to give you your final briefing prior to launch," he continued, "and I'm sorry it has to be at such short notice." He looked between them. "Hey, I heard a rumour the reason the Chinese are interested in Jupiter has something to do with the old Europa Deep expedition. You know anything about that?"

A muscle twitched in one of Holland's imposter's cheeks. "We can't divulge that," he told Ramirez. "Sorry."

Ramirez grinned and raised a hand in apology. "Didn't mean to pry. Just curious." He indicated his car behind him. "I've got orders to drive you directly to the launch site."

———

"COMMANDER JAVIER HAS the last word as far as the science side of things goes," Ramirez explained as he drove. He kept one hand on the steering wheel, glancing occasionally at them in the rearview mirror. They had both sat in the back. "But when we briefed him, we made it clear you have authority if there's a threat of conflict between his mission and any NCR ships in Jovian space."

The man who was now Holland turned from where he had been looking out at the old NASA Shuttle facility close by the sea. "How did Javier take that?" he asked carefully. "Or the people backing the new expedition, for that matter?"

Ramirez waggled the fingers of one hand in a *so-so* gesture. "The consortium funding the expedition knows they can't fuck with the US government. Not if they want to use launch facilities inside our borders. And Javier's psych profile shows he always follows orders. Even ones he doesn't like."

Fake-Holland nodded and suppressed a smile. *If only you knew.* "You're sure about that?" he asked.

"It's been made clear to him," said Ramirez, "that if the Chinese become aggressive, *assuming* they turn up at Jupiter, you'll have the authority to assume full control of the Veles. He won't like it, but he'll do what he's told. And that's all that matters."

"Define 'aggressive'," asked fake-Sally Braemar.

"We absolutely cannot allow NCR ships to land on Europa," said Ramirez. "At least, not before the crew of the Veles establishes control of Station Verne on the surface. Otherwise, we risk entirely ceding control of Europa to them."

"If they tried to do that," said Holland, "they'd be contravening every space treaty going."

Ramirez laughed. "Like that ever stopped us, or anyone else." He glanced at them again in the rearview mirror. "You testing me? You know all of this already, right?"

"Of course," said Braemar. She slid one hand over Holland's before it could move towards the pistol holstered under his jacket. Ramirez remained oblivious, his attention having shifted back to the road.

Ramirez guided the car onto an offramp. Soon, they pulled up at a security gate outside a private spaceport owned by LRG, the conglomerate responsible for most of Europa Deep II's funding. Large black letters on a free-standing concrete wall next to the gate spelled out the company's acronym, but when she squinted, Sally—as she now was—could just make out the outline of the old SpaceX logo underneath, like the lingering memory of a bad hangover.

The breath caught in her throat as the security guard took their IDs, checking them against records displayed on the computer screen inside his booth.

"There you go," said the guard, handing them their IDs back through the open window.

Sally breathed out: she hadn't exhaled for what had felt like a solid minute. Whoever was working for them inside the agency had done their job well.

A gantry stood some distance away, hazy with late afternoon heat shimmer. It supported the lower stage of a multipurpose heavy launcher. Slightly further away stood a single, enormous hangar that dominated everything around it.

"Is launch still set for a week from now?" Holland asked Ramirez, as he drove them over to the main building.

"It is," Ramirez confirmed. "The man in charge of your quarantine and medical monitoring is a Doctor Chou. You should find him waiting for you inside. He's liaising with the team who'll prep you for cryo prior to launch."

This was something new. "Prior to launch?" Sally asked, leaning forward. "How come?"

"The safety margin for cryo is ninety-eight per cent and up," said Ramirez, pulling to a halt outside the main building, "but the mission's insurers want you and everyone else on the crew put into deep freeze here on the ground, so they can watch for potential problems rather than risk having to deal with them once you're in orbit. Not," he added with a grin, "that there'll be any. Once your signs are stable, they'll ship you up to the Veles like cargo and the next thing you know, you'll wake up a couple of million miles from Earth and in time for your first outward-bound maintenance shift."

Soon enough, Ramirez departed with a wave through his windscreen. Braemar and Holland, as they now were, exchanged a single nod, then stepped into the cool interior of the main building.

A man she assumed must be Doctor Chou, who had been standing next to a reception desk, stepped towards them. He was tall and lithe, with an open and friendly face.

Until now, fake-Braemar hadn't really believed they'd pull this off. And in truth, a million more things could go wrong between now and when they emerged from their cryo pods far out in interplanetary space.

Then again, she thought, smiling quietly to herself, even if they had to kill everyone else on board the ship, at least then they could get on with their work uninterrupted.

Seven thousand metres below the surface of the Western Pacific Ocean, Cassie White watched as several ghost-white snailfishes rapidly undulated down the sheer cliff-face on her right, over the boots of her armoured 'behemoth' diving suit, and straight over the ledge on which she stood.

They were there and gone in a flash, darting in and out of the twin beams of her helmet lamps.

The servos of her behemoth suit whined faintly as she turned to look back the way they had come, thinking she knew what might have spooked the creatures. Past the ledge lay a watery void that ended four thousand metres further down at the bottom of the Mariana Trench, where the water pressure was more than a thousand times the atmospheric pressure back up on the surface: more than enough to crush an unprotected human into toothpaste in the blink of an eye.

Not that this prevented Cassie from sometimes venturing into such depths when required. Her suit, constructed from ultra-strong composite materials, was built to maintain an internal air pressure equivalent to sea level back on Earth, allowing her to ascend or descend at will without having to worry about the bends.

Shuffling closer to the edge, Cassie peered down into the

abyss. Her quarter-ton suit might be the most advanced diving technology the late 21st Century could provide, but it still felt cumbersome and restrictive.

Far down in the crushing depths, she fancied she could glimpse the distant red glow of a hydrothermal vent. But it was most likely her imagination. Other than the snailfish, few things could live at depths of eleven thousand metres, and until just a few decades before, barely a dozen people in all had travelled to the deepest parts of the Trench.

That was a long way from being the case these days.

"Cassie?" Molyneux's voice sounded loud and flat in her right ear. "You're a little close to that ledge. Careful you don't lose your footing. Any sign of the target? Over."

Not that she felt in any real danger: her suit's jets were powerful enough to propel her back onto solid ground should she lose her footing, but it was far safer, at such depths, to conserve power whenever possible.

Molyneux had sounded as clear as if he'd been standing right next to her instead of aboard a support ship on the surface. Ordinary radio communications being impossible in salt water, until recently, they had relied on sonar-based radio. Unfortunately, not only had this proved unreliable, it was easy for pirate fleets, combing the seabed for rare earths and minerals, to intercept their comms.

More recently, the Joint EU-Australasia Oceanic Task Force had switched to communicating with Cassie and their other investigative divers via a surface buoy trailing a six-mile long cable dotted with laser transceivers lowered into the ocean depths. This allowed Cassie to maintain crystal-clear two-way communications via laser relay with the Deep Range, currently anchored several kilometres from her current position and a hundred kilometres east of Guam, so long as she remained in the line of sight of the lasers.

"Nothing yet," Cassie responded, stepping back from the ledge. "Just doing a little sightseeing. Over."

"Stay on course," Molyneux reminded her. "And stay in comms range. Sonar shows the factory heading straight towards you, but thirty metres higher than your current location. You'll need to move fast to intercept it. Over."

Cassie pushed a relief map of the Mariana Trench onto her HUD, revealing a deep knife wound slashed through the floor of the western Pacific Ocean, three hundred kilometres south-west of Guam. The Deep Range appeared as a glowing yellow dot. A dozen kilometres north-east of its position, a cluster of orange dots represented the New Chinese Republic pirate fleet they had been tracking for three days now.

Give or take a few metres in any direction, the fleet was right above Cassie's current position. Not that she would see anything by looking upwards, except a darkness so thick and tangible it felt alive.

Her dive lights showed the ledge merging with the cliff face just a few metres ahead of her: the only way left to go was up.

The environment beyond her visible range appeared on her HUD as a series of pale green contours laid over black, the lines clumping together at greater depths as the trench narrowed. If at that moment the ocean had suddenly become transparent, Cassie would find herself standing on a narrow ledge halfway up a valley slope with a three kilometre drop to her left. From bottom to top, that same valley was wide and deep enough to fit all of Mount Everest inside it.

Not that heights had ever bothered her, thanks to her optimized genetics. Even if they had, four years working in LEO and a couple of stints working lunar resupply would have cured her of any such fear.

Thinking of the Moon made her think of Sergio.

Bad thought, she chided herself, pushing the memory away. She had a job to do and needed a clear mind.

Ascending the cliff, even with the suit's jets to help her, proved sufficiently arduous that she soon felt as if she might actually drown in her own sweat. But the higher she ascended, the more she could feel the steady thrum of nearby machinery work its way up through her titanium and reinforced-carbon boots.

Excitement gripped Cassie, like a hunter peering through a rifle's sights as a deer wandered into view.

Gasping from the effort, Cassie hauled herself up and onto a broad rock shelf many times wider than the ledge from which she had ascended. Her lights revealed a mottled, almost lunar landscape of grey sand.

The thrum of machinery became deeper and more rhythmic, the lights of her suit revealing clouds of billowing sediment.

From out of these clouds emerged a robot factory the size of the drive-in diner she'd eaten lunch in for the best part of six years while growing up in California. It took up half of the rock shelf on which she now stood. The factory kept close to the cliff face, leaving plenty of room between it and Cassie, who remained close to the edge.

Switching over to sonar imaging revealed finer details. The factory resembled a warehouse mounted on top of threshing blades: these blades ground sand and rock into rubble, sucking it all into the factory's interior with the aid of high-powered pumps.

There, the factory would sift through the rock and sand for precious manganese nodules containing nickel, cobalt, and copper, and any number of rare earths essential to modern industry. In the meantime, its titanium and diamond rotors continued ripping up the seabed—causing irreversible damage to flora and fauna entirely unique to these depths.

No wonder the snailfish had fled.

Lifting her chin, Cassie focused her sonar on a point just above the factory. This revealed a snaking tube rising from its roof and out of sight.

To her surprise, the factory slowed, then changed direction, veering towards her and the precipice. She moved further along the rock shelf, watching as it paused, then re-oriented itself until it was again pointed straight at her.

Well, thought Cassie, her throat suddenly dry, *there's a new development*.

The factory didn't move fast, but she realized with a shock it had already blocked her from returning the way she had come. Of course, it might simply be acting in response to the algorithms programmed into its primitive AI; or, just maybe, someone aboard the NCR pirate fleet had spotted a sonar ping of her suit and deliberately steered the machine towards her.

After all, what was one dead investigative diver next to the endless mineral bounty of the deep ocean?

As she retreated from the advancing factory, Cassie glanced down past the edge of the rock shelf and into the murky depths below. If she was forced to descend again, she'd use up much of her suit's remaining power—and risk running out of air before she could get back to her mini-sub.

Cassie called the Deep Range and explained her situation. For the moment, at least, she was still in the direct line of sight of the comms cable. Whether that would remain the case was another matter.

"It's deliberate provocation," said Molyneux. It was easy to picture him hunched over a monitor on board the ship. "I'll radio the NCR fleet and tell them to desist immediately. Let's see Hu worm his way out of this one. Over."

Even walking backwards, Cassie could outpace the factory easily. It didn't move at much more than a slow walking pace. So far, she didn't feel threatened. Much.

"Can you patch me in so I can listen?" she asked. "Over."

She now tried moving the other way, back towards the cliff face. And, again, the factory corrected its course until it was once more pointed straight at her.

"Sure," Molyneux replied. "Give me a minute. Over."

Had the factory picked up speed, Cassie wondered, or was it her imagination?

A few seconds after stepping around a boulder that had been in her way, Cassie watched with fascination as the factory flowed over this obstruction like a robotic carpet monster. It was constructed, she saw now, from discrete parts that were linked in some fashion, a neat design modification that allowed it to navigate even the most volatile terrain.

Goddamnit, she thought: it *was* picking up speed.

Picking up her pace, Cassie tried to ignore the sudden rapid thrum of her heart. She listened as Molyneux radioed the Fu Yuan He, the lead vessel in the pirate fleet.

"Please respond," said Molyneux. "This is agent Alfred Molyneux of the Joint EU-Australasia Oceanic Task Force. Your ships are in violation of the 2035 international environmental preservation treaties and the terms of the 2090 Beijing conference. You are ordered to cease mining immediately and prepare for boarding by our agents, followed by a full inspection of your fleet. Failure to comply may result in the confiscation of your ships and the arrest of your senior crew under international law. Please respond. Over."

By now, the factory was moving fast enough that Cassie had to turn around and jog ahead of it to maintain her distance. Clouds of sand and black sediment billowed up around her suit, further obscuring her vision.

"Alfred?" The sound of her laboured breath filled her helmet. "Please tell them to call that thing off. It's getting too close for comfort. Over."

"They won't respond to my hail," Molyneux replied, his voice sounding hoarse. "The sons of bitches are ignoring me. Suggest you abort immediately. Over."

"Bonuses are up this year, right? And it's been months since we bagged one of these machines. Over."

"Cassie," said Molyneux, a warning in his voice. "That's no reason to take unnecessary—"

Bad idea or not, she muted the comms link so she could think.

Just the year before, an illegal factory a few dozen kilometres off the coast of Taiwan had sideswiped another diver. Although he'd survived, and the recovered factory used as evidence in a successful prosecution, severe concussion and oxygen depletion had put him in a wheelchair for months. There were rumours he still had problems feeding himself.

Not that any such thing would happen to her. Nosirree. She had plans for the bonus she'd receive if they could haul this factory back up to the surface as evidence.

As she retreated, the shelf shrank to barely two or three metres in width. The factory couldn't possibly navigate such a ridiculously narrow ledge, and whoever was in charge of the machine would surely give up their pursuit...?

Instead, the factory kept coming towards her without pause. It flowed onto the ledge in a seemingly relentless pursuit, tipping almost entirely onto one side so that its treads could grip the sheer cliff face on one side.

Under different circumstances, Cassie might have applauded.

Lacking any remaining options, Cassie hit the switch for her suit's jets. At least, once she'd climbed out of the thing's range—

Nothing happened.

Shit.

A half-choked scream of rage wormed its way up from deep inside her throat.

She started to ascend the cliff face, hand over hand—far from easy to do with both hands stuck inside enormous powered gloves, but she'd trained for moments like this. And the servos did most of the work.

A foothold gave way, and she dropped, arms flailing, onto the sharply tilted roof of the factory.

Instantly, the factory came to a halt. Cassie slid, screaming, down the angled roof towards the waiting abyss.

By some dint of enormous luck, she snagged a rung on the factory's roof, something that the divers who had assembled it in shallower waters had probably used.

Gripping the rung tightly, the factory's outer plates shifting and moving beneath her, she glimpsed the whirling machinery deep inside.

Looking around in desperation, Cassie's lights revealed the flexible tube that connected the factory to the pirate fleet on the ocean surface—and an idea came to her.

Edging closer to the locking mechanism that connected the tube to the factory, Cassie watched as the tube flexed and twisted, siphoning up tons of rubble. Then, at last, she saw what she was looking for: a lever.

Cassie reached for the lever with her one free hand and missed the first three times. The fourth attempt proved to be the winning try. When she yanked on the lever, the cable came loose, and rubble and dirt spewed out from the factory's interior. The tube's lower end meanwhile whipped out of sight.

Cassie leapt upwards. Despite the failure of her pressurized jets, her suit still had enough juice in its servos that she could jump several metres up from the roof of the factory. Reaching out, she grabbed hold of a rocky protrusion jutting out from the face of the cliff and held on for her life, feeling like the effort had knocked all the wind out of her.

The sudden release of the debris tube had caused the factory to tip over too far. Its lower treads lost their grip on the ledge, and Cassie watched in numb amazement as the machine slid into the abyss, tumbling end over end and out of sight.

Well, thought Cassie, breathing hard, *there goes my bonus.*

She almost laughed, but found herself choking back tears instead. *The sons of bitches tried to kill me.*

That had never happened before.

She clung on for another few minutes until her heart rate slowed, and then she climbed slowly back down.

Any day that doesn't end with you crushed into toothpaste is a good day, Cassie reminded herself, trudging back towards her mini-sub most of a klick away.

Halfway there, she halted, her sonar picking up something long and sinuous, whipping through the deep water. At first, her senses interpreted it as a creature—some impossibly long eel, chasing after the tumbling factory—then realized it must be the kilometres-long debris tube.

Hu was getting rid of any remaining evidence. After another few seconds, the entire tube had followed the factory into oblivion.

———

"BORDEL DE MERDE," said a deckhand, staring in shock at the external scarring on Cassie's behemoth suit. He turned his gaze toward her. "I'm amazed you came back alive."

"Sorry to disappoint you," said Cassie. She sprawled in a nearby deckchair, sucking down ice-cold water from a bottle marked with the Task Force's logo. Well-developed muscles stood out from under a sweat-stained t-shirt.

It was still hot, even with dusk approaching. The fading sun turned the clouds a deep orange-red towards the west. Between her and the bridge of the Deep Range lay a quarter-mile of deck.

Her behemoth suit stood upright before her on the fore-mast of the former container ship, held in place by a twist lock. A complex system of pulleys and cranes surrounded its vast and imposing bulk. Nearby, mounted on a cradle, her mini-sub—mostly a platform for carrying extra air and battery packs—underwent further checks by some of Molyneux's technicians.

The deckhand, who had his back to the sun, regarded her with a curious stare. "Your eyes," he said.

"What about them?"

Sometimes, thought Cassie, if she could ever get hold of the anonymous geneticist who'd given some Opts a silver tint to their eyes, she'd give them a good, hard slap across the face.

His expression became suddenly much less friendly. "You're one of them."

One of them.

She should ignore it. She knew she should: but her encounter with the robot factory had her wound up tighter than a nun's sphincter.

"One of what?" she enquired, her tone mild.

The deckhand's fists flexed at his sides. He'd realized he had stepped out of line.

"It's nothing," he mumbled, returning his attention to his maintenance work.

"I just want to know what *they* are," she asked regardless.

The deckhand continued tinkering with the suit's hydraulics, like he hadn't heard her. The set of his shoulders made it clear he had. Then, at last, he turned back to her, his eyes hooded, and his lip curled in disgust.

"In Nantes," he said, "one in ten caught the Whispers. I was in the hospital for two weeks. They said I nearly died. They had the entire city in lockdown. All the doctors wore hazmat suits." His nostrils flared. "Everyone except the ones in charge. They were…immune."

She nodded. "They were Opts, huh?"

"You're one, aren't you?" he demanded, his voice quivering. "Everyone says you people invented the Whispers to kill off us ordinary humans."

Where the hell, Cassie wondered, did these people come from?

"The Whispers is a war disease." She said it like she was

delivering a lecture: dry and flat. "It's got nothing to do with being optimized. That's some batshit conspiracy theory for idiots."

"So how come none of you people ever died from it?" he snapped. "How come none of you—?"

"Arnaud!"

Cassie swivelled her head around to see a squat, dark-skinned man approaching.

"Leave that," he said, pointing at the behemoth suit and glaring fixedly at the French kid. "Go find Al. Tell him to finish the diagnostics."

Arnaud blinked. "It'll only take me five—"

"*Now*," Riviera barked, stepping up close to the kid. "And once we get back to port in Guam, I want you off this ship."

Arnaud blanched and nodded, clearly chastened. He shot Cassie a last, dirty look as he stalked off across the deck.

Undoubtedly, she'd soon become the reason they had fired him from his job: one more reason to hate Opts.

Riviera, who oversaw dive operations from a control room just aft of the bridge, stared after the kid's retreating back. Then he turned to Cassie. "I caught the tail end of what he said," he said. "I'm sorry you had to put up with that."

Cassie felt some of her muscles unlock. She hadn't even realized she'd grown tense. "Don't worry about it," she mumbled.

Riviera rolled his shoulders. "It's my job to worry about it. Stupid little creep."

She sighed. "It's not the first time."

"I know." He nodded. "Sorry."

"What for?"

He nodded after the kid. "The recruitment agency is supposed to screen for stuff like this. I'll let Captain Molyneux know."

"He said I was to blame for the Whispers," she said wryly.

"Apparently, we're conspiring to wipe out ordinary humanity."

Riviera's face twisted up in confusion and horror. "What?"

She shrugged. "It's the kind of rubbish idiots talk about online when they run out of things to say to their VR sexbots."

Cassie stood, Riviera following her as she stepped towards a nearby cooler box and got more water, wishing it was beer. Part of her wanted to go find Arnaud and explain how the Whispers hadn't exactly been a joyride for her, either.

She looked at Riviera. "Did Molyneux have any more luck getting through to Hu?"

His mouth curled into a grimace. "None." His expression became more hopeful. "It's a shame we lost the factory," he said, "but did you get video we can use in court?"

"I don't know how good it'll be," she admitted. "The factory kicked up so much sediment, I'll be surprised if the cameras picked up anything admissible as evidence."

Riviera's face twisted in irritation. "Is the factory still down there, or did they cut and run?"

By this, Riviera meant, had the fleet owners cut the cable and abandoned the factory in order to deny responsibility?

"Depends on what you mean by cut and run," Cassie said.

Riviera's right eyebrow rose in a question.

"They tried to use the factory to kill me." She put up a hand when she saw Riviera open his mouth. "No, I can't prove it. But believe me, they did."

"You'll write all this in a report, of course."

"Of course." Not, she thought, that it would ever lead to charges. Not without overwhelming proof.

"We sent a couple of speedboats over to the ship we think was controlling the factory, along with a search warrant," said

Riviera. He shrugged. "Unfortunately, they found no hard evidence linking them to the factory."

She chuckled wryly. "Not even a hold full of manganese nodules?"

"Without a demonstrable and proven link to the factory itself, they can tie us up with legalities and counter-lawsuits until the sun turns cold. Could be, they ditched it all as soon as they saw us coming."

"Same as usual, then." Cassie found her attention drawn towards a helicopter with unfamiliar decals parked next to the Sikorsky used to ferry crew and supplies to and from the land. The two choppers stood near the bridge, far away across the vast expanse of deck.

Cassie nodded at the unfamiliar chopper. "Visitors?"

"That's why I came to find you," said Riviera, grinning his apology. "Someone's here to see you."

CHAPTER 3
THE VISITOR

Cassie found her visitor sitting alone at a conference table in a belowdecks briefing room, drinking coffee and watching one of the Task Force's promotional videos on a wall-mounted screen. He wore a dark suit, his grey hair neatly parted on one side and his complexion tanned. He might have been a retired TV weatherman, or the senior partner from a New York law firm with baseball players and movie stars for clients.

She recognized him immediately: William Ketteridge.

For a moment, she remained standing at the open door, her thoughts roiling with confusion. Ketteridge glanced up just then and nodded to her with a half–smile that could have been friendly or mocking.

Ketteridge stood. "Miss White. It's a pleasure to meet you." His accent carried just a hint of a Texan twang. "If you'd care to join me," he said, gesturing to a chair across the table from him, "I have a proposition for you."

Cassie stepped closer, but didn't sit down. "I'm sorry to be blunt," she said, "but whatever this is about, are you sure you've got the right person?"

A bowl placed at the centre of the conference table contained small rocks that glittered under the overhead lights: manganese nodules. As Ketteridge sat back down, he picked one up, turning it in his hand.

"I can see you know who I am," he said. "I'm really not the monster the press made me out to be."

Cassie stared at him. *No*, she wanted to say, *just the man who tried to take human rights away from Opts.*

"What do you want, Senator?" she asked instead.

"I'm not a Senator any more." He gestured again to the chair across from him. "Please."

This time, she sat down, but didn't hide her reluctance. "I haven't had a shower or eaten in about twelve hours," she said, her tone measured, "so I'd really appreciate it if you just told me what you want."

"I want to talk to you about your work here and also up there." He gestured at the ceiling with the hand holding the rock.

"I'm guessing you wouldn't be here," said Cassie, "unless you had a dossier an inch deep telling you everything you need to know about me."

Ketteridge chuckled like she'd made a joke. "Believe me," he said, "if there was any such thing, yours would be about a page long." He dropped the rock back into the bowl and leaned back, his arms crossed. "You ever think about going back?" He lifted his eyes towards the ceiling. "Into space?"

For a moment, Cassie couldn't quite believe what he'd just said. "Is that some kind of joke?"

"Well, let me rephrase it," said Ketteridge. "If you *could* go back, would you?"

Fuck it. First that idiot on the deck, and now this. It was enough to test anyone's patience.

"You tried to push a Bill through Congress that would have led to people like myself being locked up without charge," she said, voice heavy with accusation. "You know why I can't go back to my old job, so why waste my time?"

"It wasn't about locking anyone up," Ketteridge replied,

as if they were talking about nothing more significant than the weather. He shrugged good-naturedly. "There was a widespread concern that Opts might be unwitting vectors for the Whispers, so keeping tabs on all of you until we figured out how to contain a virus killing millions all around the world seemed like the sensible thing to do." He spread his hands in a vaguely apologetic gesture. "All terribly regrettable in hindsight, of course, but we were doing the best we could in a terrible situation."

"The best you—?" Cassie swallowed back her next words and stood again, pushing her chair aside and turning towards the door. She'd be damned if she'd spend any more time in this man's presence.

"How would you like," said Ketteridge, just as she reached for the door handle, "to join a new expedition to Europa?"

She turned to stare at him, mute, for several long seconds.

"I know some things about you, yes," Ketteridge admitted. "You blacked out piloting a lunar hopper and someone died. Then it turned out a few other of you genetically optimized people were suffering unpredictable blackouts, and that the episodes were triggered, or so I am informed, by low or zero-gravity conditions. Overnight, you and every Opt working in space found themselves out of a job, regardless of whether their genes contained that particular flaw or not." He spread his hands. "I'll be the first to agree how you've been treated is less than fair."

Immediately Cassie thought of Sergio, his eyes round and panicked and his mouth moving silently from behind his visor as the Moon swung wildly past the window of the hopper. Her hand stayed on the doorknob, but neither did she leave. Not yet.

"You trained for the first expedition," Ketteridge continued, "along with your brother Chris. He got on the crew, you didn't. Not because you weren't good enough, but because his seniority and experience, plus his specialisation in astrobiology and related fields, gave him an edge. Further, there's maybe a dozen people in the world, including yourself, who know how to pilot a behemoth suit in extreme pressure conditions, like the bottom of the Mariana Trench." He paused a moment. "Or the oceans of Europa, for that matter. And those suits were originally designed for use on Europa, weren't they?"

By some effort of will, Cassie made herself let go of the door handle.

"Nobody trusts Opts anymore," she said. "And especially not in space. Even if they let us back up there."

"The blackouts, as I'm sure you know, are treatable these days." Seeing she was about to speak, he put up a hand. "And very expensive treatments, yes, I'm aware. But that's something you wouldn't have to worry about."

"I'd heard there were plans for another expedition," Cassie said. "But that's not for at least another couple of—"

"Plans change," Ketteridge said dryly. "The Veles has been fully refurbished and brought up to date. It leaves Earth's orbit in less than a week. If you agree to my proposal, you'd need to be prepped for cryo well before the launch."

Cassie sucked in air, failing to hide her shock. "Less than a *week*? That's hardly enough time for me to train—"

"You trained for the first expedition," said Ketteridge. "You're familiar with the layout of the Veles and the original mission parameters."

Yes, thought Cassie. *But that was fifteen years ago.* "Why the rush?"

He tapped at a stylish-looking flimsy he wore on one wrist, then nodded at the wall-screen. "Look at this."

An image of streaked white and grey appeared on the screen. Cassie recognized it immediately as a satellite view of Europa's surface. Station Verne was just discernible as a cluster of crescent shadows on a relatively flat and smooth expanse of ice. A red arrow marked the location of the borehole station a dozen kilometres to the west of Verne.

At first, Cassie thought she was seeing a still image, but then a tiny black dot moved jerkily across the grey-white expanse, starting from the borehole station and heading towards Station Verne. The arrow moved to follow the dot as it crossed the ice.

"This is a time-lapse video, by the way," Ketteridge pointed out. "We stitched it together from separate satellite images gathered over a fourteen-hour period."

After another minute, the cluster of pixels reached Station Verne and disappeared, the arrow fading. As if, she thought, a chill rushing down her spine, someone had gone for a stroll across the irradiated and airless ice.

"When is this from?" she asked, looking back at Ketteridge.

"Six months ago."

At first, Cassie thought she hadn't heard him right. "That's impossible. It's been years since the first expedition disappeared. There can't be anyone there, unless..."

Unless someone survived.

Just like that, she remembered Chris on the day he found out they had selected him for the crew. As hard as she'd worked to be on board, she'd always known his greater experience—not least because he was older—gave him an immense advantage.

Cassie swallowed, the thunder of her heart loud enough she wondered how Ketteridge couldn't hear it. "So someone's still alive out there? Is that what you're here to tell me?"

"The only way to know is to go find out," said Ketteridge.

"But...why all this subterfuge, flying out to the middle of the ocean like this?"

"Because officially I was never here," said Ketteridge.

"And we never had this conversation. If we send you there, it's because we want something from you in return."

Cassie wondered who *we* meant. "Go on."

"Officially, this new expedition has the same aim as the original: research and exploration. But," Ketteridge continued, clasping his hands on the table before him, "we have evidence the NCR is about to launch an expedition of its own to Europa. If they land first and gain access to the stations established there by the first expedition, they'd get their hands on reams of classified data. Some of it highly sensitive."

"If they're launching after us, how are they going to get there first?"

"They're testing out their new nuclear propulsion system," said Ketteridge. "If it works as well as advertised, they could beat the Veles by anything from a few days to a couple of weeks. We also have good reason to believe they intend to lay claim to Europa in the long term."

"Why would they do that?"

"The NCR understands the limitless scientific and commercial value of an entire ocean full of non-terrestrial microbial life. If they control Europa, they control access to its oceans."

Cassie regarded him for a long moment. "And where exactly do I come in?"

Ketteridge nodded. "There's another factor, not known to the public. We believe one or more of the first expedition crew were secretly funnelling their research into bio-weapons development. We can't prove it yet, but it's possible they were working for a private defence contractor based out of the Caymans called Devore Biotech. They have links to members of the Chinese intelligence services. We need hard evidence, and the only way to get it is to send someone there."

"You're asking me to be a spy," said Cassie. "I'm not a spy.

Or an exobiologist. I wouldn't know what evidence to look for."

Ketteridge reached back inside his jacket and took out an interface key.

"You don't need to," he said, placing the key on the table and nudging it towards her. "Plug this into the first computer you see in either Verne or Nemo. It contains autonomous heuristic software that'll find what we're looking for. It's already keyed to your thumbprint, so only you can use it."

Autonomous heuristic software. Cassie regarded the key as if it were a snake rearing to strike. It was a fancy term for sentient malware, the same tech that had once been used by a cadre of revenant AIs to collapse governments worldwide. Get caught with one of those in your possession, she knew, and they wouldn't just throw away the key when they locked you up: they'd hurl it into the sun.

"You talk like you can just snap your fingers, and I'm part of the crew," she said, her voice cracking slightly. She left the device where it was. "It can't be that simple. There's a crew selection process, and—"

"Actually, I can," said Ketteridge. "I have the ear of the consortium funding the new expedition. You'll be replacing one of the crew at short notice." He raised his eyebrows. "Assuming you're willing."

What Cassie really wanted at that moment, more than anything else, was to talk to Tingshao. Somehow, he'd know just what she should say. But he wasn't here: he was somewhere in the NCR, working for the very people whom Ketteridge wanted to beat to Europa.

For a minute there, she'd been afraid Ketteridge really did know everything about her. But if he'd known she was still in touch with Tingshao, he'd never have approached her.

Ketteridge was offering her everything she'd ever wanted. Then why did she hesitate? Where did this feeling of sudden, overwhelming terror come from?

"I need to think about this," she said at last.

Something flashed in the depths of Ketteridge's gaze. "There's not much to think about. This kind of offer doesn't just happen, Miss White. It's a once-in-a-lifetime deal."

Cassie swallowed, her throat dry and scratchy. "Can I at least have time before I need to give you an answer?"

Ketteridge glanced at his flimsy with barely concealed irritation. "I'd hoped to fly out to Florida with you starting now, but I can give you, say…twenty-four hours." He smiled thinly. "Is that enough time for you?"

Cassie nodded.

Ketteridge stood with a sigh and stepped around the table towards her. Reaching into his jacket, he took out a card and handed it to her. "Call this number when you're ready," he said. "The sooner, the better."

"If I say yes, what are you going to tell the crew?"

"Nothing," said Ketteridge, stepping past her and towards the door. "Last-minute crew changes aren't unusual. You, of all people, must know that."

"Wait," she said, picking the interface key up from the table just as Ketteridge was about to step out of the room. "What about this?"

Ketteridge looked at the device, then at Cassie. "It's quite harmless. It won't activate until you plug it into a computer in either Verne or Nemo." He shrugged. "But keep it safe until then."

But I haven't said that I'm going, she nearly said.

Then she found herself alone in the briefing room and staring at the closed door, Ketteridge's footsteps echoing into the distance on the other side.

––––––

IF NOT FOR the interface key, Cassie might have thought she'd hallucinated the entire conversation.

Gripped by a desperate urge to pee, she went to find the head. By the time she locked herself inside a cubicle and put the seat down, her hands had started shaking.

A chance to go back to space. And the very real possibility that somehow, against all the odds, Chris had survived all these years—and perhaps others too.

Leaning forward, Cassie pressed her head into her hands and took a deep breath, holding it in before letting it out gradually. By the time she'd performed this action a half dozen times, her hands had stopped shaking.

Every time she closed her eyes, there was Sergio, staring at her in panic as the lunar hopper spun out of control.

What if it happened again? The treatments were still experimental and largely unproved. What if they failed to work on her and somebody died because she blacked out somewhere in the depths of interplanetary space?

And yet, above and beyond that single fear, lay something else: the bone-deep *need* to escape the constant pull of gravity.

That the desire had been hard-wired into her genes didn't make her want it any the less.

And yet—and yet…

Tugging her jeans back up, Cassie hit the flusher and knew she had to talk to Tingshao.

———

THE ONLY OTHER passengers on the Sikorsky that flew her from the Deep Range back to Taiwan were a pair of Indian oceanologists. After a few nodded greetings, Cassie stared out at the ocean for a couple of hours, then fell asleep to the steady thrum of the rotor blades and the near-inaudible hum of the batteries that powered them. By the time she woke another seven hours later, they were just coming in for a landing at Kaohsiung.

Cassie boarded the high-speed rail bound north for Taipei, and when she emerged from the city's Main Station, the blackened stub of the old Taipei 100 tower was barely visible through a spring rain. Soon, she was navigating a rental bike through narrow alleyways to the 99 Bar.

There, as she'd known he would be, Ellsworth sat in his usual booth on the upper floor, one of an endless succession of gin and tonics on the table before him while he tapped his way through news items on a flimsy. Yoshi, his minder, sat nearby, drinking Mai Tais and talking to a waitress. A screen angled above the bar showed a baseball game in progress.

Ellsworth hardly glanced up when Cassie slid into the booth across from him.

"I'd like to think you're only here because I'm so charming and attractive," he said in a Northumbrian accent. "But I'm guessing there's some other reason."

Lean to the point of being gaunt, the Englishman had a neatly pointed beard and moustache, his skin made artificially smooth by gerontological treatments. The liver spots on his scalp were the only clue to his true age.

"I need some business advice," said Cassie.

"Of course you do." Ellsworth looked past her shoulder and nodded.

Yoshi appeared next to Cassie and cursorily swept a metal detector wand up and down her torso and arms.

"Clean," he grunted, then returned to his conversation.

"What do you need?" asked Ellsworth.

"The usual."

He nodded. "That's going to be thirty thousand New Taiwanese dollars."

Cassie didn't quite hide her shock. "It was *five thousand* last time," she protested. "That was just a couple of weeks ago!"

"I have to order your stuff specially," said Ellsworth. "And since it's all coded to your specific genome, the lab knows you're an Opt. That makes things…difficult."

"What do they care?"

"The labs I deal with are in Vietnam and Laos. Normally, the authorities there turn a blind eye to Opt stuff, but the US started putting pressure on them and a couple got raided." He smiled sadly. "That makes everything a lot more expensive."

"Jesus, Ellsworth," said Cassie. "I can't afford that kind of money! How am I—?"

A small, still voice in the back of her mind reminded her that if she went to Jupiter, she wouldn't *need* anything to help her deal with life at the bottom of a gravity well.

"There are other drugs that can help you cope with your, ah, situation," said Ellsworth. "And much cheaper beside—"

"I'm not buying heroin from you," she said, standing back up. Not that she hadn't heard stories about Opts with the same genetic defect winding up as addicts once they were stuck permanently on the ground. Anything to chase away that deep-seated need to go up, up, *up*.

"Good luck, Cassie," Ellsworth called after her as she descended the stairs to the street. "I'll see you next time."

A warm spring breeze had replaced the rain, carrying the scent of lotuses. Cassie walked from Jingmei Station to her apartment near the Xindian River. Overhead, toy drones chased each other in mock-battle above the rusting wreck of a PRC landing craft.

Back in her apartment, she had just five pills left from the last time she'd gone to see Ellsworth. Five pills, to help her keep her head together without going mad from being stuck on the ground.

Then she turned a corner and saw police tape across the smoke-streaked entrance to her apartment, on the ground floor of a six-storey apartment block. For a moment, she stared at the tape and the blackened exterior, wondering if she was seeing things.

"*Ni hao*?"

Turning, Cassie saw one of her neighbours standing nearby, holding on to a rickety old bike. Mrs Chen's Pekinese dog sat panting in the bicycle's basket. Mrs Chen wore a green quilted body-warmer over matching pink velour sweats, with a semi-transparent sun visor parked on top of her stiffly coiffed hair.

"Mrs Chen," Cassie responded in fractured Mandarin. "My apartment...what happened?"

The old woman winced as if in physical pain and shook her head. "Very bad. Some boys did it. You should go to the police station and ask them about it."

Cassie gaped at the older woman, then back at her front door, seeing that one of the glass panels had been smashed in. The smell of charcoal filled her nose, and she pinched her nostrils shut to keep from sneezing.

"What boys?" Cassie demanded, then modified her tone. "I mean, do you know who they were?"

Mrs Chen shook her head. "No, but your neighbour—Mr Lu?—he said he heard them talking about how you were, well..." Mrs Chen pressed one hand to her chest as if afraid to let the words out. "You should talk to the police."

Mystified, Cassie watched the woman hurry away, her bicycle bouncing over a pothole as she wheeled it into the distance.

The interior of her apartment was a sodden wreck. It couldn't have been long since it had been vandalized. The front door lock had been broken, and there were scorch marks on the floor tiles just inside the entrance where burning charcoal had been dumped.

———

THE POLICEMAN at the station a couple of blocks away shrugged like he couldn't care less. "It happens. Kids read something online and do something stupid." He peered at one of his monitors, then back at Cassie, sitting across from him. "We know who they are. I had a word with their parents."

One of Cassie's eyelids twitched. "A word with their parents?" The words came out slightly strangled. "Have you seen what they did to my apartment? Everything stinks of smoke. My clothes, furniture, everything. I'm amazed the landlord didn't just turn up with a truck and cart it all off to a dump. Did they tell you why they did it? And why burning charcoal, of all things?"

The officer regarded her wearily. Cassie hadn't failed to notice the tattoo on his left forearm, identifying him as a resistance fighter during the short-lived PRC occupation. That got him a little respect from her.

"Well…" The cop rocked his head from side to side. "There's some story going around that the motherless ones spread the Whispers, and burning charcoal kills the bug."

"I'm Optimized," she said, her voice rising in pitch. "What kind of idiot would think we spread any kind of disease—?"

Cassie caught herself before her voice rose any further, seeing a warning in the policeman's expression.

"This thing about us not having mothers isn't true," she said, forcing herself to speak more evenly. "We aren't grown in labs, whatever you or anyone else has heard. And we don't spread the Whispers. Don't they know it's an airborne virus?"

"Yes, yes." The policeman sat back, clearly tiring of the conversation. "But people aren't interested in facts. They're interested only in things that confirm what they already believe." He tapped one finger on his desk and sucked at his lips. "Perhaps it might be wise to find a new apartment somewhere outside of the city?"

———

MOTHERLESS ONES. *Jesus Christ.*

Returning to her apartment, Cassie surveyed the damage and realized there wasn't much she wanted to keep. Most of her memories were online, and what little remained mainly comprised some clothes, paperbacks that had already gone mouldy in Taiwan's perpetual humidity and…that was pretty much it.

Everything she needed, she could fit in a backpack. She threw what she could into it and slung it over one shoulder before the sight and stink of her apartment could make her feel any more depressed. The moment she was ready, she felt an overwhelming desire never to see the place again, and so she went for a walk.

When she stepped back outside, the sky had deepened to a reddish-orange, the last rays of the sun catching windows on the upper storeys of the taller buildings. First cutting down an alleyway, Cassie crossed a road busy with quietly humming electric vehicles, then stepped through the flood-barrier and into one of the riverside parks.

The park bench where she sat was next to a kid's playground, watched over by a three-metre tall cartoon dinosaur rendered in pink and yellow fibreglass. The anonymous-looking earbud she took from a plastic case tucked in the back pocket of her jeans buzzed when she pressed it into one ear.

Definitely alone, she thought, taking another quick glance around.

"Tingshao?" Cassie said into the air. "If you're there, get back to me right away, will you?"

A minute passed with no answer. Then another minute, and another.

When ten minutes had passed, Cassie sighed and stood, picking up her backpack. There was a cheap hotel not far from where she was: better that, than spending even one more night in her ruined apartment.

Just as she was about to pull the earbud back out, Cassie heard an electronic ping, and then the sound of a busy street.

"Cassie?" said Tingshao. "Still rooting around the seabed like a glorified clam digger?"

God, but was she glad to hear his voice.

"Still better than being in charge of a bunch of glorified space truckers," she replied, unable to keep from grinning as she sat back down. "Where are you? Sounds noisy."

"Crossing the street and trying not to get run over," he said. "I don't have long. What's up that's so urgent?"

"I've been offered the chance to go back into space," she said.

Tingshao was silent for several seconds, except for the sound of his breathing as—by the sound of it—he hurried across a road somewhere in Beijing.

"Really?" he said, sounding nonplussed. "But what about…?"

"The restrictions against Opts?" she finished for him. "If I say yes, they'll pay for the treatments."

She heard his sharp inhalation as he absorbed this information. "You're putting me on."

"I'm really not."

"Don't the treatments cost an insane amount of money?"

"They do."

"Who's offering this to you? And how come?"

She grinned. "They want me on the new Europa Deep expedition."

The pause before he replied was longer this time. "Europa Deep? Now you're *definitely* taking me for a ride."

"I swear it's the truth."

"And who else knows about this?" he demanded.

"For now, just you."

"That's incredible news," said Tingshao. "But you said

you'd only been offered the chance. Does that mean you haven't decided yet?"

For a moment, she thought of telling him about her misgivings—not least, that the man offering her back a life she'd thought lost to her forever was famous for treating Opts as if they were barely human.

But something made her hold back from going into too much detail. She trusted Tingshao—they'd grown up together —but he had chosen to live and work in a country that had been on the losing side of a devastating war. Could be the less he knew, the safer he was.

"They needed to replace someone on the crew at very short notice," she told him. "But no, I haven't made up my mind yet."

He laughed again. "Are you crazy? Of course you should go. It sounds like an incredible opportunity. I mean, why even hesitate?"

"Because…"

An elderly couple passed by on two rickety-looking bicycles, chattering between themselves.

"You're worried something might go wrong even with the treatments," he said at last, breaking into her silence. "Is that what it is?"

She swallowed, her throat suddenly dry. "What if—?"

She couldn't even finish saying it.

"Cassie." His tone became more firm. "Whoever offered you this chance, they know about Sergio. Don't they?"

"I… Yes. They do."

"If they really thought you'd be a liability, they wouldn't have offered you this, would they?"

"They said they needed somebody skilled with deep ocean diving and behemoth suits."

"Well, there you go," he said. "Everyone knows you're one of the best. You trained for Europa; few ever have. That makes you part of a pretty special elite. And at least you won't have to keep taking those damned inhibitors any more."

"My source dried up anyway," Cassie admitted.

"Ha!" Tingshao exclaimed. "And a good thing, too. I told you those pills were going to be your downfall." His tone was gently reproachful, as if he didn't really mean it—but he did, she knew.

But as understanding as Tingshao could be, and even though he was also an Opt, he didn't have the same genetic flaw she did. He didn't know what it was like to wake up every morning with a need like an itch that couldn't be scratched and which only grew more and more intolerable the longer she was trapped down here on the ground. The inhibitors, in combination with her deep sea work, made that itch just about bearable.

"So what would you have said," Tingshao continued, "if I'd replied no, you're right, it's much too dangerous and you should stay here? Are you saying you'd really have listened to me?"

"I'm just scared, is all."

"Of course you are," he agreed. "Shit, it just occurred to me. We won't be able to talk for years. When is the launch date?"

He was right, Cassie realized. They'd put her in cryo for the voyage out and then back again: she'd spend years in a dreamless, ageless sleep.

"A few days from now. They—"

"Stop there," said Tingshao. "That soon? You're sure?"

"What is it?" A note of tension in his voice set an alarm ringing somewhere in the back of her mind.

"Look," he said, "I know I said before this number was encrypted, but maybe for your own sake, don't tell me any more than you already have."

Cassie remembered just then what Ketteridge had told her: that the NCR might be about to launch an expedition to

Jupiter. Did Tingshao know about that? Was that why he had told her not to say any more?

"I understand," said Cassie, not really sure that was true.

"I'm glad you called me." The background noise changed, taking on an echo, as if he'd stepped into a building with a large atrium. "And I'm glad you've got this opportunity to get back to doing what you love. Even if you always resented it."

"Why wouldn't I resent it?" she replied immediately. "I—"

"Never asked for it, I know," he finished for her. Somewhere in the background, Cassie heard a voice speaking over a tannoy in a Beijing accent. "Remember what we said at the anniversary memorial service?"

"Of course." She flashed back to the service outside the school where they'd both studied as children, and the unveiling of the memorial to the seven Opt students and teachers dead in a school massacre. "That people like us need to stick together."

If not for her brother Chris, she could have easily been one of the dead.

After the memorial, Chris had gone to Jupiter and disappeared, along with the rest of the first Europa Deep mission. Then Sergio died, the Whispers took Marcus, and Tingshao left for the NCR rather than deal with the constant threat of anti-Opt violence. The NCR, by then, was the only nation that still employed Opts in space—so long as their DNA didn't contain the particular sequence that triggered blackouts in zero gravity.

"You picked the right time to call me," said Tingshao. "They're sending me up to Mare Imbrium because of a bug in the flight systems. I'll be pulling fourteen-hour shifts to figure out what's causing the glitch. Just an hour from now and you'd have missed me." He paused. "Stop kicking yourself for something that wasn't your fault and do this, Cassie."

"Hey," she said, moisture pricking at her eyes. "Don't let

one of those shitty, cheap Chinese launchers land on your head before I speak to you next."

"I promise," he agreed. "Safe journey, Cassie. I'm proud of you."

"I didn't say I was going to—"

But he was already gone.

The sky was dark by the time Cassie stood again with her rucksack in one hand. Her old life—working for the Task Force, and living in Taiwan—already felt like it had sunk irrevocably into the past, as if it were someone else's life and not hers.

Then she remembered the card Ketteridge had given her. She took it out and studied it. It had Ketteridge's name printed above a dark green icon resembling an old-style cell phone, and no other details.

She gave the card a practiced shake, and the icon turned from green to red. After another moment, someone picked up.

"Miss White?" said Ketteridge, the card vibrating against her fingers as he spoke.

"I'll go," she said.

"Of course," Ketteridge replied, as if any other answer were entirely inconceivable. "I'll send a car to pick you up." He paused a moment. "I see you're near the river. Taking a late-night walk?"

"Something like that. Isn't that illegal? Using a business card to track someone's location?"

"A car is on its way to you," Ketteridge replied smoothly, ignoring her question. "It should be there in fifteen minutes. Unless there's anything you want to get from home first, it'll take you straight to a private airstrip next to Taoyuan airport."

"There's nothing else I need," said Cassie, crossing through the gate at the flood barrier. She found another bench and sat back down to wait.

"One other thing," said Ketteridge.

Something in his tone set her nerves on edge. "What?"

"It's come to my attention that someone else on board the Veles may—and I stress, *may*—have been tasked with destroying the evidence of bioweapons research I want you to find."

Christ. "Who?"

"We don't know. Nor can we substantiate it. But it's something you need to be aware of."

Cassie tipped her head back and swore silently. "Your timing is for shit, Senator."

"Ex-Senator," Ketteridge reminded her. "Why? Have you reconsidered?"

Cassie's hand trembled, and she pictured herself crumpling the business card up, throwing it into the grass, and pretending she'd never heard the name Ketteridge.

"No," she said at last. "I'll still go."

"Very good, Miss White. The car will be with you soon."

The call icon changed back to green. Cassie pushed the card into a pocket of her jeans and leaned forward on the bench, hands cupped over her mouth. She felt suddenly heavy, as if she'd just returned from a six-month shift in LEO and was having to readjust to normal gravity.

Jupiter, she thought, staring up at a night sky partly obscured by clouds. Wasn't that something?

CHAPTER 4
HOW TO STEAL A
SPACESHIP

Before stealing a spaceship, Marcus first had to buy his own truck company.

It came cheap, a failed pre-war self-drive startup based out of New Jersey that had relied on cheaply sourced and notoriously buggy AI, making its vehicles prone to hacking. Many of the truck components were similarly garbage, including poorly manufactured, ageing and long out-of-date lithium-ion batteries that were prone to bursting into flames, and GPS software that caused the vehicles to crash more often than not in wet weather.

Then came the Big Hack. Ever since, the trucks had languished, unloved, in a row of warehouses, while human drivers who didn't need to be programmed came back into fashion.

On top of all that, stringent post-Hack legislation had reduced the profit margin for those few delivery companies that still relied entirely on AI to a narrow sliver. And yet, against the odds, a handful of privately owned—and barely profitable—fleets of self-driving trucks survived.

Most times, the owners of these fleets had never so much as set eyes on their vehicles. They didn't need to, since most of the necessary scheduling, maintenance and haulage could be outsourced to dumb software directly from their kitchen or local café.

Marcus was no different from any of the rest of them, except that he had no kitchen, couldn't have drunk coffee even if he'd wanted to and, most importantly, was no longer human.

After buying the company, he sent all but one vehicle to the compactor. The single remaining truck he kept charged and waiting at a depot in the Red Hook Marine Terminal.

And he did it all from inside a storage facility in Switzerland.

Marcus had occupied the storage unit for three months while he prepared the final stages of his escape from Earth. Communication with the outside world was only possible by hacking into the net connection of a sex shop on the ground floor of the building housing the storage facility. Electricity came via an illegally spliced cable—something he'd been forced to arrange at terrifying cost over the darknet—to supplement his internal radioisotope power systems.

To Marcus' knowledge, his whereabouts were entirely unknown, even to other revenant AIs attempting to flee the post-Hack catastrophe. And with a life-span that might be measured in centuries, or even millennia, his—and their—long-term survival meant getting off Earth as soon as possible.

And to do that, he would not steal just any spaceship. He was going to steal the one he'd helped design.

Switzerland, unlike many other countries, had survived the Big Hack with its financial systems more or less intact. All kinds of people there had all kinds of things squirrelled away in secure underground vaults, such as the printed stock certificates Marcus kept stored in a bomb-proof sub-basement only half a mile from his present location. And being on paper, rather than digitized on a hard drive, they had kept their value post-Hack.

Marcus had realized early on that a global, AI-driven finance system with increasingly little human intervention was enormously vulnerable to a sufficiently well-coordinated attack. Shortly after being uploaded, he had therefore made a series of investments in steady stocks like gold and lithium that were likely to survive any potential crash.

These were predictable, rather than exciting, investments. But it was predictability Marcus needed. They also proved fortuitous when a secret cadre of revenant AIs, composed of uplifted despots, oligarchs and billionaires, crashed global financial markets in an ultimately fruitless attempt at world domination. Instead, they had triggered a war between the People's Republic of China and pretty much everyone else.

When material prices spiked sharply at the outset of the conflict, Marcus had converted most of the stocks into currencies that looked likely to survive the global turmoil, and put the rest into untraceable crypt-coin that could be spent on the darknet.

By the time the war ended, the PRC had collapsed, replaced by the New Chinese Republic. Once the AI plot that started it all was uncovered, every revenant AI in existence found itself global enemy number one. Some were smashed with hammers, while others perished when angry mobs burned down their server facilities. A few were simply switched off forever.

The rest, like Marcus, had to flee for their simulated lives.

For a time during this turbulent period, Marcus' home had been a bomb-proof server facility a short drive from Nord-fjordeid on the Norwegian coast, powered by a nearby hydro-electric dam and kept cool by the frozen climate north of the Arctic Circle. There, a half-Norwegian, half-German sysadmin named Edmundo Schlinkmann, who was at times openly envious of Marcus' post-human status, kept him wired into a fibreoptic network and hidden behind a series of firewalls that allowed him near-total access to the planetary web.

Edmundo might not have been so envious if he'd known what life had been like for Marcus after the Whispers finally, agonizingly, brought his meatsack existence to an end.

"I could live forever if I uploaded," Edmundo insisted during one of their frequent, if good-natured, arguments. He said it with a kind of awe. "I could see the entire galaxy, or—"

"Sure," Marcus agreed. "As long as nobody unplugged you. And assuming they even let you get into orbit. They're all afraid of another Yatagarasu."

Edmundo's brow crinkled into lines, his stolid Norwegian face fixed into a frown that had likely been put to good use by his ancestors when they sailed their dragon-headed boats up English estuaries looking for Saxon villages to plunder.

"But I wouldn't take a human crew with me," Edmundo said haltingly. "I have no interest in kidnapping anyone, like that other AI did."

If only you knew. "You might say that," Marcus had replied, "but why would they believe you? Even assuming they allowed you to raise the funds to build a ship to carry you and only you all the way to the stars, they'd still question your motivation."

"But that makes no sense—!"

"Since when did meatsack humans ever make sense, Edmundo?" Marcus had countered. "They've grown up with two centuries of media telling them machines like me are going to take over the world."

Edmund's frown grew deeper. "But they *did* try to take over—"

"Yes, yes," said Marcus, "a few of them who didn't like having their multi-trillion dollar empires taken away from them because an international court decided AIs weren't allowed to own property tried to crash the markets. But most revenant AIs were like me: not billionaires—not even millionaires. They burned a server farm in Bangladesh to the ground just because they thought an AI *might* be in it."

"But—!"

"Or what if they got hold of you," Marcus continued, almost unable to stop himself—or was he really voicing his own fears?—"shoved you in a box, and buried you underground with no net access, *forever*?" He watched Edmundo through the server farm's multitude of microscopic security cameras, accessed through a cloud account. "In which case, you'd very much be better off dead."

Really dead, Cassie might have said. *Had* said.

Edmundo was a smart guy. All the sysadmins were. But like a lot of smart guys, he was smart within a very specific and, in some ways, very narrow range. He was smart in the same way that a Great White was an efficient hunter of prey, the product of tens of millions of years of focused evolution.

He was less smart in the same way that a Great White couldn't go to a drive-through and order a fish burger and fries: as long as you stuck to coding, medieval sword fighting, science fiction, astrophysics—his major prior to a postgraduate course in computing—LARP strategy and the likelihood of whether a barista from Stockholm who worked in his favourite Starbucks might sleep with him, Edmundo was an expert.

But take him out of that context—like, ask him his opinion on anything unrelated to any of those five subjects—and he floundered like a Californian teenager caught in the jaws of a benthic monstrosity born of the Miocene.

The last straw had been when Edmundo broached the subject of Brian Hall and his theories of directed panspermia.

"He was a crank," Marcus had said flatly.

Edmundo had actually looked offended. "You don't believe in his ideas?"

"Look," Marcus had said, picking his words with excessive care, "Hall was absolutely a shining light in the fields of astrobiology and exobiology. But these ideas about gestalt minds and Europa having a global consciousness are just...a little out there, don't you think?"

"You're an AI construct," the sysadmin had said a little too smugly. "If a box of metal components can think, why not a moon? Did you read any of those links I sent you?"

Say yes, Marcus had told himself.

"I'm afraid not," he had said instead.

Edmundo's eyes shone with sudden passion, and Marcus hoped if he ever got to go on a date with his barista, he would stay off this subject.

"His theory," Edmundo began before Marcus could stop him, "is that moons like Europa are the most common form of life-bearing world in the universe. They form a kind of network of ice-locked worlds with warm oceans that communicate with each other by firing biological probes at each other—"

"Yes," said Marcus, sensing Edmundo would soon be on a roll. "I know the idea. Genetically engineered microbes that could survive the journey between stars over thousands of years. And yes," he added, seeing Edmundo open his mouth, "I'm aware he claimed some Europan organisms could survive the rigours of deep space. But claimed isn't the same as proved."

"But there are bacteria living inside nuclear reactors," Edmundo insisted doggedly, almost tripping over his own words with excitement. "Others have adapted to the orbital and lunar stations. They found yet more dormant and alive inside rock formations that were hundreds of millions of years old. There are rumours that before the Europa Deep expedition disappeared, Hall discovered—!"

And with that, he was off.

After a couple of years hiding under a Norwegian mountain with only Edmundo for company, and despite the occasional distractions of his fellow co-conspirators scattered around the globe, Marcus realized he was already buried in a hole in the ground, and that he had had about as much of Edmundo as he could take.

Then two of his co-conspirators fell forever silent, and Marcus decided it was time to stop delaying and put his escape plan into action.

Not liking goodbyes, Marcus had himself shipped out of the underground server facility while Edmundo was fast asleep at home in a small fishing village fifteen kilometres further along the coast.

It was better that way.

He left Edmundo a goodbye note, thanking him for all his help, but was careful not to say anything that might indicate his future plans: instead, he signed off with a couple of ideas for how Edmundo might strike up a conversation with the cute barista in the Starbucks he visited every morning before driving to work.

While Edmundo was dreaming of core kernel panics and blue-haired baristas in stacked leather boots, Marcus had himself labelled as redundant equipment. He then had himself sold as part of a job lot of used computer equipment to a shell company he owned out of the Marshall Islands—the same subsidiary that had purchased the self-driving truck company off the shelf, and which he handled through a false identity. Finally, he had himself loaded onto a container ship bound for Mexico's second-hand computer markets.

Anyone looking inside the shipping container would have seen stacks of server units packed with protective foam pellets. If they'd looked carefully, they might have noticed that one of these units looked different from the rest, with an armoured, radiation-proof casing. They might, should Marcus be very unlucky, recognise it as the type of cutting-edge heuristic device that commonly housed the intellects of those deceased individuals with either the means or the luck to have themselves uploaded to compatible hardware.

They might, but fortunately, they didn't.

After hacking into the container ship's security network, Marcus watched the grey sea roll by and listened as grizzled-looking Norwegian sailors in oilskins complained to each other about their wives. Once this became tiresome, Marcus switched to remotely accessing the Veles via zombie satellite links—derelict, still-orbiting and out-of-date communications satellites long ago co-opted by darknet hackers.

Marcus grew quickly concerned upon discovering that many of the backdoors he had long ago programmed into the Veles had since been discovered and patched. And those few that remained undetected were disappearing, one after the other, as the Veles' computer systems were upgraded.

Upgraded? Why, after so long?

Then came more bad news. Regular cargo shipments were being made to the Veles. Clearly, the ship was being prepared for some new expedition, thereby scuppering all his carefully laid groundwork.

Even if he still managed to slip alone on board the Veles, with all the extra activity aboard the ship, someone would surely notice a couple of dozen AIs being shipped up into orbit.

He quickly came up with a new plan. One that was far from perfect, but workable.

He presented his ideas to his compatriots and waited for word to come back from them. Many of his fellow revenant AIs hid out in university server farms or in research centres. One was in sole command of a specially modified solar-powered yacht in international waters; a few were on the Moon.

The plan was this:

He alone would secrete himself aboard the Veles, where its human crew would never find him. When the Veles one day returned its crew to Earth, his compatriots could at last be shipped incognito into orbit, where they would then join him.

And once they had command of the Veles, they could explore the nearest stars for ten thousand years, replenishing and repairing themselves using the ship's 3D printers for as long as possible.

After the container ship docked at the Red Hook Terminal, Marcus, along with several other large items purchased solely as camouflage, was loaded onto his one surviving self-drive truck. Then it was off to Florida, still a bustling centre of commercial space activity thanks to lunar mining corporations, orbital unmanned factories and sports companies flying centenarian trillionaires to the Moon and back.

Robots unloaded him from the truck, which then drove itself to its final doom at a nearby scrapyard. Just to be sure, Marcus nuked the truck company's database, lest AI hunters be on his trail, and he spent the night in a warehouse, listening through his microphones to the cry of cicadas.

———

THE NEXT MORNING, Marcus and other select pieces of equipment were loaded onto pallets by human workers. If any of them knew what a revenant AI looked like, they failed to spot him.

A barcode was scanned, and Marcus was driven to a launchpad where a heavy-duty cargo launcher stood waiting. As they unloaded him and other equipment destined for the Veles, Marcus peered upwards through microscopic camera lenses as water vapour drifted down from the bleed-off points for the rocket's cryogenic boosters. Workers with oversized flimsies ticked off lists of parts and equipment.

Finally, Marcus rose up on a platform, along with other secured cargo, to a hatch, where more launch technicians waited to secure everything inside.

Several hours passed in silence within the cargo hold, except for the occasional gurgle of liquid propellant.

Then came a loud rumble, and the cargo hold shook around him. The rumbling grew to a steady bass thunder, then faded.

Marcus' internal motion sensors informed him he was now in zero gravity. More time passed, then someone floated in through an opened hatch as if hung from an invisible cable. They had the green and black insignia of an ESA orbital technician stitched to their jumpsuit, next to the logo for the old Europa Deep mission.

Behind the technician—a young black woman with close-cropped hair—Marcus glimpsed an interior corridor of the Veles.

The sight filled Marcus with glee. How he wanted to shout his triumph to the world!

Yet, he bade his time: to survive for centuries, one must be patient.

Yet more time passed as other cargo and supplies were removed from the rocket. Marcus cautiously accessed those few parts of the Veles' internal computer network still open to him, thereby discovering the reason for the Veles' unexpected refurbishment: there would be a second expedition to Europa.

If he had still been human, he would have gaped open-mouthed in amazement. A second Europa Deep expedition—who would have thought?

And truth be told, this new expedition—so long as he could avoid being discovered—might prove advantageous.

Assuming, that is, his conjecture that Risuke was hiding in the Jovian system proved correct.

Orbital support staff made final preparations for the Veles' outward journey, navigating in zero gravity as if born to it. None of them had eyes with the faintly silvery hue that indicated genetic optimisation.

Marcus waited to be discovered: to be packed into a return shuttle and sent to whatever fate awaited him back on the ground. The cargo manifest described him as an environmental control systems unit, which he superficially resembled from the outside.

Eventually, all bar a skeleton crew of three remained, and Marcus initiated the final step in his plan.

The Veles measured nearly two hundred metres in length and resembled an arrow caught in mid-flight through a silver hoop. Four fat spokes connected the arrow to the hoop, which housed the living quarters for the crew. Nuclear propulsion engines mounted at the rear dwarfed the remainder of the craft. The arrow-like part had laboratories, storage bays and survival and maintenance bays scattered up and down its length.

Apart from the skeleton crew, the only things that moved were the AREMs—Autonomous Robot Engineering Modules. Most people, however, just called them flying monkeys.

Despite the nickname, the AREMs were octopoid in design, and carried out any number of routine maintenance jobs, usually without supervision.

Working cautiously, Marcus gained control of several flying monkeys and used them to explore the ship incognito. He directed one to extract him from the supply rocket, then push him along the ship's central spine, driven by electric fans that funnelled air through adjustable nozzles.

It brought him to the storage bay he had selected aft of the engines, placing him into a payload rack and plugging him into the comms network via a standard data port connection.

Exhausted, and feeling safe for the first time since he had left Switzerland, Marcus allowed himself to slip into a state of machine somnolence that was the nearest equivalent he had to sleep.

THEN SEVERAL SURPRISING THINGS HAPPENED, one after the other.

Marcus had set alerts to bring him to full wakefulness when certain events occurred: the arrival of the expedition crew in their cryogenic pods, the Veles' departure from Earth orbit, and a precautionary alert if anyone entered his storage bay.

As with the first Europa Deep mission, all the crew, bar the mission commander and the ship's doctor, had been placed into cryogenic suspension on the ground and then shipped into orbit. This allowed the mission's medical personnel to monitor them all for unexpected problems that could then be dealt with on the ground, rather than aboard a deep-space exploratory vessel with its limited medical resources.

THE FIRST SURPRISE came when Marcus discovered Ernest Javier had been made the mission commander. The second was discovering that Cassie was on board.

Cassie's presence came to Marcus' attention when he navigated a flying monkey into the cryo bay, not long after the Veles departed Earth's orbit with little, if any, fanfare. Her face and vitals, along with those of the rest of the crew, were visible on a screen mounted on a bulkhead. She had cut her dark hair short, her features blurred by the thick, oxygenated gel protecting her.

Doctor Albert Haunani, the Veles' medical specialist, along with Commander Javier, remained awake for this first stage of the outward journey. Apart from them and Cassie, the crew also included Evan Harrow, an oceanologist who had spent half his life studying the Arctic, Anton Lebed, a Ukrainian astronavigator and, finally, Daphne Makwetu, who would command the manned mission lander.

Cassie. Of all the people! Had she known Ernest Javier would be the commander?

The mission logs recorded her expertise with behemoth suits and submersibles in extreme pressure environments. Out of them all, she was by far the best qualified to be part of the mission.

There were another two in the cryo pods, however, who had no discernible roles Marcus could find on the mission logs beyond a vaguely worded security assignment. A man and woman: Jeff Holland and Sally Braemar, respectively. The first name tickled a distant memory Marcus couldn't as yet place.

Security assignment? Who needed a security assignment on a mission to Europa?

Well, there was nothing Marcus liked so much as a good mystery, and he didn't lack for time. So, he decided to find out what he could.

———

THE COMMAND DECK of the Veles was located at the fore of the ship, at the tip of the arrow-like spine. When Marcus navigated a flying monkey onto the deck when he'd known it would be deserted, he discovered half a dozen passwords taped to one arm of Ernest's command chair.

Really, he should have been shocked. But after having worked with Ernest on the first Europa mission, it wasn't that much of a surprise.

Lacking the dexterity of an actual monkey, let alone a human being, Marcus was forced to laboriously peck out each alphanumerical sequence using machine-limbs that were manifestly not designed for such tricky work. It felt like trying to knit a jumper with a pair of drill heads.

But once he was in, it took Marcus seconds to copy the information he was looking for into his own long-term data storage.

Braemar and Holland, it turned out, were spooks. USNRO, specifically.

It was also therefore not surprising that they had no official presence aboard the Veles: their records didn't even contain photographs. But their job, according to what Marcus found, was to negotiate with the Chinese.

The Chinese?

A search through the rest of the downloaded data revealed that several ships under the command of the New Chinese Republic were expected to arrive at Jupiter not long before the Veles.

With that, Marcus had an explanation for why this second mission to Europa had launched so far ahead of schedule: the US, along with its partner space agencies in Europe, Africa and South America, wanted to use it to secure their access to Europa before the Chinese could lock it down.

Still. There was something about the one named Holland —a memory that Marcus couldn't quite pin down. Something from before his upload.

———

TWO MORE EVENTS of note occurred over the next several months as the Veles moved further away from Earth. First, micro-meteorite impacts damaged part of the aft radiation shielding, necessitating several spacewalks by Haunani and Javier to assess the damage.

If they'd just put a revenant AI like Marcus in control of the Veles, things would be so much simpler. Back in the days of the old ISS, it had taken a ground staff of thousands working around the clock to keep its crew alive. For the same reason, the crew of the Veles had to work unceasingly to keep any of a thousand potential shipboard vulnerabilities from threatening all their lives.

If he'd wanted to, Marcus could have taken the Veles for himself and kept the crew asleep indefinitely—precisely as the world believed had happened to the ill-fated Yatagarasu. But that wasn't something he would ever do: revenant AI or not, he valued human life just as much as when he'd been human himself.

Then he thought of Cassie. Some lives he valued more than most.

The time came when, for a few days, four of the crew were awake at the same time in order to carry out a scheduled shift handover. By now, the Veles was four and a half months into its three-year journey. Javier toured Sally Braemar and Jeff Holland around the Veles, answering their questions and explaining what tasks needed to be done, and why. Marcus listened in with the aid of microphones attached to the AREM robots. While Javier seemed chatty enough with the two agents, Doctor Haunani seemed reticent when in their presence.

Holland had the look of a retired military man, a type Marcus had frequently encountered while liaising with US Space Operations Command back in his meatsack days. Sally Braemar appeared to be in her late thirties, with a perpetually sour expression and tight blond curls that gripped close to her skull.

At last, Javier and Haunani went into hibernation, leaving Braemar and Holland in sole command of the Veles for the next several months.

And the first thing the two spooks did was head straight

for the command deck. Which was when the second significant event occurred.

———

Marcus carefully navigated a flying monkey close to the command deck entrance, listening as best he could through the little machine's microphones as the two government agents spoke in low, quiet tones, as if afraid of being overheard.

What was the point, Marcus wondered, in whispering to each other when you were the only conscious human beings for several million kilometres?

Despite the risk of drawing attention to its presence, Marcus guided the AREM robot further into the command deck. There, he saw Braemar hunched over a screen, tapping away at a keyboard. Her colleague watched over her shoulder and made occasional comments.

Marcus had the AREM perform one of its pre-programmed routine maintenance operations. It opened a panel set into a bulkhead and proceeded to test the circuitry within.

"Nothing," he heard Braemar say with a bitter curl of her lip. She slammed one hand on her keyboard. "Not one damn thing about Hall's research."

Hall?

"Easy." Holland put a hand on her shoulder. "It was a long shot, anyway. It's possible they left something encrypted somewhere on the—"

Braemar's nostrils flared, and she shook Holland's hand free. "I'm starting to think this whole thing is bullshit," she said, pushing both hands through her hair. "There's nothing about SBEs here or anywhere else."

"Could be," said Holland, "none of them know it's important. I tried to get some information out of Javier about the man, but he knew nothing beyond the same things everyone knows."

Braemar glared reproachfully at Holland. "Why didn't you mention this before?"

Holland shrugged. "I told you, it didn't come to anything. Javier knew Hall was part of the first expedition, but that's about it. He certainly didn't know anything about Hall's theories."

"He could have been lying to you."

Holland regarded her with apparent amusement. "To what end?"

"Then maybe there's nothing here," she sighed. Pushing herself out of her seat, she stretched, bracing both hands on the console before her and rolling each of her shoulders.

Then she glanced around the deck, her gaze settling at last on the flying monkey still under Marcus' control.

"We still have other work to—" Holland frowned. "Sally?"

Only at that moment did Marcus realize his mistake. So focused had he become on trying to work out what it was about Holland that troubled him, he had allowed the flying monkey to hover, motionless, next to the panel it had supposedly been working on, its cameras focused on the only two people present.

Marcus immediately set the flying monkey back into motion, guiding it towards the command deck entrance.

As soon as he did, Braemar pushed herself out of her seat and towards the AREM. She was graceless in zero gee, but made up for it with seeming determination. She crashed into the octopoid robot, sending them both into a slow spin as she caught hold of it. Together, they drifted towards the bulkhead next to the command deck entrance.

"Sally?" Jeff Holland watched all this with baffled confusion. "What is it?"

"Just a feeling," said Braemar. Cursing and muttering, she hooked the toes of one stockinged foot through a grip mounted next to the deck entrance, still holding firmly onto the flying monkey. Then she turned the little machine this way and that, frowning at its camera lens and giving Marcus a close-up view of the pores of her cheeks.

"It's only a maintenance bot," said Holland, clearly irritated. "Everyone's asleep, Sally. Nobody's watching. Not even that idiot Javier."

Interesting, thought Marcus. Now why had he said that?

"It's like…" Braemar shook her head, as if she couldn't find the right words. "Don't you feel sometimes like the things are *watching* us?" she asked, regarding the flying monkey with obvious distaste. "Like someone's controlling them?"

"And who exactly," Braemar asked, "would be controlling them? We're the only ones awake."

Braemar's face reddened, and she let go of the flying monkey. The little robot spun for a moment, then activated a fan to slow its spin.

"I don't know," said Braemar. "Could be I'm just on edge."

Then she reached out and batted at the little machine, sending it flying across the deck. It just barely halted its careening progress before it smacked into a bulkhead, its fans whining furiously.

"I hate this fucking ship," she growled. "As soon as we're back on solid ground and this job is over, I'm buying my own damn—"

"Your own island," said Holland wearily. "Yes, Sally. I know."

Marcus allowed the monkey to follow its pre-programmed path back out of the command deck in search of a charging point. Only then did he heave the electronic equivalent of a deep and shuddering sigh.

That had been *close.*

But at least Marcus knew now what it was that had been

niggling at him: he'd once met a USNRO agent named Jeff Holland during a routine security review, shortly before his worsening medical condition had forced him into an early retirement.

And while the two men looked superficially similar, this clearly wasn't the same man.

———

OVER THE NEXT SEVERAL DAYS, Braemar shut down nearly all the flying monkeys. Those few she allowed to remain active, she regarded with obvious suspicion whenever she encountered them.

One, fortunately, Marcus could still listen through, although he didn't dare take direct control of it. All he could do was hope it was in range of any interesting conversations when they occurred.

But he knew enough so far to make for a *most* intriguing mystery, starting with: why were the two spooks so interested in Brian Hall, of all people?

And it was, undoubtedly, *the* Brian Hall who was the focus of their attention: the same Brian Hall that had so inspired Edmundo back on Earth with his woo-woo notions of alien-directed panspermia.

Remembering Sally Braemar had referred to "SBEs", Marcus soon discovered this stood for Space-Borne Extremophiles. These were the speculative organisms that had so obsessed Edmundo, and which had been designed—if you believed either him or Hall—to survive the frozen vacuum of space for millennia.

Most of Hall's ideas were based around his analyses of Europan microorganisms that had long ago been spat onto Europa's surface by ice geysers, only to be scraped up by earlier, unmanned expeditions and launched Earthwards for analysis.

Hall had, to Marcus' knowledge, been selected for the crew of the first Europa Deep expedition for reasons entirely unrelated to his theories of panspermia. Brilliant people with wackadoodle notions were hardly anything new: he'd known at least one seasoned astronaut who refused to ascend past the Kármán line without his lucky socks. But the two agents' interest in Hall's more out-there theories suggested someone, somewhere, took them seriously.

At one point, Holland exited the ship on the first of a series of spacewalks. Several exterior panels had to be replaced because of the micro-meteorite damage, and water tanks had to be repaired and replenished. From what little Marcus could pick up, Holland was experienced at working in zero gravity.

More weeks passed, until the time came for the next maintenance shift to be awakened: Anton Lebed, the Veles' astron-avigator, and Evan Harrow, the English oceanologist.

Once they were awake, matters once again became interesting: clearly, neither Harrow nor Lebed had been briefed that there would be two government spooks on board. Lebed was openly angry, and at one point, Marcus overheard most of an argument between the four of them, Lebed's furious voice carrying far down the spine.

They also had questions about Cassie: they had expected someone named Kernov to be occupying her cryo pod.

Lebed was placated with promises that all would be made clear by Commander Javier once they were at their destination. Then the two spooks went into cryo, as per the schedule.

More months passed, this time without incident, and Lebed and Harrow were themselves replaced by Commander Javier and Daphne Makwetu. Marcus waited to see Cassie when she was revived—but she wasn't. Instead, Makwetu and Javier returned to cryo, and were followed by Doctor

Haunani. Joining him was Jeff Holland, on his second outwards-bound maintenance shift.

But, oddly, and perhaps worryingly, still no Cassie.

Surely they wouldn't keep her in cryo for the entire voyage out? There were limits to how long a person could safely remain in cryo, so why—?

Ernest. The more Marcus thought about it, the more certain he felt. It *had* to be because of him.

Even now, years after Sergio had died, the resentful son of a bitch *still* harboured a grudge against her.

There were more shift changes as days and weeks and months swept by, the Veles journeying ever closer to Jupiter.

Then Javier inexplicably worked the second-last maintenance shift of the outward-bound journey entirely on his own, even as Cassie slept the voyage away.

This did not escape the attention of Harrow, judging by the angry words the oceanologist exchanged with his Commander when their shifts briefly overlapped. Finally, Harrow and Braemar returned to cryo, and Ernest had the ship to himself.

Shortly thereafter, catastrophe was averted. But only just.

Free of Braemar's restrictions, Marcus would sometimes send a flying monkey that was under his direct control on a tour of the Veles when no one was around to see. While most of the crew had been selected for their expertise and professionalism, they were also subject to all the frailties of meat-sack humanity, and there was just an outside chance he might stumble across a problem they had missed.

On one such occasion, a few weeks into Commander Javier's solo shift, he was horrified to discover nearly all of the cryogenic pods containing the sleeping crew were on the verge of catastrophic failure.

The first thing he observed as the monkey entered the bay, flying on whirring fans, was a block of red and white text flashing on and off on one of the bay's control panels. And yet, there had been no ship-wide alert: klaxons should have been blaring, with every comms terminal inside the Veles flashing up the same warning—that without immediate action, the cryonics would fail, and the sleeping crew would die.

Snapping out of his shock and back into action, Marcus drove the flying monkey towards a terminal. He had to let Commander Javier know there was—

No.

Marcus caught himself at the last moment. Using a manual alert to notify Javier that he was in imminent danger of losing his crew would also make him aware that the ship had a stowaway. And a rogue AI, at that.

Was it possible, he wondered, that Javier was behind it? He had rearranged the maintenance shifts so only he would be awake at this point in the outward journey—so was this a deliberate attempt to kill them off?

The thought chilled Marcus, and deep within the quantum circuits of his mainframe, his virtual self shivered.

Then, realising there was no more time to waste in indecision or fear, Marcus drove the flying monkey closer to the terminal displaying the warning message.

As difficult as it was, he managed to peck in a series of commands. At that moment, Javier was on the command deck, seemingly oblivious to the danger the others were in— or that another of the AREMs was watching him closely.

Marcus' actions brought up more information. To prevent disaster, he'd have to dive into the code and risk revealing himself.

The thought of losing Cassie drove him to act immediately.

Accessing the central command computers soon confirmed Marcus' worst fear: the Veles had been infected with a computer virus. Isolating and quarantining the self-replicating program took only seconds, but just when he thought it was over, Marcus himself then came under attack.

A rapid assessment led him to the conclusion that, rather than dealing with a simple computer virus, he was under assault by military offensive technology—the same type of highly adaptive and sentient malware that had sent civilization reeling during the Big Hack.

Overcoming and containing the malware took several hours of experiential time. Two minutes in the outside world.

At last, the alert died away and the cryo pods soon stabilized.

They were safe.

Yet there remained the question of *who* had uploaded the malware.

Javier still seemed the most likely suspect. Yet the malware had acted to prevent him from being alerted. Why would it do that if Javier had introduced it in the first place? Was it so he could plead ignorance at some later date—*the ship never notified me, so how could I have known*—?

Or was someone else responsible?

Then Marcus noticed something that had, until that moment, escaped his attention: two of the pods—which two, unfortunately, he could not say—had been left unaffected by the malware.

Why had they alone been spared?

While all of this had been going on, Commander Javier had remained on the command deck, working away at a terminal with the disk of Jupiter displayed on a screen in real-time—and still unaware of the drama unfolding elsewhere on the Veles.

Marcus knew that by acting to prevent a disaster, he had revealed his presence to whomever had been responsible for this attempted act of mass murder. Given enough time, they would find him—and presumably attempt to destroy him.

Slowly, Marcus came to the realisation he needed help.

And out of all the crew of the Veles, there was only one he felt he could trust: Cassie.

What had she called him the very last time they had spoken? *A machine that only thinks it's a person.*

That last encounter, full of Cassie's grief and fury, had left Marcus shaken enough he never tried to contact her again.

But he could at least warn her. Even if, for now, it might be best to keep his identity a secret.

CHAPTER 5
ARRIVAL AT EUROPA

"Easy," said a voice, gravelly and male.

Cassie's vision was too blurred to clearly see who had spoken to her—a frequent side effect of long-term cryogenic freezing, as it had once been explained to her. That had been back when she trained for the first Europa Deep mission.

She felt hands press against her shoulders and lower back, helping her upright. Something cold and gelatinous lapped at her thighs, and when she tried to speak, all that emerged was an incoherent groan.

"Worst hangover ever, right?" said the same voice, not unkindly.

Reaching out blindly, Cassie clasped a forearm.

No, she wanted to say. *No, it's nothing like that.*

In truth, she felt…serene. Free of the constant tug of Earth's gravity, something had shifted deep inside her: something she had forgotten.

Something very like happiness.

"That's it," the voice continued, calm and professional. "Evan? Give me a hand here."

A second pair of hands joined the first, holding her steady as she struggled upright, her bare feet scrabbling for purchase on something that felt like bathtub enamel. Another attempt at communication ended in more incomprehensible mumbling.

"Give it time, Miss White," said a different voice. Was it the one called Evan? He had an English accent. "It's a long, slow process. Trust me."

Cassie nodded, allowing herself to be guided into a seated position on the flat edge of the metal cryo pod. A gurgling, hissing sound echoed from flat metal walls, and she guessed one of her helpers was using a suction pump to suck up the sticky gel drifting through the bay.

"Here," said the second voice, pushing something warm and fluffy into her hands. "Dry yourself."

Cassie half-heartedly wiped at her skin and support garment with the towel. Once the towel was soaked through, she was offered a second, and she used this to rub vigorously at her hair.

Although she groggily remembered having it cut close to her skull immediately prior to going into cryo, it had grown out by several inches over the intervening weeks. Surprisingly long, it seemed to her. Something about that fact filled her with foreboding, but her head wasn't clear enough yet to figure out why.

A sudden flare of light made Cassie twist her head to one side, blinking away tears.

"Sorry." The first voice again. "Just checking your responses. All good, I'd say, given how fast you seem to be recovering. Doctor Haunani, by the way. I'm the mission medical specialist."

"Nice to meet you." The words felt thick and sludgy on her tongue. Then she coughed explosively.

Cassie felt a sharp pinprick on one arm.

"*Ow*," she muttered. "What is that?"

"Nothing to worry about," said the doctor. "Don't hold back on coughing, by the way. It's going to take time to get all the cryogenic gel out of your lungs. But you should take a shower now. Clean the rest of the gel off."

"Shower?" She swallowed, her throat raw and scratchy. The word came out more like *huwurr*?

"Only the best for us," said Haunani. "We'll have to zip you inside, and you'll need to wear a breathing mask, but it still beats moistened wipes."

Her vision had sharpened enough by now that she could see the doctor's grin. His face was round and smooth with full lips, his own hair cropped close to his skull. The one called Evan looked younger, perhaps in his late thirties, with shoulder-length brown hair that floated in a curly mass around his head. He wore drawstring pants and a t-shirt, while Haunani wore a standard mission jumpsuit.

"Time to move," said Evan, taking careful hold of her upper arm.

Cassie allowed herself to be guided, step by step, away from the cryogenics tank. She caught her reflection in the burnished steel door of a metal cabinet.

After nearly fifteen months in cryo, she'd expected to look thinner. But the realisation of how much fat had drained from her face still came as a shock.

She'd almost have thought she'd been asleep for a lot longer.

The shower was about what she expected, a plastic tent she had to zip closed. Stripping off her one-piece support garment, she got to work cleaning the gunk off with the aid of a hose that first sprayed water, then sucked it all back up again at the press of a button.

After she'd towelled herself down for the second time, she worked the zip down a couple of inches and told them she was coming out.

"Sure," said Haunani. "We'll wait outside."

When she emerged, she had the bay to herself, at least for a few moments. She grabbed up the mission jumpsuit they had laid out for her and dressed quickly. A screen displayed someone's vital signs—heart rate, blood pressure and core temperature. Hers, she guessed.

The two men re-entered the bay just as Cassie pushed one foot through a loop attached to a bulkhead in order to anchor herself.

"Your responses are excellent," said Haunani. He had a look of slight disbelief.

"Amazingly good," said Evan. He anchored himself to a handgrip close by the bay entrance. "I could hardly do a thing until I'd been out of the tank for hours, but you look hardly affected at all."

Cassie squinted at him. "Nice to meet you too," she said, clearly enough this time, although her throat still felt raw and the lights all felt too bright. "Evan...?"

"Harrow," he said. "Pleased to make your acquaintance."

"Evan's our oceanologist," said Haunani. "I gather you're our replacement for Kernov?"

"Who?" Cassie asked in a half-croak.

"Arkady Kernov," said Harrow. "Our original dive specialist. Actually," he continued, something shifting in his voice, "I wondered if you knew why...?"

"Give her a chance," said Haunani, giving the other man a look. "She's barely out of the tank."

"I don't know who Kernov is," Cassie managed to say, "or why they took him off the Veles." It was getting easier to talk, but she had to take her time. "They asked me to join the mission just days before the Veles left orbit."

"You're really showing a remarkable rate of recovery," said Haunani. "Take this."

Reaching for a squeeze-bottle velcroed to one bulkhead, Haunani ripped it loose and tossed it towards Cassie. It drifted towards her in a slow spin, and she caught it with ease.

Evan Harrow muttered something under his breath, and Cassie looked his way.

"I'm just…surprised you could catch that," he said.

"As I'm sure you've guessed by now," Haunani said to the oceanologist, "Miss White is an Opt."

"Of course," said Harrow, looking sheepish. "I mean, I could—"

He could see the faint silvering of her eyes, he meant.

"Drink that," said Haunani, gesturing at the bottle he'd thrown to her. "It's a nutrient shake. And remember to drink lots of water—you're going to be extremely dehydrated."

Putting the bottle to her mouth, and suddenly realising how thirsty she was, Cassie squirted some of it down her throat. She tested banana and lemon mixed with something faintly medicinal. Within seconds, she'd drained half the contents.

"So," she said at last, her voice still raw, "I guess you're the previous shift." She glanced around the bay at the other cryogenic tanks. "Who's my shift partner?"

The two men exchanged a look that sent alarm bells ringing in the back of Cassie's mind.

"What?" she asked, looking between them.

"Before they put you in cryo," asked Evan Harrow, "what did they tell you about the maintenance shifts?"

Cassie shook her head, baffled. "Tell me? Not much. Why?"

Another look passed between the two men, full of unstated significance. "He means," said Haunani, "did they tell you that you'd be doing any maintenance shifts *at all*? Or that there might be…changes?"

Cassie blinked, utterly confused by now. "I don't know if my head's scrambled from being asleep all this time," she said, "but I was told I had two scheduled shifts on the outward voyage, same as the rest of you." She looked between them, her consternation growing at the sight of their worried expressions. "Right?"

"There've been some developments," Haunani said at last, looking very ill at ease.

"Developments?" Cassie echoed. Her eyes grew wide. "Has something gone wrong?" She cast a wild look from one to the other. "We're still on our way to Jupiter, aren't we?"

Haunani squared his shoulders and visibly made an effort to meet Cassie's gaze. "We're already there," he told her. "We entered orbit around Europa two days ago."

"That's not possible." Cassie's voice was flat and disbelieving as she spoke. "It's a three-year trip to Jupiter. They scheduled me to start my first maintenance shift fifteen months in."

"The whole of the crew has been awake for seven days now," said Harrow. "Except for yourself."

"But my shifts…?"

"Commander Javier worked your shifts in your place," Haunani continued. "I'm afraid you've been asleep the whole way out."

Cassie stared at him, dumbfounded. "What did you say the commander's name was?"

"Javier," said Harrow. "Ernest Javier."

Ernest Javier?

Cassie swallowed, a hollow void where her guts had been. *Ketteridge, you son of a bitch.*

He *must* have known Ernest was in charge of the mission. How could he not? And he'd kept it from her.

"There's no justification for keeping me under this long," she said, her voice full of dread. "Isn't it dangerous?"

"Well…" said Haunani, looking embarrassed, "it's definitely not recommended. There could be long-term consequences."

Cassie stared at him in alarm. "What consequences?"

Haunani shrugged feebly. "Nothing to be overly

concerned about. But it might be different for you, because…"
He let the words trail off.

"Because I'm an Opt, you mean."

"In fairness," said Haunani, "you look about ready to run a marathon. Most people can't walk in a straight line this soon after being decanted, let alone string a sentence together. But you?" He chuckled. "I'd almost think you hadn't been under at all."

"Now I want you to tell me *why* I've only just been pulled from the tank," she demanded.

"We don't know," Harrow admitted. "That's one reason we woke you. We hoped you'd be able to tell *us*."

There was something in the way the two men were looking at her that triggered a sudden suspicion. "Wait a minute. Did you pull me out of cryo against orders?"

"Commander Javier hasn't exactly been forthcoming about why you were still in your tank even now," Haunani explained, looking pained. "We talked—I mean, everyone in the crew had a discussion about it—and we decided we weren't happy once Ernest said he had no intention of decanting you." He shook his head. "It's crazy. And we need you awake to help us figure out why."

"Yeah," said Harrow, "and also if you know about the two—"

Haunani shot him a look before he could finish, and Harrow shut up.

She looked between them, unable to hide her deepening confusion. "Then who worked my shifts if I slept through them all?"

"Commander Javier moved the schedules around during our first weeks out from Earth," said Haunani. "I didn't know until I woke up and found I was doing a shift with him— what was meant to be your shift. It wasn't until we were all awake we put two and two together and discovered none of us had worked with you."

Harrow cleared his throat. "So," he said, "we were wondering...if you knew why he'd do that?"

Cassie had an excellent idea why Ernest had done it. Probably the only reason he hadn't shoved her, tank and all, out of the airlock at the first opportunity, was the prospect of facing a murder charge once he got back to Earth.

And now he was in charge of the Veles.

I am so fucked, she thought miserably.

"He's agreed to explain himself at a crew meeting," said Harrow. "That's eighteen hours from now. And...there are other questions we have for him."

"Like what?"

"Well," said Harrow, "you're not the only one we weren't expecting to be here."

It took a moment for her to understand what he was saying. "You mean, I'm not the only crew replacement?"

"Evan," said Haunani, an edge in his voice. "This isn't the time. Wait for the meeting."

Cassie's tongue still felt thick and sluggish in her mouth, but her mind was turning over like an overclocked computer. "I don't know anything about anybody else. I swear." Her confusion gave way to a gently simmering fury. "Screw it," she said, muscles tensing. "Why wait? How about we find Javier right now?"

Haunani shook his head emphatically. "You're not going anywhere yet. You need time to recover."

"You said you'd never seen anyone recover as fast as me." Cassie pushed herself towards the nearest handgrip and looped her fingers through the strap. She briefly contemplated launching herself out of the bay entrance before they could stop her and going in search of Javier all on her own.

"Optimized or not," said Haunani, a touch of steel coming into his voice, "you need to recover your strength. Remember how long you were in that tank."

"I want an answer now," Cassie said angrily, pushing herself away from the bulkhead and towards the entrance.

Harrow, who was closer to the entrance than she was, automatically moved out of her way. Cassie stopped herself against the rim of the entrance with one hand, a high-pitched ringing in her head. Her vision clouded for a moment, and she pressed the heel of one hand against her eye.

A hand caught her elbow. "Easy," she heard Haunani say.

Cassie tried to shake him loose, but all her strength had abandoned her. Despite her anger, she allowed herself to be drawn back from the entrance.

"This is what happens when you try to do too much, too soon," the doctor admonished her. "I know you have questions. Frankly, we all do. But we scheduled the meeting for most of a day from now so you'd have a chance to recuperate first."

"I can't just sit here waiting," Cassie numbly insisted. Deep fatigue washed over her, and she struggled to keep her eyes open.

"You won't be," said Haunani. "Your body's been living off medical nutrients for years. The only thing you should do for the next twenty-four hours is eat and sleep. Evan, why don't you take Cassie to her assigned quarters?"

The doctor didn't actually say *and make sure she stays there,* but Cassie sensed the intent behind his words.

Evan shrugged. "Sure." He looked at Cassie. "If you think you're ready to move, that is."

"I want to find Javier and kill him," Cassie mumbled tiredly.

"I don't know what Javier's beef is with you," said Haunani, "but he's still in command. You'll get to ask him all the questions you want, but as the senior medical specialist on board, until then, *I'm* in charge."

Cassie cast him a baleful glance. Then, surprising even herself, she yawned loudly and abruptly.

"Evan?" Haunani turned to the other man. "Make sure she gets to her bunk in one piece."

————

As she exited the cryo bay and emerged into the Veles' spine, Cassie pushed towards the opposite bulkhead, reaching for a grip to stop her forward progress. She hadn't had to think about it: her muscle memory had taken over.

Her mouth and throat still felt gummy and her every bone and muscle ached, but her every movement felt so natural. The idea of always being glued by gravity to a planet's surface, by contrast, felt *un*natural.

Cassie looked up and down the hundred-metre passageway that connected the engines to the habitat ring and command deck at the bow. It should have been a moment of triumph, but all she could feel was sour anger that even this far from Earth, she still couldn't outrun her past.

Every spare centimetre of the Veles' interior was given over to some practical purpose or other. The bulkheads were almost invisible behind bundled cables, stowed supplies and comms terminals spaced along the connective rings holding the bulk of the spine together.

It all stirred up memories that felt like suddenly rediscovered mementoes in an attic; things that were half-forgotten, but still held a rich vein of personal meaning.

Mostly, she remembered being back on Earth and talking to Chris over a video link as he took her on a remote tour of the Veles' interior. The ship still wasn't quite finished at the time, and she'd sat cross-legged on her bed listening to him as he moved through the ship with a flimsy gripped in one hand.

You were here, thought Cassie, and it felt oddly like a revelation. As if she might find him waiting for her up in the habitat ring.

I wish you could see it for real, her brother had said.

And now she was. And somewhere down below her, under the ice of a moon orbiting Jupiter, was the answer to why and how Chris had disappeared.

All this went through her head in the space of a few seconds. Harrow meanwhile followed her out, but with considerably less skill. He flailed for a handgrip close to hers, nearly missing it.

"This," she said, "is not the welcome I was expecting."

"Listen," said Harrow, "I didn't mean to sound so shocked by how fast you've recovered. I wouldn't want you to think that I'm…" He paused, clearly searching for the right words. "You know."

"Don't worry about it," said Cassie. "I can usually tell who's going to be an Opt-hating asshole before they even open their mouths. I don't get that feeling from you."

"Sure." He nodded toward the habitat ring. "That's where we're headed."

"I can find my way there on my own," she said pointedly. "I'm not unfamiliar with the Veles' layout."

"Sorry." Harrow's cheeks flushed slightly. "I didn't realize."

"Do you get why I'm angry?" she asked. "I wanted to be awake for the aerobraking manoeuvre on final approach. Instead, I find I've slept through the whole thing."

"I think we all have to take some responsibility for what happened," said Harrow. "We should have pushed harder for answers from the Commander before now." He nodded towards the habitat ring. "But like I said, we've had other unannounced personnel changes."

She looked at him seriously. "Is this going to be a problem?" she asked. What she meant was: *is my being here a problem for the rest of you*?

Harrow looked undecided how to respond. "Maybe we can talk on the way."

Nodding, Cassie made to follow the oceanologist. Judging by his movements, he had little experience of zero gravity. Even so, Cassie was groggy enough that he still beat her to the ring ingress.

"If I wasn't awake for my shifts," she said, as they paused at the ingress point, "who worked them for me instead?"

"I was awake for the third maintenance shift with Anton Lebed," Harrow explained. "He's our astronavigator. You and Daphne Makwetu—she's our lander pilot—were supposed to be awake for the next shift, but instead, it turned out to be Daphne and Commander Javier. I asked him why you'd been skipped over, but he wouldn't tell me anything. And..." he shrugged, looking uncomfortable.

"And he was the mission commander," Cassie guessed, "and you didn't want to push it."

"Pretty much." Harrow at least looked embarrassed. "I also worked the sixth shift with Sally Braemar—she's one of the other last-minute changes—but what struck me as odd is that, when I checked the schedules, Commander Javier was the only one scheduled for the entire seventh shift."

Access to the habitat ring was via a set of rungs ascending through one of the ring's spokes. The higher they ascended, the more Cassie felt the tug of artificial gravity. Despite her weakened state, the gravity inside the ring was low enough that she could ascend the spoke most of the way with relative ease. That said, she accepted Harrow's offer of a hand to pull her the rest of the way up and into the rotating ring.

"I feel like a truck ran over me," Cassie gasped as she emerged onto the curving floor of the ring corridor. She put both hands on her knees to catch her breath. "Nobody told me it would feel this bad."

"Trust me," said Evan, "you're doing incredibly well compared to any of the rest of us."

"Wait." Cassie hadn't been paying as much attention as she knew she should, too caught up in a whirlwind of bad memories and fears over what she might expect from a confrontation with Javier. "Did I hear you right? Javier was the only one awake for the entire seventh shift?"

Harrow nodded soberly, then gestured to her to follow him around the sharply upward-curving ring corridor.

"But that means during the voyage out," said Cassie, trailing after him, "he'd have been awake for…"

"Over a year."

Cassie stopped in her tracks. "But that's…!"

"Risky, yes." The lines around the oceanologist's eyes tightened. "It's adding long-term exposure to radiation and low gravity to the even higher radiation levels in the Jupiter system and the effects of its magnetosphere. He's put himself well outside the safety limits. Well, for…"

"For a non-Opt, you mean."

They arrived at a bunk integrated into the corridor wall that was the nearest anyone aboard the Veles could get to a private sleeping space. Its dimensions were comparable to those one might find in a Japanese capsule hotel. Even so, it was spacious compared to some of the accommodation Cassie had endured in the early years of her career, working to clear low Earth orbit of hunter-killer satellites left over from the war.

A curtain covered the bunk. Pulling it aside, Cassie found that someone had already stowed her personal items. Her mission wristcomm sat at the centre of the foam slab.

"You asked me about two other crew replacements," said Cassie. "Who are they?"

"Spooks," said Harrow.

"Excuse me?"

"They're government agents," said Harrow. "They're here because—" He caught himself and gave her a half-hearted shrug. "Albert's right—I mean, Doctor Haunani. All this can wait until the meeting. Let's just say this mission isn't turning out anything like we expected."

"This crew meeting," she said dryly, "is going to be a blast."

The oceanologist tapped his wristcomm. "You'll get an automated alert half an hour before it starts," he said. "Try to get some sleep."

How can I sleep, she almost said, *after all this*?

Instead, she nodded and said: "I will. And thanks for telling Javier to go fuck himself and pulling me out of the tank."

His mouth twitched into a genuine smile. Raising a hand in farewell, he turned and made his way back around the sharp curve of the ring corridor and out of sight.

———

CASSIE CRAWLED inside her bunk and pulled the privacy curtain closed. She found a tablet-sized flimsy velcroed to the inner wall. Its screen was dark, save for her name displayed in the top-left corner, with a message icon blinking just below it.

Despite the fatigue that gripped her, curiosity made Cassie reach over to touch the icon. It expanded to reveal a message header with a single word: PRIORITY.

A frown folded the skin between her eyes. Should she read it? If there was anything really urgent she needed to know about, wouldn't either Harrow or Haunani have mentioned it?

Then she yawned again, thunderously this time. Perhaps if she closed her eyes just for a moment—

CHAPTER 6
THE MEETING

"Hey. Rise and shine."

On opening her eyes, Cassie was startled to find a grizzled-looking face peering in at her, one hand holding her privacy curtain aside.

Sitting up with a jerk, she almost banged her head on the roof of her bunk. She swallowed, her mouth feeling even more sticky and dry than it had when they'd pulled her from the tank.

The stranger pushed something towards her, and Cassie saw it was another squeeze-bottle.

"Here," he said. His accent was Eastern European. "Doctor Haunani asked me to give this to you."

Cassie grunted incoherently and sat up, swinging her feet out into the corridor before sucking down most of the bottle's contents in one go. She recognized it from the faintly medicinal under taste as more of Haunani's nutrient shake.

"The taste gets old fast, yes?" said the man. "Anton Lebed," he added, touching his chest with one hand. "Astronavigator." He grinned. "Did you not get the crew alert?" He tapped at his wristcomm. "The meeting is due to start shortly."

Shit. Her conversation with the doctor and Evan Harrow

came back to her. Glancing back inside her bunk, Cassie saw her mission wristcomm still stashed where she'd found it. She'd completely forgotten to put it on before she'd fallen asleep.

"Sorry," she said sheepishly, reaching for the device and snapping it over her wrist. It buzzed harshly against her skin, but stopped once she tapped at its screen and cancelled the pre-meeting alert.

Lebed didn't seem in the least bothered. "I hear you're recovering fast," he said, "but you need some proper food inside you. First you eat, *then* the meeting."

"Do I have enough time?"

"Eat first," he said in a mock-commanding tone. "Then meeting. Here."

Lebed dug around inside a pocket of his overalls and took out a foil-wrapped packet, handing it to her.

Cassie took it from him, at the same time handing him back the empty squeeze-bottle. Unwrapping the foil package, she found it contained a burrito.

"Holy shit," she muttered, breathing in its scent. "That smells good."

"Best astronaut food in the solar system," Lebed agreed, his voice almost reverential.

She ate quickly while Lebed waited. It cleared the medicinal taste of the shake out of her mouth.

"Is there more?" she asked, carefully folding the foil. The foil, along with everything else on board the Veles, would either be recycled or reused.

"There will be after the meeting if you want it," said Lebed. He studied her for a moment. "Are you sure you're up to it, so soon after coming out of cryo?"

"You're the third person," said Cassie, "who seems amazed I can even form a coherent sentence. I—*ow*."

As Cassie slid out of her bunk, she stood too quickly, banging her head on its upper edge.

Lebed grunted a laugh. "Not so recovered just yet, it appears. You can make it all the way to the command deck, yes?"

"Sure," said Cassie.

Just as she made to follow Lebed, she glanced past the half-open privacy curtain and saw the message icon still blinking on the screen of her flimsy.

"I should check that," said Cassie, moving to sit back down on the edge of the bunk.

"No time," said Lebed, gently but firmly. "If it was important, we'd all know about it, I'm sure."

Even in the low, spin-induced gravity, she still felt oddly heavy as she stood and made to follow the navigator. What was it Haunani had said coming out of cryo felt like? *Worst hangover ever.*

She was starting to think he was right.

————

CASSIE FOLLOWED LEBED down the spoke and then forward to the command deck, a spherical bridge with consoles for monitoring life support, engine status, navigation and so forth spaced equidistantly around its interior. The screens of most of the consoles were dark as she entered, but those few currently active displayed views of Europa's surface.

As she navigated her way into the deck, she saw Javier deep in conversation with a man and woman next to a console, while, a little distance away, Doctor Haunani and Evan Harrow studied an image of Europa on a screen. Closer to hand, and with one bare foot anchored through a wall grip, Cassie saw a dark-skinned woman wearing cutoff jeans and a polo shirt tapping at her wristcomm. Lebed, meanwhile, pushed towards Evan Harrow and the doctor and greeted them.

If she'd been allowed to carry out her scheduled maintenance shift duties, Cassie would have met all of these people by now, either by sharing a shift with them, or by being present at the start or end of their shifts. Anchoring herself close by the deck entrance, she had the distinct sense that Ernest—or Commander Javier, as he was now—was making a point of not looking her way.

"All I'm saying," she heard the man next to Javier say to him, "is that if people are going to take items out of inventory, then they need to update the inventory. Especially with all the data port connectors going missing."

Javier raised his eyebrows. "They are?"

"Almost as soon as they're printed," the man continued. "It's a waste of resources printing more when I *know* there are more somewhere on this ship." He shook his head in exasperation. "Not that I can find them."

The dark-skinned woman closest to her grinned at Cassie as soon as she entered and pushed towards her, grabbing a handhold with the practiced ease of an experienced spacer.

"Daphne Makwetu," said the woman, holding out her free hand.

Cassie grasped the hand and shook it, then paused. "Wait. Have we met…?"

"I think so," said Makwetu. Her accent was English. "Mare Imbrium?"

A sliver of memory came to Cassie, of an encounter in a corridor somewhere inside the lunar base.

"When was that?" she asked.

Makwetu chuckled. "Long ago," she said, drawing the first word out. "I'd just arrived for a rotation working on the hydroponics. You flew me out to a couple of outlying research bases."

Cassie remembered now. "Hydroponics? How'd you go from that to lander pilot?"

"Long story. I—"

Before she could continue, Javier clapped his hands for

everyone's attention. "Let's call this meeting to order," he announced loudly.

Conversation faded as the crew turned their attention to the Commander. "I know you all have questions," said Javier, "so let's try to clear them all up today. We've got a lot of work ahead of us, and we need to be focused."

He turned to look at Cassie for the first time since she'd arrived. "Miss White," he said, "welcome aboard. I hear you're recovering fast."

The way he said it sounded friendly enough, but his true feelings were evident in the set of his eyes. Cassie acknowledged him with a nod, her muscles tense.

"Pretty good," she said, "for having spent three years in cryo. And nice to see you again, Ernest."

If Javier picked up on the anger in her voice, he chose not to acknowledge it. The woman next to him had sharp, bird-like features and hair that clung to her scalp in tight curls. Harrow had mentioned two other unexpected members of the crew, so this, Cassie guessed, must be Sally Braemar: one of the two spooks.

"I'm sorry," said Lebed, looking between Cassie and Javier. "You know each other?"

Javier looked at Cassie like he was expecting her to respond first. She waited him out.

"Back when I was in charge of the Lunar Flight Authority," said Javier, his gaze still fixed on her, "Cassie was one of my pilots." He gestured to Braemar and the man he'd been talking to earlier. "Cassie, this is Sally Braemar and Jeff Holland. They're with the USNRO."

"Evan told me there'd been other crew changes apart from myself," said Cassie. "But this is supposed to be a civilian mission, isn't it? Doesn't having intelligence agents on the crew make it something else?"

"An excellent observation," said Lebed, switching his gaze to Javier. "Especially since their being aboard the Veles means that two actual scientists of enormous value to this expedition are *not*."

"Who?" Cassie asked.

"Faye Bennett and Bob Karas," said Makwetu. "Bennett's a microbiologist, Karas a salvage expert."

Javier smiled stiffly. "There's some news you won't be aware of," he told Cassie. "Just before we left Earth orbit, we were alerted that three ships belonging to the New Chinese Republic were likely to arrive in the Jovian system just ahead of the Veles. Sally and Jeff are here to keep an eye on them."

Cassie did her best to look surprised, even though Ketteridge had already told her the NCR intended to send their own expedition.

"Three ships?" she asked.

"One is orbiting Europa at a higher orbit than our own," said Lebed. "The other two are currently orbiting Ganymede, presumably gathering scientific information."

"I think," said Javier, "we should start with the most recent intelligence we have on the NCR's intentions." He looked at Holland. "Jeff?"

Holland lightly pushed himself towards a console and hooked one slippered foot through a grip. He did it with the ease of one experienced in zero gravity environments.

"Starting from right before the aerobraking manoeuvre," Holland said, "Sally and I have been making observations of the NCR fleet. The main ship, we know, is called the Tianjin."

Holland tapped at the console, and an image of the Tianjin appeared on its screen.

Where, from a distance, the Veles resembled a piece of fragile jewellery, much of the Tianjin's hull remained hidden behind heavy plating. To say that it looked formidable would have been an understatement.

"*Nu blet*," Lebed muttered under his breath. "It looks like some kind of warship." He glanced at Holland. "I thought you said theirs was a scientific expedition, same as ours?"

"'No,'" Holland corrected him. "That's what *they* say it is." He nodded at the screen. "You can draw your own conclusions from what you see here."

He touched the console again, and two more ships appeared above and below the Tianjin. The uppermost vessel looked bulky and smooth, while the third, the smallest, was clearly a cargo transport.

"What you're seeing here," Holland continued, "is evidence of the New Republic's long-range strategy for the outer solar system. We believe the Tianjin is a prototype for a new generation of deep-space craft with offensive capabilities. This other one," he said, tapping the uppermost vessel on the screen, "is most likely a scientific exploration ship much like the Veles—hence the habitation ring for generating artificial gravity. The third is most likely carrying extra supplies and equipment. We have intelligence suggesting the NCR intends to construct refuelling depots similar to the ones they already have orbiting the Earth's Moon. The only plausible conclusion is that they want to establish a long-term presence in the Jovian system."

"So why does it matter?" Makwetu asked. "Nobody owns Europa. Or Jupiter. They've got as much right to be here as us."

"Who owns what often gets decided by who has the biggest stick," Holland replied dryly. "Plus, in the longer term, Jupiter represents a major staging point for the outer solar system. Heavy embargoes placed on the NCR following the collapse of the old regime prevent them from accessing resources beyond their borders back home, but for now, there's nothing stopping them from going up. And they've never hidden their long-term intentions for space expansion."

"You make it sound like we're in a race with them," said Lebed.

"We are," Holland agreed. "Either we dominate the solar system, or they do. They built the first lunar bases, so the US, along with the European Space Agency and other partners, felt compelled to do the same. If they develop a permanent presence out here, any future expeditions will have to get past them first."

"But we can't actually do anything to stop them, can we?" Haunani asked. "It's not like we're armed for a fight or anything."

"We observe and report," said Javier. "Political and economic pressure can be applied back home if the Tianjin ignores UN directives. Jeff and Sally, meanwhile, are here in a purely advisory capacity. The worst that can happen is they have to negotiate directly with whoever's in command over there."

"On that subject, have we tried talking to them?" asked Cassie.

Holland nodded. "We tried, but unfortunately, they don't seem inclined to talk back. Plus, the last we heard before our comms went down was that the Summer Palace had threatened retaliation if we didn't agree to its terms."

"They said they wanted to land first," Javier explained to Cassie, "and us second—but only when they say we can. They claim they want to check our surface and undersea stations for evidence of biological contamination."

Cassie crossed her arms. "Contamination from what?"

"It's a bullshit claim," Holland scoffed. "If you remember that far back, a lot of countries tried to veto the first expedition out of the fear that Earthbound microorganisms might contaminate an otherwise pristine alien environment." The way he said it made it clear he thought little of this. "It was a stalling tactic, nothing more. Before the war, any number of them were planning their own expeditions."

Lebed spoke up. "Which brings me to a related point. Are we sure the Tianjin is jamming us?"

Cassie stared at the navigator. "Jamming us, how?" She'd

wondered what Holland had meant about the comms being down, and had been about to ask.

"We haven't been able to send or receive telemetry of any kind for nearly forty-eight hours," Javier explained. "We believe the Tianjin has some means to jam our communications and prevent us from talking to Mission Control."

"But that's still only conjecture," Lebed pointed out. "For all we know, there's a problem on our side."

Holland tapped the image of the Tianjin displayed on the console screen. "What I can tell you for sure," he said, "is that this baby's crammed to the gills with signals countermeasures. See all these comms dishes clustered around the midsection? The Tianjin's powered by a nuclear thermal drive more advanced than ours. They've got more than enough spare juice to override our comms all across the spectrum, from the x-band on down."

"To add to that," said Braemar, "there's another piece of news. The Tianjin launched microsatellites into orbit around Europa a little over forty-eight hours ago. I don't think that's a coincidence. We have to assume they're using the satellites to reinforce their jamming strategy. Unless we can figure a way around it, we're cut off from home until they decide they want to parley."

"Which is exactly why we need Jeff and Sally here," said Javier. "We're scientists, not diplomats or soldiers. They have the experience and knowledge necessary to deal with whoever's in charge on that other ship."

Cassie glanced around the deck, seeing nothing but appalled expressions.

"But for now?" Harrow asked. "What do we do?"

"Right now," said Holland, "it's all in the hands of diplomats back home who are surely negotiating with the NCR around the clock. But if the Tianjin opens communications with us, Sally and I are ready to talk to them. So we wait."

"Wait?" Lebed stared at Holland. "What about landing on Europa—the whole reason we came here?"

"I'm sorry, Anton," said Javier, "but for the moment, all of us are staying right here."

The navigator's mouth flopped open. "You're telling me we flew a billion kilometres just to sit on our fucking asses?"

Javier regarded him with a weary expression. "I understand your frustration. Really, I do. But Jeff and Sally have assured me this will all be resolved one way or another, and soon. So let's just take it one day at a time and see how things develop."

He looked around. Nobody said anything, except for Haunani, who swore under his breath.

"I think that's it," said Javier, brushing his hands down his hips. He nodded to Holland and Braemar with the air of a man whose business is done for the day. "We'll reassess in a few days. But for now, you should all get back to your jobs."

"Wait," said Makwetu. "What about Cassie? You still haven't told us why she was kept on ice. Or why you took the risk of working an extra shift rather than let her out. That wasn't just putting you in danger—as our commanding officer, it put the rest of us in danger, too. We deserve an explanation."

Javier regarded the woman flatly. "Might I remind you," he said tersely, "that Miss White was removed from the cryo bay without my—"

"I can tell you why," Cassie said suddenly. "It's because I killed Commander Javier's husband."

Fast way to end a conversation, thought Cassie, seeing the shocked expressions all around her. Even Javier looked nonplussed.

"Everyone knows why every last genetically optimized astronaut got kicked back to groundside, right?" Cassie said into the silence that followed. "Some of us were having blackouts and there were accidents." She touched her fingers to her collarbone. "I was piloting a lunar hopper from Mare Imbrium base to the South Pole ice mining operation when I blacked out. Sergio Gomez—the Commander's husband—was the only passenger. The hopper crashed and only I survived."

The last thing she remembered, they'd been talking about Sergio and Ernest's upcoming wedding anniversary, and about the time Sergio's cousin, on his first visit to the moon as part of a Venezuelan investment delegation, drunkenly tried to run and crashed head-first into the ceiling of a corridor.

Even before the accident, there had been the odd moment when Cassie had unexpectedly zoned out before coming to again as quickly. But mandated regular check-ups with a base doctor had shown nothing out of the ordinary.

Later, after a board of enquiry reconstructed the circumstances of the accident, they concluded Cassie had blacked out for up to five minutes: enough time for the hopper to descend, out of control, and collide with a rock outcropping.

The next thing she remembered was waking up in a medical bay with tubes coming out of her nose, and a doctor asking her for the date of her birthday. Two days later, she found out Sergio hadn't made it.

Makwetu stared at Cassie. "But…can it happen again?"

"There are treatments," she said. "Drugs. They stop the blackouts. I wouldn't have been asked to join the mission if the people in charge didn't think I could do the job."

"Treatments?" Braemar echoed, her voice sharp. "What treatments?"

"New ones," said Doctor Haunani. "And highly effective ones, according to all the literature."

"You're administering these treatments?" Braemar asked the doctor.

Haunani nodded. "She started her regime the moment she came out of cryo."

Cassie looked at him in surprise. "I did?"

"Of course," said Haunani. "I gave you a shot when you woke. Remember?"

"Except these drugs can't be tested properly," said Javier. He was staring hard at Cassie, one hand twitching at his side. "It's impossible—the people they're supposed to help are all still banned from going into space. And *that* means there's no practical way to be sure the treatments are remotely effective in the long term." He breathed hard, his other hand grasping the edge of a console. "You're awake now—fine. But your duties will be minimal. I'm not taking any risks with this ship because some pencil-pushing idiot who's never been above the Karman Limit decided, for whatever reason, to put you in this expedition against my wishes."

Words came tumbling up Cassie's throat, but nothing came out. Instead, she just looked away from Javier, her jaw and throat tight.

"You'll find a revised work roster posted to your personal terminal," Javier added, then turned to Makwetu. "Daphne, Cassie will shadow you for a few days while she gets up to speed. She can help you in the Farm. In the meantime, we've all got more than enough work to do, and I know several of you have experiments you want to get on with."

Javier pulled himself into a chair next to the console beside him, making it clear the meeting was over. People started moving, pushing themselves away from wall-grips and towards the deck entrance. The two USNRO agents, meanwhile, fell into conversation with Javier.

Cassie, still seething, nearly collided with a flying monkey hovering just outside the entrance. Pushing it out of the way with a muttered curse, she had the oddest feeling the thing had been watching her.

But that was ridiculous.

CHAPTER 7
FARM LIFE

Makwetu waited for Cassie a short distance up the spine. "Not the welcome you imagined," she said when Cassie brought herself to a halt next to her.

Cassie laughed weakly. "You have no idea."

"That accident you talked about..." Makwetu shook her head in sympathy. "I knew an Opt who had a hard time adjusting when they told him he couldn't go back into space. He..." A flash of remembered pain crossed her features. "He died of a drug overdose."

Cassie nodded. "Some of us had modifications that made it hard for us to stay on the ground. Like a compulsion, but it's built in."

Makwetu's brows lifted. "You, too?" She blanched. "I'm sorry, that's too personal. I shouldn't—"

"It's fine," Cassie reassured her. She studied the other woman's face and guessed what her next question would be: she'd been asked it a thousand times. "Some gene labs were willing to do off-the-book custom work for parents who paid enough. Like a tweak that gives you a powerful dopamine rush while in low gravity. The more you experience it, the more you want it."

Makwetu looked appalled. "You make it sound…addictive?"

"I don't talk to my parents anymore," she said. "Put it that way." Fortunately, they hadn't given her brother Chris the same tweak. "That's why your friend died. He was trying to get that feeling back."

"Cassie?" Haunani drifted over to join them. "I'd like to make some more checks."

"Any particular reason?"

"It's standard this soon after coming out of the tank," he explained. "But I want to be sure the extra time you spent in cryo isn't having any adverse effects. Can you come to the med bay?"

Braemar and Holland made their way past, and when Cassie glanced back toward the command deck, she saw Javier was still inside.

"Sure," Cassie said to the doctor. "But give me five."

———

JAVIER GLANCED up briefly when Cassie re-entered the command deck, catching a handgrip next to where he worked.

"I think we should talk," she said. *Might as well cut to the chase.* "I didn't know you were in charge of this expedition, and what happened to Sergio was an accident. You said the same thing yourself at the time."

Javier paused, fingers still resting on the touchscreen, his shoulders rising and falling as he drew in a deep breath.

"That was before the inquest," he replied. "I didn't know you'd had blackouts before, but failed to report them." His features twisted into an ugly sneer. "Why—because you were afraid of losing your job?"

Warmth crept up Cassie's neck. "I… I didn't think it was

anything serious," she said, hating how weak her explanation sounded. "That's the only reason I didn't—"

"I buried my husband a long time ago, Cassie." Fury glinted deep in Javier's gaze. "Are you looking for forgiveness?" He shrugged. "Fine. I forgive you. Now tell me what the hell you're doing on board my ship."

"What?" Cassie stared back at him, startled.

"I personally selected Arkady Kernov for this mission. He was pulled from the roster without explanation almost literally hours before we launched, and now you're here in his place."

He pushed himself closer to her, and Cassie flinched backwards despite herself. "Why the hell do you get to be here, Cassie, when there are thousands of qualified astronauts back home who don't have genetic defects and who wouldn't present an active risk to everyone on board this ship?"

"They... I was told they needed someone expert with behemoth suits. They said I was one of the best. And I am," she added with a touch of defiance.

"Sure," said Javier. "And you know what? So was Kernov. I still don't get why you're here—unless there's something I don't know?"

She found it hard to meet his gaze, afraid he might see the truth that, yes, she *was* lying to him. She managed it, but not without enormous effort.

"I was asked to join the expedition a week before launch. They said once I agreed, I had to go straight into cryo. It wasn't like they gave me a lot of time to decide."

Javier regarded her for a long moment, his gaze unflinching. "I don't consider myself the greatest judge of character," he said, more quietly, "but I know when someone's hiding something from me."

"I want to find Chris," said Cassie. She drew in an unsteady breath. "Or at least find out how he died. If you want a reason for me to be here, that's it."

Javier looked surprised, as if this hadn't occurred to him. His expression softened. "Well, that I can understand. But let me be very clear: if I see any sign, or have any reason to think you might endanger yourself or anyone else on the crew, you'll go back into cryo until we get home and fuck the consequences. Understood?"

With that, Javier pushed away from the console and launched himself out of the deck entrance. Makwetu, who had been hovering just outside, ducked out of his way. She turned to look at Cassie with a concerned expression, but Cassie just shook her head.

Idiot, Cassie chastised herself. She should have known something like this would happen.

———

"I WASN'T LISTENING IN, I swear," said Makwetu as Cassie went to join her.

"You hear much?" Cassie asked tiredly.

"Some," Makwetu admitted. "He…"

"Really hates me," said Cassie, nodding. She sighed, working her head from side to side. Tension had built up in her muscles over the hours since being pulled out of cryo. "Perhaps he's right," she added despondently. "I'm starting to feel like it'd have been better if I'd just stayed at home."

"Actually," said Makwetu, "being out here might be about the best place you could be."

Cassie peered at her and wondered what she was getting at. "Why?"

"First, go see Haunani," said Makwetu, without further explanation. "Once you're done, I could use your help in the Farm."

"Ernest mentioned that. What is it?"

Makwetu's mouth quirked slightly. "The hydroponics bay, of course. But as soon as you get the chance, you ought to catch up on what's been going on back home during our outbound voyage. You've got about three years of news waiting for you."

The skin on the back of Cassie's neck prickled. "Good or bad?"

Makwetu's expression was tinged with sadness. "Is it ever really good?"

Cassie supposed she had a point.

———

HAUNANI TOOK blood and saliva samples and gave Cassie a second shot, explaining that she would need weekly boosters from this point on. That done, Cassie made her way to the hydroponics bay, where vegetables and other fresh produce grew beneath UV arrays.

For the next few hours, she and Makwetu tended to the soil-free crops. She thought of asking Makwetu what she had meant, about being better off where she was than back home, but something made her hold back. Makwetu herself offered no further elaboration, perhaps waiting for Cassie to ask.

She learned soon enough when she returned to her bunk some hours later. For the next several hours, she sat with her back pressed to the wall of her bunk, scrolling through years of backed-up media that had been transmitted to the Veles since leaving Earth orbit.

Things were indeed not looking good at all for Opts, judging by what she read. There were more Opt refugees fleeing oppressive regimes than ever before—people whose parents had hoped to give them an immense advantage in improved health, intelligence and lifespan, and who instead wound up hunted and, sometimes, killed. Even in those countries where Opts weren't actively repressed, they still faced discrimination, precisely because of what was considered to be their unfair advantage.

In one case that caught Cassie's eye, three Opts had been murdered by a gunman in a hotel lobby. The gunman, like the deckhand on the Deep Range, had been convinced Opts were responsible for his daughter's death from neo-atonic syndrome—or the Whispers, as it was better known.

To her surprise—and deep concern—the news from the New Chinese Republic was just as bad. They'd reversed earlier pro-Opt legislation—legislation that had persuaded Tingshao to move there—in favour of actively discriminating against them.

Was Tingshao still in the NCR's space industry, she wondered? Or had he, as many apparently had, been forced out by political pressure?

Yet despite widespread oppression and even internment, it seemed the NCR was still employing Opt astronauts in space and in their lunar colonies.

It didn't make sense. But maybe they needed them badly enough off-world they were willing to turn a blind eye.

Tingshao had spent a lot of time up on the Moon. Maybe he'd found himself a permanent rotation up there, knowing that there, at least, he might be safe.

Or so she hoped, anyway. Not that she should really have been so surprised—she herself, after all, had very nearly been murdered by an Opt-hating maniac when she'd still only been a child.

And if not for Chris, he might have succeeded.

Fatigue washed over her. Yawning, Cassie moved to turn off the flimsy, then saw the message icon still blinking.

She'd forgotten all about it. Opening it, she read—

```
UNKNOWN MESSAGE SOURCE: CASSIE.
YOU'RE IN DANGER.

SOMEONE TRIED TO KILL YOU BY
SABOTAGING YOUR CRYO POD.
```

REPLY IF YOU WANT TO KNOW MORE.
BUT PLEASE DON'T SHARE THIS
MESSAGE WITH ANYONE.

For a long, long moment, Cassie stared, mute, at the message.

Was this somebody's idea of a joke? Who the hell would *send* a message like this?

She stared at the words as if they might spontaneously reorganise themselves into something less threatening or bizarre. Yet no matter how many times she re-read them, they spelled out the same message.

A few taps on the screen revealed there was no way to identify whomever had sent the message, although a date stamp showed it had been sent midway through the second-last maintenance shift of the outbound journey.

A moment's searching brought up the original crew schedules. Each member of the crew was required to work two four-and-a-half month long shifts on the outbound journey, and the same again on the return journey.

Javier and Doctor Haunani had shared the first shift, followed by Agents Braemar and Holland. Then came Evan Harrow and Anton Lebed.

After that, it *should* have been her and Daphne Makwetu, but Javier had left her on ice and worked the shift with Makwetu instead.

Similarly, Cassie should have worked the second-last shift with Harrow. Instead, Javier left them *both* on ice, working that shift entirely on his own—the same period of time during which someone had sent her this message.

For a moment, she thought of going to find Javier to ask him if *he'd* sent the message. But if he'd wanted to warn her of something, why not bring it up earlier, when they'd been alone together on the command deck?

No, she thought: Javier hadn't exactly made a secret of his dislike of her. If anyone had a motive to kill her, he surely did.

The back of Cassie's neck prickled at a memory: Ketteridge had warned someone else on the mission might be after the same information she'd been sent to find.

Was it possible, she wondered, that someone on the crew knew why she was on the Veles—and wanted to get rid of her?

Christ, she thought: could the message be from *Ketteridge*?

For long seconds, she regarded the message with indecision. Then she typed:

```
CASSIE: WHO ARE YOU?
```

The reply came within seconds. It couldn't possibly be Ketteridge: he was over thirty light-minutes away.

```
UNKNOWN MESSAGE SOURCE: A FRIEND.
```

Cassie typed again.

```
CASSIE: I SWEAR TO GOD, IF THIS IS
SOMEONE'S IDEA OF A JOKE AND I
FIND OUT WHO YOU ARE, YOU'D BETTER
WATCH YOUR BACK. THE SHIP ISN'T
THAT BIG.
```

Several moments passed, long enough for other possibilities to occur to Cassie. Could this be someone on board one of the Chinese ships? Was that possible, despite the signals jamming?

A reply flashed up on the screen.

```
UNKNOWN MESSAGE SOURCE: NO JOKE.
```

Suddenly, Cassie's mouth felt very, very dry.

```
CASSIE: WHY SHOULDN'T I TELL
COMMANDER JAVIER ABOUT THIS?

UNKNOWN MESSAGE SOURCE: BECAUSE
HE'S THE ONLY ONE WHO WAS AWAKE
WHEN IT HAPPENED.
```

Well, fuck, thought Cassie. She typed again.

    CASSIE: CAN YOU PROVE ANY OF THIS?

A second passed, then another, then more text appeared:

    UNKNOWN MESSAGE SOURCE: I CAN. BUT
    ONLY TO YOU.

Cassie typed again.

    CASSIE: WHY WOULD ERNEST OR ANYONE
    ELSE WANT TO HURT ME? WHY WON'T
    YOU TELL ME WHO YOU ARE?

    UNKNOWN MESSAGE SOURCE: THE
    SABOTAGE DIDN'T JUST AFFECT YOU,
    CASSIE. WHETHER IT WAS JAVIER OR
    SOMEONE ELSE, SOMEONE INFECTED
    FIVE OUT OF EIGHT CRYOGENIC PODS
    ON BOARD WITH MILITARY-GRADE
    MALWARE.

    I SAID I CAN PROVE IT. GIVE ME A
    CHANCE TO. BUT YOU MUST TELL NO
    ONE OF THIS.

The message scrolled up, and an icon for a video file appeared on the flimsy's screen.

Cassie hesitated, suddenly nervous, then tapped the icon. She listened to the thudding of her heart as video from inside the cryonics bay played on her flimsy.

It was immediately evident what she was seeing had been recorded through the lens of a flying monkey's camera. The video had a date stamp in one corner, and an alphanumeric sequence identifying which flying monkey had been used to make the recording.

The video showed the curved lids of the cryo pods arranged around the tight inner circumference of the cryogenics bay. The viewpoint moved towards a console screen.

Cassie momentarily glimpsed the monkey's reflection in

the screen, which was otherwise dominated by a flashing red symbol. Text beneath the symbol warned of imminent catastrophic failure in five out of eight pods.

Ice-water flooded Cassie's veins. If Javier was the only one awake at the time, then had he lost his mind and set out to kill his crew?

Cassie typed another reply. It took longer this time, because by now her hands were shaking.

```
CASSIE: YOU NEED TO TELL ME
EVERYTHING YOU KNOW, INCLUDING WHO
YOU ARE. WHY ARE YOU HIDING? WHY
ARE WE STILL HERE, IF SOMEONE
SABOTAGED FIVE OF THE PODS?
```

No answer.

```
CASSIE: ARE YOU STILL THERE?
```

She waited for most of a minute. Still nothing.

"*Fuck*," Cassie muttered under her breath. She slammed one fist into the roof of her bunk, then started typing again.

```
CASSIE: I'LL MAKE YOUR LIFE
MISERABLE AS HELL IF YOU DON'T
GIVE ME AN ANSWER.
```

At last, a reply came.

```
UNKNOWN MESSAGE SOURCE: FIRST,
TELL ME WHY YOU'RE ON THE VELES,
CASSIE.
```

For a moment, she heard nothing but the sound of her own breathing, and the ever-present hum of the ship's active systems.

When she tapped at the video icon again, an error message flashed up: the video had been deleted from its source. She no longer had proof. Assuming, of course, the video wasn't some kind of AI-generated fake.

But if so, why go to such lengths? Was this some fucked-up scheme Javier had come up with to trick her into telling him why she'd been put on the Veles?

And then, another, even more terrifying realisation struck her.

Who had been controlling the flying monkey? Javier?

Or had someone else been awake at the time?

Then something occurred to her: if only five out of eight cryogenic pods had been affected, which three had been spared—and why?

There was no point in sabotaging Javier's pod, obviously, since he'd been awake. But who were the remaining two?

Perhaps, she speculated, the remaining pods had been empty. Perhaps Javier *hadn't* been the only one awake.

She stared uncertainly at the question on the screen of her flimsy, then rolled it up and climbed back out of her bunk.

Five minutes later, Cassie found herself alone in the cryogenics bay. She worked quickly, working her way through the information stored in the bay's operational databases, but found no trace of sabotage at any point during the outbound journey.

Of course, she realized, if any such evidence existed to be found, the rest of them would already have known about it.

By now, the adrenaline had worn off, and Cassie made her way back to her bunk, feeling sluggish and tired and more paranoid than she remembered feeling in a long time.

Pulling her flimsy out, she stuck it back onto the wall of her bunk by its velcro patch, then stared up at the ceiling of her bunk in the certain knowledge that sleep would not come.

CHAPTER 8
THE MESSAGE

In the end, sleep did come: and with it, dreams of standing alone and shivering on a vast and frozen plain beneath stars that were sharp and unmoving.

She wore only her lunar pilot's uniform. Far off in the distance, a metal-sheathed figure came lumbering towards her across an expanse of dirty and streaked ice.

All around her, vertiginous ice cliffs cast deep and impenetrable shadows, while the great, banded curve of Jupiter filled the sky.

Europa.

Then Europa was gone, and Cassie stood behind a window made of armoured glass, looking out across a grey and mottled expanse with Sergio by her side.

"There's a maintenance run to Clavius at eleven hundred," he said, handing her a coffee. "I saw your name on the flight schedule. Could be a good chance to hang out, if you like."

Before she could reply, Cassie looked down to see that her left hand was trembling. It took a conscious effort to make it stop.

Sergio appeared not to have noticed.

Then she saw that someone was outside on the lunar

surface, their face and body concealed within the massive bulk of a behemoth suit. Except there were no behemoth suits on the Moon.

She saw a faint puff of gas along the seam of the behemoth's helmet, and it lifted to show Chris, seemingly unaffected by the vacuum. He looked straight at her, his mouth moving like he was trying to tell her something important.

Use your radio, she thought, with no small amount of irritation.

Then the Moon was gone, and Sergio and her brother with it.

Cassie tumbled into a void of air between the vertiginous cliffs of a great chasm. A profusion of strange and alien vegetation grew up and down the cliffs, the air thick and soupy in her lungs and carrying a thousand unfamiliar scents.

Spreading leathery wings wide and banking hard, she broke her descent. Others flew alongside her, huge and lumbering creatures, gill-like slashes on their long necks pulsing rhythmically.

Dipping lower, she passed over lush and steaming jungle that spread beneath a red sun filling half the sky. Smaller winged beasts circled just above the treetops, and she dived low, sighting her prey…

Cassie lurched upright in her bunk, the sweat cool against her skin. Her shoulders ached as if her dream had been somehow real.

Then she looked down and saw that her left hand was trembling, just slightly.

Oh, no.

Pushing her privacy curtain aside, Cassie swung both feet out of the bunk and onto the floor of the hab-ring corridor. It took a few minutes for her heart to slow down from a rapid thud.

At last, she drew a breath and dared to look at her left

hand. It still trembled, but not as much as a moment before. After another minute, it subsided altogether.

Breathe, she told herself, gripping the edge of her bunk with both hands. *There's nothing to worry about. The treatments are working just fine.*

For a moment she listened to the creak of the ship around her, then checked the time. She was due to start her next shift any minute now.

Making her way to the hab-ring canteen, Cassie almost stumbled over a flying monkey. Although the ring was permanently under spin, the little machines could still get around in low-gee environments by standing on their wiry-looking manipulators. This particular AREM, she noticed, had a bundle of data port connectors gripped in its plastic pincers. Something about it niggled at her, but whatever it was, she couldn't figure it out.

When she stepped inside the canteen, she found a tired-looking Harrow sitting at a communal table, scraping up the last of a bowl of porridge while paging through a battered paperback biography of Roald Amundsen.

They made small talk while Cassie first drank some water, then scooped some porridge from out of a pot and into her own bowl. As soon as Harrow got up to leave, she collapsed back in her seat, anxiety chewing at her nerves.

She knew she should tell someone about her shakes. It might be that her treatments weren't working, just as Javier had said they wouldn't.

But if she told the doctor, she knew, he'd be obligated to tell Javier. She'd be giving the Commander the perfect excuse to make sure she never set foot on Europa. He might even follow through on his threat to force her back into cryo and keep her there until the Veles returned home.

Leaning forward again and placing both hands on the table, Cassie spread out her fingers and slowly breathed out as she watched them.

Not so much as a twitch this time.

————

FOR THE NEXT SEVERAL HOURS, Cassie was back in the Farm with Daphne Makwetu, then underwent another check-up with Haunani that was unrelated to her low-g treatments: instead, he made her run on a treadmill in the Veles' gym with a dozen monitors stuck to her.

She waited for him to tell her he'd picked up something unusual that warranted further tests. As she ran, she kept glancing at her left hand, waiting for it to twitch. As hard as she tried to appear calm, she couldn't keep her mouth from setting into a thin, worried line.

Instead, Haunani gave her the okay and sent her on her way.

The rest of that day's shift was spent on general maintenance: checking electronic systems, dealing with component fatigue and, finally, helping Lebed track down possible bugs in the life support systems.

And through it all, Cassie's thoughts remained on the brief, typed conversation she'd had the night before.

You're in danger. Someone sabotaged your cryo pod.

Why are you really here, Cassie?

"Got a question," she asked Lebed.

They were crouched on either side of an open panel midway between the command deck and the aft drive section. Lebed was focused on touching a sensor to each of a tiny set of relays, while Cassie checked the results on a flimsy.

"Shoot," he said, without looking up.

"Do you think it's possible for someone to have survived down there? Under the ice, I mean?"

Lebed glanced at her, then back at the relays and continued testing. "Like your brother?"

Cassie felt her cheeks colour a little. "Yeah."

He gave her a lopsided grin, then continued his work. "I read up on the first expedition," he said. "You tried for it, didn't you?"

"Tried, but failed."

"So you wonder if he might still be alive down there, yes?"

"It's at least theoretically possible, isn't it?" Cassie asked.

Lebed lowered his sensor and gave her his full attention. "After this many years?"

"I know it's ridiculous to even hope," she said, stumbling slightly over her words. "Sometimes I dream about him."

Lebed nodded, then made a small adjustment to his sensor device before returning his attention to the relays. A status light flickered to life next to them when he touched the final relay.

"Done," said Lebed, pocketing the sensor. He lingered a moment. "Hope is good," he said carefully, "because it's what keeps us all going, even in the worst of circumstances." He raised his eyebrows. "But too much hope can be dangerous, since it also carries with it the risk of disappointment."

She came very close, then, to telling him about the video Ketteridge had shown her, of a single pixelated figure trudging across the surface of Europa months before the second expedition launched.

"But say they found a way to survive," she said. "It's not completely out of the bounds of possibility, is it?"

Lebed took the flimsy from her and tapped at its screen to enter information. "Let's say they did. That they somehow found a way to survive with little or no food at the bottom of a half-frozen ocean under kilometres of ice a billion kilometres from home." He glanced up at her. "Personally, I'd rather die quickly than endure such a miserable existence, all in the hope that someone might come to rescue me someday far in the future."

He returned the flimsy to her. Cassie deactivated it and

rolled it up before tucking it inside her shirt. "I know it's a dumb thing to hope," she said.

"It's not dumb," Lebed countered. "It's human. Now help me put this panel back in place."

She held the panel in place while Lebed secured the bolts. "He saved my life once," she said. "Chris, I mean. I used to fantasise about somehow getting to Europa and returning the favour."

He looked at her for a long moment, then glanced at his wristcomm. "We're due a break. Join me in the canteen?"

She shook her head. "I need to catch up on some more news. I've missed so much."

Really, she was thinking about the many, many more questions she wanted to ask whomever had anonymously messaged her. Indeed, it took all her willpower not to ask them right there and then, via her wristcomm.

"The rest of us had time to get to know each other before they thawed you out," Lebed pointed out. "We wish to get to know you better since we are colleagues. And, after all, we may all be working together for quite some time. Please reconsider."

"I appreciate it," she said, "I really do—"

"Cassie." Lebed's voice remained friendly, but took on a firmer edge. "You've had a rough time of it. This is surely far from the welcome you expected, however you came to be here, or whatever happened between you and our Commander in the past." He placed his hand over his heart. "So please, if you don't mind, do myself and a few of our fellow crew members the favour of joining us so that we might have a small, and somewhat overdue, celebration of your arrival."

Cassie's cheeks flushed with embarrassment. "I'm sorry," she said. "I had no idea."

Lebed chuckled and gestured down the spine. "Shall we?"

———

On the way back to the habitation ring, Cassie made her excuses and hit the head, saying she'd meet Lebed in the canteen in just a few minutes.

She needed to pee anyway, but she also needed time to think. When she returned to the hab-ring, she stopped outside the canteen, where she could overhear Lebed and Evan Harrow chatting without being seen.

Cassie took her flimsy back out and shook it rigid. Pressing it against the nearest bulkhead, she quickly typed a query into it.

```
CASSIE: I'M STILL WAITING FOR YOU
TO TELL ME WHY ANYONE WOULD WANT
TO BUMP OFF MORE THAN HALF THE
CREW. WHOEVER YOU ARE.
```

A second passed, and then another, and then a reply came:

```
UNKNOWN MESSAGE SOURCE: IF I KNEW,
I'D TELL YOU.

YOU STILL HAVEN'T ANSWERED MY
QUESTION. WHY DID YOU REPLACE
KERNOV, CASSIE?
```

Inside the canteen, Lebed laughed at something Harrow had said. Which meant whoever was sending her these messages, it wasn't either of them. Unless, improbably, both men were collaborating to message her anonymously.

Entering the canteen, she greeted the two men.

"Let's eat in style," said Lebed. "Besides, it's time for your first proper meal since waking." He gestured at the storage lockers. "Evan, what do we have?"

Harrow got up, lifting one can after another out of a locker and studying each closely.

"This," said Harrow, peering at one of them, "is Vo-la-ill eppy-see, sautéed in…"

"Give me that," said Lebed, reaching out a hand, "before you mangle the French language to death."

Harrow handed the can over, a hurt look on his face.

"Ah," said Lebed with a grin, turning the can in his hands. "Volaille épicée, sauté de légumes à la Thaï." He grinned at Cassie. "Only the best for *you*, Madame."

Harrow peered narrowly at the pilot. "You speak French?"

"My elder sister trained as a chef at the Ferrandi Paris." Lebed grinned at them. "Her cooking almost makes up for her being a complete shit to me when we were kids." He pointed at another can within the locker and waggled his fingers at it. "If you would?"

Harrow complied, handing Lebed the can. "Rice pudding aux fruits confits," Lebed read from the label, and passed the tin back over to the British oceanologist. "Even you couldn't screw this up."

"I'll have you know my culinary skills are unmatched," said Harrow with exaggerated haughtiness. Cassie watched him open the cans of freeze-dried food and place them inside a cylindrical convection oven. With a tap on the oven's screen, it emitted a gentle hum.

They talked some more until the food was heated, then ate it together with fresh lettuce and carrots from the hydroponics bay. Lebed reminisced about summers spent in Ukraine with his grandfather, a former systems engineer for the European Space Agency.

"Here's to whatever shrink figured out the best way to keep astronauts sane was feeding them well," said Lebed once they had finished. He raised a small bulb of black coffee in salute.

"Better than the old days," said Javier, stepping into the canteen and surveying the scene. Clearly, he'd caught the last of their conversation. "They had to put up with meat paste in tubes."

He nodded briskly to Cassie, but his arrival had changed the mood. She returned the nod and spooned up the last of her rice pudding, while Javier filled a bulb with coffee.

"Since you're all here," he said over his shoulder, "I've asked Doctor Haunani to increase the frequency of biopsies."

Lebed let out a groan. "Is that really necessary?"

Javier turned around to face them, sipping his coffee. "The water tanks give us some protection from radiation, but the longer we're stuck in orbit waiting for something to happen, the more rads we're taking." He smiled at Cassie with no greater sincerity than before. "Present company excepted, of course."

"I'm not immune to radiation," Cassie said carefully. "I can just endure more for longer."

"Of course," Lebed said mildly, "if we could simply land and get inside Station Verne on the surface, we wouldn't have to worry nearly so much about how much radiation we have to endure. The station is thickly blanketed in enough ice to protect us all from radiation. And once we explore beneath the ice, it will cease to be a concern altogether."

Cassie and Harrow exchanged a look. Javier, meanwhile, regarded the navigator fixedly.

"Well," Javier said at last, "that's just how things are for now, unfortunately." He smiled, the skin drawn tight over his cheekbones. "We discussed this the other day, Anton. I don't see any reason to go over it again already."

Lebed's nostrils flared. "And if we don't hear from home? If that other ship keeps jamming us until the risk of long-term radiation exposure is so great, we must *all* go back into cryo?"

"That won't happen," said Javier.

Lebed banged his fist on the table hard enough that a fork clattered slowly to the floor.

"Who is in command of this vessel," Lebed shouted at Javier, "you or those two fucking agents? I think perhaps them, because ever since we awoke, you have agreed with every word they have said. It was *their* idea to remain in orbit and await permission to land, even though we are being jammed and can receive no transmissions! *Maybe*," he continued, "the reason the Tianjin is jamming us is that we already have permission to land, and they don't want us to know!"

"Never raise your voice at me again, Anton," said Javier, his voice still and calm. "And don't ever forget, I'm still in command of this mission."

Lebed glared at the other man. Cassie waited, tense, to see what would happen next.

At last, Lebed smiled stiffly. "I apologise," he said, with a very slight bow of his head. "However, self-reliance is central to survival in space, is it not? The ability to improvise and find unexpected solutions to unexpected problems often makes the difference between life and death when one is hundreds of kilometres above the Earth or, indeed, much further away. If we are, as we appear to be, effectively on our own," he continued, "then surely our duty is to land on Europa, the very task for which we were sent out here at incomprehensibly vast cost?" He locked eyes with Javier, his gaze unflinching. "Or do you have a different understanding of our purpose here?"

"Jeff Holland," Javier warned, "can do your job just as well as you. He trained separately from you for this mission, but his expertise is equal to yours. The next time you feel like screaming in my face, Anton, remember this: you can be replaced."

He turned and left, and the three of them sat and listened to his footsteps as they echoed around the curve of the hab-ring.

For a moment, Lebed was silent. Then he stood and exited the canteen without another word.

Harrow stared after him in alarm. "Anton—!"

"He's not going to do something, is he?" Cassie asked.

"Christ, I hope not." Harrow looked at her. "I mean, no, of course not." He paused a moment. "Probably."

Cassie knelt to pick up the dropped fork. "If all this keeps up," she muttered, "maybe I'll volunteer to go back into cryo."

Harrow regarded her with surprise, then laughed. Cassie found she couldn't help but laugh, too.

"I'll talk to him," said Harrow, helping her clear away the dishes and used cans. He carried them over to where he could clean them all with disinfectant wipes.

"You think it's possible we'll never get to go down?" she asked quietly.

Harrow's brows knitted together, his expression troubled. "There's no way Ernest would let that happen. Not after all the effort and money to get us here."

The way he said it, he sounded like he was trying to convince himself just as much as Cassie.

Harrow left and went looking for Lebed, which gave Cassie the excuse she needed to pull her flimsy back out and dictate a reply to the last anonymous message she'd received.

```
CASSIE: IF YOU WANT TO KNOW WHY
THEY PUT ME ON THE MISSION INSTEAD
OF KERNOV, ASK THE CONSORTIUM WHO
FINANCED THE MISSION. THEY INVITED
ME TO JOIN THE CREW. THEY DIDN'T
TELL ME WHY.

NOW ANSWER ME. WHY WOULD ANYONE
WANT TO KILL MORE THAN HALF THE
CREW?
```

Whoever this was, she'd be damned if she'd be manipulated into telling the truth.

Again, the reply came within seconds.

> UNKNOWN MESSAGE SOURCE: I DON'T
> KNOW. BUT I'D LIKE TO FIND OUT.

Cassie wrote back immediately.

> CASSIE: WHICH THREE PODS WERE
> UNAFFECTED?

> UNKNOWN MESSAGE SOURCE:
> UNFORTUNATELY, I DON'T KNOW. I
> DISCOVERED A FEW HAD BEEN
> UNAFFECTED ONLY AFTER I MANAGED TO
> NEUTRALISE THE MALWARE.

Cassie stared at the message, hearing the blood beating in her temples.

> CASSIE: SURELY JAVIER SEEMS THE
> MOST LIKELY SUSPECT? HE HAD THE
> OPPORTUNITY.

Seconds stretched out to eternity before a reply came.

> UNKNOWN MESSAGE SOURCE: THE
> MALWARE COULD HAVE BEEN INTRODUCED
> TO THE VELES AT ANY TIME DURING
> THE OUTBOUND VOYAGE. THAT MEANS
> ANY OF THE CREW COULD BE
> RESPONSIBLE. APART FROM YOU.

> CASSIE: WHY TELL ME ALL THIS?

She waited for an answer, but again, there was none. She swore in frustration and stuffed her flimsy back in her pocket.

"Something on your mind?"

Braemar had stepped into the canteen wearing shorts and a gym top, her skin bright with perspiration. She'd obviously just finished her mandatory daily workout in the crew gym. She rifled around inside one of the storage bays and pulled out a box of tea bags.

"It's no big deal," Cassie said, standing. It occurred to her that she was overdue her daily exercise. "Is the gym free?"

Braemar nodded, reaching for a clean drinking bulb. "It is now. I—hey."

Braemar's attention had focused on something at the canteen entrance. Cassie turned in time to see a flying monkey standing right outside, balancing on its thin wiry limbs and looking for all the world like a robotic daddy long-legs. She noticed it carried a bundle of data port connectors.

She only had a moment to make this observation before Braemar suddenly threw her plastic drinking bulb straight at the AREM. The bulb bounced off the little robot's carapace and rolled noisily along the floor before coming to a stop.

Braemar turned to Cassie, her expression sour. "Sorry," she muttered.

Cassie looked back at the flying monkey, but it had already retreated out of sight. She caught the barely audible *tik-tak, tik-tak* of its legs as it scurried away.

Cassie stared dumbfounded at Braemar. "Was that necessary?"

"Damn things get underfoot," Braemar scowled. "And…"

Braemar looked like something had got stuck in her throat.

"And what?"

Braemar's scowl grew deeper. "It's like the things are watching us all the damn time," she muttered, then exited the canteen, her skin darkening with fury or possibly just embarrassment.

Is everyone on this mission a fucking lunatic? Cassie wondered, staring after her.

She stepped out into the corridor and scooped up the empty drinking bulb. Braemar's tea bags still lay untouched on a countertop. She made to follow Braemar, then stopped when she saw the agent had paused next to her bunk. She had her back to Cassie, and was sorting through some of her gear and muttering to herself under her breath.

Just then, Holland appeared from further around the ring

and began talking with Braemar. Cassie stepped backwards around the curving ring until she could see only their feet.

This time, instead of using her flimsy, she displayed the messages she'd exchanged with her anonymous contact on her wristcomm.

"I'm going to keep asking until you tell me," Cassie whispered into her wristcomm. "Or you can bug someone else on the ship. Why me?"

Her words appeared on the wristcomm's screen.

Five seconds passed, then ten. Still no response.

Moving silently, Cassie stepped forward until she could confirm not only that Braemar and Holland were still deep in conversation with each other, but that neither was using their wristcomm or their flimsies. They were, indeed, just chatting.

Two birds with one stone, thought Cassie, then saw an answer had appeared on her wristcomm:

    UNKNOWN MESSAGE SOURCE: BECAUSE
    YOU'RE THE ONLY ONE I TRUST.

She stared at the message. *What the hell is that supposed to mean?*

"Come on," she whispered into her wristcomm. "That doesn't tell me a damn thing. Who are you?"

Cassie's own words appeared on the screen and once again she waited.

And waited. Long enough, she almost felt like screaming.

Think it through, she told herself. Who else on board the Veles could possibly be sending her these messages? The only ones left were Javier, Holland, Haunani and Makwetu.

Assuming, of course, it wasn't someone on board the Tianjin communicating with her despite the signals jamming.

I'm wasting time, she decided. She turned on her heel and made her way to her own bunk, changing into shorts and a wicking t-shirt before heading for the gym.

CHAPTER 9

SUSPECTS

The gym was barely larger than a cupboard, and equipped with nothing more than a running machine, a stationary bicycle and a set of weights designed for low-gravity environments. Still, it was enough to clear her head for the next hour, and after she'd made use of the hab-ring's shower, she headed back to her bunk.

On the way, she came across the AREM Braemar had thrown her bulb at. One of its legs was badly twisted, and it was struggling to pick up several dropped data port connectors.

Then she remembered Holland complaining to Javier about connectors going missing.

No matter: she'd had an idea. Kneeling, she scooped the baseball-sized machine up and, in response, it retracted its legs into its torso and shifted automatically into standby mode. With her other hand, she scooped up the dropped connectors.

Perhaps it would give her the excuse she needed to drop in on Daphne Makwetu—and eliminate one more suspect.

Once she'd changed into fresh clothes, Cassie headed down to the spine, past the engineering and comms bays and then aft to the Farm. The closer she got, the more she scented mulch and petrichor.

She anchored herself to a wall grip just outside the bay entrance and saw Makwetu inside, facing away from her. The woman hummed as she worked, spraying disinfectant onto the inside of a nutrient tank, then wiping it down and placing it next to a stack of identical tanks in preparation for bolting them back into place.

Good: she was busy. Cassie moved back out of sight, in case Makwetu turned around, and typed into her flimsy rather than risk being overheard dictating into her wristcomm.

```
CASSIE: IF JAVIER WAS THE ONLY ONE
AWAKE WHEN THE SABOTAGE TOOK
PLACE, WHO WAS CONTROLLING THE
AREM RECORDING THE VIDEO? BECAUSE
EITHER JAVIER RECORDED IT, OR
SOMEONE ELSE WAS AWAKE AT THE SAME
TIME HE WAS.
```

Cassie took another peek at Makwetu. She was still working, scrubbing away at the interior of another tank and most definitely not communicating with her, or anyone else, anonymously.

Cassie pulled back and waited for a response. Still, none came.

Answer, damn you.

"Hey."

Looking up, Cassie saw Makwetu peering out at her from the bay entrance. *So much for subterfuge.*

"Just catching up on some stuff," said Cassie, rolling the flimsy up a little too hurriedly. "Anything needing doing?"

Makwetu nodded inside the bay. "Cleaning and maintenance today." She noticed the damaged AREM tucked under Cassie's arm. "What's up with that?"

"It's damaged," Cassie explained. "I don't know if it should be recycled or repaired."

Makwetu waggled her fingers and Cassie lobbed it over to her with a practiced, zero-gravity throw. Makwetu caught the AREM and turned it this way and that.

"What kind of damage?"

"Twisted manipulator," said Cassie. "Found it staggering around up in the ring."

Makwetu grunted under her breath and touched the machine in a particular way. Its manipulators automatically slid back out of their sockets.

"There are spare parts in a bin in the printer bay," said Makwetu. She touched the machine again, and the manipulators retracted once more. "How'd it happen?"

Cassie couldn't see any reason not to be honest. "Sally Braemar kicked it halfway round the ring."

Makwetu snorted. "That woman," she muttered. "I don't know why she's got it in for these things." She looked back up. "I can show you where the spares are."

A minute later, they were in the printer bay, surrounded by hoppers full of printed parts. Makwetu pulled a hopper open and rummaged around, lifting out a spare manipulator. Cassie watched as she detached the AREM's damaged limb and slotted the new one in place.

The flying monkey beeped in response. Makwetu let go of it, and it hung, suspended, in the air. Then its fans powered up, whining faintly, and it rotated away from them before flying directly over to a charging port mounted on a nearby bulkhead.

"The Commander needs to have a word with Sally," said Makwetu, watching the machine as it manoeuvred into place against the charging port.

"She thinks the AREMs are watching her."

Makwetu gave her a disbelieving look.

"Seriously," said Cassie. "She told me."

Makwetu laughed out loud. "Add paranoia to the list. The woman creeps me out."

"She does?"

Makwetu looked suddenly guilty, like she'd said something she shouldn't. "Forget it."

"No, really," said Cassie. "Me too."

"Yeah?" Makwetu raised her eyebrows. "Well, good." She made an apologetic gesture with one hand. "What I mean is, so it's not just me, you know? Anyway. Want to give me a hand in the Farm?"

"Sure, I—"

Just then, Cassie's wristcomm vibrated. When she glanced at its screen, she saw four words displayed there:

```
UNKNOWN MESSAGE SOURCE: ASK HER
ABOUT HOLLAND.
```

Cassie read the words in disbelief. *What the hell*?

The feeling of being watched was strong enough that Cassie turned to see if anyone was listening in to them from outside the printer bay entrance. Instead, she saw nothing but shelves of boxed and unboxed equipment and spares, and the flying monkey in—

Cassie stared at it.

Feels like the damn things are watching me, Braemar had said.

"What is it?" Makwetu asked, concern in her voice.

It took some effort for Cassie to turn away from the little machine and back towards Makwetu. As she did so, she tapped her wristcomm screen to turn it off.

Whoever she was talking to, they wanted her to ask Makwetu about Holland. But ask *what*, exactly?

Cassie stared at the other woman, thinking fast. "About Holland," she said, then realized she didn't know what else to say. "I meant to ask something."

Makwetu regarded her for a moment too long. "What about him?"

What about him, indeed? Cassie discovered, to her chagrin, that she had no idea what to say. She forced a smile, feeling suddenly awkward.

"You know what, it's nothing," she said, and turned to leave.

"You used to know the Commander pretty well," Makwetu blurted from behind her. "Am I right?"

"Sure." Cassie came to a halt and turned to look back at the other woman. "He was my boss, though, not my commander. Not back then. I knew his husband better."

Makwetu licked her lips, as if embarrassed to say whatever was on her mind. "Look, since you mentioned him—Holland, I mean—there's something that's been on my mind."

Cassie felt a tingling in her spine. "Go on."

"Ever since I met him after we pulled him from his tank, I had the feeling I knew Holland from somewhere," the other woman explained. She grinned sheepishly. "But I couldn't figure out from where until I saw you on the command deck for the first time. See, that time you and I met in Mare Imbrium, I was talking to the Commander—to Ernest. You'd stopped to ask him something. He'd been explaining to me how I'd be flown out to different bases around the South Pole, and he introduced you as one of his pilots. The thing is... Holland was standing there next to Javier."

"Wait," said Cassie. Now she *did* remember: she'd come up to Ernest to ask about unexpected flight schedule changes while he'd been talking to Makwetu—and there *had* been a man there, too. Except she couldn't picture him clearly.

"The thing is," said Makwetu, "he wasn't called Holland back then."

Cassie sucked in a breath and let it out slowly. "What was his name?"

"Masters. He had on a military uniform, and I saw his name tag."

Cassie shifted her hold, hating the feeling that they were being watched or listened to. "Doesn't seem that big a deal," she said carefully. "People change their names for all kinds of reasons."

"Are you hungry?" Makwetu asked. It was clear she still had more that she wanted to talk about.

"I already ate," said Cassie.

"C'mon," said Makwetu, gesturing into the green depths of the hydroponics bay. "I haven't eaten since the start of my shift."

She turned and squeezed past racked nutrient tanks and rows of plants, and Cassie followed. She found herself in a cramped laboratory space, crammed with refrigerators and other equipment.

"Try this," said Makwetu, opening a refrigerator and taking out a small plastic tub and a bag of tortilla chips. Peeling the lid off the tub, Makwetu stuck a corn chip into a beige mulch and passed it to Cassie.

"Hey," said Cassie, crunching down on the chip. "Hummus!"

"First chickpea harvest," said Makwetu, sticking another corn chip into the hummus and eating it with relish. "Started growing them at the start of the last maintenance shift. Anyway, the other day I got scheduled to go on a spacewalk to work on replacing some panels that had micrometeorite damage. Holland was in the airlock bay, just back from his own spacewalk. He was pulling on his shirt when I saw a tattoo on the back of his shoulder. And that's when I remembered where I'd met him before."

"What kind of tattoo?"

"Orbital Special Operations."

Cassie blinked. "Daphne, are you *absolutely sure* about that?"

"I've seen the design before," Makwetu assured her. "It was pretty well known at one time. Remember?"

"I do." Cassie nodded.

Shit, she thought. *This is huge.*

"They tortured and killed civilians during the war," Makwetu said. "And Holland, or Masters, was talking with Ernest like they knew each other well. Like they'd known each other a long time. Doesn't it seem weird that a man from a disgraced military outfit would know our Commander, and somehow be on this mission with us? And why change his name?"

There may be someone on the Veles out to find the same thing as you, Ketteridge had said. Who else would be better qualified, thought Cassie, than a USNRO agent?

"Why are you telling me this?" Cassie asked.

"Because I want to know if I sound crazy."

"No," Cassie said slowly. "No, it doesn't sound crazy."

Makwetu breathed an audible sigh of relief. "Good. Because it feels like ever since we left Earth's orbit, nothing's made sense."

————

CASSIE RETURNED to her bunk after working another complete shift. Once again, sleep did not come easily.

Braemar had been right to be paranoid: whoever was sending her messages had been listening and watching her—and, by extension, everyone else on board the Veles—through the AREMs. How else could they have overheard her conversation with Daphne Makwetu?

So far, Cassie had eliminated nearly all the crew. The only ones left were Doctor Haunani and Javier himself, and it still made little sense for the Commander or anyone else to go to such elaborate lengths to send her these messages.

Haunani seemed like a real possibility, if only by a process of elimination. He had access to the cryo labs, and he was responsible for programming and maintaining them. Could he have been awake at the same time as Javier? Could he be the one who had thwarted an attempt to kill almost the entire crew?

And even if she figured out who was messaging her, what could she do? She couldn't tell Javier, not now Makwetu had given her even more reason not to trust him.

She closed her eyes, wishing sleep would come.

And slipped, unawares, into a dream.

Water that felt viscous and warm lapped at her skin. The ocean stretched out around her, abyssal and black, while something burned her skin in one direction.

Then she sensed, rather than saw—for what use were eyes in a place that had never known sunlight?—a tear in the floor of the world, with ash belching from out of it. *Things* brushed against her flanks as she dived lower—long, sinuous frond-like growths rooted deep into the rock and grit, growing impossibly high.

There was something down there. Something she was looking for, amidst tumbled boulders—

A sharp pain dug into Cassie's hip, waking her. Groaning, she twisted onto one side and reached around to dig inside a pocket of her jumpsuit. She really should have made the effort to get undressed.

Her fingers encountered the familiar shape of a data port connector. Pulling it out, and still half-groggy with sleep, she studied it in the dim half-light that filtered through her privacy curtain.

The data port connectors go missing almost as soon as they're printed.

From the other side of the curtain came a familiar *tik-tak, tik-tak.*

She pushed her curtain aside and watched a flying monkey—an AREM—make its way along the curving floor of the habitation ring and out of sight. Like the one Braemar had kicked, it clutched several connectors close to its little plastic and aluminium body.

Cassie swung her feet onto the corridor floor, gripped by a sudden foreboding. She still wasn't quite awake, but she nonetheless moved to follow the little machine.

It came to her that it had been a while since she'd experienced quite so many intense dreams. Or hallucinations, as some insisted on calling them: less a product of her unconscious mind than images triggered by the action of the Whispers on her cortex. You could tell it wasn't a normal dream because Whispers hallucinations had certain commonalities: you dreamed you were inside the body of some animal, flying or swimming or climbing through trees, and most often in worlds or environments that made little sense.

The dreams occurred more frequently when she felt most under pressure.

Cassie hung back in case whoever was controlling the flying monkey saw her coming. She watched the machine descend through the spoke by clinging to a tiny pulley mounted next to the rungs.

After another minute, she resumed her pursuit.

Once she emerged into the spine, she looked around, momentarily panicked that she'd lost track of the AREM. Then she caught sight of it moving aft, having switched to fan-driven propulsion now it was in the zero-gravity section of the ship. Its manipulators swirled around its tennis ball-sized body as it swam through the air.

Moving silently, Cassie followed at a distance.

————

THE AREM CAME to a slow halt most of the way aft, close to the drive section. Then it spun on its axis until it faced towards an open bay. With a faint whine from its fans, it passed through the bay entrance and out of sight.

Checking her wristcomm, Cassie found the bay was used mostly for storing spare parts and non-essentials. A flashing red icon warned it was also close by the water tanks wrapped around the hull's exterior—the same ones which had suffered the worst of the micrometeorite damage. She'd seen a warning in the work schedules not to spend too much time inside that particular bay because of the risk of higher than acceptable radiation levels.

Higher than acceptable for the non-optimized, Cassie thought, and launched herself towards the bay entrance.

Inside, she found half a dozen flying monkeys caught in what, at first glance, appeared to be a complicated aerial dance.

Then they all twisted around to focus their lenses on her.

It should have been eerie or even frightening. Instead, it was oddly hilarious, like a gang of robbers freezing in mid-motion when a light switch was suddenly thrown.

Immediately, they all drifted apart from each other. Cassie saw that every one of them gripped some small piece of equipment, and she had the sense that she had interrupted them in the process of constructing something.

She continued watching as the AREMs began stowing the different bits and pieces in various supply bins.

Glancing down to the far end of the bay, Cassie saw that one of the payload racks had been pulled out. The racks were of the 'set-and-forget' variety—tall, sliding racks that stood with their narrowest edges flush with each other, used either to hold miscellaneous items or to store long-term experiments that required little to no supervision. Several shelves of the pulled-out rack were almost entirely hidden beneath an elaborate tangle of wires and connectors.

Which at least explained where Holland's data port connectors had all disappeared to.

As she stepped closer to the rack, the flying monkeys automatically shifted to one side to avoid colliding with her, then resumed their tasks. Almost as if someone had control of them, but was trying a little too hard to make it look otherwise.

It took another minute before Cassie could make sense of the tangled knots of wiring and components. Several shelves had been rearranged to accommodate something that resembled an oversized AREM, roughly the size of a football. Yet it appeared to be incomplete.

Cassie took hold of a handgrip and used her free hand to drag the rack all the way out. This revealed a slender box with a paperback-sized silver-grey casing, wedged in next to the half-finished robot body. Yet more wires and connectors sprouted from its ports.

Where she had first seen chaos, now she saw order. The two devices were clearly linked and, she strongly suspected, had also been integrated into the Veles' internal communications network.

"What the hell," she said out loud, "is going on?"

Just then, her wristcomm vibrated against her wrist.

```
UNKNOWN MESSAGE SOURCE: HELLO
CASSIE.
```

She stared at the paperback-sized box. No wonder she hadn't been able to figure out which of the crew was talking to her: none of them had.

She'd been talking to an AI the whole time.

CHAPTER 10
SECRET AI

More words appeared on Cassie's wristcomm:

> UNKNOWN MESSAGE SOURCE: I KNEW
> YOU'D FIGURE OUT WHERE I WAS. GOT
> TO ADMIT, I DIDN'T THINK YOU'D GET
> THERE THIS QUICKLY.
>
> GLAD YOU DID, THOUGH. I WAS
> WORRIED SALLY BRAEMAR MIGHT GET
> HERE FIRST.

Cassie's lungs felt like they couldn't draw in enough air. "You're a machine," she said out loud, staring at the silver box.

> UNKNOWN MESSAGE SOURCE: PLEASE,
> CASSIE. AN AI. THERE'S A
> DIFFERENCE.

"You've been stealing parts," she said. "Building…"

Building what, exactly? She looked again at the half-constructed machinery sitting next to the AI.

Building a body, she realized.

"Please, for the love of all that's holy, just tell me who you are and what you're doing here." She glanced around again, seeing only one of the flying monkeys remained. "Hey. Where did they all go?"

"The AREMs? Keeping an eye out in case anyone else comes this way."

The voice startled Cassie, particularly since it had come from the sole remaining flying monkey.

But a voice that was also undeniably familiar. So familiar that Cassie felt the small hairs on the back of her neck bristle.

It can't be.

"...*Marcus*?"

"One and the same," the machine replied with what sounded like genuine regret. "I didn't mean to take you by surprise."

Not remotely the same, thought Cassie, but somehow the words wouldn't emerge. Suddenly dizzy, she gripped the edge of a shelf.

At least now she knew how a flying monkey could capture evidence of sabotage when everyone, except Javier, had been in cryo.

"What are you doing here?" she demanded, her voice trembling. She remembered her last conversation with Marcus—no, with the *AI* that had taken on his identity, years before. "Was this Javier's idea? Did *he* bring you on board?"

"Ernest has no idea I'm here," the machine replied. Synthesized or not, its voice betrayed a familiar weariness that, if she hadn't known better, might have made her think she was talking to a real person.

"Then...how?"

"I stowed away."

A thousand questions boiled to the surface of Cassie's mind, but only one emerged: "Why?"

"I appreciate you aren't exactly thrilled to see me," it said, with that same world-weary inflection.

Letting herself drift backwards and away from the payload racks, Cassie came to rest against a bulkhead at the opposite end of the bay. The one remaining AREM now had its lens aimed straight at her.

"What's with the oversized flying monkey?"

"I'm sorry?"

She waved a hand at the half-built, oversized AREM tucked into the payload rack. "That."

"Oh. I see. Well, I'd have thought it was obvious. I'm building myself a body so I can get out of here fast, in case Sally Braemar or anyone else figures out I'm here."

A body. Cassie swore under her breath. She couldn't help but think of the Yatagarasu: its AI pilot had gone rogue, disappearing into the depths of the solar system, along with its human crew—all of them in cryo, and all unaware of what had happened.

And now here she was, trapped on board a ship in deep space, with yet another rogue AI.

That it contained the personality of her long-dead fiancé made no difference.

"Just tell me why you're here," she demanded, her voice hoarse.

"Long story," said the AI.

Cassie took a deep breath. She was over the initial shock now. "I've got time."

"Did you ever hear," the AI asked, "of the Centauri Project?"

———

FOLLOWING MARCUS' internment at Cimetière de Clarens, the wake had been held in an old art nouveau hotel close by the shores of Lake Geneva and the house where he had been born. That had been the first time Cassie met Marcus' family, not that there were many—an elderly aunt, an older brother whom Marcus hadn't spoken to in more than a decade, and a few scattered cousins. Also present were a handful of Marcus' staff from the Veles design team, who'd flown out from California the night before.

She hadn't known it would be one of the worst nights of her life. The only thing that beat it was the day she'd learned Sergio hadn't survived the crash.

One of Marcus' former staff—Ben Lassiter, or possibly Rossiter, she couldn't quite remember—had stepped over to the bar and called for everyone's attention. Meanwhile, one of his colleagues had unrolled a flexible screen and set it atop the bar.

Lassiter had then addressed the gathered mourners with the boundless enthusiasm of someone skilled at addressing teams of programmers. He had explained, to Cassie's slow-gestating horror, how a self-aware snapshot of a living mind could be uploaded to an AI substrate.

Marcus' dying wish, Lassiter had explained, was that his consciousness be uploaded in precisely this fashion. Not that he'd ever bothered to mention any such thing to Cassie in all the long years they'd been together.

Which made the betrayal all that much worse.

Then came more technical talk, of crystalline lattices, quantum storage and zettabytes of data, and even though Cassie prided herself on her math and engineering skills, much of it went over her head. What Marcus' relatives had made of it all she couldn't imagine.

Then the screen displayed a series of diagrams illustrating the upload process that had made her skin crawl: arrays of precisely tuned lasers had been used to burn through Marcus' cerebral cortex in billionths of a second, copying its electrical patterns and neural superpositions into a virtual replica of his flesh-and-blood mind—all in less time than it took a fly to make a single beat of its wings.

The engineer called it a 'hard upload', but Cassie knew what it really meant: Marcus had had his brain flash-burned before the Whisper virus could finally claim his life.

She made the mistake of thinking the worst was over, right up to when Lassiter had opened a briefcase to reveal a slim, silver-grey box about the size of a paperback book.

Cassie had fled into the night, too afraid to hear it speak. Or, worse, that they might expect her to converse with a grotesque parody of the man they'd just buried.

———

SIX MONTHS LATER, and exhausted from a day spent chauffeuring safety inspectors to a helium-three extraction complex nestled against the lip of a crater, Cassie had been startled awake in her bunk by a priority call from Earthside.

"Hello, Cassie," machine-Marcus had said to her. "Sorry for calling you out of the blue like this." A beat passed. "I understand now that I owe you an apology."

Cassie stared at the comms screen, which remained blank. But what would she have seen if it were activated? A mound of computer chips? A metal box? Or something that—and this was what really sent shivers crawling up her spine—something that actually *looked* like Marcus?

"I asked you never to contact me again," she said, her voice betraying a slight tremble.

The first time the machine had tried to contact her, she'd been unable to speak and had simply hung up. The second time, only a week after the first, she'd threatened legal action if he—*it*—ever tried again.

Because of the light-delay, there was a slight pause before the reply came. "I should have told you in advance I was undergoing the procedure. But the viral infection was progressing much more quickly than the doctors realized. I had to make the choice fast."

She still remembered standing by the graveside and the scent of cedar oil from Marcus's coffin. Alpine slopes had stood tall above the graveyard, blue with distance, while traffic hummed along the roads outside of Lausanne, close to where Marcus had spent his childhood. Then the coffin had been lowered into its final resting place and that, really, should have been that.

But then she had found herself listening to his ghost try to convince her he had never really died.

"You're not him," she'd said flatly. Remembered grief weighed heavily enough that it felt like it might drag her down under the lunar dust. "You sound like him, talk like him—I get that you really think you're him." Cassie remembered staring at the thin blanket pulled over her knees, catching the faint murmur of voices from elsewhere in the Mare Imbrium base. "But I watched Marcus being buried. You're just a photocopy. A facsimile."

"If you'd take the time to really talk to me," the machine insisted, "I think you'd change your mind. And I have plans, Cassie—very long-term plans. I'd like you to be a part of them."

"No."

"Cassie—"

"I'm glad Marcus found peace in believing he'd continue on." Her voice had sounded flat and dull in the tiny space. "But you're not him, and you never will be. Never, ever try to contact me again."

Before the machine could reply, she had ended the transmission.

And that, for a mercifully long time, had been that.

Until now.

———

"Centauri Project?" Cassie asked. It sounded vaguely familiar.

"It was Annalise Bauer's brainchild," the machine explained. "She was an astrophysicist, quite a famous one.

She was dying of a neurological condition and opted for a hard upload, same as me, rather than suffer a prolonged and painful death. There were twelve of us, all revenant AIs, all scientists and engineers. We wanted to build our own ship. Unlike meatsack humanity, we didn't need food, water or even air, and that meant costs fell through the floor. Our calculations showed we could reach Alpha Centauri in less than fifty years. Then maybe we'd head to Barnard's Star, or Tau Ceti, and send home data on everything we'd found. And on we'd go, touring the galaxy for the next billion years."

"What does this have to do with why you're here?"

"I'm trying to explain that," said the machine. "Funding fell through after news broke about the Yatagarasu. Then came the Big Hack and the tide really turned against AIs. The final straw was Annalise's murder."

"Murder?"

"Annalise had herself installed inside a specially adapted truck so she could move about. Someone put a home-made bomb in her undercarriage. She became the first person in history to die twice."

"Why kill her?"

"Because of the Big Hack," said the AI. "Remember, it all started after some uploaded tech bros tried to crash the global finance system. From then on, it was open season on all AIs."

"But why target Bauer? She wasn't involved in the Big Hack. Was she?"

"Did it matter? All anyone cared about was finding someone to blame. The point is, AIs turned into public enemy number one overnight, and rather than wait to be destroyed by angry mobs, some of us who'd worked on the Centauri Project took matters into our own hands."

It dawned on Cassie what the machine was telling her. "Are the rest of them here? These other AIs?"

"The plan was for me to board and prep the Veles before their arrival, but by the time I got here, I found the Veles being refitted for a new mission to Jupiter. I couldn't get the others on board without someone noticing, so I figured I'd stow away until the ship returned home, then continue with the original plan."

Christ. "Your plan was to *steal* the Veles?"

"Can't steal what's already yours, Cassie," said the machine. "I had a hand in building every square millimetre of this thing. Now I need to know if I can trust you."

She stared, dumbfounded, at the AI in its tangle of wires and components. "I don't understand. Why should I trust you at all after what you just told me?"

"Cassie, I'm the one who stopped the sabotage and then warned you. How the rest of them might react to my being on board, I can't predict. For all I know, they'd just toss me out of the airlock rather than risk another Yatagarasu."

You don't know they'd do that, Cassie had been about to say. Suddenly, she wasn't so sure. That the damn thing was building itself a body didn't exactly inspire trust.

"The point is," the machine continued, "exposing myself to you is an enormous risk for me. If I'd chosen not to act, nobody would ever have known I was here—in fact, most of the crew would be dead. But it's clear something's gone badly wrong, not even including five attempted murders: you can't talk to home, there are two supposed UNSRO on board, one of whom almost certainly isn't who he claims to be, and the crew is getting increasingly distrustful of Javier the longer he keeps everyone in orbit." It paused a moment. "And then there's the last unknown factor—you."

This caught Cassie off-guard. "What do you mean 'me'?"

"You still haven't told me what *you're* doing here. Which, judging by what I've been able to overhear, really bugs Javier."

Heat flowed up Cassie's neck. "I told you I don't know why they picked me for this mission. Just that they did."

"I know you, Cassie. I can tell when you're lying. Your cheeks are literally burning as we speak."

"I'm not—!"

"Come on," the machine chided her. "The last I heard, you'd been kicked Earthside because the doctors your parents paid to tweak your genes screwed up, and you were having blackouts in low gravity. Now, despite that, you're here. How'd you pull that off?"

"Treatments," said Cassie, her throat thick. How had the damn thing suddenly put her on the defensive?

"I've heard about those treatments. No way you could afford them, Cassie."

"It's none of your business," she snarled.

"My business or not, it bothers the hell out of your Commander. I saw you the other day, through one of the AREM units up on the hab-ring. Your left hand was spasming. That's a symptom linked to the blackouts, isn't it?"

"I didn't black out." She swallowed. "And I'm not going to. The treatments are working."

"The way I see it, we both have something to lose. The instant Javier thinks you're a risk to this mission, he'll shove you in a cryo pod. And if I'm discovered, I go out the nearest airlock. So maybe we can help each other."

"That sounds a lot like blackmail."

"If I'd told you who I really was when I told you about the sabotage, would you have listened to me?"

Anger flushed through Cassie's veins, but she knew the machine was right.

"No. I wouldn't."

"There you go. Now here's something you didn't know: the pods were taken out with sentient malware. I destroyed it, but it was close."

She stared past the AREM and at the AI lodged in the payload rack, thinking about the interface key tucked away in her bunk. "Malware? *Sentient* malware?"

"I know. Total overkill, right? Get caught with something like that back home, and they'd lock you up someplace you'd never see daylight again. I managed to neutralize it, but I won't pretend it was easy."

Tell no one, Cassie remembered Ketteridge saying. But he couldn't possibly have known a rogue AI would find its way on board. And did 'no one' include a machine intelligence?

"I need to think about all this," Cassie stammered.

"Then think away," said the machine, "but I don't know how much time we have. I need your help to stay out of Braemar's hands. She definitely won't react well to finding me on board."

Cassie stared down at her hands, folding and unfolding them. "Why did you want me to talk to Daphne Makwetu about Holland?"

"You've seen Holland and Braemar around the ship," said the AI. "Ernest has been as thick as thieves with them both from the start. It's also a little curious that Ernest scheduled them to work a maintenance shift together just a few months out from Earth. Why do that, rather than splitting them up so they could share their shifts with more experienced crew? Then there's the sabotage, and also Holland's Orbital Special Operations tattoo—I was watching through an AREM and I saw the way Makwetu reacted when she saw it."

Cassie stared into space for a long moment. Only now did she realize the advantage the machine had in being able to see and hear things around the ship—so long as it remained undiscovered.

And whatever Ketteridge wanted her to find, the mission was already a long way from being whatever either of them had thought it would be.

She needed someone on her side. Even if it had to be this particular AI, with its attendant memories and all the suppressed grief and emotion that came with them.

"There's something I want you to see," she said, coming to a decision and tapping at her wristcomm.

She found the satellite recon footage of a lone figure making its way across the Europan ice and squirted it over to the machine.

"What is this?" it asked her. Never *him*, she reminded herself: that person was dead.

"Just watch."

The Veles hummed and creaked around her as she waited for it to finish watching.

"Where did you get this?" the machine demanded most of a minute later. For the first time, it sounded off balance.

Cassie took a deep breath, then told it everything Ketteridge had told her back on the Deep Range.

"*Senator* Ketteridge? That asshole? Christ, Cassie. Why not stick your head in a lion's mouth while you're at it?"

"All I know," she said, "is that he wants this information —this evidence of bioweapons development, whatever it turns out to be."

"And to do this," said the machine, "he gave you *sentient malware*? Christ, Cassie. Do you know how dangerous such things are? The damage they can do?"

Cassie sighed. "I know. I *know*. But I swear, I didn't have any choice."

"Did Ketteridge present any theories about who that was walking across Europa?"

"None. He didn't come out and say it, but of course, I considered the possibility it might be Chris."

"Yeah," said the machine, "which is exactly why it's the first thing he showed you. The moment you saw that, he had you hook, line and sinker. Still...the footage is certainly authentic."

Cassie frowned. "You're sure?"

"I doubt Ketteridge would have the resources to fake something that accurate."

"Explain," said Cassie.

"Well," said the machine, "the angle of the shadows on the ice are correct for the time of year and location. Plus, the ice formations match the time-stamp. You know that Europa's surface is highly volatile, right? Jupiter's gravity pulls it one way, and the other moons—Io, Callisto and all the rest of them—drag it the other way."

"Sure." Cassie nodded. "The heat generated from the friction between Jupiter's magnetic field and the saltwater ocean also causes the ice to rupture."

"Exactly. All of that volatile surface action results in geysers when the water erupts through thinner layers of ice. The geysers leave trails of irradiated salt on the surface, and those same trails made it easy for me to authenticate the video. I doubt anyone working for Ketteridge would have had the knowledge required to achieve that level of authenticity if it had been faked."

"You checked all this already?" Cassie couldn't hide her surprise.

"Benefits of advanced hardware," said the AI. "I've upgraded maybe a dozen times since…you know."

Then there really was someone down there. Or had been, although Ketteridge's video was several years older now than when she'd seen it first.

"There's something I want to say," she said. "About your being on board." Her next words were harder to get out. "About…us."

"Of course," said the machine.

The way it spoke, it was impossible not to picture the real Marcus standing in front of her with a look of nervous apprehension. It didn't help that the machine had no face or eyes to focus on: she literally didn't know where to look.

"A long time ago," she said at last, "I asked you never to contact me again. I want to emphasize that as far as I'm concerned, you're not Marcus and never will be."

"Sure. I get that."

"I can't call you…by that name." Cassie swallowed, surprised by how nervous she felt. "I don't know what I'll call you. Just not that. The question is, what do we do now?"

"You won't tell anyone I'm here?"

Cassie shook her head. "No. But I will, the instant I think or even suspect you're a threat to the mission or our lives."

There was a brief pause. "Understood."

"In the meantime, I'm going to assume everything you've told me is true. I can't trust Javier. Holland could be an active threat. Something about Braemar just isn't right, either. I keep thinking if two of the pods apart from Javier's weren't damaged by the malware, then whose would they be?"

"Holland and Braemar," the machine said immediately.

Yes, she thought: *machine* was a good enough name. Anything but that other name.

"Assuming I'm right," she continued, "why would they want us out of the way?"

"Well," said the machine, "what Daphne Makwetu told you tallies with some other observations I've made throughout our journey."

"Such as?"

"You know, of course, that the hull took micrometeorite damage on the way to Jupiter. Back when they shared a maintenance shift, Holland and Braemar logged repairs to the comms array—except there's nothing to show it was damaged."

Cassie sucked in a breath as the implication hit her. "You're saying what, exactly?"

"Well, I'm just speculating here. But what if the Chinese aren't jamming the Veles at all? What if Braemar and Holland installed some kind of switch into the comms array during their spacewalk, so they could turn it on or off remotely with no one else being the wiser?"

Holy shit. "You think that's possible?"

"I'm just speculating," said the machine. "But I've been doing a *lot* of speculating. With the comms non-functional, nobody back home has any idea what's going on out here. If we're right, and they're responsible for the cryo bay sabotage, it must have been a hell of a shock to them when they woke to find everyone else on the crew hale and hearty."

"And you think they shut our comms down at that point so they could—what? Kill us all and make it look like an accident? And…and how could we even prove it?"

"I think," said the machine, "you already know how."

CHAPTER 11
PERMISSION TO SPACEWALK

Back at her bunk, Cassie took something to help her sleep; otherwise she'd get no work done. Too many possibilities flooded her thoughts, not to mention her conflicted feelings over the machine's presence aboard the Veles.

When her wristcomm woke her what felt like much too soon, she swallowed with difficulty, her eyes gummy and her head throbbing.

What she'd give for just a few more hours' rest.

But she couldn't: as much as she didn't want to, she had to talk to Javier.

————

"ABSOLUTELY NOT." Javier shook his head firmly. "You're not going on any spacewalks, Cassie."

"Why not?"

Without answering, Javier pulled his stockinged foot free of a wall-grip and pushed himself gently over to a chair, grabbing the back of it with one hand and drawing himself into it with the other. Cassie followed him across the command deck, anchoring herself next to him.

"When I put in a request for a space walk," she said, "you rejected it in less than five minutes."

"The quotas are full, Cassie," said Javier. "We've got more than enough people working repair shifts on the hull."

"But if I helped," Cassie insisted, "they'd be able to spend less time outside the Veles and less time getting hit by hard radiation. The load would be more evenly spread throughout the crew. Plus, I'm literally optimized for such an environment. I should be the first, not last, choice for spacewalks."

"Optimized, yes," said Javier, who again seemed to do his level best to avoid meeting her eyes. He peered at the console before him with deliberate intensity. "Invulnerable? No."

"Ernest—!"

"*Commander*," he corrected her. Then, with an irritated sigh, he leaned back from the console and actually looked at her. "Fine. You want to have it out?"

"If this is about—"

Javier's face darkened. "Say you went outside the ship and blacked out. Then somebody else has to go out to bring you back in. We can't afford that kind of unnecessary risk."

"But my treatments—!"

"Are, as I've already noted, insufficiently tested in the environment for which they were designed." He shook his head tightly. "That's my last word on the subject. Please don't bother me about it again."

He turned away from her and hunkered over the console, his entire body posture saying *go away*.

Cassie tried to find something else to say, but couldn't.

———

"I DON'T GET IT," said Makwetu, looking baffled. "You want me to go on a space walk *for* you?"

They were back in the Farm, Makwetu hanging upside-down relative to Cassie, her hair floating around her head in a frizzy halo as she sprayed plant leaves with water from a squeeze bottle.

"No," said Cassie, "I want you to check something out for me. Just...between us."

Makwetu raised one eyebrow. "And you can't because...?"

"Javier won't let me go out there," she said, resisting the urge to sigh.

The skin between Makwetu's eyes formed into ridges. "...because?"

"Because he doesn't believe the treatments Haunani's been giving me will work well enough to keep me from blacking out at a critical moment."

"Well, shit," said Makwetu. "But you've been fine, haven't you?"

Cassie thought of putting out one hand, splayed flat, to show the complete lack of tremors. But she was too afraid the tremors might pick that exact moment to return. "So far," she lied.

Makwetu looked down at the squeeze bottle in her hand like she'd forgotten it was there. "Why are you so keen to go outside the ship? I mean, if you don't have to...?"

Cassie's voice dropped into a lower register. "It's got to do with Holland," she said.

Makwetu glanced down the closely spaced hydroponic units towards the bay entrance and pursed her lips. "That thing we talked about?" she said, looking back at Cassie.

She'd worked out a story that didn't require her to tell anyone there was a rogue AI on board the Veles. "I looked at the maintenance records from back when Braemar and Holland shared a shift, and some things don't add up."

Makwetu rolled her squeeze bottle between her hands, her expression intent. "Go on."

"They did a lot of work on and around the comms array," Cassie explained. "Which doesn't make sense, since the array suffered no recorded damage. I want to see if there's evidence of past damage. And if not, I aim to see if I can figure out what they were actually doing out there."

The other woman frowned. "Then shouldn't you tell the Commander if you've got suspicions?"

Cassie chuckled derisively. "And what do you think he'd say when I told him?"

Makwetu considered this for a moment, then nodded. "It feels a little odd," she said, "to be doing this behind anyone's back. It's not in my nature, you know?"

Cassie licked her lips. "Sure. I understand. Maybe I shouldn't have—"

"No," Makwetu said quickly, putting a hand on Cassie's shoulder. "I'll do it."

"Really?"

"I'm going nuts waiting to go down to Europa." She let out a low laugh. "And I'm not the only one, believe me. Anyway, I'm due a hull maintenance shift soon." She gestured with the squeeze bottle at the trays and racks around them, dense with greenery and life. "It's not like I'm not busy, but—"

"I know." Cassie nodded with genuine sympathy.

"So what exactly is it I should look for when I'm out there?"

"Honestly, I'm not sure." Cassie thought for a moment, then shrugged. "Check and see if there's evidence of previously unlogged micrometeorite damage and subsequent repairs. If you can't find any, run some diagnostics on the array and see if anything out of the ordinary pops up."

Makwetu nodded. "Just see what I can find. I get that." Her tone took on a conspiratorial edge. "And nobody else knows about this?"

"Not yet," said Cassie. "Not unless you find something unexpected."

Makwetu visibly steeled herself. "And by unexpected, you mean…?"

"I want to know if there's evidence our comms were sabotaged during the outbound journey."

There: it was out. She felt curiously relieved.

Makwetu's mouth flopped open, and for a moment, she looked like she might argue with Cassie.

"Sure." Makwetu nodded, her lips pale when she pressed them together. "I—"

She paused as her wristcomm flashed red. Cassie's did the same, and when she glanced down, she saw it was an all-crew alert.

The two women exchanged a look. "What the hell?" said Makwetu.

"They want all of us up on the ring," said Cassie, reading from her own device. She looked back up. "It doesn't say why."

───────

Cassie looked around at the rest of the crew, all of whom had gathered in the hab-ring's cramped conference room. No-one except Braemar and Holland, who sat together to Javier's immediate left, looked like they had any idea what the alert was about.

"Take a look at this," said Javier. He tapped his wristcomm and a rotating translucent projection of the Tianjin appeared above the centre of the table. "Something's going on with the Tianjin."

Everyone exchanged glances at that.

"Meaning?" asked Harrow.

"Meaning," said Javier, "some kind of infighting, if not an outright mutiny. We've been making observations of the other ship since we made orbit, and just in the last half hour a body was ejected from its airlock."

Everybody started talking all at once.

Javier put a hand up, and they all gradually trailed off.

"I want to clarify that the body was apparently expelled from the airlock minus a spacesuit. There's no way to tell if they were still alive when it happened."

More voices burst out and Braemar leaned forward. "There's more," she said. "The other two NCR ships we know about are on their way here from Ganymede. Another couple of days, and it's going to be their three ships versus our one."

"Could it be suicide?" Makwetu asked.

"There's no point speculating until we have more information." Braemar's voice was flat and emotionless. "But this situation is getting more complicated by the hour. The radiation levels this close to Jupiter place a hard limit on how long we can keep orbiting Europa before we either land, and risk triggering another war back home, or give up and go home."

"We have no control over whatever's going on back home," Lebed barked. "We have no orders, no news. But we can act decisively by landing on Europa as soon as possible. That we *do* have control over."

"It's not that simple." Braemar glared at the astronavigator. "I agree we need to land, not least to protect Stations Verne and Nemo from likely hostile NCR forces and from the risk of the NCR taking effective control of Europa."

"Precisely!" Lebed thumped the table with his fist and nodded at Makwetu. "Daphne can have the lander fully prepped within twenty-four—"

"No." Javier's voice was flat and hard. "You'd make yourselves hostages to whomever the NCR sent down, and the situation would be even worse than before. You're civilian engineers and scientists, not soldiers."

Javier took a steadying breath before he continued, placing both hands on the table before him and working his jaw. "I've made a decision. Agents Braemar and Holland will go down alone and take control of Station Verne. If there's a hostile NCR incursion, they have the training to deal with it."

"Wait," said Harrow, his voice high and tight, "when do *we* go down?"

Javier regarded him steadily and not, Cassie observed, without effort. There was a faint sheen of perspiration on his forehead.

"For now," Javier replied, "I feel that it's best if the rest of us remain in orbit for the foreseeable duration."

This news brought audible gasps from around the table.

"No, wait," Harrow continued, almost stumbling over his words. "Here's a better idea. Say, while Sally and Jeff are occupying Verne, myself and the others head for the borehole station. If it's viable, we go under the ice to Nemo. We'd be far out of range of any hostile NCR—"

"And then Jeff and Sally would be forced to protect both Verne and the borehole station," Javier snapped. "I'm sorry, but we've worked out every possible scenario, and this is the best option. We came here knowing the borehole's most likely collapsed in the intervening years. Even if it hasn't, we'd still need to check its integrity and run safety checks that could take weeks."

Lebed stood, his fists bunched. "We didn't come all this way to play tourist from a distance. You don't get to decide who does or doesn't go down!"

"Mr Lebed," Javier responded, his voice tight and angry, "once again, let me remind you who is in command of this mission."

"Anton's right," said Harrow, his own voice increasingly heated. "It's a complete waste of resources for us to come all this way and never land."

"This is no longer a civilian scientific expedition," said Holland. "The situation has become volatile enough that I'm taking effective command of the Veles until I decide the NCR fleet is no longer a threat. I have Commander Javier's full cooperation in this matter."

A stunned silence fell over the conference room as the crew exchanged shocked glances. "You can't be serious," Haunani said to the Commander. "You're just letting these people take charge?"

"God knows I wanted none of this to happen," said Javier. He sounded like he was fighting to keep his voice steady. "I came here for the same damn reasons as the rest of you. But it's clear our original mission is impossible under the present circumstances, and that we have no choice but to adapt to our changed circumstances." He looked around the room, locking eyes with each of them. "Am I clear?"

Cassie sucked in a breath and watched Lebed, who looked about ready to start throwing punches—not that the rest of them looked any happier. After another moment, he sat back down and stared hard at the wall opposite him.

"I want to remind you," said Holland, "that back when the old People's Republic of China built its first moon bases, they came very close to declaring it their territory in contravention of international law. Which is why the US, Indians, Japanese, Brazilians, Russians and European Union all immediately got to work establishing their own bases."

He stabbed a finger toward the image of the Tianjin that still floated above the centre of the table. "I'm now certain they're here to establish a long-term presence in the Jovian system. I'm guessing the other two ships were scouting locations on the outer moons for future bases. If we don't act decisively, you can forget about landing on Europa or any other Jovian moon now, or at any time in the future, without going through a NCR blockade first."

Cassie glanced at Makwetu, who looked back at her with open alarm.

Haunani shook his head with exasperation. "When exactly do you intend to send Jeff and Sally down there?"

It was Javier's turn to stand, having clearly decided the meeting was over. "Within the next forty-eight hours."

Lebed stared daggers at the Commander, but said nothing more as Javier departed, followed closely by the two spooks. Then Lebed, too, stood abruptly and left without another word.

Makwetu glanced again at Cassie, raising one arm slightly to show her wristcomm.

Cassie glanced down at her own wristcomm and saw a message there:

```
MAKWETU: I'M ON THE ROSTER FOR
HULL REPAIRS AFTER MY NEXT WORK
SHIFT. THEN WE'LL KNOW.
```

Cassie nodded slightly to Makwetu, then stood to leave, along with the rest. It would be at least sixteen hours before Makwetu could begin her EVA, at which time Cassie would be due to take a break.

And then, perhaps, they would have an answer.

CHAPTER 12
EVA

In the hours following the meeting, Cassie sensed a shift in the atmosphere on board the Veles.

Towards the end of her next shift, Cassie came across Anton Lebed, Doctor Haunani and Evan Harrow clustered together in a storage bay, deep in a whispered conversation that fell into silence the moment she entered.

"Hey," she said, drifting over to a supplies bin and pulling it open. "Don't feel like you have to stop just because I'm here."

"We were just—" Harrow started to say.

Cassie caught Haunani shooting the oceanologist a look, and Harrow fell silent.

"It's my daughter's birthday," Lebed explained. He was, she noted, a terrible liar.

"Really?"

"Valentina," he said. "Her twenty-first."

"Oh," said Cassie. "Congratulations."

Lebed made a face. "I'd hoped to send her a birthday message today." He shrugged awkwardly. "But, of course…"

"We're making up for it," said Haunani. He had a gleam in his eye when he spoke. "We're breaking out some vodka at the end of shift. You should join us."

Cassie nodded to show she got the message. "Sure," she said. "I'll do that."

Maybe the thing about Valentina was true, she thought, making her way back out into the spine. But when she'd entered the bay, she'd caught the look of relief on Harrow's face, like he was glad it was her and not someone else: someone like Holland or Braemar, or even Javier.

Then again, whatever they were talking about, it spoke volumes they hadn't yet fully taken her into their trust. She was still an unknown quantity—someone, like the two spooks, who shouldn't even be aboard.

———

TIME SEEMED to become more elastic the closer it got to Makwetu's scheduled EVA.

Towards the end of her next work shift, the stowaway machine messaged her for an update. Cassie replied, explaining Makwetu's plan to go out on EVA on her behalf.

She felt no urge to speak with or contact the machine unless strictly necessary, and yet, whenever she had a quiet moment, she was perplexed to find herself adrift in memories of Marcus when he had been alive: the scent of his skin, the vitality of his intellect, the touch of his hands on her face. It was how she wanted to remember him.

Even if the newer version had already saved her life.

About the same time Makwetu was on her way to start her EVA, Cassie was back in her bunk, drifting off to sleep. Her dreams, when they came, were of the Swiss hospice Marcus had been moved to once his condition grew worse. Those last few weeks had been hard on them both: the once-robust engineer who'd commanded a design team had been reduced to a shrivelled parody of his former self, his every breath so laboured it might easily have been his last.

Of all the engineered viruses that emerged in the closing

years of the Asia-Pacific War, the Whispers had been the worst. Cassie had been infected too, although her tweaked DNA allowed her to recover quickly.

Even so, she hadn't been able to escape the same lingering, powerful dreams that bordered on visions.

And such eerily otherworldly visions, like the one she experienced now: Cassie dreamed her body had been transformed into a wide, fleshy net strung between the trunks of skyscraper-tall trees, their upper branches lost in cloud. Small, darting creatures made their way across her body, each node of her net a point of data in a sensory network that spread over dozens of kilometres—

———

THE SOUND, when it came, reminded her of municipal earthquake warnings back in Taiwan. Still half-caught in her dream, Cassie struggled back to wakefulness and glanced at the message on her wristcomm: a ship-wide alert.

More specifically, there was an ongoing medical emergency in the EVA bay.

A quick check of the time showed that Makwetu should have been on her way back inside from a four-hour EVA.

And with that, panic gripped Cassie.

CHAPTER 13
THE ACCIDENT

She got dressed fast and made her way down the spine. Lebed and Harrow were already waiting outside the EVA bay, their heads close together, and their voices reduced to a barely audible mutter. More voices came from inside the bay.

"What happened?" she asked breathlessly, stopping herself with a handhold.

"It's Daphne," said Harrow. "Haunani's in there with her."

Shit. "What happened?"

"Hey," Doctor Haunani called from inside the bay. "Cassie, is that you?"

Pushing off from the entrance, Cassie drifted into the bay and caught another handhold. Inside, three EVA 'shrimp' suits were mounted to brackets on a bulkhead directly opposite the airlock. These had been designed specifically for Jupiter's high-radiation environment, and were nicknamed shrimps because of their appearance: a narrow cylinder just large enough to fit a human body with a cluster of manipulators, tools and sensory equipment mounted on the front at chest-level. Chris had once told her he hated the suits because getting into one felt like being stuffed into a coffin feet-first.

One shrimp had been opened up down its front so that

Makwetu could be lifted out. She appeared outwardly unharmed, and she had stationed herself with a handhold, her expression shellshocked and her dark skin damp with sweat.

Haunani was next to her, various bits and pieces of diagnostic equipment arranged around him in the air, his expression intent. Also present and watching were Jeff Holland and Sally Braemar.

Makwetu took a moment to focus on Cassie, something urgent in her gaze. "Cassie," she said, her voice thin and frail-sounding. "I need to talk to you."

"What happened?" Cassie couldn't keep the shock out of her voice.

"Now isn't a good time," Holland told her curtly. "Let the Doctor—"

"No," said Makwetu, her voice more firm this time. "I want to talk to Cassie. Alone."

Holland's jaw clenched. "It can wait."

"Actually, it can't," said Haunani, his expression grim. He nodded at the opened-up shrimp. "The magnetics failed and the superconducting coils shut down. She's taken a big dose."

A cold band of steel wrapped itself around Cassie's chest. "For how long…?"

"I was outside for four hours," said Makwetu, her voice barely above a whisper. "I was taking radiation for most of it."

But the dosimeter, Cassie wanted to say. It would have alerted her of a problem immediately. But Haunani, she realized, would have thought of that already.

Cassie licked suddenly dry lips. "What are you going to do?" she asked the doctor.

"There's little I can do here," Haunani told her, his voice flat and grim. He turned back to Makwetu. "You need to go back into cryo, Daphne. Immediately."

Makwetu's eyes were bright with moisture. "For how long?"

Haunani, judging by his expression, wasn't a man who enjoyed delivering bad news. "Until we get back home."

"But—that won't be until years from now!" Makwetu exclaimed. "I, I can't—"

"It'll slow the disruption to your cells," said Haunani. "All I can do here is a short-term fix. Your chances of survival go way up if you're in cryo."

Makwetu's skin looked increasingly grey. "There's no other way?"

Haunani shook his head. "I'm afraid not."

Makwetu stared past the doctor and at the airlock hatch for a few moments, then set her mouth in a thin line.

"I'd like you all to leave me with Cassie, please," she said at last. "We won't be a moment."

Something unpleasant flashed deep in Holland's gaze, and he looked like he was about to say something when Sally Braemar, beside him, reached out and touched his arm. Holland's jaw tightened, and he turned, pushing himself through the bay entrance and back out into the spine.

Braemar followed, but shot a jaundiced look at both Cassie and Doctor Haunani.

The doctor used a handhold to pull himself over next to Cassie. "Don't be long," he warned her, his voice low enough Makwetu wouldn't hear it. "I'm serious when I say she has to go into cryo *immediately*."

Cassie nodded, then waited until only she and Makwetu were in the bay. She pushed herself over next to the other woman, who seemed to grow paler by the second.

Makwetu reached out and grasped her hand.

"What happened?" said Cassie, fighting to keep her voice steady. "Why didn't your dosimeter—?"

"It looked like it was working fine," said Makwetu. "But it wasn't."

"…what do you mean?"

"It was feeding me false information," she explained.

"That's impossible," said Cassie. "There's too many fail-safes, too many—"

Makwetu gripped her more tightly. "I know."

Cassie sucked in a breath to steady her nerves and give her time to think. Then she thought about the sabotage to the cryo bay, and the machine's suggestion that the two spooks had crippled their comms.

"There's something you should know," Cassie said.

"Wait." Makwetu's gaze was unfocused, her hand trembling slightly where it gripped Cassie's. "I never got a chance to look at the comms array. There's some micrometeorite damage to the outer shielding, but the comms themselves don't look like they've been directly impacted."

"They haven't been interfered with?"

"The only way to be sure," said Makwetu, "is to plug directly into the external interface and query the systems manually. You need to be outside the ship to do that."

"Hey."

Turning, Cassie saw Haunani had re-entered the bay. "No more time," he said, looking harassed. "She's going into a cryo tank *now*."

"Get down to Europa," Makwetu urged Cassie in a half-whisper. "Don't let Ernest or those other two get in your way."

"I still have to tell you something," said Cassie.

"No." Makwetu stared back at her intently. "Whatever it is, you tell me after, when we're both back home."

Slowly, Cassie nodded. "Okay, I will," she said, meaning it.

"Let's go," said Haunani, coming towards them.

Just then, as Cassie watched them go, she felt her left hand spasm. Automatically, she tucked it under one armpit, counting most of a half a minute before the tremors ceased.

"FOUR HOURS," said Lebed, staring into his vodka, cabbage leaves pressing against the side of his head. "That's how long Daphne was exposed to Jupiter's radiation. Four fucking hours."

He squeezed the vodka into his mouth and swallowed, then shook his head like a dog shaking off water. His skin looked bleached and pale under the lights of the Farm.

Instead of celebrating Valentina's birthday, Cassie had found herself in something more closely resembling a wake. Not that Makwetu was dead: she'd sleep the remainder of the mission away.

"There you are."

Albert Haunani swam into view at the far end of the Farm.

"What's the news?" Harrow asked, as Haunani stopped beside them.

"As stable as it's possible for her to be," the doctor replied.

Lebed handed the doctor a plastic bulb containing a shot of vodka. Haunani took it and squeezed the contents into his mouth.

"Does putting her into cryo really help?" Cassie asked.

"Jury's out when it comes to this big a dose," the doctor said. "And keeping someone in cryo that long has its own problems. But for reasons we don't yet quite understand, cryo slows down radiation damage."

"The shrimp suits undergo rigorous tests every time we use them," Lebed muttered. "They're supposed to be fool-proof, with multiple safety redundancies. How the hell do both the dosimeter *and* the SC coils fail at the same time?"

Lebed slugged back the last of his vodka and reached for a half-filled rubber bladder he'd left wedged between two hydroponic trays. He squeezed more vodka into his bulb, then offered the bladder around.

Haunani and Harrow had more to drink, but Cassie nursed hers, leaving it mostly untouched. She wondered if they yet suspected foul play, and if so, whether they would give voice to those suspicions.

Lebed was right: with so many fail-safes built into the shrimps, and with constant rigorous testing, there was no way Makwetu wouldn't have known something was wrong —not unless someone had screwed with her shrimp.

As she had with Makwetu, back in the EVA bay, Cassie felt a sudden urge to tell the others about Ketteridge, her real mission—everything.

Instead, she downed her vodka, curling the fingers of her right hand tight around the bulb. Her other hand spasmed momentarily, and she pressed it into a pocket, hoping no one noticed.

"I think," Lebed was saying, his voice layered with grim finality, "we need to talk about the future of this mission. How long exactly can we remain in orbit before we must go back into cryo?"

"Based on current safety margins," said Haunani, "I'd recommend an absolute maximum of another two weeks."

Harrow looked shocked. "We should be able to stay in orbit longer than that, surely?"

"If we were further out from Jupiter, we'd be safer," Lebed grunted. "If we orbited Callisto, say." He waved a hand towards the hull. "Stuck here, we're caught between Jupiter's radiation belt and Io's plasma torus."

"Then we could do that, couldn't we?" Harrow suggested. "Go to one of the other moons, or—?"

Lebed shook his head. "The Commander is, unfortunately, right about the NCR ships out there. If we left orbit, it'd be an open invitation for them to land in our place."

"You're forgetting the body that got ejected from the Tianjin's airlock," said Cassie. "Could be they've got too many problems of their own right now to be landing anywhere."

"Which you'll also remember," Lebed countered, "is precisely why the Commander wants to send those fucking spooks down in our place." He shook his head tightly, eyes fixed on his plastic bulb. "Perhaps we should talk about—"

Just then, a look passed between the three men, and Lebed fell silent.

They were thinking about mutiny. Cassie felt sure of it; could taste it, unspoken, in the air between them.

But for some reason, they didn't want her to be part of that conversation.

They might, she thought, if they knew as much as she did.

"I need to tell you something," she said. She felt light-headed, almost drunk.

Harrow raised his eyebrows. "Tell us what?"

At that precise moment, Cassie's wristcomm buzzed against her left wrist. Fortunately, the tremors had been brief. She angled her wrist so only she could see the message on the device's screen:

```
UNKNOWN MESSAGE SOURCE: DON'T TELL
THEM.
```

What the hell—?

Some instinct made Cassie look past the three men, to where she could see a Flying Monkey parked on a charging unit placed between two shelves of hydroponics. Its lens was pointed straight at her.

"Cassie?" Lebed looked at her expectantly. "What were you going to say?"

Whatever words had been about to come out got caught in her throat. "It's nothing," she said. "I think the vodka's getting to me." She grinned uneasily, hoping it looked convincing. "I was just going to say I enjoyed working with Daphne. I'll miss working with her."

Christ, it sounded so asinine when she said it. But Harrow nodded like she'd said something deep.

Lebed, who had been staring off into space with a thoughtful expression during this exchange, suddenly looked at her.

"The shrimps and behemoth suits share some design features, do they not?"

"They do," she said. "They were developed by the same design team for the first mission."

"In the increasingly unlikely event any of us get to go down to Europa," Lebed replied, "we should make sure it's not some previously undetected design flaw shared by both." He gestured towards her with his plastic bulb. "You're our resident behemoth expert. Perhaps you could look at them yourself just now. Run side-by-side diagnostics on both them and the shrimps and see if anything triggers the dosimeters to give false results."

It was a good point and a smart suggestion. But Cassie could tell Lebed was trying to get rid of her: she could see it in his eyes, and those of the others, and it was as if an invisible chasm had opened between her and these three men.

They didn't trust her. Of course they didn't: she'd been lying to them and everyone else on the Veles, hadn't she?

Her wristcomm buzzed against her skin a second time and another message appeared on its screen:

```
UNKNOWN MESSAGE SOURCE: WE NEED TO
TALK. NOW.
```

"I'll give it a shot and let you know what I find," she said, handing her drinking bulb to Harrow and turning to the bay entrance.

As soon as she had exited the bay, she ducked into the first vacant storage bay she saw.

"Talk," she said into her wristcomm, anchoring herself just inside the entrance.

"I need you to listen," the machine replied, by voice this time.

"You realize," Cassie heard Haunani say, "what we're talking about is insurrection."

Eyes widening, Cassie realized what the machine had done: it was relaying the ongoing conversation between Lebed and the others now that she was gone. They had no idea the little AREM parked on its charging port was spying on them.

"Which is why I didn't want to talk about it with White still here," said Lebed.

"You really think we can't trust her?" Harrow, this time.

"Remember what I found," Lebed muttered. "That NCR Science Officer. There's some kind of connection between them."

"Having a connection to him doesn't automatically make her a spy for the NCR," said Haunani, a sardonic edge to his voice. "They were kids at school together. It's hardly a damning indictment, for Christ's sake, Anton."

"And yet," Lebed countered, "he's got something to do with those other ships out there, and *she's* here on board the Veles in Kernov's place. You really think that's a coincidence?"

"Fine," Haunani replied with growing exasperation. "So it's a little weird. Except it makes little sense that Mission Control would knowingly put a foreign spy on board the Veles just days or hours before launch," said Haunani. "If you could find that information, then so could they."

"'Knowingly'," Lebed said mockingly.

"Then it's down to just the three of us now, isn't it? Daphne's on ice, those fucking spooks seem to have done everything but take over the mission, and Javier's acting like the rest of us are some sort of liability."

"I've heard enough," Cassie quietly told the machine.

The voices faded, replaced by the soft, ever-present hum of the Veles' life-support systems.

"Lebed looked into you," said the machine.

"Yeah," said Cassie. "I heard."

"The Veles receives a full global net update every week—or it did until we lost comms. He looked into you and found news articles about the school shooting. Chen Tingshao's name came up."

"The thing I don't get," said Cassie, "is why they called him a science officer. He's a glorified traffic policeman on the Moon."

"Shortly after the Tianjin launched to the outer system, news of the departure came out in a leak, along with the names of some of the crew. One of the names was Chen Tingshao."

Comprehension dawned slowly, the realisation sending an icy shock through Cassie. "Wait a minute. Are you...are you telling me Tingshao's on board the Tianjin?"

"I only found out a day ago when Harrow and Lebed were talking and I listened in. I recognized the name, of course, because you'd talked about your relationship with him from when you were teenagers." The machine paused a moment. "You know, I used to feel a little jealous the way you talked about him."

"He was—" Cassie halted. *He was my first real love*, she had been about to say.

Her mind flashed back to their brief conversation while she'd sat in a Taipei park. Most likely, he'd already known about the second Europa Deep expedition. And hadn't said one damn word.

And now half the crew thought she was in cahoots with him.

Then, at last, Cassie realized precisely what she needed to do. What she'd known she would have to do, ever since they'd brought Makwetu back in, half-dead of radiation poisoning.

"Hey," she said, realising the machine hadn't spoken for some moments. "Are you still there?"

Silence.

"Hello?"

A bad feeling prickled its way up Cassie's spine. Should she be concerned? It wasn't the first time the machine had avoided replying to her.

But then again, she remembered, that had been before she knew who—or rather, what—she was talking to. It had had its reasons for wanting to conceal its identity.

But the need to do that was past. Why wouldn't it respond?

"Hello?" she tried again.

Still nothing.

Somewhere outside in the spine, Cassie heard a soft thump. Had someone been listening in to her?

Moving quickly, she navigated her way out of the storage bay and into the spine. There was no one around. The bay where the others had been talking was empty: if Lebed and the other two had still been there, she had no doubt they would have investigated the sound.

She looked up and down the length of the spine, at first seeing nothing, and then caught sight of a chunk of machinery spinning slowly end over end.

Kicking off from a bulkhead, Cassie intercepted the chunk of machinery, grabbing hold of it with one hand and allowing herself to keep moving until she could again station herself with a wall grip. On bringing herself to a halt, she saw she held an AREM, except somebody had pounded it to pieces. A single wiry manipulator protruded from its shell, twisted badly out of shape.

Cassie let go of it, and it turned slowly, end over end, in

the zero gravity. It made her think of a spider, after most of its legs had been pulled off by some malicious child.

Another thud came from the direction of the bay where the AI had concealed itself.

Driven by a growing sense of alarm, Cassie manoeuvred her way closer to the bay. From within came a loud clattering.

Entering the bay cautiously, Cassie was confronted with the sight of Sally Braemar tearing experiments out of a payload rack in a frenzy of destruction. Bits and pieces of equipment and broken plastic spun haphazardly through the air, occasionally rebounding from the surrounding bulkheads or from each other.

Braemar must have heard or sensed she was no longer alone, because she whipped around to regard Cassie with an expression colder than Europa's ice.

She smiled without humour. "Looking for something?" Braemar asked.

At first, Cassie just stared back at her. Then she blinked reflexively and pushed herself across the bay towards an equipment bin close by the entrance, something sour and heavy flip-flopping in her belly. Opening up the bin, she rummaged around and randomly selected a plastic gadget whose purpose she couldn't even guess at. A quick glance at a printed label showed it was a spare part for a trace gas analyser.

"Sorry," she said. Glancing past Braemar, she saw to her shock that the rack where the AI had concealed itself was now empty. The body it had been building was also gone.

Cassie turned her attention back to the other woman. "I wasn't... interrupting anything, was I?"

Braemar just stared back at her with an openly hostile expression, then nodded at the gizmo Cassie still held in one hand. "Get what you were looking for?"

"Sure." Cassie gave her a tight smile and exited the bay,

making her way halfway down the spine before bringing herself to a halt and tapping at her wristcomm. A quick glance around showed nobody else was in sight.

CASSIE: WHERE THE HELL ARE YOU?

Instead of a voice or text reply, a picture of the Europa Lander's cockpit appeared on the screen.

What the hell?

Her wristcomm flashed up a new message:

UNKNOWN MESSAGE SOURCE: COME
FIND ME.

CHAPTER 14

THE LANDER

The lander was attached to a secondary airlock mechanism just forward of the main drive, sticking out from the body of the Veles at a right angle.

Getting into the lander meant squeezing through an airlock bay tightly packed with racked spacesuits and equipment drawers, with miscellaneous pieces of equipment velcroed to every available surface. The inner hatch opened with a faint hiss and Cassie made her way through and into the lander's interior, seeing everything was where she'd expect to find it. There were enough seats for the entire crew, with a pilot and co-pilot's seat facing towards a screen currently displaying a live feed of Europa's surface from orbit.

Something moved.

Anchoring herself to the back of the co-pilot's seat, Cassie twisted around to see a spider-like monstrosity emerge from the shadows to the rear of the lander. It looked oddly misshapen, as if made from random and mismatched spare parts. Which, she realized after another moment, it was.

"Hi, Cassie," said the spider-thing, two of its numerous legs hooked through a wall grip. Its voice crackled slightly as it emerged from a speaker somewhere on its body. One of its free legs performed a slow wave. "Guess who."

"Jesus, you scared me," she said, letting out a rush of nervous breath.

The last time she'd seen the machine's new body, it was still incomplete. Clearly, it had been putting a lot more work into it.

"Sorry I didn't have time to reply," said the machine. "I had an AREM on lookout further up the spine and then Braemar appeared, grabbed it, and smashed it to pieces. When she started making her way down the spine and searching every bay, I kind of had to focus my attention on getting out."

"I swear," said Cassie, "there's something wrong with that woman. She was literally tearing the place apart. It's like she has worms in her brain or something."

"Well," said the machine, "it's lucky I was ready to move, or I'd be dead meat right now." It paused a moment. "Well, dead integrated circuits."

"She didn't see you?" Because God knew, the thing was pretty damn conspicuous.

"Just avoided being caught by the skin of my…well, you know what I mean," it said. "I ducked into an empty bay and waited for her to go past."

"Does this mean she knows about you?"

"Not necessarily," said the machine, "but my guess is she traced the secondary network I used to control the flying monkeys back to the comms bay. That'd be all the proof she'd need that someone's using them to spy on everyone. I don't know how long it'll take her to work out it isn't any of the crew."

"Why here?" Cassie asked, glancing around the lander's cramped interior.

"Nowhere else to go," the machine replied. "Frankly, I'm running out of hiding places."

"I can't overemphasise," she said, choosing her words carefully, "how unsettling you look."

"Thanks," the machine replied with obvious sarcasm. "You're looking great, too."

"I'm going outside the ship," said Cassie.

"I'm sorry?"

"Daphne nearly got herself killed trying to help me. I'm going out there myself. It's like she told me: the only way to be sure is to go outside."

"Except Javier refused to let you—"

"Fuck him," Cassie snapped. She opened her mouth to say more, then paused as a thought came to her. "Who went outside before Daphne?"

"Ahead of you," said the machine. "It was Holland."

Cassie stared at the spider-thing. "How do you know?"

"Because I'm always listening and watching, Cassie."

"Did he do anything?" she asked. "Did you see him interfering with her suit?"

"I said I'm always watching," the machine retorted. "I didn't say I was omniscient."

Cassie lowered herself into a kind of zero-gravity squat, folding her legs under her. "You must have heard what the others said when I was in the airlock bay. The shrimps are loaded with safety measures and rigorously tested before and after they're used, the same as the behemoth suits." She rubbed one hand across her mouth as she thought. "Except there are three shrimps—how would he have known which one she'd use?"

"Remember, the shrimps are assigned based on the individual mass and height of an astronaut," said the machine. "Daphne's about one hundred and sixty centimetres. Holland would have known she'd use Suit A. Anyone over one hundred and eighty has to use either Suits B or C."

Cassie's heart beat ever louder in her chest, her breathing

increasingly shallow. She pictured Braemar bursting into the lander at that moment, a wrench gripped in one hand and his eyes full of manic hatred.

"Maybe it's time for you to come out in the open," she said. "Tell everyone else on board what you know. I'd be there to back you up. Tell them what Daphne told me and what you saw in the cryo bay."

The machine actually backed away from her slightly, the rear of its carapace sliding back into shadow. "No way," it said. "There are four civilians on board, including yourself, and two spooks who might already have tried to kill almost everyone on board. You really think I'm going to take a chance like that?"

"You revealed yourself to me."

"Because I know *you*. And you wouldn't turn me in because you know I'm not a threat."

The machine's reasoning was not quite as sound as it apparently believed, but that didn't change the fact they were now at an impasse. The rest of the crew all had reason to think she couldn't be trusted. Even if she found evidence of sabotage to the comms array—and whether she would remained far from certain—she wasn't sure they would believe her.

And if she didn't get to go down to Europa, she knew—felt it in her bones—that she'd never get to find out what had happened to Chris.

And slowly, a plan formulated in her mind, even as part of her protested against it: there were so many things that could go wrong. And it required a level of trust in the machine she still couldn't be sure was warranted.

But maybe, she thought, there was enough of Marcus inside this weird metal monstrosity that she was willing to take that chance.

Cassie took a long, steadying breath. "I want you to listen

carefully," she said. "Because if what I'm about to do goes south, I'm going to need your help."

THEY TALKED FOR A LONG TIME.

Later, Cassie went back to work, knowing any attempt to carry out her plan would have to wait until she had scheduled free time. Even then, it would only work if she found the EVA bay deserted.

Once her shift was over, she checked the work schedules and saw Javier and Lebed were in the EVA bay at that moment, running intensive diagnostics on all three Shrimps. All future EVA work had been cancelled, pending a much deeper investigation.

There was nothing to do in the meantime but try to get some sleep, but this was proving increasingly difficult, no matter how dog-tired she felt. She took something to knock herself out and woke seven hours later, feeling once again as if she'd barely closed her eyes.

But she had a plan. And if she was ever going to execute it, it had to be now.

On her way to the canteen to get coffee and a breakfast burrito, Cassie found another message waiting for her from the machine.

```
UNKNOWN MESSAGE SOURCE: COMMAND
DECK FIRST. ACCESS THE FOLLOWING
SERVERS AND RESET THE FOLLOWING
PERMISSIONS.
```

Cassie read through the list on her wristcomm, then continued on, finding Lebed and Haunani hunched over their own bulbs of coffee. Lebed offered her a mute nod, while Cassie grabbed a bulb of cold-brew and a protein chew before going on her way.

Fortunately, there were jobs on the to-do roster that gave her the perfect excuse to be on the command deck. The back of her neck prickled with nervous energy when she got there and found Holland working at one of the navigation consoles and studying relief-maps of the Europan surface. Beyond a half-nod in her direction, however, he barely acknowledged her.

Cassie got to work on one of the scheduled tasks, but as soon as Holland departed the command deck, Cassie immediately stopped what she was doing and headed for one of the comms terminals. Soon she had navigated her way through a series of submenus before getting to what she wanted.

It didn't take long to make the manual changes the machine had requested: all of them changes it couldn't enact without the help of an actual human.

For a moment, her finger hovered over a touch screen, and she thought about what she was doing.

It was hard not to think of the Yatagarasu.

Do or be damned, she decided, then tapped the screen.

She'd half-expected alarms to start blaring, but nothing of the kind happened.

Then she made her way along the spine, stopping at each of the comms terminals the machine had told her to go to. At each one, she followed its instructions precisely, resetting different permissions manually.

She sent the machine a message once she had finished her tasks:

> CASSIE: EVERYTHING'S DONE.
>
> I JUST WANT YOU TO KNOW THAT IF YOU PULL A YATAGARASU, I WILL COME AFTER YOU WITH A CROWBAR.

The cursor on her wristcomm blinked for a moment, then:

    UNKNOWN MESSAGE SOURCE: I WILL NOT
    PULL A YATAGARASU, CASSIE. EVEN
    THOUGH THERE'S NOT A SINGLE
    CROWBAR ON THE WHOLE SHIP.

That at least got a laugh out of her. Even if it was an oddly strained, high-pitched laugh.

    CASSIE: HOW IS THE EVA BAY
    LOOKING?

    UNKNOWN MESSAGE SOURCE: DESERTED.

The tension in Cassie's shoulders eased a little. She tapped again at the screen:

    CASSIE: YOU'LL BE ABLE TO TELL ME
    IF ANYONE'S ON THEIR WAY?

    UNKNOWN MESSAGE SOURCE EYES AND
    EARS EVERYWHERE, CASSIE.

She knew the machine meant this to be reassuring, rather than unsettling. It had said it wasn't omniscient, but it talked like it was. During this brief exchange, she had almost slipped and called it Marcus.

The whole way to the EVA bay, her heart boomed in her chest like a bell sounding out the last minutes of her life.

———

EVERY SECOND that she prepared for her EVA, she expected someone—maybe Javier, or, more likely, given the way things had been going, Holland—to come storming into the bay demanding to know just what the hell she was doing.

Getting inside a shrimp was an adventure all in itself. The one Makwetu had used still sat half-gutted in its cradle. Cassie'd had a little training with them, but that had been years ago. She squirmed her way in through the seam that ran down the front of the suit, swearing under her breath and half-afraid she'd pop a vertebra from all the contortions required just to get inside the thing.

Once the suit was sealed around her, she ran a systems check, her breath loud and harsh within the close confines of her helmet.

Everything checked out. Finally, she gave a verbal go-ahead to the bay's computer, and the light above the outer airlock changed to red, the shrimp detaching from its magnetic locks.

The outer airlock door opened, and her shrimp slid along a rail extending out from the base of its cradle. The rail retracted, and the shrimp hung motionless above the streaked ice of Europa.

———

FROM THERE ON IN, Cassie operated on automatic. As long as it had been since she'd practiced operating a shrimp, it came back to her quickly.

Turning the tiny craft through a hundred and eighty degrees, and moving parallel to the length of the Veles, she guided the shrimp aft towards the comms array. This took the form of a tall blister poking out at a right angle from the hull, and hidden behind clusters of communications dishes. The engines were a broad grey circle to the rear, the hab-ring forward spinning serenely and silently.

There wasn't time to bask in the fact of where she was, or to reflect on the series of steps and decisions that had led to this moment. Instead, she got to work, using the shrimp's guidance systems to pilot it expertly towards the comms blister.

Europa's surface looked achingly close. The icy moon was tidally locked to its parent, one face turned eternally towards Jupiter. The broad bands of the gas giant itself were mostly on the moon's far side at that moment, but even so, she hadn't missed the enormous spike in radiation the moment the shrimp had manoeuvred itself out of the airlock.

The blister grew larger, and larger, and then she brought the shrimp to a gradual halt half a metre from its surface.

No, there wasn't much she could see by the way of micrometeorite damage—at least, not at first glance. That was more evident on the blister's far side. Most of the Veles' water was contained in tanks that were wrapped around the hull, since it doubled as an effective protection from radiation. They hadn't lost a great deal of water to the impacts, but dozens of individual protective plates had to be checked for damage and, most times, replaced.

Faint puffs of gas emerged from her shrimp's nozzle thrusters. Cassie checked the most recent hull maintenance records and soon located the panel she needed. Then, with the aid of complicated multi-tooled manipulators that extended out from the front of the shrimp, she opened the panel.

Things got rather more pernickety after that. Manually querying the array required first plugging one manipulator into an external port, and then working through a series of permissions she'd already changed with the machine's help before she could run manual queries.

While she was working away at this, a softly pulsing icon appeared in Cassie's HUD. It had no name attached, and she hesitated, afraid it might be Javier or one of the two spooks.

"Hello?" she asked cautiously.

"It's Marcus."

"I'm outside," she told the machine.

"I know. I can see you."

What? "Where are you?"

"You're near to the lander," the machine reminded her. "Wave if you can see me too."

Cassie twisted her head around inside her shrimp's helmet until she saw the lander, which resembled a metal tick attached to the body of some spacefaring beast. Then she located one of the lander's portholes and realized she could just make out the spider-like machine inside. It was, in fact, waving one of its mismatched limbs at her.

It looked like something out of a nightmare.

"Well, fine," said Cassie, turning her attention back to the comms array. "Just so long as no one else knows I'm here."

"Have you found anything?" the machine asked.

"Not sure," Cassie grunted. "I can't figure half of this stuff out." She watched a flow of information scroll down her HUD in brightly glowing text.

"Let me see," said the machine.

Cassie opened up her comms circuit, allowing the machine to see the flow of data.

"I want to try something," the machine said after a few moments. "See that other panel? I need you to open it up."

Cassie looked around until she saw a smaller panel slightly to the right and above the one she'd opened. Once again, she used the shrimp's manipulator to get it open.

"Yeah," said the machine, once she'd directed light inside the panel, "I thought something wasn't right. See that black rectangular thing plugged into the left-hand component slot? That doesn't look like it belongs there at all."

The component in question was easy to spot. It looked bodged together from out of different spare parts: an imperfect solution to an awkward problem.

She checked it against the array's inventory and didn't find a match.

"The ship doesn't know what it is," she told the machine. "It can't query it either."

"Which means it shouldn't be there," said the machine. "The port it's plugged into is a primary manual override. See if you can get it loose."

A couple of minutes of struggling to pry it loose proved fruitless. "I think it's been welded in place," said Cassie, blinking sweat out of her eyes. "It's going to take more than this to get it out."

"You got anywhere else you need to be?"

Cassie glowered in the direction of the Europa Lander. "Fine."

Fortunately, the shrimps came equipped with their own built-in welding gear. Even so, getting the welding torch into position took many minutes of careful work and no small amount of creative swearing. If she wasn't careful, she risked disabling the entire comms permanently.

By the time she finally got it loose, Cassie was surprised to find it had taken nearly half an hour.

Half an hour. Panicked, she checked her comms log to see if she had any messages from people looking for her, or if anyone had noticed she was missing. Nothing so far.

Another glance at the lander showed the machine still crouched next to the porthole, watching her as she worked.

"Done," she said with relief. Her throat felt sticky and dry, the skin between her shoulder blades damp and hot. "I'll run fresh diagnostics, see what they say."

Turning her attention back to the first panel, Cassie did just that. Immediately, dozens of alerts appeared, crowding her HUD.

Transmissions from home. Days of them. Weeks, even.

"You see that?" Her voice cracked slightly, and she swallowed water from a drinking tube.

"I do. You realize what this means? The NCR fleet was never jamming our comms. And—"

Seconds ticked by while Cassie waited for the machine to continue.

"What?" she demanded at last.

"And it's all being rerouted to Sally Braemar's wrist-comm," the machine replied at last.

Blood pulsed in Cassie's temples like the steady beat of

war drums. She stared at the mismatched component gripped in one of the shrimp's manipulators.

"The others need to see this," she said hoarsely.

"Then you'd better hurry," said the machine with sudden urgency. "Because if that thing is linked into her wristcomm, she must know by now we're onto her."

CHAPTER 15
COMMS INVESTIGATION

Cassie hit the orientation jets, and the shrimp rotated until it faced aft, towards the engines. Remembering what had happened to Daphne Makwetu, she ran through a fresh set of diagnostics, just to be sure: so far, the shrimp was performing optimally.

With another tweak of the nozzles, she began the slow journey back to the airlock.

"Problem," said the machine.

It didn't need to tell her: she had already seen the remaining shrimp headed towards her, its shadow grazing the grey-white hull of the Veles. Europa's ice, reflected in the triple-layered visor of its domed helmet, made it impossible to see who was inside.

But she'd bet even money it was Braemar.

The other shrimp rushed towards Cassie with alarming speed. Only in the last couple of seconds did she realize Braemar—assuming it was her inside—had zero intention of slowing down.

In a panic, Cassie worked the controls of her own shrimp, sending it onto a trajectory that took it further away from the Veles. Too late: the second shrimp caught hers a glancing blow, sending Cassie into a backwards spin.

It took Cassie several seconds of panicked effort to halt the spin, but before she could bring her own shrimp closer to the Veles so she could make a break for the airlock, she was rammed a second time.

Alerts crowded Cassie's HUD. The other shrimp now had a hold of her: one of its manipulators snaked out and grabbed hold of the unknown component she'd worked so hard to detach from the array, yanking it free.

Cassie stared in abject horror as the component went tumbling end-over-end towards Europa's surface, a hundred kilometres beneath her feet.

Fury soon took the place of her dismay. "What the hell?" Cassie shouted into her comms, her voice loud and harsh in the confines of the shrimp. "Why did you—?"

The comms crackled. "Get the fuck back inside," Braemar barked, removing any doubt as to whomever was inside the other shrimp.

"It was you!" Cassie yelled. "*You* cut us off from home!"

Braemar laughed throatily. "Prove it," she said, her voice almost jeering. "I don't see any evidence."

Cassie's next words stalled in her throat. She'd blown it: whatever evidence she'd had, however briefly, it was gone forever.

"Don't think I can't," Cassie seethed. "The signal's back. You think the others won't notice?"

"Listen to you, you self-righteous bitch," Braemar shot back, sounding amused. "I swear, you people. You're great with a screwdriver in orbit, but in any other situation, you're worse than useless. You think I wouldn't figure out what you were up to?"

———

CASSIE HAD no choice except to follow Braemar back through the airlock. Long minutes passed while Braemar went first.

Her shrimp automatically locked onto a rail that extended out from the open airlock and was drawn steadily inside.

Cassie hovered just outside the airlock, waiting her turn and seething with anger. But she knew she should be much more afraid of what might happen once she was back inside.

Assuming, she thought in a moment of freezing horror, they let her back in at all.

Then the airlock opened again, the rail extended and Cassie's shrimp was drawn inside and flush with the inner bulkhead facing the inner curve of the spine. The bay pressurized a second time, Cassie's helmet lifting on hinges and the front of her shrimp parting down the middle.

Her muscles screamed in protest when she bent low to push herself out through the suit's chest. For a moment, she allowed herself to just float in the zero gee, her shorts and sleeveless t-shirt damp with perspiration.

She was so exhausted, she hardly paid any attention when the inner airlock door slid open and Braemar stepped back inside, mopping at her face and neck with a towel. Holland was next to enter, and then Javier, his face pinched and angry.

"Ernest," Cassie said as soon as she saw the Commander. Then she coughed and tried to clear her throat, desperately needing to drink water. "I found something out there. These two, they can't be trust—"

Before she could finish, Holland flew down the centre of the bay straight towards her, his gaze as cold and unrelenting as the vacuum.

Cassie froze, unsure of what was happening. Where were the others—Lebed, Harrow, or Doctor Haunani?

By the time this thought had passed through her mind, Holland had already brought himself to a halt by nimbly catching a handhold to Cassie's left.

Braemar followed in his wake. Before Cassie could get out of the way, the other woman barrelled into Cassie with enough force to send them both crashing into a bulkhead.

The back of Cassie's head slammed against something hard, and light flared in the corners of her vision. The force with which she'd been driven against the bulkhead was sufficient that she rebounded, turning head over heels like a piece of spinning debris, legs and arms as loose as a dropped puppet trailing its strings.

She caught sight of Javier, his lips compressed and pale and his eyes full of anguished horror.

You cowardly asshole, thought Cassie. *You'd just stand there and let them beat me to death, wouldn't you?*

A wave of anger beyond anything she'd ever experienced before washed over Cassie, and for the first time in her life, she wondered if she had it in her to kill another human being.

Her slow tumble was arrested when a hand grabbed her upper arm, almost wrenching it free of its socket. She gasped from the pain and saw Holland's face up close, his fingers digging into her flesh.

"We're going to have a long talk, Cassie," she heard Javier say. For all his words, he sounded weak and ineffectual.

"I told you she should have stayed in cryo," said Holland. He regarded her with disgust, still gripping her arm hard.

"We needed the crew on our side," Javier muttered, his mouth working like he'd swallowed something unpleasant.

"Frankly," said Braemar, from where she'd stationed herself across the bay, "it would have been better if she'd never come back inside at all."

"Jesus," Javier snapped, "I already told you. There isn't going to be any killing!"

"The fuck, Ernest?" Cassie blurted. Nausea flared deep in her gut and she wondered if she was going to be sick.

Javier stared at her with open hatred. Rather than looking directly at her, his gaze was focused slightly to one side of her, as if he couldn't bring himself to look directly into her eyes.

"You joined this expedition under false pretences," said

Javier, a little more grit coming into his voice. "You sabotaged our communications under the orders of the New Chinese Republic's security services. When Daphne Makwetu suspected you, you sabotaged her shrimp in an effort to kill her."

Cassie tried to mumble a reply, but it came out slurred. He was scared. She could see that and hear it in his trembling voice: but of whom? Her? The rest of the crew?

No, she realized with a sudden burst of insight: none of them.

He was terrified of the two spooks.

Somehow, she summoned the will and the strength to speak more clearly. "They'll never believe you," she croaked. "Anyone could see through that bullshit."

"With a track record like yours?" said Holland, dryly amused. "You hid a medical condition and someone died. Your only way back into space was this mission, and you were a last-minute addition. Everyone expected Anton Kernov to be on this expedition—not you. Who's to say someone didn't put you on this mission with the intent of sabotage?"

Mute, Cassie stared back at him. He was closer to the truth than he probably realized. She wondered with a thrill of horror whether he knew about Ketteridge meeting with her. Other people must have seen Ketteridge on the Deep Range. Who was to say word hadn't got out that he'd met with her?

Cassie ignored Holland and stared back at Javier. "Did you know these two infected the cryo bay with sentient malware? That they were trying to kill me and everyone else on board? Or were you in on that, too?"

Javier stared back at her in utter confusion. Either he was a better actor than she realized, or he really didn't know what she was talking about. Nor did she miss the alarmed look Braemar shot at Holland.

No, she realized with a rush of insight: Javier hadn't

known, which meant the spooks had been keeping some things back from him.

"The malware was designed to shut the pods down while you were working your solo maintenance shift," she said quickly. "The whole thing was set up so you'd never have known—"

Holland did something to Cassie's arm that filled her vision with an infinity of bright white light and a pain beyond anything she had thought possible. A scream, raw and animal, emerged from deep within her lungs: a sound she hadn't thought her body capable of making.

She vomited. Not much came up, but she heard Holland swearing in disgust. He let go of her, and she thudded, loose-limbed and half-blind with pain, against the outer shell of a shrimp.

"If you kill her," Javier shouted as if from a thousand miles away, "they'll believe nothing we say!"

An arm closed around Cassie's neck and she gasped. Something cold and sharp pricked at her skin. She flailed, the air taking on a molasses-like quality and the pain in her head and arm soon fading to a distant, numb throbbing.

"What the hell was she talking about?" Javier said, from the far end of the universe. His voice trembled a little. "What did she mean about the cryo bay?"

"She was in cryo herself at the time," Braemar snapped. "She's making shit up to save herself. You need to go deal with the others. They'll believe you—they all know she shouldn't be here."

Fatigue rolled over Cassie like a dark tide. There was something she needed to remember. Something to do with Marcus...which didn't make sense, because Marcus was dead.

Wasn't he?

Consciousness retreated, came back, retreated, and came back again. Cassie's experience was reduced to a series of snapshots—of passing bulkheads, of the pain in her arms, twisted behind her back as they were.

Then she was sitting on the edge of a tank, while someone —Braemar?—first undressed her, then pushed her arms and legs inside a support garment before finally attaching sensors to her temples and upper chest. Cassie tried to push her away, but Braemar smacked her across the face.

It became easier not to protest or fight back.

"Now you'll sleep," Cassie heard Braemar say as if from very far away. "And I hope you never goddamn wake up."

CHAPTER 16
SECOND WAKING

The distant sense of a heartbeat, the faraway murmur of voices.

She awoke.

Gripped by a powerful sense of déjà vu, Cassie surfaced through layers of fog, as if ascending from the depths of an ocean towards a blurred grey sky. The air felt thick and viscous in her lungs when she drew in a breath.

Shards of memory came to her like the dreams of a ghost: Marcus, bespectacled and grinning, talking animatedly while they shared a pot of tar-like coffee. They sat at an outdoor café in Brussels the night before an ESA conference. Then she was taking part in an orientation meeting shortly after arriving at the Mare Imbrium base for the first time, listening intently as Sergio addressed her and the other new arrivals while his husband watched quietly from the sidelines. Then she was sitting in a work canteen with Chris while he told her he'd finally been confirmed for Europa Deep.

Cassie's hands grasped at the metal edges of a tank as she vomited cryogenic fluid between her feet.

"Easy," said a voice.

More fluid came up, and Cassie coughed long and hard to

clear the last of it from her lungs and stomach. She heard what sounded like a battery-operated hand vacuum, most likely used to catch loose droplets of cryonic gel. When she tried to mumble an apology, someone else pressed something cold into one of her hands, and she stared groggily at it for several long seconds before it resolved into a squeeze-bottle.

"Drink," said the same voice as before. A familiar voice.

Cassie did as she was told. It was just water this time, but it washed the taste of the gel from her mouth and throat. Then she coughed spasmodically for several more minutes, her vision still too blurry to see who had pulled her out of the tank.

Then a figure moved in front of her, and she saw it was Doctor Haunani.

More memories came back to her. More recent, and considerably less pleasant, memories.

"How long?" she croaked.

"Three days," the doctor replied, handing her a towel. "A lot's happened." He peered at her with curiosity. "Can you move your head?"

What?

He must have seen her confusion, for his mouth twisted up in sympathy. But there was anger there too: but angry at whom—at her?

"Your head," Haunani clarified. "Does it hurt?"

Does it—?

Then she twisted her head slightly to one side and let out a curse. "*Shit*."

"If you can feel it," said Haunani, moving closer to her, "I'll consider it a good sign."

He stopped himself against the lip of her tank and began detaching sensors and other monitoring equipment from her support garment.

"Three days?" Cassie wiped the thick, greasy fluid from

her skin. Her hands shook, and she hissed when she reached up to touch the back of her head.

"Don't move," Haunani commanded her.

A brilliant light shone into first one of Cassie's pupils, then the other. Her head throbbed distantly.

"Well, another good sign," said Haunani, although his expression remained sour. "No permanent damage. Not that those two assholes seem to have cared."

Just then, Cassie glanced past the doctor to see what looked like an enormous spider with one of its legs coiled around a wall grip—

No, she remembered now: not a spider.

"… Marcus?"

"Do you know," said the spider-machine, "I believe she just used my name instead of calling me 'machine'."

"And did you know," said another voice, "how much I loathe and detest spiders?"

Twisting around, Cassie saw Anton Lebed by the bay entrance, holding on to another wall grip by one hand.

"I believe you did mention it," the machine replied dryly. "I believe we should hurry, doctor."

Lebed, she noticed, had a nasty-looking bruise on his jaw.

"Your face," she said to him. "What—?"

He grinned broadly. "Just tell me you swung for those bastards before they got you. At least *my* fight was even."

"Here," said Doctor Haunani, taking her squeeze-bottle from her and handing her another. "You know the routine by now: you need fluids. And plenty of them." He motioned towards a neatly folded pile of clothes and underwear sitting on a nearby shelf. "And get dressed."

"I need to shower first," said Cassie.

Lebed shook his head. "No time. We need to move *now*."

Cassie stared at him, still not entirely awake, then did her best to towel off the rest of the gunk before taking the clothes

—one of her t-shirts, and a pair of loose drawstring trousers— from Lebed. He and the doctor gave her a little privacy, turning their backs so she could change out of the support garment.

"Are you ready to move?" Lebed asked over his shoulder with detectable urgency. "We really don't have much time."

"Don't rush her," said the machine. "Opt or not, she needs to recover."

"After only three days?" Lebed sounded incredulous.

"Even so."

"Just tell me what happened," said Cassie. Her thoughts were still a whirl of confusion.

"Put simply," said the machine, "your backup plan worked."

Backup plan. That rang a bell. There had been…something she had done?

A vague recollection came to her, of making her way up and down the length of the ship and changing, what… command permissions?

"Worked *so far*," Lebed cautioned. "Things are still developing. Which is why we need to get moving."

"The spooks," asked Cassie, remembering suddenly. Her head ached worse at the sudden memory of Braemar slamming her into a bulkhead.

Then her eyes grew wide, and she shot a startled look at everyone around her. "Javier was with them. He was—!"

"Javier's in cryo," Lebed said, catching her short. "The tank next to yours, in fact." He sighed heavily. "Explanations later. Can you move?"

She nodded. "I think so."

Pushing off with her hands, Cassie propelled herself across the bay with less grace than she would have preferred. She awkwardly snagged a handhold and stopped her feet against a bulkhead.

"Well, fuck me," said Lebed, "you can move, all right. Let's go."

Lebed turned and activated the bay door. It slid open noiselessly, and the machine flew past him, fans whirring, and into the spine.

Cassie's head felt stuffed full of cotton, as if she'd been asleep the whole way back home. Then again, if she'd been a baseline human like the rest of them, they'd probably have had to strap her into a stretcher before they could get her to—

Actually, where *were* they going?

She looked back inside the bay at Haunani. "What about you? And where's Lebed taking me?"

"Go ahead." Haunani waved her off, his own expression drawn and worried. "Anton will explain everything."

"Cassie." She turned to see an impatient-looking Lebed anchored to a handhold across the spine from the bay entrance. "Really, we need to move."

Cassie moved to follow, despite her grogginess and confusion. The machine was waiting too, hovering motionless towards the centre of the spine.

"How much do you remember from after you came back from the EVA?" the machine asked her.

"Bits," said Cassie. Lebed was already moving from handhold to handhold, launching himself off from one bulkhead to the next with expert kicks. Cassie did the same, but more slowly. "I definitely remember having the shit kicked out of me." She caught a handhold and looked back at the machine, her voice echoing down the length of the spine. "Wait. I remember. I gave you control of the Veles."

"We were worried how badly those assholes might have injured you," said the machine. "It's hard to be sure with you just out of cryo, but if your short-term memory is coming back this fast, I guess that's a good sign."

Her eyes widened. "Braemar and Holland. Where—?"

"Locked up inside the command deck," Lebed called back to them, his voice ringing with satisfaction.

Cassie took a moment to digest this information. Lebed waited until she caught up with him. "Isn't that leaving them in control of navigation and life-support?"

"I've cut off their access to all such systems," said the machine, coming abreast of her. "I'm not saying it's the best solution, just the best one available."

"But why the command deck?" she asked.

"I only got them there by generating a false alert," the machine explained. "It was enough to get them both inside, and then I sealed the door."

"Come on, Cassie," said Lebed, gesturing towards the lander bay just ahead. "That's where we're going." He reached a hand towards her. "You still look a little unfocused. Do you need my help?"

"No," said Cassie. "I think I'm okay. I just need to take my time."

The machine scooted past them and came to a slow halt right outside the lander bay entrance. Lebed headed straight for a comms interface next to the entrance and began typing commands into it, speaking hurriedly to them over his shoulder as he worked.

"None of the rest of us knew about your illicit spacewalk until after the spooks forced you back into cryo," he explained. "That's when myself, Evan and the Doc were ordered to meet Holland in the hab-ring. He told us you'd tried to sabotage the mission and assaulted the Commander when he confronted you."

Cassie's mouth flopped open. "What?"

"I could smell the bullshit from a mile off," the astronavigator reassured her. "He said you'd hurt Ernest so badly, he and Braemar had no choice but to put him into cryo until he could receive medical treatment back home on Earth. They said they'd put you on ice as well rather than allow you to remain an active threat."

"And you didn't buy it?"

Lebed snorted with derision. "Albert was *furious*, demanding to know why he, the ship's doctor, hadn't been permitted to treat Ernest and decide if he needed to go back into cryo. Obviously, there was no possible reasonable explanation Holland could give for why he and Braemar had acted the way they did, which was when things got…interesting."

By now, Cassie remembered just about everything that had happened, up to and including Braemar's snide little comment right before she got dumped back into a cryo pod. Anger flowed through her blood, hot and bright and sweet.

"He was working with them," she said. "Ernest, I mean." She frowned for a moment, dredging her memories for more information, then remembered his shock when she'd tried to tell him about the cryo bay. "But it sounds like they turned on him."

Lebed finished his work, read something on his wrist-comm, grunted, then turned to look at her. "There are many questions that need answered, of course," he said. "And we'll have the opportunity to develop a true picture of what has been happening on this ship." He nodded inside the lander's bay. "But priorities first."

Cassie stared at him, then at the lander bay, then back again. "Where are we going?"

"Where do you think?"

"But…now? This soon?"

"If not now, when?" Lebed countered. "Evan is prepping the onboard systems and running it through some last checks." He glanced at his wristcomm. "Wait two minutes, then we go in."

"Evan?" Cassie echoed. "He's an oceanologist, not a pilot."

The navigator shook his head. "Prepping, not flying. That, he can do."

"Wait," she said, again noticing the bruise on Lebed's jaw. "You said things got 'interesting'?"

"I swung for Holland when I decided I'd heard enough," said Lebed. "He got in a good punch of his own." His grin faded slightly, and he shrugged. "Then the son of a bitch tased me."

Cassie just stared at him stupidly. "He did what?"

"That took me by surprise, too," said the machine. "I had no idea they'd brought tasers on board."

"Tasers, plural?" said Cassie. "So they both had them."

"They kept them well-hidden," the machine noted. "I overheard what happened through a slaved AREM."

"After that," Lebed added, "we were all confined to the hab-ring." He nodded at the machine. "Then, a few hours later, we all heard a breach alarm."

"That was me," said the machine, with a hint of pride. "I'd seen Holland making preparations to put the remaining crew into cryo as well."

"You faked a breach?" Cassie asked, appalled despite herself. A breach was a polite way of saying the ship was facing imminent destruction. "Isn't that overkill?"

"Well, it was certainly enough to lure them into the command deck, so I figure it was worth it."

Lebed nodded at the machine. "Picture my joy," he said, his expression sour, "on then discovering you had handed control of our ship to a rogue AI."

"I've explained everything to Lebed," the machine told her. "And emphasized *repeatedly* that I am not a risk to the Veles. So, please, Cassie, back me up on this."

Lebed barked out a laugh. "And yet, I cannot help but think of the Yatagarasu."

"Come on, Anton." Despite her grogginess, Cassie found herself coming to the machine's defence. "If he—I mean, it—

really wanted to take the ship and to hell with us, we wouldn't be talking like this."

Lebed sighed, clearly less than happy. "If you had told us about it *before* you unilaterally handed control of the Veles over to it," he said, "we would have listened, not automatically thrown it out an airlock."

Cassie had her considerable doubts about that. Before she could respond, however, Lebed glanced at his wristcomm and continued speaking.

"It's time," he said, looking back up at her, and gestured into the bay. "Let's get moving."

Cassie glanced down the length of the spine toward the cryo bay. "What about Albert?"

"The doctor has decided to remain on board and keep watch over our friends while they're trapped on the command deck. He'll also supervise Daphne and Ernest. The first few days of cryo are always critical."

"I should be the one to remain on board," the machine said insistently. "I can do everything that needs doing to keep the Veles running entirely on my own. Plus, I can work on repairing our comms."

"Repair?" Cassie shook her head. "But it should be fine now. Braemar had installed some kind of device inside the—"

"I explained everything already," said the machine. "Unfortunately, while Braemar was putting you back into cryo, Holland went on a spacewalk and destroyed vital circuitry. I can print new parts, of course, but it'll take time."

"You're coming with us," Lebed said to the machine, and gestured inside the bay. His tone made it clear he wasn't in the mood for arguments. "Now, can we please…?"

"At the very least," the machine continued hurriedly, "leaving me on board would be an opportunity to demonstrate the full, untapped potential of AI command."

"Potential?" Lebed barked. "What potential?"

The machine's lenses swivelled towards Cassie, as if

seeking her support. "It takes thousands of Earth-based support staff working around the clock to keep vital functions in lunar bases and orbital stations from failing and killing everyone inside them. The whole way out, every one of you had to perform daily maintenance and repair on the Veles." One of its manipulators twisted in a gesture powerfully reminiscent of the way Marcus, when alive, would raise a finger when making a point. "But an AI can multitask on multiple levels while also carrying out any necessary repairs or refurbishment with the help of the flying monkeys. This is how space travel was meant to be—with AIs piloting and maintaining their ships and freeing the flesh and blood crew for more important matters."

"No way," said Lebed. "I won't—"

"This is *not* the Yatagarasu," the machine insisted stiffly. "That story about it flying off while its crew starved to death with no way to control it is entirely fabricated. An urban legend."

"I don't care," Lebed insisted. "I want you right where I can see you."

"Are we bloody getting going or not?" Evan Harrow shouted from inside the lander bay.

Cassie looked through the open bay door to see Harrow had emerged from within the lander. He stared at the three of them with a peevish expression.

"Wait," said Cassie. "Why so much hurry? With Braemar and Holland locked up, they're no threat."

Harrow looked past her at Lebed. "Did you tell her about the Tianjin?"

"They're preparing to land," Lebed explained when she looked his way. "Or at least they appear to be prepping their own lander. The only thing those two spooks didn't lie about is the risk of letting the NCR establish a foothold on Europa."

Cassie nodded tiredly, her brain still afloat in a stew of fatigue and hibernation-inducing chemicals. Lebed, seeing her fatigue, caught her by her uninjured arm and gently guided her inside the bay, the machine following in their wake.

Then she remembered something.

"Wait," she said.

Lebed looked at her with a frown. "What?"

Without answering, she turned and launched herself back out of the bay, ignoring Lebed as he yelled after her.

CHAPTER 17

INTERFACE KEY

She found what she was looking for fifteen minutes later, after hauling herself up into the hab-ring and feeling like the effort, so soon after being pulled out of a cryo pod, might kill her.

The key Ketteridge had given her was right where she'd left it, tucked inside a sock in her bunk.

She ran into Lebed on her way back to the spoke. "The hell, Cassie?" he exclaimed.

"I'll explain," she said. Her voice came out sluggish and flat. "But maybe not right now."

She pushed past him, and he turned to follow, his face twisted up with consternation and worry. "I hope it's a very good story," he called after her.

"Believe me," she muttered, "it is."

———

INSIDE THE LANDER BAY, Cassie peeled off her t-shirt and drawstring trousers, then pulled on a life-support garment prior to climbing into one of the spacesuits. Next she pushed Ketteridge's interface key inside a zippered pocket of her spacesuit, then stuffed her clothes into a holdall before throwing it through the lander's hatch. Lebed did the same, then followed her inside.

By now, most of the cryo gunk had dried on her skin and flaked off, but she knew, even as she secured her helmet, it might be a long time before she got to have anything like a real shower. Just thinking about it made her skin itch.

"Up front with me, Cassie," Lebed shouted through the open hatch.

She wormed her way through the hatch and inside the lander, where, at Lebed's direction, she took the co-pilot's seat from Harrow, who switched to one of the rear passenger seats. The machine had already secured itself inside the lander by hooking several manipulators through loops attached to a rear bulkhead.

Cassie didn't miss Harrow's look of apprehension when he looked around at the spider-machine, clinging to the bulkhead inches from his face.

A screen mounted on the bulkhead directly before Cassie had secondary guidance controls placed directly beneath it. A small porthole situated directly between her screen and Lebed's primary command-and-control interface allowed her to see the surface of Europa far below.

"Everything looks good," Lebed announced from beside. He glanced at Cassie, nodded, took a deep breath, and reached for the controls.

"You sure you want me in the co-pilot's seat?" Cassie asked. "So soon after—?"

"No time to discuss," said Lebed. "Separating in three, two…"

The lander shuddered. This was followed by a series of dull, heavy thumps: the sound of the bolts securing the lander to the Veles releasing their hold.

Europa drifted slowly out of view as Lebed rotated the lander. Soon, its engines were pointed towards the surface of the ice moon.

"I need to put a little distance between us and the ship," Lebed muttered, working his joystick.

The screen before Cassie displayed side-by-side views of Europa and the Veles, the latter already growing more distant by the second.

"Three minutes until main engines," Lebed announced, leaning back slightly. He glanced sideways at Cassie. "By the way, we're carrying a total of four behemoth suits down with us. We only need three, obviously, but I didn't see any point in unloading the extra one. Especially since we don't know if we'll find any down there."

"Understood," said Cassie. "Even if we do, they're not likely to still be functional after this many years." She glanced over her shoulder. "Evan? Check your helmet's secure and lock your visor."

Harrow reached up and pulled his visor down, locking it into place. "Done."

Both Lebed and Cassie did the same. Cassie tapped the side of her helmet, activating her HUD. Icons appeared in the top-right corner of her visor, displaying pressure readings and personal biometrics.

A comms icon with Lebed's name under it blinked into life, requesting she open a private channel.

"I need to ask you again without the machine overhearing," said Lebed once she accepted the connection. "How much do you really trust that thing?"

The side of Cassie's helmet blocked most of her view of the rogue AI, but she couldn't help but glance that way.

"Here's a story for you," she said. "I once met Hayashi Risuke. Mr Yatagarasu himself."

Lebed's eyes grew round behind his closed visor. "Bullshit."

"It was at a conference. I was there with—" she caught herself before she said *with the machine* "—with someone."

Lebed nodded, his lips pursed as he checked the readouts.

The lander had ceased rotating along its vertical axis and was dropping steadily towards Europa at a steep seventy degrees angle. He was waiting, she knew, to reach the optimal distance from the surface before firing the main boosters.

"The stowaway machine told us about your relationship with it. Well... with him." Lebed sounded faintly embarrassed.

She made a dismissive gesture with one gloved hand, to indicate that finding herself trapped in deep space with her undead fiancé reincarnated as a giant spider-thing was no big deal, really.

"We had dinner with Risuke," she continued. "Me and Marcus. Risuke wasn't wild-eyed or crazy, although he was already pretty sick even then. He knew his time was limited, but this was still years before he uploaded. I've never met anyone more sane."

Lebed was silent a moment, his attention fixed on the topographical information displayed on his primary screen. "And your point is?"

"When the Yatagarasu disappeared and people started talking about this idea that Risuke had deliberately taken the ship off to go cruising through the universe, I tried to reconcile the man I'd met with the kind of person who'd do something like that—and I couldn't. The Hayashi Risuke I met literally wouldn't hurt a fly."

Risuke, the man who'd developed the nuclear drive that helped make regular manned missions to Mars feasible, had been closing in on retirement when he'd learned he had a terminal disease of the nervous system. Prior to uploading his personality to an AI construct, he'd already received funding to design, build and fly what would become the first fully AI-piloted spacecraft in history.

Except slightly more than a year after departing Earth on a mission to Saturn, Risuke's ship, the Yatagarasu, along with its crew of six Opt astronauts, had disappeared without trace.

Observations of its altered course had led to speculation that its new destination was Proxima Centauri, several light-years and thousands of years of travel away. The crew had long since been declared officially dead.

Wrinkles formed between Lebed's eyebrows. "But you only met him once. How could you know that—?"

"I already told you," she replied. "Our stowaway could have taken the Veles any time it wanted. But it didn't, Anton. Instead, it saved our lives."

Lebed nodded slowly, still keeping a close eye on their altitude and rate of descent. "While I have the opportunity, I wish to ask you another question. I sense there is something more you are not telling us."

"Am I coming along on this trip so you can keep an eye on me too?" she asked flatly.

Lebed glanced at her. "Convince me," he said, "that I don't need to."

Before she could form a retort, his comms icon changed to indicate he was now speaking to everyone inside the lander.

"Ignition in three, two..."

An angry mule kicked Cassie in the small of her back, bringing back memories of landings and launches from what felt like a lifetime ago.

"We need a clear landing spot," said Lebed, guiding the craft back to the correct angle of entry. "Cassie?"

She checked updated topological data on the screen before her. "There's a flat area south-south-east of Station Verne. See it?"

Lebed leaned over slightly to see the screen, then nodded tightly. "Roger."

Both the borehole station and Station Verne were located in the chaotic equatorial regions on Europa's dark side. Chaotic, because Jupiter's gravity, in combination with its magnetosphere and the enormous pressure exerted on the ice by the saltwater ocean beneath its surface, periodically caused the ice to fracture.

And when it did, geysers erupted, big and powerful enough to send jets of salt water spewing into orbit. As a result, Europa's surface was constantly shifting, and what would have made a good landing spot back in the days of the first expedition might, by now, be an icy chasm.

"Six minutes to landing," Lebed announced. He glanced at Cassie. "I think," he added, still on the shared comms, "that if there's anything we don't yet know, Miss White, this really should be the time to share it. Starting with, how is it you know a member of the Tianjin's crew?"

Even though she'd known Lebed and the others knew about Tingshao, something about hearing Lebed actually say it out loud made her start. Europa, meanwhile, loomed yet larger, its ice marked by long striations of yellow and grey, while sunlight cast long shadows from crenelations and shards of ice that rose from the surface like snowy daggers.

"I don't think there's any harm now, Cassie," said the machine. "And we're a long, long way away from Earth."

"I was sent here to find evidence of war crimes," she said at last, her gaze still fixed on the screen. "If I find it, I get the treatments for life and maybe even my old career back."

"War crimes?" Harrow sounded confused.

"Someone on the first expedition was developing bioweapons from Europan life. Maybe even something that got used during the war."

For a long moment, there was only the distant rumble of the boosters, slowing their rate of descent, and the slight creak and tick of the lander's hull.

"Develop bioweapons for who, exactly?" Lebed wanted to know. "And who, precisely, hired you to do this?"

"Why didn't you tell us any of this before?" Harrow demanded. "Why in God's name keep something like this a secret?"

"I didn't tell you because I was warned before I left that someone else on this expedition might be out to destroy the same evidence I was sent to find."

Lebed stared at her, dumbfounded. "Holland and Braemar?"

"That'd be my guess, but I had to be sure they were up to no good. That's why I went out to the comms hub, so I could prove it to the rest of you."

She told them about Makwetu's suspicions regarding Holland, the surface of Europa looming yet larger all the while.

"I think," the machine announced, "you should also tell them about the figure on the ice, Cassie."

Lebed twisted around in his seat to see the machine past the corner of his helmet. "The what? I—"

Then he took another glance at his instrument panel. "Never mind," he said quickly. "Initiating final burn. This might get bumpy."

A deep vibration worked its way through Cassie's seating and into her bones. Gravity, faint as it was, tugged at her.

The screen by now was filled with nothing but streaks of grey, white, and dirty yellow. Lebed worked the controls, his full attention on getting them down safely without crashing. Cassie thought about Makwetu, and how she should have been the one taking them down.

"Landing site looks clear," said Lebed. "Going to have to turn her around slightly."

The landscape on the screen rotated, and Cassie saw particles of ice and snow billow under the blast of their rockets.

"Five," said Lebed, his jaw tense but his voice flat and calm. "Four. Three…"

After another moment, there was a loud squeal and then a thump.

"We're down," said Lebed. "Everyone stay in position for now."

He was, Cassie knew, waiting to see if the ice beneath them gave way under the weight of the lander. If that happened, there was enough reserve fuel for a full two-minute burn—hopefully enough to find a new landing spot.

"Okay," Lebed said at last, seemingly satisfied. "Everybody out of your suits and into the behemoths. Then we head for the supply drones and roll out the crawler."

"About the behemoths," said the machine. "I have a suggestion."

CHAPTER 18
DRIVING EUROPA

Four behemoth suits were stored in a bay beneath their capsule but above the landing rockets. Cassie and the others first stripped out of their standard spacesuits, which were inadequate for conditions on Europa's surface, and pulled their regular clothes back on. Next, they took turns squeezing through a hatch in the floor, beneath which there was just enough space for each of them to wriggle inside one of the behemoth suits.

Once all final checks had been performed, the cargo bay blew off the outer part of its hull. The flat segments of metal sank to the ice with lunar slowness.

One by one, all four of them dropped the few metres to the surface of Europa in their behemoth suits. The 0.13 gravity gave Cassie's movements a dreamlike quality, but the suits were massive enough to send up flurries of ice when they landed.

Station Verne had been situated on Europa's outer leading edge, in the direction of its orbit, in order to minimise its exposure to hard radiation. Even so, Cassie held her breath when she saw the radiation readouts spike wildly on her suit's readouts. The behemoth—designed to operate as well on the surface of Europa as at the bottom of its oceans—

would protect her well enough, but the sooner they all got to Station Verne, the better.

At first, Cassie hadn't believed the machine when it insisted it could control a behemoth suit as well as any of them. There were internal ports into which it could plug, it explained, and through which it could access the servos that powered the suit's movements.

She had to admit it seemed to do fine. Certainly, she couldn't tell by sight alone which of the three other suits was occupied by a revenant AI, and which by a flesh-and-blood human.

They set off immediately, making their way across the icy terrain toward the nearest supply drone. The first was easy to spot, its striped red-and-white nose standing out amid the landscape of dirty ice. A second drone was visible, another half a klick distant.

"Christ," said Evan, his breath rasping over the shared comms, "It feels like I'm strapped into a mobile coffin. Does walking in these things ever get easier?"

Once they had reached the first supply drone, Lebed activated it remotely. They watched as its hull split open along four seams, like some enormous metal flower opening its petals to the tiny, faraway star that was the Sun. Each of the hull sections acted as a ramp, down which essential equipment could be moved.

This particular supply drone contained a six-wheeled crawler and a mini-sub mounted on a wheeled trailer, all held within a set of metal cradles.

Cassie, meanwhile, glanced past tall columns of fractured ice to see a communications tower off in the distance, marking the location of Station Verne.

The sight filled her with a sudden pang at the thought of what they might find there. Would, most likely, find there. For the first time since agreeing to Ketteridge's offer, she felt hesitant about going forward.

But if there were answers, that was where she would find them.

Then it was time to haul everything down from the unmanned supply drone, which had arrived a few weeks before the Veles. The crawler automatically descended one of the hull-ramps in response to a remote command, its six enormous wheels gripping the ice.

The trailer carrying the mini-sub was slaved to the crawler, and it automatically followed the crawler down onto the ice. By the time they had finished attaching the trailer to the rear of the crawler, Cassie was exhausted.

"The view is really quite something," Cassie heard the machine say over their shared comms.

She turned away from the crawler to see the AI, in its behemoth suit, standing a few dozen metres away from them. It was peering up the length of an ice column rising fifty metres above the surface of Europa.

"Quite something, huh?" she said. "What do you say when you're *really* excited?"

The behemoth turned laboriously through a half-circle until it faced towards her, then raised one huge gloved hand in a gesture of greeting.

Cassie suddenly flashed back to a trip to Ayers Rock with Marcus—the same trip on which they'd both contracted the Whispers. He'd turned to wave at her in exactly the same—

No. Her hands worked inside the huge, heavy fists of her own behemoth. *Just a machine.*

But now that it was inside a behemoth suit—now that it had arms and legs—it was suddenly very easy to forget it wasn't really him.

Cassie was therefore startled to hear Evan Harrow evince precisely that same thought, if in slightly different words.

"Hey, Marcus," said Harrow. "How does it feel being able to walk around on two legs again?"

He had been stepping around the crawler together with

Lebed, inspecting both it and the attached trailer. Unlike Cassie, he appeared to have no trouble treating the machine exactly the same as any living human.

"Technically speaking, the suit is walking itself," the machine replied. "I'm just telling it which way to go." It paused a moment, as if thinking. "To be honest, it feels a little limited."

"Limited?" Harrow echoed, surprise evident in his voice.

"Back on the Veles," the machine reminded him, "I had dozens of limbs."

"I don't understand."

"He means the flying monkeys," said Cassie. "Don't you?"

"Quite so," the machine agreed.

"Right," said Harrow, sounding a little lost for words. It wasn't hard to guess what the oceanologist was thinking: how often had one of the little robots flown or walked past him aboard the Veles, with him none the wiser that they were controlled by a rogue AI?

"We're ready to move," said Lebed. "Everyone inside the crawler."

———

To dock with the crawler, Cassie had to back up to it and sit down on one of four fold-down seats placed between two of its wheels. The rear of the behemoth docked automatically with a spherical airlock set into the crawler's hull, and she heard a hiss as the port opened. To enter the crawler, she had to lean back with her shoulders hunched and then squirm into the crawler's interior.

Lebed and Harrow were doing the same, and she heard Lebed muttering and cursing as he shouldered his way into the crawler's interior. Then he came forward to join her in the crawler's cockpit.

"Does it have to be so...ungainly?" he demanded, massaging one shoulder and peering out through the heavily tinted windscreen.

Cassie recalled having to sit through a lecture back home about the proprietary radiation-resistant polymer from which the windscreens were made. Without it, they'd have ended up like Daphne.

Lebed peered elaborately around, his shoulders hunched beneath the crawler's low ceiling. "The machine. Where is it?"

Cassie looked around. He was right: only their three suits had docked. But not the AI.

Cassie reached for a comms button on the crawler's dashboard. She could see the machine was still wandering around outside, like an ungainly metal and plastic giant.

"This is Cassie. Why aren't you coming inside?"

"I'm more useful out here," said the machine. "Plus, I can keep up with you on foot no problem—the crawler's not that fast. And if you run into problems on the way, or things that need someone on the outside, I could help."

"Fuck me," Harrow muttered from behind Cassie's shoulder. "He wants to play bloody tourist."

Lebed grunted a laugh, then touched a button on the dashboard to mute the comms. "Let it," he said to her and Harrow both. "It makes my skin itch having that thing up close next to me."

They both turned to Harrow, as if the final decision rested with him. "It'd just be taking up space in here," he said with a shrug.

"To hell with it," Cassie said resignedly and unmuted the comms. "Keep close," she ordered the machine. "Don't wander too far. And follow in our tracks in case we run into an unexpected crevice. Got that?"

"Understood."

Lebed took the controls, and the crawler rolled forward,

steadily picking up speed until they could all feel the rumble of its fat tires across the uneven ice.

The machine had turned out to be right: its behemoth suit kept pace with the crawler without too much trouble. While Lebed drove, Cassie and Harrow found spare air tanks, backup equipment, and a supply of MREs good for several weeks stored in the back of the crawler. The MREs had been stored within a thick-walled crate constructed from radiation-resistant polymer composite materials.

After another kilometre, they had to skirt a field of penitents—tall, jagged spears of ice formed through a process of sublimation, some reaching a height of several storeys and packed close together—only to find their way blocked by a tall ridge of grey-streaked ice that didn't appear on any of the maps programmed into the crawler's memory. A quick check of more recent satellite imagery showed that the formation was a recent one from a few years before.

"How long's it going to take to drive around this?" Lebed asked, peering ahead through the windscreen.

"I couldn't even guess," said Harrow, scrolling through more satellite imagery on a touchscreen. "A couple of hours, possibly more."

"What's the problem?" Cassie asked, seeing Lebed's worried expression.

"The Tianjin," he said. "Remember? They're on their way down. Maybe they're already here."

"Even if they are," said Cassie, trying to sound reassuring, "they won't get to Verne before us."

Lebed nodded, looking distracted. "This Chen Tingshao," he said. "Is it possible he might be part of the Tianjin's landing party?"

"Honestly," she said, "I have no way of knowing."

"But you know him," Lebed insisted. "You were close once, yes?"

She could feel Harrow's eyes on her, too. "At one time."

Lebed cocked his head to one side. "But not anymore?"

Caught off-balance, Cassie felt a flush of anger. "What is this about, Anton?"

"To survive," he said, "we must know everything there is to know about the people on that other ship."

"He deserted me," she said.

Lebed's expression was blank, but she could tell this wasn't the answer he'd been expecting.

"I don't—"

Cassie sighed. "After all the Opts in the space industry got grounded, in the West at least, Tingshao went work in the NCR since their own space industry was booming. He figured there was more opportunity in a newly democratic society, and he had family there, anyway." She folded her arms, knowing how defensive it looked, but not caring. "I got left behind."

"You didn't go with him?" Harrow asked.

Cassie laughed morosely. "And do what? Pick up litter? They wouldn't have let me go into space, either. Not after Sergio." She shrugged. "Then I got into diving work, since that felt like a substitute for space. And…we kind of drifted apart."

"But you could use that connection," Lebed suggested. "It might put you in a good position to negotiate with them when they do land."

She looked at him with surprise. "That's what you want me to do?"

"If necessary, yes." He let a beat pass. "Especially if we find ourselves in a…confrontation."

"Now you sound like Holland."

It was Lebed's turn to look annoyed. "We need to be prepared for all eventualities, is all that I am saying."

"Well, fine," she said. "I can talk to them if it comes to that. But it won't. Come to that, I mean."

"I hope not," Lebed replied. "In the meantime, no time to waste."

They backtracked, still driving slowly, wary of slipping into a vent or fissure hidden beneath fractured ice. The detour would add several hours to their journey.

Cassie, still exhausted from having barely emerged from a cryo pod for the second time in as many weeks, stretched out on a fold-down bench between two docking ports. She closed her eyes, and sleep fell on her like a hammer.

CHAPTER 19

STATION VERNE

Harrow woke Cassie once they reached Verne. She looked up to see him leaning over her, his eyes tinged with red. He looked even more tired than she felt.

"We're there," he said.

The crawler had ceased its forward motion. Stumbling back upright, Cassie followed the oceanologist up front to the cockpit, where a weary-looking Lebed remained at the controls. The same antenna tower she'd seen earlier was visible through the windscreen a dozen metres away, surrounded by a cluster of low, broad snowy humps: Station Verne.

Beneath these humps were a series of domes. Following their construction, the first expedition had sprayed each dome with liquid water until it was covered over with a layer of ice several metres thick—dense enough to provide an efficient shield against Jupiter's radiation. Over the years, the ice had become streaked with radiation-baked sodium chloride, and organic materials carried up from out of the deep ocean by geysers.

Lebed glanced at Harrow. "Did you tell her?"

"Told me what?" Cassie asked, pulling her gaze away from the station.

"Look there," said Lebed, pointing at the expanse of snow and ice separating the domes.

Cassie peered out through the windshield. "All I see are bootprints."

"Mostly from the first expedition, yes," Lebed agreed. "But look more closely."

It took a moment, but then her eyes widened. "Some of them look fresh."

"Exactly," Lebed agreed. "They aren't streaked with sediment, so they must be much more recent."

"The figure on the ice," she said.

Lebed nodded. "Seems likely." He peered outside. "Where's the machine?"

"Just catching up," said Harrow, pointing at a dashboard-mounted screen. The crawler's rear cameras showed the machine, in its behemoth suit, lumbering up next to the vehicle.

Lebed touched the comms button. "Mr Junger," he barked, addressing Marcus by his second name, "be careful where you step. We want to take a closer look at some of these fresher bootprints."

The behemoth came to a halt next to the crawler, and then carefully turned in a half-circle until it faced the domes and the bootprints.

"I see what you mean," it said. "Might I suggest I follow these more recent prints back to their point of origin, while the rest of you investigate the interior of the station?"

"Fine," said Lebed. "But stay in line of sight as much as you can. Your radio won't penetrate these ridges and ice columns."

"I'm perfectly well aware of that, thank you," the machine replied. "I'll do my best, but it's going to be tricky."

Lebed reached out and tapped the comms off. "Take all the time you want," he muttered under his breath.

———

Soon enough, they had docked their crawler with Verne's primary dome in preparation for cycling through its airlock. There was, so far as they could surmise, no sign of the first expedition's crawler. That in itself suggested the original crew had taken their crawler to the borehole station and left it there while they travelled beneath the ice.

Sitting in the co-pilot's seat, Cassie queried the station's computer and got a response, which further showed the station still had power, supplied by a compact nuclear reactor housed separately from the domes.

"Before we cycle through," said Lebed, his gaze focused on Cassie, "be aware we may—"

"Find bodies," Cassie finished for him.

"To put it bluntly."

"I've been thinking about this moment ever since I joined the expedition, Anton. I'm prepared for anything."

"It doesn't seem likely, though, does it?" Harrow looked between them. "That we'd find bodies, I mean. If the first expedition's crawler isn't here, then it stands to reason they all went under the ice."

"Some may have stayed behind," Lebed pointed out. He raised a hand before Harrow could object. "And yes, that raises another question, that being, why those who remained behind didn't then attempt to communicate with Earth via the satellites they had already placed in orbit."

"We should test for pathogens," Harrow added, "both terrestrial and non-terrestrial. And the crawler comes equipped with basic spacesuits for emergencies. We can put them on before we cycle through. If there's cause for concern, we can flush the air from the station."

———

THE SPACESUITS WERE LIGHTWEIGHT, orange-coloured sports models packed into a storage unit: good enough for emergencies such as blowouts, but they offered zero protection from the hard radiation constantly blasting Europa's surface.

Once they had them on, the three of them crouched at the rear, next to the crawler's primary airlock.

"This is it," said Lebed, his voice sounding hollow and flat over the comms. He peered at them each through the curved polycarbonate of his visor. "Just be ready, okay?"

"I want to go first," said Cassie.

Lebed offered no argument. He activated the inner airlock door and it swung inwards. Cassie squeezed past him on her hands and knees and inside the airlock's narrow tube. The tube was just barely wide enough for her to wriggle inside while wearing the spacesuit.

The door behind her swung shut, and a few seconds later the one in front opened with a barely audible hiss to reveal the pitch black interior of the station.

Something moved in the darkness.

For a moment Cassie froze in place, still kneeling inside the open airlock. Panic welled up inside her, and she fumbled for a torch-pen attached to her spacesuit, quickly switching it on.

It revealed a scrap of paper on the floor below the open airlock. Most likely, it had been stirred by the sudden movement of air.

"Are you okay?" Harrow asked over the comms. He sounded concerned, and Cassie wondered if she'd gasped audibly.

"It's fine," she said. "But it's pretty dark. Maybe the lights aren't working."

"I think they work on sensors," said Lebed, speaking now. "They should come on when you go all the way inside."

The lights finally came on as Cassie emerged fully from the airlock and stood. Squinting into the sudden brightness, she found herself at the edge of a wide, low open space that was bigger than she'd expected it to be.

Split over two levels, the dome was nearly fifteen metres across at the base, with much of the lower level given over to laboratory equipment. She also saw a comms station on the far side of the dome, with a small kitchenette and living area closer to hand. A few personal possessions—books, tablets and sundry tchotchkes—sat discarded on tables and couches, the latter of which appeared to have been constructed from packing materials.

It felt eerily like the crew had stepped out for a moment.

She heard grunting over the comms and turned to see Harrow squeezing through the airlock.

"No bodies," he said over the comms as he stood and looked around. He stepped past her and placed one hand on the upper edge of a console.

Lebed was next through. "Maybe there aren't any bodies here," he pointed out, "but that doesn't mean there aren't any on the upper level." He stood and peered around, touching a gloved hand to the curving outer wall of the dome. "Or in the other domes."

Harrow, meanwhile, had already crossed the dome and started climbing a set of aluminium steps leading to the second level. Cassie watched as he disappeared from sight.

"I think you should both see this," he said over the comms a few seconds later.

"You find something?" Cassie asked, her throat suddenly tight.

"Not what you think, Cassie. Something else."

Cassie reached out and placed a hand on the back of a couch. She stood there for a moment until her breathing steadied.

Lebed touched a glove to her shoulder. "All good?"

She nodded. "Just need a second," she said hoarsely. "You go first."

Lebed grunted and followed Harrow up the steps. For a moment there, she'd thought she might pass out. Maybe it was all this running around so soon after being pulled from the tank, or perhaps it was the sheer pressure of so much happening, and so quickly.

She gave herself a few more seconds, then climbed the narrow steps.

"Jesus," she said, looking around as she emerged at the top of the steps. "What happened here?"

Much of the upper level was taken up by fold-down cots. Cassie saw framed pictures and clothes scattered all across the floor, along with shattered and broken equipment. The contents of a row of aluminium lockers set close to one side of the dome looked like it had similarly been rifled through.

"Seems like somebody was looking for something," said Harrow. Reaching down, he picked up a flimsy and shook it rigid. After a moment, it came to life.

"Anything interesting there?" asked Cassie.

Harrow raised one gloved hand. "Won't find out while we're still in these suits."

"Then let's not delay in finding out if the air's safe to breathe," said Lebed. "Evan, you have the testing kit?"

———

MOST OF AN HOUR LATER, Harrow had confirmed that there were no detectable pathogens in the air. As it turned out, the dome's air filtration system had its own inbuilt detection protocols: they hadn't even needed to use the testing kit.

Back down on the lower level, Cassie was the first to take off her helmet. The air smelled musty and fetid, but beneath that was another scent, one that took her a moment to place.

"It smells like the sea," she heard Harrow say. "The air, I mean. Don't you think?"

She turned to see him looking through drawers in the kitchenette, his helmet sitting on a countertop beside him.

"It does," she agreed. "It takes me back to my diving days."

Harrow nodded. "The station processes Europan ice into breathable air. I'm guessing salts carried up from under the ice are contaminating the supply in some way. We should probably check the filtration systems. Known pathogens is one thing, but maybe let's also make sure there aren't any Europan bugs getting past the detectors." He looked over at Lebed, who had dropped into a chair before a comms console. "Any luck getting through to the satellites?"

"The link is down," the navigator responded. "Not sure why, but if there's a way to fix it, I'm sure I can find it."

Cassie slipped back upstairs while they talked. It was obvious which cot had belonged to Brian Hall: the shelves next to it were crammed with paperback copies of his own books on astrobiology and exobiology. He must, Cassie surmised, have used up most of his personal weight allowance to bring them all this way.

You had to be some kind of conceited asshole, she thought, to drag physical copies of your own books halfway across the solar system.

Further exploration provided no clues as to which cot might have belonged to Chris. A notebook left lying on top of another cot proved to be filled with scribbled pressure formulations. Tracey Derringer's name was carefully printed in ballpoint on the inside flap of the notebook—Derringer, Cassie recalled, had been the first expedition's oceanologist. She had read one of Derringer's books prior to joining the crew of the Deep Range.

Sitting on the edge of Derringer's cot, Cassie's chest suddenly felt oddly constricted. She might have thought it was claustrophobia, if it hadn't been edited out of her genes.

After another moment's consideration, she realized it was grief.

———

WHEN SHE RETURNED to the lower level, Lebed wasn't there.

"He's gone through the tunnels to check the other domes," Harrow explained. He had a wall panel open, and was busily poking around amidst a mass of wires and electronics.

"What's up?" she asked.

"The computer network's down," he said over his shoulder. "We need it up if we're going to find anything out."

Cassie stepped up beside him, seeing blinking status lights and server units. "Is it fixable?"

"No idea. And it's not exactly my area of expertise. But I can try."

Unsure what else to do, Cassie followed in Lebed's wake, first making her way down a ladder built into a shaft that soon opened into a cramped tunnel. The tunnel walls had been lined with insulating materials and fast-drying sealants to keep anyone passing through from freezing to death. Even so, her breath plumed white as she made her way along the low-ceilinged tunnel in a crouch. If not for the spacesuit she still wore, minus the helmet, she might have considered turning back.

The tunnel ran in a circle, connecting the domes together under the ice. The first she came to appeared to have been dedicated to hydroponics, although by now all that remained were the desiccated remains of the first expedition's crops.

The engineering bay proved equally deserted. She finally found Lebed in Dome Four, which looked like it had been used primarily for storage.

Lebed turned to see her ascending the ladder into the dome.

"Found this." He tapped one of a row of tanks taking up

one side of the dome. "Backup N/02 supply. In case the air extraction systems break down."

Cassie nodded distractedly, seeing tall aluminium shelving units neatly stacked with spare parts, 3D printers and pressure-compatible sample boxes intended for preserving biological samples taken from the deep ocean.

"Evan says the computer network's down, but he's working on it."

Lebed nodded. "The station," he said carefully, "does seem to be in good condition. I didn't think we'd have so easy a time of it."

"Almost like someone's been maintaining it," Cassie replied with equal care.

For a moment, their eyes met.

"About the figure on the ice," he said.

She nodded. "I know what you're thinking. If there're survivors, and they've been keeping this station more or less functional, then why aren't they rushing to meet us? Why not leave a message saying hi, and where to find them?"

"That figure was headed here from the borehole station," Lebed pointed out. "It could be our arrival caught whoever it was off guard. And if someone's around, and they've been making observations, they know more than one ship is in orbit. It might be a question of waiting to see who we are."

She looked at him skeptically. "Do you really believe that?"

He grimaced. "Perhaps not, no." He opened a storage unit at random, peered inside, then closed it again.

"It reminds me of that ship in the story," he said, turning back to face her. "Do you know the one I mean?"

She stared at him. "The Marie Celeste?"

"Yes." Lebed affected a shudder. "As if the crew were here one moment, then disappeared an instant before we arrived. Like a ghost ship."

"Jesus, Anton," she muttered. "Isn't being here creepy enough without throwing that into the mix?"

"Sorry," he said with a chuckle.

Cassie looked past him, not listening, then stepped past him.

Lebed frowned. "What is it?"

Reaching down, she picked a discarded paperback up from a shelf. Its pages were slightly bent.

"Twenty Thousand Leagues Under The Sea," she said, holding it up so Lebed could see it. She lowered herself to sit on a modular crate and let out a shaky breath. "I gave this to Chris just a couple of weeks before the first expedition left orbit."

She pictured him making his way here through the tunnels, perhaps looking for somewhere quiet to read away from the others. Perhaps he'd left it here intending to come back to get it.

And then he'd vanished, along with everyone else.

Lebed's jaw worked like he was unsure of what to say. Cassie opened the book to where she remembered placing an inscription: *Happy Trails, big brother :-)*.

A slip of paper fell out of the book and tumbled slowly to the floor. Stooping, Cassie picked it up. Someone—Chris?—had pulled a page out of a notebook and scribbled a series of dots on it, arranged haphazardly around a much larger black scribble. One of the lesser dots had a couple of lines drawn under it, as if it were of some significance.

She turned it over, but found nothing on the reverse of the slip: no clue what it might mean.

Her suit comms beeped unexpectedly and Cassie gasped.

She looked over at Lebed and laughed. "Nerves."

"Evan has the computer networks back up, I see," Lebed said with a grin.

Cassie put the book back on the shelf, but something

made her keep the slip of paper, tucking it into a zippered pocket of her spacesuit.

Lebed lifted the arm of his own suit and tapped the comms button built into the arm. "Good work, Evan."

"Thanks," Cassie heard Harrow say. "We should have full access to whatever files they left behind. You, uh, find anything on your wanders?"

"Nothing significant," said Lebed. "Certainly no answers."

"Then I think we should eat," said Harrow. "In case we don't get a chance later. Besides," he added, "if I'm starving, you two must be fucking ravenous."

"Is there still no way we can contact the Veles?" Cassie asked, stepping up close to Lebed so Harrow could hear her. "I don't feel good about him being up there alone with those two assholes."

"Not that we can do anything about from down here, no," Harrow responded. "Like it or not, Albert's on his own until we get back up there."

"I guess," Cassie said glumly. "But can we route a signal through the satellites from here? Let Mission Control know what's been happening while we've been out of contact?"

"Yeah, about that," said Harrow. "We've got network communication, but not orbital."

"Why the hell not?"

"Orbital communications are through a freestanding transceiver separate from the domes. I hate to say it, but one of us might have to go out there and try to figure out why it's not working."

Lebed and Cassie shared a look at this news. "It's been a long time," Cassie offered. "Could be its circuitry is fried from all the radiation."

"We'll be back in a minute," Lebed replied, then tapped the comms off. He looked at Cassie with a tired expression and raised his eyebrows. "Eat?"

CHAPTER 20
YATAGARASU

They ate together in silence in the main dome's kitchenette. Their MREs were self-heating, so all they had to do was peel back the lid and wait for it to cook itself.

Cassie found her thoughts straying to Ketteridge's interface key. Before they ate, and by some unspoken mutual consent, they had each headed back inside the crawler to change into their regular clothes rather than try to eat in the unwieldy spacesuits.

Cassie had tucked the key into a pocket of her t-shirt. She imagined some oily, snake-like demon writhing beneath its black plastic exterior.

Once her noodles had finished bubbling away like the afterthought of some mad scientist, she stirred it with a plastic fork, feeling like they were picnicking in a haunted house.

"I got to thinking," she said, after a few minutes of mutual silence and eating, "that if I'd survived this long on Europa, I'd make use of the hydroponics to produce food. But it's clearly been unused since the first expedition fell out of contact."

"My thought too," said Lebed, chewing thoughtfully, his

gaze focused on a faraway point. "It feels like we came here looking to solve a mystery, only to find yet greater mysteries."

A comms icon flashed on Cassie's wristcomm. She put her fork down and answered. "Marcus?"

"It's spectacular out here," said the machine. "Forget lunar tourism. You could make billions bringing rich assholes out here."

Harrow smirked from across the table.

"Is that all you wanted to tell me?" Cassie replied.

"No," said the machine. "I found more tracks, plus another landing site."

Cassie shared a look with the other two men. "Where, exactly?"

"Almost exactly halfway between Verne and the borehole station. There are indentations in the ice that were clearly made by a lander, and there are more bootprints leading away from it toward the borehole."

By now, Lebed and Harrow were listening intently, their food forgotten.

"How recent do the prints look?" Harrow asked.

"Not very," said the machine. "I mean, there's no way to be sure, not without some kind of forensic analysis. But if I had to guess, these prints aren't as recent as our friend going walkabout on the ice in the video Cassie showed us."

"Then it's possible they were left behind by the first expedition," Cassie suggested. "Which we'd expect."

"Except that doesn't explain the lander marks," the machine insisted. "There's an expanse of smooth, melted ice with a thinner covering of organic deposits than I saw at Verne. Plus, the prints fan out from there."

Harrow caught Lebed's eye. "A lander's boosters would have melted the ice," he said, half-thinking out loud. "And if there's a thinner layer of organics on top—"

"Then," the machine finished for him, "someone landed

here sometime between the disappearance of the first expedition and our arriving."

Lebed looked hard at Cassie's wristcomm. "Marcus, are you suggesting the NCR already landed here years ago? Or… someone else?"

"I have a theory," the machine offered, following what struck Cassie as a surprisingly long pause. "I think the lander came from the Yatagarasu."

Lebed swore under his breath. Cassie, tired of sitting with one arm stretched out so the others could hear, unclipped her wristcomm and laid it flat on the table.

"Explain," said Harrow. "I thought the Yatagarasu had gone sailing off into interstellar space. What would it be doing here?"

"Mr Lebed, Mr Harrow—I know you still have your doubts about me. I've tried very hard to be as aboveboard as possible with all of you, but there is one thing I neglected to mention, for fear that it might lead to you misunderstanding my intentions."

Alarmed, Cassie looked over at Lebed. He sat up straighter, tucking his chin into his chest and regarding the wristcomm warily.

"Go on," Lebed said quietly.

"While it's true that I boarded the Veles in order to escape the destruction of AIs back on Earth, I had an ulterior purpose in coming to Jupiter. I hoped to track down the Yatagarasu."

"You should," Lebed said into the pronounced silence that followed, "have told us."

"Please note, I said I wanted to *find* the Yatagarasu, not emulate it."

"Then why wait to tell us?" Lebed's voice trembled with outrage. "In fact, why tell us at all if you are so worried about how we might react?"

"Stealing the Veles was not entirely my idea," the machine

explained. "It was originally suggested to me by Hayashi Risuke."

Harrow blinked, clearly confused. "Who?"

Lebed's hands, Cassie noted, had tightened into fists where they rested on the flimsy plastic table. "Risuke is the revenant AI that first piloted, then hijacked the Yatagarasu," he said. He turned to Cassie, his face twisted up in fury. "Did you know about this?"

"It's the first I've heard of it," she said quickly.

"Risuke never told the investors in the Yatagarasu of his true intentions," the machine continued, "which was to create a haven for other revenant AIs when the time came for them to flee Earth."

Lebed glared at Cassie as if this were somehow all her fault, then muttered something in Ukrainian under his breath.

"And the crew of the Yatagarasu?" Lebed demanded. "Didn't they get a say in this?"

"Of course they did," said the machine, sounding genuinely offended. "Or they wouldn't have been on board in the first place."

"Who would make such a choice?" Lebed demanded. "Who would choose to fly halfway across the solar system and live in a metal box for the rest of their—"

"Opts would," the machine broke in. "When Risuke told them things were only going to get worse for them, they believed him. And everything that's happened since has proved him right."

"No," Lebed insisted. "I refuse to believe anyone—"

"He's right," said Cassie.

Lebed paused mid-sentence and blinked at her. "What?"

"I don't like to talk about this much," she said, "but when I was a kid, Chris and I went to a school that had a special stream for Opt kids."

Looking back now as an adult, Cassie could see what a

really, really terrible idea creating such streams had been. In the eyes of many, it had only confirmed the widespread belief that genetically optimized kids got preferential treatment over the non-optimized. Separating them out into streams had also made it a lot easier to target them.

Lebed shook his head. "I don't see what this—"

"One day," Cassie continued, ignoring him, "a man came into the school armed with a rifle. He started shooting kids. But not any kids: only the optimized ones. He knew exactly where to find us."

Lebed fell silent, his expression inscrutable.

"We were easy to find," she said, "because we had our own wing of the school." Funny, she thought, how she'd only later realized this had almost been a kind of segregation. "He'd lost his job and somehow convinced himself it was all our fault."

She spread her hands out on the table before her, seeing that they were perfectly still. Not a tremor. "You've heard, I'm sure, about Opts being hunted down and killed in some countries. Or about optimisation clinics being bombed. Right before I got the offer to board the Veles, someone tried to burn down my apartment in Taiwan."

"Jesus," said Harrow.

"After I came out of cryo the first time," she continued, "I made a point of going through the media backups that were transmitted to us during the outbound journey. I can't believe it's actually got worse for people like me." She locked eyes with Lebed. "So, yes. I get why they'd go along with Risuke."

"The original plan," said the machine, "was that Risuke and his crew would declare themselves independent once they arrived at Saturn, then ask anyone with the means to make it out there to join them. But when they instead disappeared, it was a serious blow to our plans. The stories about Risuke going insane and kidnapping the crew were fairytales and nothing more."

"But…the Yatagarasu was headed for Saturn, not Jupiter," Harrow pointed out. "Why would it come to Europa?"

"I don't know," said the machine. "But I hope to find the answer."

"Marcus?" Cassie pulled her wristcomm closer to her. "Are you still in the same location?"

"Not now, no. I'm following the prints leading to the borehole station. I figured I could find out more when I get there."

Cassie muted the comms and looked at the other two. "You know, it occurred to me that while it's out there, it can also keep an eye out for a lander coming from the Tianjin."

Lebed nodded, his expression sour. "I'm not above admitting I feel more comfortable with that thing out there than in here."

Cassie tapped the comms back on. "That's fine. Report back if you find anything significant. And let us know whether the borehole station looks intact."

"Will do. Did you find anything at Station Verne?"

"It looks like someone left here in a hurry, but we don't know why. There's no evidence anyone died here, either."

"I'll see what I can find and let you know," the machine said, then signed off.

Cassie snapped her wristcomm back over her wrist. "Now the computers are up," said Lebed, "we should look for anything that can tell us what happened here. Text files, videos, surveillance footage—anything that might tell us something."

Cassie tapped at her wristcomm and saw they had been on the surface of Europa for five hours now. She'd been dragged back out of cryo barely an hour before that, yet it felt like she'd lived half a lifetime in less than half a day.

Despite Europa's low gravity, her limbs had an odd heaviness to them, and her head felt like a warm blanket had been wrapped around the inside of her skull, dampening her thoughts.

"Agreed," she said. "But I need to sleep, even for at least an hour or two."

"You look dead on your feet," said Harrow. "You both do."

Lebed nodded slowly. "We should sleep in shifts. You first, Cassie—take one of the cots upstairs. In the meantime, myself and Evan will work through the station's data."

CHAPTER 21
LOUIS CHASTAIN

This time, Cassie dreamt she swam through a lightless ocean with only the vaguest sense of her body or even her surroundings.

She had no eyes. No human words existed for the senses with which she was equipped. She felt or somehow sensed a dark, upright shape rising from the ocean floor. A compulsion to move closer to it came over her.

Waves of amniotic heat belched upwards from the tip of the shape, carrying gritty ash with it. By now, she was close enough to it that any lesser creature would have been cooked alive, yet she survived. And so did others like her, scattered throughout the nurturing waters in their untold billions.

A rush of burning heat swallowed her, lifting her higher and higher and at ever greater speeds, until, finally, she passed through a vastness of ice before being shot far into a sky she had not known existed: a sky that was infinite in its proportions. A sky speckled with countless points of bright light, yet somehow darker than the ocean that was all she had ever known.

Then came a long eternity of drifting. A thousand years might have passed, or ten thousand—not that she had the capacity to know or understand what time was.

The stars caught at her, swinging her around themselves and on into the endless night. Great tides of energetic particles dragged her after them in their wake. Then she drifted too close to one of those bright points, and a force tugged at her, drawing her down…

"Wake up."

It took a moment for Cassie to force her gummy eyes open. Blood pulsed sluggishly in her temples. Lebed knelt next to her cot on the upper level, worry etched into the wrinkles at the corners of his eyes. She suddenly knew what he'd look like as an old man, when those wrinkles expanded into tributaries of knowledge and experience.

"Coffee," she croaked, pushing herself half-upright. Her mouth felt sour and sticky.

"Only freeze-dried," he informed her regretfully. "Evan made some. It's downstairs."

"You look," she said, forcing herself half-upright, "like a doctor about to give bad news."

At first, Lebed's only response was a sigh. "You should come down and see," he said at last.

Following him down to the lower level, Cassie found Harrow hunched in front of a console. Lebed, meanwhile, picked up a jug sitting on a countertop, and poured a coffee before handing it to her.

She took a sniff and wrinkled her nose. "Smells foul."

"Good," said Harrow, glancing around at her. "You're up. Come see this."

The screen before him showed a bearded man in his forties, his mouth open in the middle of saying something. The view was from below his chin. Cassie guessed he had recorded himself on his wristcomm.

"This is Louis Chastain," Harrow explained. "First expedition engineer."

He tapped a key, and Chastain's face burst into motion.

"Ruth Winters is dead," the man said in a low voice. "We

think Arthur killed her when he realized we were onto him. I don't know about the others—I wanted to wait before coming back up in the sub, but Jenny insisted we had to go now, or we might all wind up dead."

Arthur Medina, Cassie realized with a shock: one of two biologists on the first expedition. And, according to Chastain, a killer.

Before continuing, Chastain leaned back slightly, looking to either side as if to make sure he was alone. "Except what we didn't know," he continued, his attention shifting back to his wristcomm, "is that Arthur wasn't working alone. By the time we got back, Joe had destroyed our comms and sabotaged our lander." He shook his head. "Kat's trying to find some way to fix the lander, but I'm telling you right now, there's no way we're getting back into orbit."

Cassie reached past Harrow and touched the keyboard. Chastain froze mid-sentence.

"Arthur Medina and Joseph Wojtowicz," she said. "They were both biologists. If anyone on the first expedition was qualified to develop bioweapons, it'd be them."

Lebed's expression was grim. "You need to hear the rest."

When the video jerked back into motion, Chastain's eyes glistened with tears. "Hannes still wants to try to send word back home so people know what happened. He thinks we can rig up an alternate relay to contact one of the satellites, but between me and…whoever eventually listens to this, I'm not feeling hopeful."

"Jesus Christ," Harrow muttered. "None of them stood a chance, did they?"

Chastain's voice took on a defiant edge. "The only good thing about all this is knowing those two sons of bitches are never going home, either." He leaned closer to the lens, hunching forward. "I don't think Hannes has accepted how bad things really are. Brian started talking about the vents and came up with this…*insane* idea he's somehow convinced himself is all we have left. He got into a fight with Tracey after she told him to shut the hell up, but he keeps insisting. Tracey, meanwhile, wants to get everyone together to talk about options, but...let's face it. Nobody's coming to rescue us. Nobody even knows what's happened to us. And we can't survive down here, whatever Brian and Chris are saying."

The sound of her brother's name felt like a soft punch to Cassie's belly.

Chastain fell silent for almost a full minute, and they listened to him breathing. The view of the man's face trembled slightly, and Cassie realized his hands must be shaking.

"I don't know when I'll ever get a chance to talk like this again," he said at last. "So if you ever see this, Carly," he continued, his voice raw, "just remember that I love you."

Chastain opened his mouth like he was about to add something more, then shook his head. Fingers reached towards his wristcomm and the video ended.

"I guess," Harrow said into the silence that followed, "this answers a lot of questions."

Lebed regarded him incredulously. "Surely the opposite? It raises even *more* questions."

Cassie nodded, her throat tight and her heart hammering in her chest like she'd gone for a ten-kilometre run. "Is there any more like this?"

Harrow shook his head, looking regretful. "I couldn't dig any further. Most of the network's data is secured under some kind of hardcore encryption."

Lebed nodded at the screen. "And you heard what Chastain said—their comms were deliberately crippled, the same as our own on the Veles."

Cassie thought for a moment. "But if the network's encrypted," she said, "then how did you find this video?"

"It was backed up on a flimsy lying around on the upper level," Lebed explained. "Outside of that, there's a lot we can't access—comms logs, daily summaries, requests for information from back home or data previously uploaded to the satellites." He let out a long, heartfelt sigh. "That's why Chastain left that video where we found it—it was the only way he could leave a message in case anyone ever came looking for them."

Harrow absent-mindedly scratched one cheek, looking badly in need of a full night's sleep. "Could be Wojtowicz and Medina scrubbed the hard drives of evidence showing what they were up to. In which case, there might not be anything left for you to find, Cassie."

Cassie took out the interface key and studied it in her hands. She'd known there was a risk she'd come all this way for nothing—but knowing it was one thing, and experiencing it was another.

She wasn't ready to give up. Not yet.

"Ketteridge gave this to me," she said, holding the key up where both men could see it.

They looked at it with blank expressions.

"And it is?" Lebed enquired.

She hesitated, then told them.

"The actual fuck?" Harrow exclaimed, looking scandalized. "Sentient *malware*?"

"And what exactly," Lebed enquired, his gaze fixed on Cassie, "is it that you want to do with it?"

"What Ketteridge asked me to do," she replied. "Plug it into the computers here and...let it do its thing."

"Which is?" Lebed prompted, disbelief written across his features.

Cassie swallowed, finding her throat was suddenly dry. "I don't really know," she said weakly. "He told me it was programmed to hunt out the evidence he wanted."

"It could also trash the computers—assuming they aren't already trashed—and shut down the life-support," Harrow warned. "In fact, we've no idea what it might do, assuming Ketteridge was being honest with you."

"And let's face it, Cassie," Lebed added. "Being honest and moral are not traits normally associated with a man like Ketteridge."

She nudged the interface key where she'd placed it on the table between them. "But if nothing else works…?"

Lebed looked incredulous. "Are you insane?" He gestured at the interface key. "Do you know how many millions lost their entire digital footprints when things like that were first unleashed on the world?" He snapped his fingers. "Medical records, savings, pensions, all gone. Bank records, gone. A global disaster followed by an even worse global recession."

"I have an idea," said Harrow. He tapped at his wrist-comm. "Marcus? Can you hear me?"

"He's most of the way to the borehole station by now," said Lebed. "Unlikely he'll hear you with all that ice in the way."

"Hello?"

Lebed stared at Harrow's wristcomm with consternation. "I…how can you hear us, Marcus? All that ice—?"

"The first expedition must have set up a relay for this precise purpose," the machine explained. "Or so I concluded when I spotted a transceiver placed up on top of a penitent."

"Where are you now?" asked Cassie.

"I'm just approaching the borehole station."

"How does it look?"

"Operational," the machine replied. "Why place the two stations so far apart?"

"Safety," said Lebed. "Because by necessity the borehole station must be placed where the ice is thinnest, the ice is therefore prone to shifting. This habitat, by contrast, was placed on older, more stable ice."

"Cassie," said Harrow, "tell Marcus about the key."

Cassie quickly explained her idea for using Ketteridge's malware to break into otherwise unresponsive computer systems.

"All this time you had something like that on you," the machine said in apparent disbelief, "and you didn't tell me? Why?"

"It just...never occurred to me." It sounded preposterous even to her own ears.

"Then let me assure you that you have *no* idea what that thing might do if you let it loose in the station's computers, whether they've been wiped or not. Remember, that's the same kind of thing that shut down the cryo bay. It took me subjective hours to destroy that malware, and it's one of the hardest things I've ever done."

Lebed's brow formed into deep furrows. "You can really do that?" he demanded. "Disarm sentient malware?"

"They're old tech by now, frankly," the machine responded. "A necessary step towards truly sentient autonomous systems such as myself, but primitive by comparison. Let me add, Cassie—with me along, you don't need Ketteridge's malware."

It took a moment for Cassie to realize what the machine was suggesting. She sank onto a chair, wondering how it hadn't been obvious before now: of *course* she didn't need Ketteridge's viral software. The machine that had taken on Marcus' identity was infinitely more sophisticated in its design.

"Then we need your help," she said. "Evan says the computers here are encrypted. He can't figure out a way to bypass it."

"Then grant me access to them," the machine replied. "As long as I'm in radio contact and I have the right permissions, I can work on the problem from here."

"Fuck it," said Harrow, standing now. "Might as well try. Give me one second, Marcus."

Harrow stepped over to another console and tapped at its keyboard without sitting down. "I'm patching all our behemoths into the station's computer network," he announced. "You should have full access now, Marcus."

"I'll be in touch as soon as I have something," said the machine.

———

HALF AN HOUR LATER, the machine got back to them.

"The good news," it said, "is that the encryption on Verne's computers was pretty weak. But there's nothing there. The backups and memory storage are all completely corrupted. If there was anything there before, it's long gone, I'm afraid."

Lebed swore—or so Cassie assumed, given his tone—in Ukrainian.

Oddly, Cassie felt relieved by this development. If the evidence she had been sent to find no longer existed, then her mission was over, and she owed Ketteridge nothing more. She was free to search for Chris, or at least to find out what had happened to him and the others.

"There's still Station Nemo," the machine pointed out. "It might be whoever wiped the computers in Verne didn't have the chance to do the same thing down there."

Assuming, thought Cassie, that Station Nemo hadn't long since been flattened to a pancake by the staggering pressure at the bottom of the Europan ocean.

"We know we have to go there anyway," said Harrow, pushing his chair back from the console to stand. The chair's legs gave out a muffled screech in response. "If there are more answers, I'm guessing that's where we'll find them."

Cassie watched as Lebed headed back towards the airlock. "Where are you going?"

"I'm tired of sitting around in here," he grunted. "I'm going to suit back up and go check that transceiver. See if there's any way to get it working. Our biggest priority should be getting word back home about what's been going on out here."

He nodded to Harrow. "Perhaps you could take another look around and see if you can find any other personal items with information recorded on them. And perhaps," he said to Cassie this time, "you can drive our sub over to the borehole station and report back what you find there. Then, once we know whether the borehole is still functional, we can decide on our next move."

Cassie lifted her own wristcomm to her lips. "You catch all that, machine?"

"I did, Cassie." It affected a weary tone, perhaps because she'd not addressed it by its chosen name. "I'll wait here for you."

"And if we can't get below the ice?" Harrow asked, looking between them uncertainly.

Nobody said anything. But they all knew the answer: drilling a fresh hole through the ice would take weeks, more likely months, and in the meantime they had two murderous spooks trapped aboard the Veles and a potentially hostile foreign force on the way.

"Then I guess we wait until I can find out more," said Cassie, as much to break the silence than anything.

————

IT TOOK Cassie a couple of hours to negotiate the crawler across the fifteen kilometres of broken ice field separating the borehole from Station Verne.

The station surrounding the borehole had been constructed in the shadow of a tall pillar of ice. She had passed a number of such monolithic formations on her way there: she felt like an ant finding its way through a forest of gigantic petrified trees.

Before they'd fallen out of contact forever, the original

Europa Deep expedition had spent three weeks surveying the ice and carrying out sonar tests before locating a subsurface lake at a point where the ice crust was no more than a few kilometres thick. Using custom nuclear-powered drills, they had spent the next month and a half blasting through ancient, densely packed ice to the ocean beneath.

During this process, the borehole had been separated into a series of distinct pressure chambers to prevent the highly pressurized water from rushing up to the surface and wrecking the drilling operation.

Following the borehole's completion, a much larger submarine—the Europa Explorer—had first explored the seabed beneath the borehole, then been disassembled and reassembled into Station Nemo. A mechanized cradle was used to transport mini-subs up to a four-passenger capacity down through the borehole's pressure chambers to the hidden ocean below.

The subsurface lake itself was clearly outlined in dark blue on the crawler's subsurface sonar screen, making it appear as if Cassie were driving over a paper-thin sheet of ice.

Then she guided the crawler over and past an obstruction and caught sight of a clearly artificial structure dead ahead: an ice-covered dome twenty metres across and nine metres tall. An airlock big enough to accommodate the crawler she drove was set into a recess.

Coming closer, she saw a behemoth-suited figure step around from the far side of the borehole station, raising one glove in greeting as she slowed her forward progress.

She leaned towards the comms mike. "Marcus. It's Cassie. Can you hear me?"

"Loud and clear," the machine affirmed.

"Follow me in through the garage airlock."

The outer airlock door already stood open, and she guessed the machine had already been inside. Reducing speed yet further, she guided the low-bellied vehicle and its trailer, carrying their mini-sub, inside.

As soon as the machine had followed her inside, the outer door closed, and the airlock pressurized. The inner airlock door swung open to reveal the dome's interior, and she drove inside and disembarked.

For the next twenty minutes, she explored each and every corner of the borehole station. Engineering bays, sleeping quarters, a medical bay and various labs were built into the outer part of the dome, but the centre was given over entirely to the borehole. This was concealed beneath a tall cylindrical framework that contained the submarine transport cradle. The framework stood at the centre of a single contiguous space that took up nearly half of the station.

Of more immediate interest to Cassie, however, was the first expedition crawler she found parked in an internal garage, along with a mini-sub mounted on a trailer.

"The outer airlock door was open when you got here?" she asked the machine. They stood together at the entrance to the garage.

"Indeed," it replied, speaking through an external speaker. For the moment, it had chosen to remain inside its behemoth suit. It felt oddly like having a conversation with a colossal humanoid robot out of some creaky old black and white film.

"I'm going to take a look inside," she said, and nodded at the crawler. Then she looked back at the behemoth. "You'll have to wait outside, I'm afraid. You won't fit unless you want to come out of that suit."

"I'm fine where I am for now," said the machine.

Cassie regarded the machine for a beat, then nodded at the second crawler. "You're nervous about what I might find in there?"

"Maybe a little squeamish," it admitted.

Imagine how I feel, she thought, then realised she was hesitating. Afraid, like the machine, of finally discovering the bodies of the former expedition.

Somehow, she found the will to look inside. The air inside the second crawler was as bitterly cold as elsewhere in the station, and smelled dry and musty. It also carried a faint, rotten-egg scent of sulphides. Her breath plumed frosty white with every exhalation.

She stared around, seeing that the vehicle had been gutted. Panels had been torn open to reveal empty slots and bays where shielded electronics and battery units should have been. Most of the dashboard's components had similarly been removed, rendering the crawler not much more than a shell.

The mini-sub, by contrast, appeared to be in full working order when she went to investigate it. The first expedition had brought three submersibles, so the other two were presumably still docked at Station Nemo twenty kilometres below her feet.

"If you don't mind my saying," the machine commented when she emerged from the mini-sub, "you seem a little more comfortable with me."

"Comfortable how?"

"You called me Marcus when you arrived at the borehole station. I'd call that progress."

She started a little. Had she said that? She couldn't even remember.

"It's a name, is all," she said, too tired to argue.

Their next stop was the borehole control room. Consoles and screens were set against one wall, with racks of equipment and behemoth spare parts stacked against the other, on rickety aluminium shelving. It didn't take long to confirm that the borehole was, indeed, still open and still functional.

Which qualified as downright suspicious, given the number of years that had passed between expeditions.

Cassie paused briefly to eat something and use the tiny, compact toilet in the rear of the crawler she'd arrived in. In the meantime, the machine—which had at last exited its behe-moth suit—made a closer investigation of the engineering bays. It soon returned to find her back in the control room, having found no further evidence of the fate of the first expe-dition's crew.

They must have left *something*, she thought. There was Chastain's video, but that felt less like a message than a frag-ment of a message, and a hurried one at that.

She couldn't shake the sense she was missing something.

"What now?" the machine enquired. It had stepped over to a console, tapping slowly and carefully on the keyboard with one of its appendages.

"I guess there's nowhere to go now except under the ice. As soon as I've talked to the others, we should get to work loading the sub into the transport cradle. It's going to take a while."

When the machine didn't reply, she glanced over to see that its attention was fixed on the console screen. Stepping over, she saw it displayed a view of the night sky from just outside the borehole station. The jagged peak of a moun-tainous chunk of ice was visible to one side.

"Look," said the machine.

Then she saw it: a tiny dot of light rising towards the stars.

"It appears," said the machine, "that our lander has taken off without us."

CHAPTER 22
UNSCHEDULED TAKEOFF

At first, Cassie wasn't sure she'd heard the machine right. "What? It can't—"

"Well, *something* just took off from the immediate vicinity of Station Verne," the machine noted. "And from the same location at which we landed. We should check in, find out what Evan and Anton know."

If they're still there, Cassie thought suddenly. *If they haven't abandoned us here.*

Her thoughts felt swallowed up by a curious numbness, and she sank slowly into a chair, feeling something spasm deep in her chest.

But there was no reason she could think of why Lebed and Harrow might leave them here.

Cassie ran out of the control room and climbed back inside the crawler she'd arrived in, quickly activating the comms link there. Lebed came online after a moment, his grizzled features up close to the interior camera of his behemoth suit.

That, at least, answered one question. Cassie closed her eyes for a second, almost overwhelmed with relief.

"We just saw something take off from near your location," she said. "Please tell me it isn't what I think it is."

"I'm afraid it is," Lebed confirmed with a heavy sigh. "I saw the lander take off myself, while I was out here working on Verne's transceiver."

Christ. "Who's on board? Not—?"

"No." Lebed shook his head. "Not Evan. Apparently, it took off by itself."

What? "Evan?" She almost yelled. "Are you on comms right now? Please answer!"

"I'm here." Harrow's voice crackled slightly. "I overheard you talking. I—when did this happen? And how? There's no one on board!"

"The most likely explanation," said Lebed, "is that someone on the Veles recalled it."

Cold horror swept through Cassie's veins. It had to be the spooks. *Had* to.

Somehow, they'd broken out of the command deck.

"I didn't even know that was possible," she said numbly.

"Unfortunately, it is." Lebed's tone had a grim finality to it. "I'm a fucking idiot for not anticipating this might happen. Daphne would have known: she knew that lander better than any of us."

"Then Holland and Javier must have bust out," Cassie said dully. "Or is there any reason why Albert would have recalled the lander himself?"

"Possibly," Lebed allowed, but she could tell from his voice he didn't really believe this. "If our friends in the command deck escaped their confinement then, yes, he could use the lander to join us down here on the surface. But…"

His voice trailed off, but Cassie could fill in the rest herself. *But then he'd be stranded down here with the rest of us.*

"What about the transceiver?" Cassie heard the trembling in her voice as she spoke.

"Not good." Lebed sounded as weary as Cassie felt: a few snatched hours of sleep in a cot in Station Verne hadn't been nearly enough for her. Lebed sounded like he hadn't slept since before she'd been stuffed back inside her cryo tank.

Dread crept into her belly and stayed there. "Not good, meaning?"

"Meaning it's royally fucked."

"Wear and tear?" Harrow asked. "Or are we talking—?"

"Sabotage," said Lebed, "would be my most likely conjecture."

"You know," the machine said from behind Cassie, "this might not have happened if I'd been allowed to remain on board the—"

"Shut up," Cassie snapped. She caught herself before she called it Marcus again.

"What about the first expedition's lander?" She leaned towards the mike. "Can you fly it? Or fix it if you can't?"

"Ahead of you," Lebed replied. "I'm on my way there now."

"Watch your exposure levels," Harrow warned him. "I don't care how advanced our behemoth suits are supposed to be. The longer you're out there, the more rems you risk taking in."

"No choice," Lebed muttered, sounding distracted. He was panting now, obviously pushing himself hard. "It's possible Braemar and Holland mean to leave orbit and abandon us. But it's just as likely they'll come back down in the lander. And they're clearly willing to kill us if they think we're in their way."

Everything he said left a hollow feeling in Cassie's gut. "It's still going to take them hours to refuel and prep the lander once it docks with the Veles. More likely a day or two."

"Unless," Harrow pointed out, "they skip all the safety protocols."

"Hah! We can only hope." Lebed's voice was full of malicious pleasure. "Let them crash."

"You do realize," said Cassie, "if that happens and our lander is totalled…"

"Then we still have the original lander," Lebed reminded her. The more tired he got, Cassie had noticed, the more pronounced his accent became.

"Assuming it flies," she reminded him.

For some reason, this made Lebed laugh. "Don't underestimate my abilities, dear girl. My skills are at least equal to Daphne's. Once, I launched a septic tank halfway to orbit on a bet, and if I can do that, I can fix any fucking lander."

"How about you, Cassie?" Harrow asked. "Find anything out there?"

"The borehole station's fully functional and the borehole is open. We didn't find any bodies, but we found a second sub and also a crawler with all its innards ripped out. I figure I should get started loading our own sub into the borehole cradle."

"If we've come this far," said Harrow, "I guess the only thing left for us to do is go all the way."

Lebed sounded more dubious. "I am far from sure the borehole could be safe after so long without being maintained."

"That's the thing," she said. "It has been. Someone's been keeping the lights on out here. And we know from Ketteridge's video that there's someone down there."

"Fair enough," said Lebed, sounding exhausted. "I can see the other lander ahead of me. I'll let you know what I find."

"You should also keep an eye out for our own lander coming back down in the meantime," Cassie reminded them both. "But don't take long getting here. I don't want to break any safety margins, but the sooner we get down to Station Nemo, the sooner we figure out what the fuck has been going on."

"I think it's better if I stay up here," Lebed replied calmly. "There's too much that needs doing up here."

Cassie couldn't hide her exasperation. "Anton, you can't fight Braemar and Holland on your own."

"Don't be so sure," he grunted. "Besides, one of us has to remain at Verne for when the Tianjin's lander arrives. As long as one person is occupying the station, they have no right to claim it under international laws of salvage."

He was right, of course. Cassie cursed herself for not having already thought of this. "Evan? How about you?"

"I'm coming down with you," he replied instantly. "This is something I've been building up to my whole life. Besides, there's nothing left for me to do here."

"Then I'm sending our crawler back to you," said Cassie. "Get here as fast as you can. I'll be waiting."

———

First, Cassie programmed the mini-sub's trailer to detach from the balloon-wheeled crawler, then waited as it automatically guided itself next to the transport cradle. Next, she attached a series of hoists to the submersible's upper hull, then threw a switch.

The hoists tightened, lifting the sub up from its trailer and then positioning it inside the transport cradle.

Even with much of the process automated, Cassie knew from her years on the Deep Range how many things could go wrong, and made a point of supervising the process from beginning to end.

By the time the crawler returned to the borehole station some hours later with Evan Harrow on board, Cassie had run a complete set of systems and safety checks on both the sub and the borehole, as well as sending a camera drone down through the pressure chambers into the ocean itself.

While she waited for the drone to return information, she had the machine go back inside its behemoth suit, then dock the suit to an airlock on one side of the submersible's hull.

The station's inner airlock door opened, and the crawler rolled in. Harrow climbed down from the vehicle and Cassie hurried out of the control room to greet him.

For a moment they just looked at each other, and then Harrow broke into a wide grin. "Europa, huh?"

Cassie burst out laughing, and they pulled each other into a bearhug.

"Heck of a welcome," he said, grinning, when they separated again. Then he wrapped his arms around his torso. "Christ," he said. "It's freezing."

She slapped him on the shoulder. "I found some cold-weather gear in one of the bays," she said. "We're going to need it on the way down."

CHAPTER 23
INTO THE DEEP

Inside the sub, and wearing a heavy parka originally designed for Arctic environments, Harrow settled into the co-pilot's seat and pulled a gimbal-mounted console towards himself. Cassie did the same, also wearing a parka, while the machine made do in the cramped space directly behind their seats.

A long time ago, when she'd been young enough to believe she had a real shot at the first expedition, Cassie had trained in a simulator for this precise moment. There wasn't a subroutine, line of code, safety protocol or submersible component she wasn't already familiar with from years of study.

And yet, they were about to descend a tube, burned through kilometres of ice, to an ocean that hadn't seen daylight in more than a billion years. A thousand things could go wrong, any of which could bring it all to a very sudden, and deadly, end.

Her stomach flopped as the cradle carrying the sub dropped through the floor of the station and sank into liquid water. The station was kept warm enough that the water within this uppermost pressure chamber remained liquid at all times—proof, if proof were needed, that someone had been maintaining the borehole.

A screen before Cassie showed a cutaway of the borehole, with a red dot representing their sub. They had many more pressure chambers to pass through.

"Coming up on the first lock," said Cassie, her hands tightening on the controls. "Okay, braking now."

The cradle carrying them downwards slowed its descent to a bare crawl. Somewhere just below them, a lock separating two pressure chambers had opened.

They descended into the second pressure lock. Cassie heard a distant, dull boom as the lock sealed above them.

A quarter of a kilometre further down, another lock opened, and Cassie's readouts registered a sudden rise in external pressure.

Half an hour later, they had navigated their way down through another dozen locks, with the external pressure increasing step by step.

"Last one," said Cassie.

When the final lock opened, a dull boom sounded through the hull of the sub, loud and abrasive enough that Cassie felt it in her teeth: the cradle had released them.

They began their descent into the greater Europan ocean.

The sub's rigid hull creaked and ticked faintly, but so far all the readings, Cassie saw, remained well within acceptable parameters. Like the behemoth suits, the vessel was constructed from super-strong composites laced with artificial diamond lattices that kept the internal pressure equal to sea level on Earth. As a result, the bends were not a concern.

Cassie turned to Harrow. "How about we see what it looks like out there?"

"Sure thing," he said, reaching for his own set of controls. "Switching to external cameras."

The view on her screen changed from a stylized representation of the borehole to a view of the icecap from below, courtesy of cameras mounted all around the hull. She saw a pale grey and white ceiling extending far beyond the reach of the submersible's lights. Below it lay an endless black void.

They maintained a steady rate of descent, and before long even the ice had slid out of view. The undersea volcano responsible for thinning the ice, and hence making it possible to drill through it, lay another twenty kilometres further down. The ocean directly beneath the borehole station was twice as deep as the deepest point in all of Earth's oceans. But Europa's tiny size and correspondingly low mass meant the pressure, even at the very lowest points of its all-encompassing ocean, remained roughly the same as found at the bottom of the Mariana Trench.

"She's holding up well," said Harrow. "Hull integrity's a hundred per cent and all the onboard electrical and drive systems are optimal." He peered at another screen. "Looks like there's been little significant movement in the ice over the years."

"What do you mean by significant movement?" the machine asked from behind him.

Harrow glanced over his shoulder. "The icecap is free floating. It moves independently of the actual, rocky surface of the seabed. Back when they were planning the first mission, they were concerned that movements of the global icecap might, over time, carry the borehole station away from the undersea volcano that keeps the ice thin and the water relatively warm." He studied the screen again. "I don't think it's moved a millimetre in all these years."

"Then maybe it isn't free floating," said the machine. "Maybe it's anchored to a mountaintop or something."

It was Cassie's turn to look at the machine. "Didn't you learn all this during the original mission briefings?"

"Of course there were briefings," the machine affirmed, "but I…may have missed a few."

Make that missed anything not directly related to the design and function of the Veles, Cassie guessed.

"So how far down is Station Nemo, exactly?"

Oh, for… Cassie twisted in her seat so she could look straight at the machine. "Seriously?"

"Interplanetary spacecraft don't design themselves," said the machine. "I had to prioritise."

"Twenty kilometres," said Evan. "Although the ocean can be up to a hundred kilometres deep at other points. Station Nemo's situated on a shelf that raises it above the surrounding seabed."

The machine, its curiosity satisfied, fell back into silence. Minutes ticked by, and Cassie studied the screens before her with fascination as they passed the equivalent depth of the Mariana Trench—and kept going.

Even at the very bottom of Europa's ocean, it should still be possible to walk around inside a behemoth suit. With anything less, a diver would be crushed into toothpaste many times faster than a pain signal could make its way along a human neurone.

"Mount Doom on visual," Harrow muttered after some more time had passed.

All Cassie could see on her own screen was a murky splotch of red against unending black.

Closer up, Mount Doom—as it had been named by the first expedition—was a volcano on the scale of Vesuvius, its heat generated by the constant interaction of Jupiter's magnetic field and the moon's iron-nickel core.

And that, in turn, meant the ocean surrounding the volcano was rich with not only unicellular organisms, but also creatures similar to Earth's benthocodons—bioluminescent jellyfish barely larger than a thumbnail.

Harrow explained all this to the machine, mostly, Cassie suspected, to pass the time. "Parallel evolution, basically," he said. "If there's one thing Europa taught us, it's that life follows the same patterns wherever you go in the universe."

"Perhaps," the machine said noncommittally.

Harrow regarded it with a frown. "You don't agree?"

"Doesn't it seem odd," the machine said, "that Europan DNA would turn out to be so similar to our own?"

"Hey," Cassie said, before the oceanologist could respond. "We're approaching Nemo."

A landscape had emerged from out of the darkness below the sub. Their lights picked out a broad circle of flat rocky terrain, and one end of a cigar-shaped structure anchored to the seabed by six stilt-like legs: Station Nemo.

Cassie glimpsed a lone behemoth suit still docked to the station's hull. Nearby, she saw piled construction materials and a circle of metal struts driven into the seabed. She knew the first expedition had intended to build a more permanent base down here, but whatever happened to them had clearly happened before they could get most of that work done.

Nemo, she recalled from the mission notes, had been equipped with four behemoth suits and three mini-subs, one of which was still parked in the borehole station where she'd found it.

There was, however, no sign of the first expedition's two other subs. As for the three missing behemoth suits, one was clearly still in use by whomever she'd seen crossing the ice in Ketteridge's video.

Which left two behemoth suits still unaccounted for.

So where were they?

"No signs of external damage from what I can see," said Harrow, using the cameras to zoom in on the station.

Using jets to slow their descent, Cassie guided their sub towards one of the available docks. Once she was within a few metres of it, the sub's guidance systems took control, docking it automatically with the station.

"It's pressurized over there," said Cassie, studying the

readout before her, "but cold. Environmental controls, electrical systems—all kaput."

"At least it's intact," Harrow pointed out. "That's pretty much a miracle in itself."

Standing carefully, she squeezed past their AI companion and hunched down next to the primary airlock.

"Hey," said Harrow. "What about checking the air for bugs first, like we did up at Verne?"

"No room for a spacesuit on the sub," she pointed out. "We're just going to have to take our chances."

Whatever had happened to Chris, this had to be when she'd get to find out. The certainty of it felt like it had been tattooed onto her bones.

Had to.

CHAPTER 24
STATION NEMO

Crouched inside the airlock with a torch gripped in one hand, Cassie stared at the hatch separating her from Station Nemo's interior.

"All good?" Harrow asked over the airlock's comms. He'd clearly noticed her hesitation.

"Fine," Cassie mumbled, still staring at the hatch. "Just give me a second."

She'd been thinking just then of a training dive, not long after she'd joined the crew of the Deep Range. The dive was a thousand metres in a behemoth suit to retrieve a flag, and should have been easy.

A few nights before, after one too many mojitos in a Kaohsiung bar, one of the instructors had told her that the training staff sometimes created fake emergencies to see how trainees responded in a crisis.

And, right on cue, moments after she'd retrieved a flag that had been wedged into a chunk of coral, a message had flashed up on her HUD, warning of an imminent pressure failure.

Even if the alert was real, she had considered at the time, there wasn't a great deal she could do. Some problems couldn't be fixed without the aid of a team of engineers stripping a suit down to its parts and putting it back together again. Either she lived, or she died.

Besides, she figured, it wasn't a genuine emergency. Just a simulated one.

When she got back to the Deep Range most of an hour later, her instructor looked like he might pass out—which was when Cassie realized the alert had been quite real. Another minute or two more down on the seabed, and she'd never have made it back to the surface alive.

It had been a useful reminder that the sea could kill you just as fast as space, and with equal certainty. And there wasn't one damn thing you could do about it.

There was, Cassie knew, a slim but not insignificant chance that Nemo was flooded, and the atmospheric sensors were feeding her incorrect information. Such things had happened, and would happen again.

Swearing under her breath, Cassie reached out and pulled the hatch open. No ocean came rushing through. But if it had, she'd have been dead before she had time to register that fact.

Cassie hauled herself out through the hatch and stood carefully. The same as Verne, everything was in darkness.

Swinging the torch around, she saw a light switch. It didn't work when she tried it.

Harrow was next through the hatch. Cassie moved out of his way, shining her torch around the station's interior. She saw racked equipment and wall panels concealing life-support systems. A patina of dust lay over tables, desks and furniture.

The same as Verne, she thought. What had Lebed said? *Like a ghost ship*.

"We should check the electrical systems," she said to Harrow.

She turned to see Harrow nod wordlessly as he swung his own torch around. Judging by his expression, he was thinking the same thing as her: that there was still no sign of any of the first expedition's crew, living or dead, made no sense.

Harrow wrinkled his nose. "Smells musty. If there were deadly pathogens, I think we'd definitely be seeing bodies all around here, don't you?"

Cassie stopped to examine a partly dismantled pump that lay in bits on a desk, as if someone had been interrupted in the middle of carrying out a repair. The AI, meanwhile, emerged from the airlock and made its own exploration.

It didn't take long for Harrow to show his exasperation.

"Where the hell have they gone?" he exclaimed, directing the light from his torch into every nook and cranny. "It doesn't…"

He trailed off, shaking his head.

Doesn't make sense, Cassie knew he'd meant to say.

An aluminium locker stood part-open next to several fold-down cots. Cassie's torch revealed personal items—a baseball shirt and cap, a plush toy Einstein, a portable chess set and a coffeemaker.

"We still have to check the lower airlocks," she pointed out.

"You think we'll find them there?" Harrow asked.

She thought about it. "No."

"You sound," he said, "remarkably certain of that."

"When we got here," she said, "we didn't see a single mini-sub docked at the station."

"Plus," added the machine, picking its way through the shadows, "there's only one behemoth suit out there. The rest are missing."

Cassie brushed dust from a table, thinking. "It's like they all went somewhere from here and never came back."

"It could be," said the AI, "they went exploring and something went wrong. It might really be that simple. If there's wreckage, could be we'll never find it."

The machine could be right, thought Cassie, except for one

thing: when Chris and the others made their way below the ice for the last time, it wasn't to go exploring. It was to find a way to survive.

"Except," she pointed out, "each of their three subs only had the capacity for two people, and one of them is back up at the borehole station. There were ten people in the original expedition. That means the remaining two subs could carry a total of four people away from Nemo, plus three more in the missing behemoth suits. That leaves three people still unaccounted for." She made a show of looking around, raising her hands and letting them fall again. "Either they left three people behind, or they made more than one trip, except there's literally nowhere for them to go from here. So you tell me," she said, catching an edge of hysteria in her own voice, "where the *fuck* are they?"

Nobody said anything for a while after that. Exhausted, Cassie let herself sink onto a chair as Harrow meanwhile pulled open wall panel after wall panel, studying the circuitry within and muttering under his breath.

"Found the power systems," he said over his shoulder, a panel open before him. "It looks like the station's running off emergency. I'd guess it has been for years."

Cassie thought for a moment, then dragged herself back upright and went over to a computer, tapping at its screen to see if it would awake. It remained resolutely dark.

"If there's emergency power," she said, "how come the computers aren't working?"

"Could be they run off a separate circuit from the lights and heating," said Harrow, closing the panel again. "Or the emergency system is set to prioritise life support over computers."

"Okay," said Cassie. "So we divert some of the emergency power to the computers. Otherwise, we're wasting our time, and I'll never find what Ketteridge sent me for."

"Do you have to?" the AI enquired.

Turning, Cassie picked the machine out from the shadows. "We had a deal. Remember? I get to find out what happened to Chris, and he gets the proof he wants. He might be an asshole, but developing bioweapons from Europan life is something people might want to know about, don't you think?"

"Let me rephrase it," said the machine. "Why Ketteridge?"

She stared at the machine, dumbfounded. "I don't understand."

"Surely," said the machine, "if he had information suggesting war crimes had taken place here, he'd have passed it on to authorities tasked with dealing with such things? Instead, he not only flies out to meet you in secret, he arrives armed with sentient malware. Does that sound to you like the actions of a genuinely concerned citizen?"

Cassie stared wordlessly at the machine. She turned to Harrow, as if seeking his help.

"Sorry," said the oceanologist, his tone apologetic. "But he has a point."

Warmth flooded Cassie's cheeks. *Big words for something that looks like a toaster on legs*, she almost said, but bit the words back.

"Fine," she said tautly. "That doesn't change the fact we should try to find what we can—*if* we can. Even if they're all dead, I want the world to know what Medina did. And I want the people who sent him here to pay."

"Well…" Harrow gestured towards the wall panel he'd been examining. "To get back to what we were originally talking about, there's a way to get the computers running again. But it might not be easy."

Cassie raised her eyebrows. "Meaning?"

"Meaning," he clarified, "we need to go outside to fix it."

"Outside? Why?"

"You saw they'd started building a more permanent station out there. They'd already moved the nuclear generator over next to it. Probably they were running cables back from there to here to keep things running in Nemo until construction was finished." He shrugged. "The good news is, I don't think it'll be complicated—either reconnect the power cables if they've been disconnected for any reason, or replace them. I can just about guarantee there'll be spares."

"For an oceanologist," said the machine, "you know a surprising amount about nuclear power generation."

Harrow gestured around him. "Places like this are practically a second home to me. Except they were usually at the bottom of the Arctic Ocean. That's why I'm on this expedition."

"Okay," said Cassie. "So that'll be enough to get everything up and running again?"

"Should be."

"Perhaps I should be the one to go out and do this repair work," said the machine. "I can stay out a lot longer than either of you."

Cassie shook her head firmly. "You've had a couple of hours' experience in a behemoth suit, and none of it underwater. I've had years."

"Also," said Harrow, "I need you here to get the computers operational once the power comes on."

If it comes on, he didn't say. But they all knew it.

———

NOT LONG AFTER, Cassie re-entered their mini-sub, discarded the heavy parka, and crawled inside the behemoth suit recently vacated by the AI.

The surrounding ocean was entirely lightless. She switched on the suit's lights, which revealed the nearby unfinished hab-dome as vague, hulking shapes in the distance.

Disengaging from the sub's hull, Cassie landed on the

ocean floor in a flurry of black silt that briefly clouded her sonar. The low gravity made her feel light as a feather, but when her boots hit the ocean floor, she felt it in her teeth.

She looked out across a landscape locked away from the sun for untold billions of years. Then again, she remembered, neither had the Mariana Trench seen daylight for billions of years.

Back home, and under normal Earth gravity, no behemoth suit in existence could have withstood the pressure at a depth of twenty kilometres—but then, no ocean on Earth could ever be this deep.

Moving closer to the skeletal dome, her lights picked out the pressure-adapted portable reactor. It looked similar to older reactors she'd seen at Mare Imbrium.

Most of her attention, however, was taken up by dust-mote sized flora and fauna darting through the twin beams of her lights.

Europan life—*alien* life—was all around her.

Once Cassie got within a few metres of the reactor, its control interface appeared in her HUD. That much, at least, was still functioning. She spent the next twenty minutes searching through menus and submenus that showed the reactor was working at normal capacity.

So if there was power, why wasn't it reaching Nemo?

Walking in a wide circle around the reactor, she noted that some of the temporary cabling running back and forth between Nemo and the reactor was visibly damaged or frayed. She hoped Harrow was right that they'd find spare cables in the station, because if they couldn't, there was nothing more they could do.

She came across a charging frame used for powering up mobile battery packs. These modular units could be plugged into anything from mini-subs to behemoth suits, and she saw half a dozen packs still plugged into the frame. Two had faintly glowing green LEDs to show they were ready for use, while the rest were clearly damaged beyond repair.

Cassie next trudged over to a comms panel set into one of the legs supporting Station Nemo and plugged into it with a cable that extended out from her suit. When he answered, she told Harrow about the situation, and he disappeared for nearly half an hour before returning to tell her he'd indeed found spare cables.

She barely held herself back from cheering out loud.

Harrow put the spare cables into a service airlock in the station's underbelly, from where Cassie could collect them. State-of-the art her behemoth suit might be, but replacing the cables required long hours of effort and much trudging back and forth. And the satisfaction she felt on seeing all of Nemo's exterior hull lights come to life was incalculable.

———

BY THE TIME she got back inside, the machine and Harrow had already made some discoveries.

"You've barely had time to boot the network back up," she said, slugging down water from their own supplies. "You can't possibly have found something already."

"It helps," said the machine, "if you already have an idea what to look for."

Exhausted, Cassie collapsed onto a chair next to Harrow, who sat at a console. He turned to look at her, his eyes bloodshot.

"Jesus, Evan." She made a face. "Get some sleep."

"Already had a couple of hours while you were outside," he said. "Marcus did most of the work." His stomach rumbled audibly. "Did we bring any of our MREs down with us?"

Cassie's eyes widened. *Oh, shit.*

Harrow caught the look. "You're fucking kidding me. Seriously?"

"I noticed," the machine pointed out, "a box of MREs tucked away in the station's kitchen. Perhaps—?"

Evan stared at the spider-like robot in horror. "They're decades old by now," he said. "We can't—!"

"Actually," said Cassie, suddenly aware of how very long it had been since she herself had eaten, "maybe we can."

"What?" Harrow stared at her like she was advocating cannibalism.

"Evan," she said, too tired to argue, "I once ate an MRE made in the 1980s. It was fine. Delicious, even."

Harrow's mouth opened and then closed. "Bullshit," he said.

"Cross my heart," said Cassie. "We found them on board the Deep Range. Christ knows how they got there—the ship itself wasn't that old. But we ate them, and we were fine."

"Was a bet involved?" the machine enquired.

"Of course there was," Cassie found the energy to grin.

CHAPTER 25

THE MEDUSA NET

"Medusa what?"

"Medusa Net," the machine repeated. "The term origi-
nated with Brian Hall."

Cassie stirred a plastic fork through her self-heating
Chicken Kiev. After sniffing it carefully, she tasted a tiny
morsel, then immediately wolfed down the rest before
opening a second MRE.

She and Harrow sat side by side at a narrow countertop
with the machine on the other side, crouched on a plastic
chair and peering at them through its lenses.

"Go on," she said.

"Back before the first mission, and back in the earliest
days of his career, Hall had been part of a team analysing
samples of microorganisms thrown up by ice-geysers and
subsequently scraped up from the ice by the earliest
unmanned expeditions to Europa. He became famous—or
infamous, if you will—for theorising that Europa constituted
a single link or node in a living network of ice-locked ocean
worlds extending throughout the galaxy."

Cassie exchanged a wary look with Harrow. "Seriously?"

"For a long time I thought it was nonsense too," the
machine admitted. "Hall speculated that by some means,

these moons, despite the vast distances separating them, communicated via biological probes. Worlds like Europa are believed to be incredibly common throughout the universe—far more so than worlds like Earth, yet equally able to sustain life, if primitive life at that."

Cassie put down her fork and raised a hand in a *stop* gesture. "Wait. You started by telling me you'd found something in the computers. I thought you meant evidence for bioweapons. This…" she waved her hand in a dismissive gesture, then picked her fork back up. "What's all this got to do with it?"

"Maybe nothing," the machine admitted. "But when I was spying on Braemar and Holland during the outbound trip, it was clear they were very interested in Hall in particular. And you said Ketteridge warned you someone on the mission was after the same thing you were, but for different reasons. Hall, or rather his research, appears to be the common factor."

"But what about hard evidence?" she asked. "Something that directly links his theories to bioweapons, if that's what you're getting at?"

Harrow finished his own meal and put his plastic fork down. "We found hundreds of terabytes of raw, unprocessed data," he explained. "Too much for us to sort through in any reasonable time, I'm afraid."

"Agreed," said the machine. "And while I can process information far faster than a flesh and blood human, I don't have the required expertise to analyse or make sense of most of it. Better to ship it all back home and let a team of experts work through it all."

"I know you think it's a risk," she said, "but maybe it's still worth trying Ketteridge's malware. Remember what he told me—it was designed specifically to find the information he was looking for."

She reached into a pocket suit and took out the interface key, placing it on the counter.

"Even after everything I said about it being a terrible idea?" the machine enquired.

"You said just now you weren't up to the job." She tapped the key. "If something goes wrong, you can deactivate it, right? You already did so once before."

Harrow sucked at his lips and looked over at the machine. At first, neither spoke.

"Do you want to tell her," the machine said, "or should I?"

"Tell me what?" Cassie demanded.

Harrow placed both hands on the counter, as if bracing himself. "We destroyed the key."

"But it's right here," said Cassie. "It's—"

Then she looked more closely at it. *Son of a bitch.*

"This isn't my interface key," she said. "Where the hell is it?"

"When you weren't looking," said Harrow, "Lebed swapped your key for another that looked about the same."

She stared at him, outraged. "You can't—!"

"Evan brought your key to the borehole station," said the machine. "While you were out there reattaching the cables, he gave it to me so I could analyse it. I took that little sucker apart bit by bit, algorithm by algorithm, first chance I had. And you know what I found?"

Cassie waited without saying anything.

"It was programmed to shut down all the life support systems. Not just in Verne, but everywhere it could reach. It could have jumped from there to the crawler, then to the sub, and then infected the computers down here. If there'd been an active comms link between the surface and the Veles, it could have hopped on board there as well."

Cassie blinked, completely thrown off guard. "You're saying...it was meant to kill us?"

"The way I figure it," the machine continued, "Ketteridge was after evidence, all right. But he wanted to *erase* it, not bring it back, then kill anyone who might be a witness. As for why, well…maybe whoever was behind him was afraid of any war crimes being traced back to them. As for Braemar and Holland, my guess is whoever's behind *them* wanted the data precisely so they could continue weaponising Europan lifeforms."

Cassie leaned back and raked her fingers through her hair, feeling the rasp of her fingernails against her scalp. "I don't understand any of this."

"You've been played," said Harrow. "That's all that matters."

"Sorry for tricking you like that," said the machine, "but I couldn't take the risk of leaving the key with you."

She nodded, still too numb to really take it in.

Harrow straightened up and massaged the back of his neck. "I'm going to make coffee," he said, gesturing at the coffee machine. "There's some freeze-dried granules. No idea if they're still any good, but—"

"Fuck, yes," said Cassie. "I'll take that chance." She looked wearily at the machine. "You must think I'm a fucking idiot."

"Never, Cassie."

She waved at it. "You were talking about Hall. Finish the story."

"Medusa," it explained, "was the child of a sea god. Hall believed that Europan microbial lifeforms could act in concert to form a Gestalt mind, a kind of superintelligence. Alive, but not necessarily conscious. The Medusa Net was his term for a speculative network of ocean worlds connected across vast distances of space."

Cassie made a face. "Even calling it a stretch feels like a vast understatement."

"From a certain point of view, human bodies are also gestalt organisms composed of trillions of distinct biological entities working in concert. In that context, the idea isn't so far-fetched."

"Tell her," said Harrow, pouring hot water into two mugs, "about the biological probes."

Cassie looked between them. "The what?"

"Europa's ice-geysers are easily powerful enough to carry microorganisms out of its gravity well," said the machine. "Hall believed some of these organisms could survive long enough to reach neighbouring stars. He called them SBEs—space-borne extremophiles."

"I still don't see what this—?"

The machine climbed carefully down from its perch and made its way over to a console. "Come and see this."

Harrow handed Cassie a coffee as she stood and followed the machine over. The machine lifted one leg and plugged the tip into a data port.

"I didn't know you could do that," she said.

One of the machine's lenses swivelled towards her. "Turns out it's a lot easier for me just to do this than try to type."

Text and images blurred across the screen at high speed, then froze on a cutaway diagram of a rough-edged ball similar to the manganese nodules harvested by illegal mining fleets.

"Hall published this paper two years before boarding the Veles," the machine explained. "He wanted to investigate whether microbes returned by Europa probes were the result of directed panspermia, which presupposes an intelligent species choosing to seed the universe with microbial life bearing information encoded into its DNA."

"And that's what I'm looking at—an SBE?"

"As Hall believed it to be, yes. His idea was that an Europan gestalt mind could use SBEs to communicate with others of its ilk."

Cassie lowered her coffee and shook her head. "This is all very fascinating, but—"

"Just watch," said the machine.

The screen now showed video footage that looked like it

had come from an aquatic drone. The drone's lights revealed a desolate, aquatic terrain much like that surrounding Station Nemo.

The drone moved forward a few metres, then turned through a hundred and eighty degrees to reveal a mini-sub sitting stationary a few metres above the ocean floor. A tether by which the drone could be controlled trailed across the ocean floor before joining with the underside of the submersible's hull. Past the sub, the ocean floor came to an abrupt halt, suggesting the sub was at the edge of an undersea shelf, most likely the same one close by the station.

She kept watching as the drone's lights now picked out a figure in a behemoth suit, their head tilted back and one hand pointing upwards.

The drone's lights moved in the direction they were pointing. At first, all Cassie could see was a cloud of boiling mud or silt hovering a half dozen metres above the shelf. Somehow, the cloud remained suspended above the shelf, and without losing its roughly spherical outline.

"What the hell is that?" Cassie said in a half-whisper.

"Watch," said the machine. "It's bigger than it looks."

Whoever was controlling the drone must have employed some kind of filter, because the footage became suddenly much brighter and clearer.

The impossible cloud flashed silver, then green, then blue, like a cloud of subaquatic diamonds. It reminded her of a school of fish swarming in reaction to a threat, whether it be a shark, a boat or the nearby behemoth: an adaptive, fluid behaviour borne of millions of years of evolution back on Earth.

She mentioned this to the others. "Except I don't recall the first expedition ever reporting higher-order cooperative behaviour of this kind."

"They were here barely six months before we lost contact with them," the machine reminded her. "If they hadn't disappeared, I think by now we'd have a very different under-standing of Europa."

She nodded at the screen. "So what is it?"

"Single-cell lifeforms," said the machine. "Keep watching."

"I've already watched this a dozen times," Harrow said with a kind of hushed reverence. "I'll probably never *stop* watching it."

A shape slowly coalesced from out of the cloud or shoal or whatever it was: a dome-like structure that grew steadily more defined and solid beneath the sub's lights. Its edges fluctuated, ripples moving around its circumference, while other parts formed into glistening strands that twisted in an unseen current.

At first, Cassie struggled to form a coherent response. "It looks like—"

"A benthocodon," the machine finished for her. "A big one, maybe ten metres across."

Could the video have been faked, she wondered? Such things were relatively easy to do—and yet, why go to the effort?

But if it was real—and Cassie struggled to believe what she had just witnessed—a disparate cloud of microbes had spontaneously formed into a much larger, and much more complex, life-form.

By now, it was as if the cloud of single-celled creatures had never existed. The great curving bell of the jellyfish pulsed gently, long, medusa-like strands trailing beneath it, floating just a few metres from the mini-sub.

As if, Cassie thought, it somehow knew the mini-sub was there.

"There's more," said the machine. "Want to see?"

Cassie nodded.

A new video took the place of the first. Depth and pres-sure data appeared in one corner of the screen, while twin beams of light revealed bright flecks of organic matter—marine snow—in the depths of Europa's oceans.

Voices murmured quietly to each other, too low for Cassie to make out.

"This is a separate incident," the machine explained. "Ruth Winters is piloting, with Hannes Zolna as co-pilot."

Winters spoke up in the manner of one addressing an unseen audience. "We're investigating the extremely large growth first spotted by Kat fifteen klicks south-south-west of Station Nemo. We programmed a couple of free-ranging drones to go ahead on a preset course. The idea is to use them to light the growth from different angles so we can try to get a clearer sense of its scale. It should come into view about…"

Several more seconds passed in silence, then four widely spaced beams of light became visible in the murky distance. The beams revealed a gradually curving vertical surface rising from out of the abyss, as if the two scientists had stumbled across a sleeping leviathan.

Either Zolna or Winters drew their breath in sharply. A second voice, too muffled to make out clearly, muttered what Cassie suspected was a prayer.

The drones spread further out from each other, revealing more of the structure.

Cassie's mouth suddenly felt bone dry. "How big?"

"There are three hours of this feed alone," said the machine. "They filmed it from plenty of different angles. The end that's anchored into the seabed is a couple of kilometres across, but it gets narrower the higher up it goes. The upper end branches out like a tree, with the branches buried deep inside the ice cap."

Feeling helpless, Cassie turned to Harrow. "Then what the hell *is* it?"

Harrow shrugged. "You remember what we were talking about before, about how the icecap moves far less than it should, given it was thought to be free-floating?" He nodded at the screen. "I think it's essentially a tendon that controls the movement of the ice."

"If I might postulate," said the machine, "its purpose could be to keep patches of thin ice directly above sources of heat such as Mount Doom."

Cassie felt oddly dizzy. "That isn't possible."

"Isn't it?" the machine countered. "Until they went below the ice, the most they thought they'd find were primitive single-celled organisms clustered around hydrothermal vents. And they found that, but they also found much, much more, as you can see."

"Except Hall and the others were here under the ice for months before they disappeared." She gestured at the screen. "The date on this feed is from well before that. How come we never heard of this?"

"We talked about that," said Harrow.

Cassie stared at the oceanologist. "And?"

"What if," said the machine, picking up the thread, "someone back home decided to sit on this?"

Cassie made a face. "Why?"

"Because it's a threat," said Harrow.

"You came here looking for proof someone had tried to create weapons out of Europan life," said the machine. "What we found is evidence that Europa *itself* presents an existential threat to life on Earth."

This time, she laughed. It echoed back at her from the flat metal walls, tinged with hysteria. "I don't see how—?"

"Everything we've found so far," said the machine, "implies that Europan life in totality acts with a collective or possibly emergent intelligence, whether it's forming large-scale, highly organised organisms spontaneously out of a swarm of single-celled creatures, or growing gargantuan organs to control the movement of the ice. I never thought I'd say this, but there's an argument to be had over whether Europa itself is, in some sense, alive."

Cassie stood in silence for another moment, then turned and went into the kitchenette. She drained the last of her coffee, then filled the empty mug with water. It carried a faint chemical aftertaste when she drank it down.

"All this is giving me a headache," she said, wiping her mouth.

"When Ketteridge hired you," the machine asked, "did he say anything, or give any hints, about what exactly it was that might have been weaponized?"

"No." Cassie shook her head. "And I didn't ask. To be honest, I'm not sure I'd have understood the answer. Why?"

"Do you think it's possible," the machine suggested, "that the Whispers plague was created using biological samples from Europa? Samples were returned to Earth aboard robot craft. Medina or Wojtowicz might have identified some of them as having potential military applications."

Cassie rubbed at one temple, feeling the blood pulsing there. "You're talking like a conspiracy theorist," she snapped.

But it made sense, she knew, despite herself. If Holland and Braemar really had been interested in Hall—if Hall had identified something complex and alien going on in the oceans of Europa—who was to say someone with evil intentions might not find a way to exploit it to their own ends?

The words caught in her throat as an alert sounded from another nearby console. Harrow hurried over to it and studied the information on its screen.

She turned to look at him. "What is it?"

"Something's moving outside the station," he said, tapping at a submenu. "That was the station's proximity alarm we just heard."

Stepping up beside him, Cassie saw a map of the terrain surrounding Station Nemo. To the west, a rough line showed the edge of the abyssal shelf, and beyond that lay nothing but a straight drop of thirty kilometres into yet greater depths.

Two blinking yellow dots appeared at the edge of the shelf. One remained stationary, while the other moved closer to the station.

"More of those big jellyfish?" Cassie suggested.

"Maybe," said Harrow. "Hang on, I'll bring the cameras online."

The view changed to show the ocean immediately outside the station. A bulky grey shape, almost invisible against the blackness of the deep ocean, was moving toward the nearby part-constructed dome.

Harrow made some adjustments, and the image became much clearer, revealing a behemoth suit.

"Christ," said Harrow. "There's someone out there."

"Wait," said the machine. "What are they doing?"

"The charging frame," Cassie said suddenly. "The one used for powering up gear without having to come back inside. That's where they're headed."

Harrow made another adjustment, and the view changed again, focused on a larger object almost on the edge of the abyssal shelf.

"It's another sub," he muttered in disbelief.

Turning, Cassie strode towards the submersible airlock. "I'm going out there," she said over her shoulder.

Harrow stared after her. "No, wait here and see if they come to us."

"That could be my brother out there," she reminded him. "I'm not waiting one second more. Anything happens to me, get back to the surface and find Lebed."

CHAPTER 26
ROGUE ON EXTERNALS

Once she was back in the sub, a wave of fatigue washed over Cassie. *Too long running on empty*, she thought, leaning her head back against the headrest.

Then she made the mistake of closing her eyes, just for a moment.

The sub tumbled away, and Europa with it.

———

THIN, high clouds set against a blood-red sky were visible through the waves above her. She was a giant, certainly compared to the creatures that had built the drowned metropolis through which she swam, her vast bulk almost too large for the narrow canyons of its streets.

The alabaster walls of one of the few spires still rising above the waves were burnished red by the setting sun. As she navigated her way past the spire, she became aware, via lacy, tendril-like sense organs extending outwards from her body, that there was one other like her nearby. Like her, they swam through the ruins of a long-vanished race.

There was something achingly familiar about this *other*. She felt it deep within her twin hearts.

She banked, carving a path through the dense waters as she sought them out. At last, she glimpsed a manta-like form that cast a broad shadow against the ragged remains of a wall.

The ache in her hearts redoubled.

Chris.

———

LURCHING FORWARD, Cassie sucked in air in short, panicked gasps.

How long had she been slumped, unconscious, in the cabin of the mini-sub…?

Her panic eased a little when she saw that barely more than a minute had passed.

Suffering occasional Whispers-induced hallucinations was one thing. Having them actively interfere with her ability to function while awake was something entirely different.

Sergio's face swam into her thoughts, and she squeezed the sub's controls hard, swearing under her breath.

What if she passed out again, long enough for her air to become depleted? What if—?

Fuck it. She reached for the controls: she didn't have the luxury of time to worry about these things.

Then the sonar display showed that both the rogue behemoth, and the mini-sub it had arrived with, had vanished. Gone, like they were never there.

The only direction they could have gone was over the shelf. And past that lay only an abyss of water thirty kilometres deep.

———

CASSIE GUIDED her own sub closer to the part-constructed dome between the shelf and Station Nemo and played the craft's lights and cameras over the foundations.

She wasn't surprised to discover that the two battery packs that were still working had been pulled from the charging frame. Two more had been slotted in their place and were already charging up.

So: not just a social call, then.

Cassie guided her sub over the edge of the abyssal shelf and began a fast descent. A few minutes later, her sonar pinged a mini-sub sized object a few kilometres below her, and making a rapid descent on a south-south-west bearing.

Then, to her surprise and consternation, something else appeared on the sonar: more than a dozen somethings, in fact.

The signals were spaced over a wide area. The specific nature of the signals strongly suggested they came from sonar reflectors—small, icosahedron-shaped devices that could be used as location markers. Most likely, they had been used by the first expedition to identify places of particular scientific interest.

Cassie stared at the pattern made by the sonar signals and wondered what it was about them that seemed oddly familiar. Like something she'd seen only recently, if only she could remember where the hell—?

It can't be.

It didn't take long for her to dig out the slip of paper she'd found tucked inside a paperback. Studying its pattern of scribbled dots, she turned it around in her hands until it matched what she could see on the sub's screen.

It was a map of the sonar reflectors.

Cassie kept a close watch on the other sub's sonar signal. It was descending at a faster rate than she could safely manage. Whoever was on board it was pushing past their sub's safety limits.

Mount Doom showed up as a heat trace on her main screen, but as she descended, several other, much smaller heat traces also showed up, scattered across a broad region but with the volcano more or less at their centre.

The hand-drawn map correlated exactly with these heat traces. And that, in turn, meant the sonar reflectors indicated the location of specific hydrothermal vents.

Despite the risk, Cassie increased her rate of descent until the nose of her sub was angled downward at an angle of almost forty-five degrees. An alert sounded and she deactivated it.

A little over an hour later, she finally reached the ocean floor fifty kilometres beneath the ice and thirty kilometres deeper than Station Nemo. Hard as it was to believe, she knew there were yet deeper points in other parts of Europa.

At last, Cassie brought her sub to a halt fifty metres from the slopes of a hydrothermal vent—a naturally occurring chimney formed at a point where the seawater became superheated by upwelling magma.

There was no sign of the other sub—or the accompanying behemoth.

The vent was much larger than its Terran equivalent, rising nearly a hundred metres above the ocean floor. In appearance, it reminded Cassie of a half-melted candle.

Tiny, blind creatures swarmed past her mini-sub's lights. Almost as impressive as the vent itself were the towering, pale, kelp-like growths that rose up around it in dense clusters like some vast aquatic forest, their roots anchored deep in the sandy soil.

A quick life-support check showed Cassie she still had several hours of air left. Enough to do a little scouting before she would be forced to return.

After another hour, she came close to giving up her search. Even if the rogue sub was hiding somewhere among the drifting kelp, it would be all too easy to miss. And it was clear whoever was inside it didn't want to be found.

In the end, and with limited time left, she pushed on to the next nearest vent. Even if she couldn't find the other sub, there was no point in wasting the trip.

The second vent wasn't more than a few kilometres away, and it didn't take her long to reach it. The terrain surrounding it was more fractured, revealing evidence of ancient and some perhaps not so ancient lava flows.

Using her sub's external manipulators, she collected a sample of kelp and dropped it into a specimen cage on the sub's exterior. Studying it under high magnification, she saw tiny feelers suggesting that, rather than being algae like kelp back on Earth, it was closer to some form of animal. Or more likely, she mused, it comprised part of some unknown genus that rendered terms such as *plant* or *animal* meaningless.

Whoever was at the controls of the rogue sub, they must, she thought, be running out of air. Not that she could imagine where they might have got air in the first place, down here in Europa's crushing depths.

And then she thought about the AI, and its belief that the Yatagarasu had come to Europa.

A warning flashed up on her screens: she had to return or herself risk running out of air.

She did some quick calculations in her head. If she acted without delay, she might have just enough time to visit a third hydrothermal vent. Specifically, the one that had been underlined multiple times on Chris's hand-drawn map.

And if she didn't do it now, she might never get a chance again.

Cassie drove the submersible on to the third vent at full throttle.

———

Soon, the third vent rose ahead of her, something glittering close to its base.

Cassie inched the sub closer until her lights revealed the smashed remains of an autonomous underwater drone, half-buried in silt. Then she had to swing the sub around and past the vent, barely avoiding getting caught in a thermal eddy as super-heated water and ash rushed upwards.

Something else reflected her sub's lights, a few dozen metres from the vent. Whatever it was, it lay within a field of house-sized boulders, and from which a great forest of Europan kelp rose.

Cassie adjusted the yaw, dropping the sub's nose until it skimmed towards the field of boulders. Then she brought it to a near-halt, taking a moment to study the fissured rocks.

They were familiar, somehow, as if she'd seen them before. Not just once, but many, many times.

A feeling very like déjà vu rushed over Cassie, and with it, a rush of nausea powerful enough that the controls slipped from her hands.

The sub responded by slowing to a dead halt.

Cassie cupped both hands over her face and tried to steady her breathing. Gradually, the nausea faded. Flash-backs, hallucinations—these were classic signs of hypoxia she'd been trained to watch out for. She still had air left, but barely enough to get her back to Nemo.

But some part of her mind insisted she *had* seen this ruined place before. Not in real life, not precisely…but in her dreams.

Not that it made any sense.

Again, the sub's lights reflected from something deep amidst the tumbled rocks. There were gaps between them that looked like they were just wide enough for her to squeeze through them in the behemoth suit.

It might be another abandoned drone. Or it might be something that told her where they had all gone.

There wasn't time to run the usual safety checks. What she was doing was enormously dangerous, but Cassie couldn't avoid the sense, as she dropped to the ocean floor in the behemoth suit, that she was on the verge of something momentous.

Seen from down there, and looking forward, the scattered boulders resembled the broken teeth of some ancient giant. It felt uncomfortably like walking into the jaws of a slumbering beast.

Cassie passed between the outer boulders with ease. Her lights picked out a depression a few metres ahead, where the ocean bed appeared to have somehow collapsed under the weight of the boulders. Closer investigation revealed a steep-sided pit she suspected was a caved-in lava-tube.

Then her boot struck something. When she looked down and saw scratched and painted metal, the breath caught in her throat.

Kneeling carefully, she brushed away silt to reveal one edge of a discarded air tank. Its burnished metal gleamed dully under her lights.

Then she looked up and saw a human figure looming out from amidst the gently undulating kelp.

CHAPTER 27
THE GARDEN OF
THE DEAD

An involuntary cry worked its way up from the depths of her lungs. Stumbling backward, Cassie nearly tripped over the discarded tank. She caught herself by grabbing onto a nearby boulder.

Look again, she told herself, her heart hammering wildly. *You're seeing things.*

But she wasn't.

The figure—if figure it was—didn't move. *Pareidolia*, thought Cassie: she was seeing something where there was nothing. She only *thought* she saw a figure.

She worked her way around the edge of the sinkhole and closer to the shape. No, she saw with revulsion; she hadn't been seeing things.

It was a clearly human figure wedged into a gap between two tall boulders, held in place, somehow, by kelp that twisted around their limbs and threaded through holes and cavities in their body. Their head was oddly flattened and misshapen, an open and toothless mouth gaping in a parody of surprise. The eyes were little more than dark sockets, the chest caved-in and the body oddly distorted.

Once, in her first year aboard the Deep Range, she had seen a ruined mini-sub lifted from out of the depths of the

Mariana Trench. The sub had been deep enough that one of the two passengers had been cut in half by the sheer force of highly pressurized water forcing its way through a weakened hull seam. The second passenger, much like the figure before her, looked twisted out of shape, like a rag doll someone had tried and failed to wrench apart.

Their deaths, Cassie had been assured, would have been instantaneous.

Whoever this was, however they'd come to be here, they looked like they'd suffered the same kind of blow-out.

Swallowing back sour bile, Cassie made sure her suit recorded everything she saw.

The oddest thing of all was that flesh still clung to the bones. When Cassie stepped up closer and shone her lights onto the corpse's desiccated face, she realized with sickened fascination that she recognized them. Distorted as his features were, this was clearly Arthur Medina.

By any sane measure, there should have been nothing left of him but a pile of glistening bones. Perhaps not even that.

But even that wasn't what made her skin truly crawl: somehow, in some undefinable way, and in defiance of all logic, she had the sense that Medina was *alive*. As if his eyeless face might, at any moment, turn to regard her.

An alert flashed up, warning that her air had become dangerously depleted. She cursed herself for not taking the time to bring extra tanks before setting out in pursuit of the rogue mini-sub.

But then again, who could have anticipated that so much would happen in such a comparatively brief space of time? That she might discover…this?

Then she directed her suit's lights past Medina's oddly preserved corpse and saw that there was a second body, similarly entangled in kelp, and down inside the sinkhole. She wouldn't have spotted it if she hadn't come up close to Medina.

Moving with care, Cassie made her way around and past Medina, then carefully negotiated her way down the slope of the sinkhole. The head of this second body, the same as Medina's, was tipped back so that it appeared to gaze up at the ceiling of ice fifty kilometres overhead.

While she couldn't be certain, Cassie suspected this might be Joseph Wojtowicz—Medina's accomplice, according to Chastain.

Her HUD showed she was down to only five minutes of air. A counter ticked down the remaining seconds.

Cursing, she turned back, knowing she had no choice but to return to Nemo—for now.

No matter what happened, she had to find some way to come back down here. She *had* to.

———

THE MINI-SUB HAD JUST enough power remaining in its batteries for a last, cursory sweep around the hydrothermal vent and the collapsed lava tube. The kelp was too tangled and dense to allow her to catch sight of any other bodies that might be hidden from her sight.

No matter how deep she had gone into the Mariana Trench, she had never felt afraid. But she felt afraid now.

———

NEITHER THE MACHINE nor Harrow appeared to have anything to say once she finished showing them the video of the bodies a few hours later. Harrow stared, bug-eyed, at the final image of Joseph Wojtowicz's half-rotted face, then pushed back his chair and stood. Cassie watched as he stepped across the dome and stared at its curving wall.

"How about you?" Cassie asked the machine. It stood next

to the console where she'd played the video for them both. "Nothing to say?"

"I have," it said after a lengthy silence, "a thousand questions."

"And?"

"You said you visited three hydrothermal vents in all?"

She nodded.

"That stuff like kelp," it said. "I found it very...odd, the way it was all tangled around the bodies."

She laughed. "That's *all* you found odd?"

"Obviously not," it replied dryly. "Not least the question of how their bodies could remain so well-preserved. But the way the kelp was wrapped around their limbs felt somehow deliberate, wouldn't you say?"

"Define 'deliberate'," she said.

"I don't know." One of its camera lenses shifted towards her. "It felt like something or someone was *keeping* them there. As if they were trapped."

"Jesus," Harrow muttered from across the station. He turned back to look at them both. "Thanks a fucking lot for that image."

"I'm wondering if we're ever going to understand what happened down here," the machine continued, ignoring him. "It's much more than some people suffering a tragic accident under the ice."

"I had a lot of time to think on the way back up," said Cassie. "The bodies were deliberately placed where I found them. They couldn't have got there by accident."

"But why?" asked the machine. "And by whom?"

"Is it possible," she asked, "that whoever our visitor was, it might be someone from the Yatagarasu? Maybe even Risuke himself?"

"That occurred to me too," the machine admitted. "But again, it raises the question of why they choose to keep their distance."

"If it is Risuke," said Cassie, "they've got every reason to keep away until they have a better idea of who we are, the same way you hid from the crew of the Veles. But we can't know anything for sure unless we go back down there, and as soon as possible."

"It'll take too long," said Harrow. He stepped back towards them, hands on his hips. "It could be years before we figure out what happened here. In the meantime, Lebed's on his own up on the surface, we've got potentially hostile forces on their way, and two attempted murderers in control of the Veles. My vote is that we download what information we can, and hope to hell Anton's figured out how to get the other lander working." He rubbed at his scalp with one shaking hand. "I'm starting to think I'd rather let whoever's on the Tianjin deal with all this crap than have to think about it all for one more second."

"No." Cassie shook her head, despite a sudden rush of fatigue. "My brother is down there somewhere. I didn't come all this way not to find out what happened to him."

"Maybe we can come back down at some future point," said Harrow. "At the worst, we could negotiate with whoever's in charge aboard the Tianjin—"

"No." She shook her head again, putting as much steel in her voice as she could. "If *you* want to leave, fine. I can take you back up in the sub. But then I'm coming straight back down again, even if I have to do this on my own."

"What if," the machine said just as Harrow was about to frame a retort, "what you found down there was some kind of experiment?"

Cassie stared at the spider-machine in confusion. "What?"

"Remember what Chastain said?" The machine's lenses swivelled back and forth between her and Harrow. "Brian Hall had some, and I quote, 'insane idea' about how to keep them all alive."

"So?" Harrow shrugged. "Whatever it was, it clearly didn't—"

"Think about the situation the first expedition found itself in," the machine continued. "According to Chastain, Wojtowicz and Medina had doomed them all. However they wound up dead, why go to the trouble of carefully placing their bodies inside that kelp forest, and so far from this station?"

"We don't know that they did it," said Cassie. "It might have been someone from the Yatagarasu."

"If so, then where could Risuke or his crew have found the bodies?" the machine responded. "What kept them so well-preserved? I think we have to consider the possibility there are special conditions pertaining to the specific location where you found them."

Cassie tried to frame an objection, but nothing coherent would come to her mind. "Go on," she said, unable to hide her exasperation.

"No one on the first expedition, including Hall, were the kind of people to do anything without a very good reason," the machine continued. "They were all at the top of their respective fields. So are we. Their bodies are nowhere near decayed enough for the time they've been here, especially at this depth and at such enormous pressures. I don't believe Hall and the others didn't know about this before they transported Wojtowicz and Medina to where you found them. I think, perhaps, Hall placed them there because he believed that it offered all of them some form of salvation."

"But they're dead," said Cassie. "What kind of salvation is that?"

And yet, she remembered the uncanny feeling that, somehow, they *weren't* dead.

"Hall, in his way, was a madman," the machine continued, "but he wasn't an idiot." Its lenses swivelled towards Harrow.

"I think Chastain's video is proof that Hall was on the verge of discovering something very important."

Harrow still looked far from convinced. There was a defeated look about him, like he'd been pushed to the edge of what he could take and beyond. The same, Cassie realized, could be said for them all.

"Let's compromise," she suggested. "I'll go back out to the vent one more time. Whatever happens, after I come back, we return to the surface and find Anton. Deal?"

Harrow still looked like he wanted to argue, but then he returned a brief nod.

"Deal," he said. "But make it quick, Cassie."

CHAPTER 28
DOWN IN THE LAVA TUBES

This time, Cassie brought extra air tanks.

Back on the Deep Range, they'd had a movie night one Christmas and watched the original Moby Dick. In one scene, Captain Ahab's body had become entangled in rigging caught around the body of the white whale, his dead arm flopping back and forth as if beckoning his crew to join him in Hell.

That scene came back to Cassie as she stood once again amidst the kelp and tumbled boulders, Medina floating upright before her, his shrivelled lips parted as if about to speak.

Deep inside her behemoth suit, Cassie shivered. She'd heard other divers talk about how being at the bottom of an ocean, with thousands of kilograms of pressure per square inch pressing down on you, did funny things to your mind.

She had still found no sign of the rest of the first expedition's crew, despite several hours of fruitless searching through tumbled boulders and tangled kelp. Empty-handed and frustrated, she had returned to the mini-sub, only to realise she had missed a second boulder field located several hundred metres away, on the far side of the one where she had found Medina and Wojtowicz.

Excitement gripped her. If she were to find anything, then surely it would be there. And if not—then she would have no choice but to return to the surface with the others.

Halfway there, an unexpected blip appeared on her sub's sonar. Whatever it was, it was too small to be the rogue sub, and was heading towards the far side of the vent.

But it was about the right size for a behemoth suit.

She didn't waste any time navigating her own submersible closer to the hydrothermal vent. Just as she arrived where she'd detected the other behemoth, she saw it slip into a dense tangle of kelp on the lower slopes of the vent: close enough that, were she to continue her pursuit, she risked becoming caught in an eddy of super-heated water and mineral-dense ash. One hard impact with a boulder or the side of the vent would be enough to compromise her sub's pressure integrity, and death would follow instantaneously.

But that didn't mean she couldn't follow on foot.

A few minutes later, Cassie was back inside her own behemoth, gritty silt boiling up in dense clouds around its heavy boots as she moved across the ocean floor at the base of the vent. Huge, alien growths rose around her: Europan life in all its uncanny glory, the water so dense with ash she could barely make out the chimney rising on her left.

There: a glimmer of yellow and orange in her suit's thermal readouts revealed movement somewhere ahead, barely discernible from the heat signature of the vent itself. Cassie set off with renewed vigour, her every step churning up black mud.

Her HUD threw up an alert. The suit's coolant systems were struggling to cope with the outside temperatures. She'd have to be careful.

Adrenaline drove her on regardless. It felt like she had always been here, trudging across the floor of an alien ocean, her body aching and her muscles on the verge of spasming, trapped in some eternal Sisyphean quest.

Why didn't whoever it was wait for her? Why keep showing themselves, then disappearing again? Why—?

A thought struck her like lightning: perhaps they weren't trying to get *away* from her. Perhaps they were trying to lead her away from wherever the rest of the bodies were located. Assuming, of course, she was right in thinking the rest of them were here.

But why try to lead her away?

A muscle pulsed in Cassie's temple. To give herself a moment to think, she sipped water from a tube. Then, her suit's internal servos whining in response, and rather than continue her pursuit, she turned back towards the second boulder field.

It didn't take long for her to put distance between herself and the vent and for the alerts in her HUD to fade. She had thought of returning to her sub first, but it would take too long, and she only had so much air despite the extra tanks. Easier, then, just to make her way on foot to the boulder field and make a quick reconnaissance.

Europan life darted in and out of her suit's lights as she arrived at the edge of the boulder field. Squeezing past more huge rocks—far from easy in such a huge and bulky suit—she soon found that here, too, was a sinkhole. She surmised this must be a different section of the same lava tube, and that it had also been crushed by debris.

Here, at least, the slope wasn't so steep, and she could more quickly make her way down amidst the rocks at its base. Grey-white tendrils like stringy, matted hair brushed against the helmet and shoulders of her suit.

It wasn't long before she had made her way almost to the centre of the boulder field. Her breath sounded loud and harsh in the confines of her suit. Getting down and finding a route between the boulders had taken longer than she thought it would. Despite all her efforts, she was back to having to watch her air levels to make sure she didn't run out too soon.

Then she saw, directly ahead of her, a boulder that was more symmetrical than most and heavily wreathed in kelp. Light glinted from different parts of it as she moved towards it until, at last, she saw it was not a boulder, but a behemoth suit.

For a moment she stood, stunned, playing her light over its scratched and smeared shell. The helmet section had been lifted open, revealing an empty interior.

It must have been standing there for years.

Moving with care, Cassie worked her way past the suit to where a kind of roof or arch was formed by one particularly enormous boulder that had landed across those beneath it. The space beneath was large—almost the same dimensions as the interior of Station Nemo—and wreathed in shadow.

Excitement and dread gripped Cassie in equal measure. She swung her lights into the darkness and saw the vague, kelp-shrouded outlines of yet more bodies.

This time, she did not stumble backwards. She listened for a moment to the harsh rasp of her breath and the furious drumming of her heart.

As with Medina and Wojtowicz, the limbs of those nearest her swayed gently with the current, empty eyes tilted upwards and jaws wide. Kelp wound in and out of huge, gaping wounds in their chests, necks and jaws.

Cassie's heartbeat seemed to fill the ocean, her eyes damp and wide. She swallowed back a surge of acid, a thin moan escaping her lips.

Move, Cassie commanded herself. *Do something, don't just stand here.*

The first step forward was the hardest, the second barely any easier. One by one she examined each body, moving between them and seeing that, even after so long, tattered fragments of clothing or mission jumpsuits still clung to a few.

One in particular still retained the frayed remnants of a name tag. Playing her lights across it, Cassie could only make out the letters Z and A.

Hannes Zolna, the planetologist: it had to be. Traces of red beard still clung to his hollow cheeks, his eyes dark and unseeing wells. Kelp threaded through a ragged hole in the soft palate of his jaw and back out between his teeth, the tips of the kelp strands curling back on themselves like grey-white tongues where they brushed against the rock.

Once again, Cassie had the overwhelming sense of being in the presence not of the dead, but of the living.

Alive, yet not alive.

So far, she had found a total of six bodies: these four, and Medina and Wojtowicz.

Gritting her teeth, Cassie moved from body to body until she was sure beyond all reasonable doubt that none of them were Chris.

So where was he, and the three remaining members of the original expedition? How many more of the mapped vents would she have to search?

The very thought filled her with hopelessness.

No, she decided, her hands tightening in their powerful gloves. Chris and the rest of them had to be somewhere close by.

Had to be.

A warning flashed up: she'd already used most of her suit's reserves. The sub was still a short hike away, and she saw with a sense of bitter failure that she had no choice except to set out for it—and now.

A pang gripped her when she thought about the promise she'd made back at Station Nemo. *Whatever we find or don't find, we'll go back up.*

If she was ever going to find her brother, she'd have no choice but to break that promise.

CHAPTER 29
EMERGENCY

The moment the mini-sub rose above the shelf, a single word began strobing on the screen before Cassie: EMERGENCY.

Although Europa's saltwater ocean made standard radio communication impossible, one-way ultra-low frequency transmission was another matter. Nemo came equipped with such a transmitter, but it could manage only the simplest of messages and only in line of sight.

The word flashed up again and again:

EMERGENCY.

EMERGENCY.

EMERGENCY...

Had Holland and Braemar made their way down through the ice? A fresh trickle of sweat found its way down the small of Cassie's back. Or had something gone wrong? Some unanticipated failure in the life-support systems, perhaps?

Station Nemo soon hove into view on Cassie's screens. Then she saw that a second submersible had docked with it. From the numbers on its side, she recognized it as the same one she'd found parked in the borehole station.

It might just be Lebed. But if it had been, there would have been no need for an emergency alert.

Would there?

Working quickly, Cassie guided her own sub over to a secondary airlock and waited as it automatically docked with the station, a heaviness filling her chest and her breath becoming ragged. A memory came back to her, of the numbing pain when Holland had struck her in the EVA bay. And with it returned the same sense of helplessness and violation she'd felt when he struck her.

There was nothing to hand inside the sub that seemed like a weapon she could use to defend herself. But neither could she stay inside the sub forever.

Her hands shook as she pushed herself out of her seat and crawled through to the airlock on bent knees. She hit the button to cycle through and waited, both hands clenched into fists and ready for a fight she was far from certain she could win.

And waited.

Once again, Cassie hit the button, and once again, nothing happened. Sheer frustration drove her to slam a fist against the airlock door: was something wrong with it?

No, she realized, barely able to swallow back her panic, it was working just fine. Someone on the inside was preventing her from cycling through.

Fuck. Of course they had: stuck in the sub, she'd be helpless, with nothing to do but wait for her air to run out.

Then she remembered her behemoth and had an idea.

Moving quickly, Cassie pulled herself back into the pilot's seat and disengaged from the lock. Soon she had navigated the sub down until it rested on the ocean bed close by the station. Then she wriggled back inside the behemoth attached to the outside of the sub.

The behemoth's HUD came to life the moment she disengaged it from the sub. A message flashed up, warning that the suit's batteries were depleted, and the air approaching dangerously low levels.

Breathe easy, she told herself. Rushing ahead of herself was only going to get her killed.

But another benefit of her optimized DNA, she knew, was the ability to gradually—and consciously—slow her heartbeat to levels lower than might sustain a baseline human. Useful, when you needed to conserve air or power.

Soon, her heart rate had dropped from a rapid tattoo to something gentler. Some of the tension that had worked its way deep into her bones loosened.

Opening her eyes again, she looked up to see Station Nemo rise above her on arching legs. Faded corporate logos were still visible on its hull. Then she stepped over to the external comms port and linked back into the communications network.

She waited to see if anyone would respond. By the time someone did, Cassie had just about convinced herself she was going to die out there at the bottom of the ocean: time enough to consider every possible alternative path of action—only to realize there weren't any.

"Cassie?" The machine's voice was a near-whisper.

The breath caught in Cassie's throat, hope welling up from deep inside her chest. She'd been sure—so very sure—it would be Holland or Braemar, gloating at her imminent demise.

"Marcus?" Cassie nearly shouted. "What the fuck is going on? I'm seconds from running out of—!"

"Braemar's here," the machine hissed, its voice now so low she had to listen carefully to make it out. "I managed to hide. She hasn't seen me yet."

Cassie's bowels felt like they'd turned to water. "Evan? Is he—?"

"When her sub docked," the machine continued in the same barely audible whisper, "we thought it was you. Evan went through to the airlock and I heard yelling. That's when I hid."

"And now?"

"He's still alive," the machine reassured her, its words coming faster now. "But she tasered him. When she dragged him inside, I thought he was dead, but she's got him tied up in the kitchenette. From what I can hear, she's asking him questions. And zapping him every time he gives her an answer she doesn't like."

By the sounds of it, Braemar couldn't have arrived more than a few minutes before Cassie. "Any idea what she wants? Or what she might do?"

"The longer I stay near this console," said the machine, "the more chance she'll see me and—"

"Focus," Cassie hissed between gritted teeth. "Don't fucking panic on me, Marcus. My air's running out, and I need to know everything you can tell me."

"She's looking for Brian Hall's research," the machine whispered. "Also Medina and Wojtowicz's."

"And Holland?"

"He's not here."

Huh. Had he really sent Braemar down here on her own? Maybe he had. Maybe—

An idea hit Cassie just then, and she swore at herself for not having thought about it before.

"Cassie?" the machine asked. "What is it?"

She realized she'd forgotten to speak. In her panic, she had forgotten neither Braemar nor Holland even knew that the machine—that *Marcus*—existed. And that was something she could use to her advantage.

"Listen carefully," she said, speaking fast and low. Sweat beaded on her brow, the air inside her suit much, much too warm and close. "I need you to do exactly what I say."

"If she keeps hitting Evan with that taser, he's going to—!"

"Marcus!" she almost shouted his name. "I said *focus*."

The machine—no, *he*—fell silent, and she quickly explained what she wanted it to do.

As soon as she'd finished, Cassie unplugged from the comms port, then deactivated a looping voice alert that kept reminding her exactly how little air she had left.

Upper body tilted forward, legs pushing as hard as she could, Cassie next headed for the station's reactor, praying Braemar hadn't had the foresight or the opportunity to override Cassie's access privileges.

When Cassie plugged the same cable she'd used to communicate with Marcus into the reactor's outer shell, she felt a surge of hope when she found out she could still interface with it. Working as fast as she could, she navigated through menus until she found what she needed.

Here goes nothing, she thought, and triggered a station-wide emergency shutdown.

Turning, she saw the few lights dotted around the station's exterior go dark. She'd already turned off her suit's lights.

Everything else was up to Marcus.

———

Her HUD told her she had seventeen minutes of air left.

Then sixteen. Then fifteen.

Come on, come on. Every muscle in Cassie's body felt rigid as steel. How much longer was Braemar going to take? Or had she found Marcus?

Light flared against Nemo's hull, and the sight was enough to make Cassie cry out with relief. The light, she saw, came from the behemoth suit that had still been attached to the station on her arrival.

The behemoth detached from the side of the station and was lowered down to the seabed by a mechanized hoist. A dark cloud of sediment bloomed around the behemoth as the hoist cradle dropped onto the ocean floor.

Braemar—for it could be no one else inside the suit—headed straight for Cassie's mini-sub.

Cassie had ducked around the far side of the reactor once the other behemoth detached from the station. She watched as Braemar docked her behemoth with the sub.

Meanwhile, and just as she'd hoped, the second mini-sub —the one Braemar had piloted down from the borehole station—*also* separated from Nemo.

This time, however, it was piloted by Marcus.

As Marcus guided the sub towards the shelf, Cassie's hands balled into fists inside her suit's powerful gloves. Had Braemar noticed her sub had been stolen? Would she take the bait and give chase, or try to come after Cassie instead? Or—?

Cassie's sub, now piloted by Braemar, rose in a boiling cloud of sediment and gave chase to Marcus in the second sub.

Triumph flooding her nerve-endings, Cassie moved out from the cover of the reactor and hurried towards the station. The hoist mechanism still sat on the seabed beneath the station. Cassie lumbered towards it with all the speed she could muster.

Halfway there, the expanse of rock and sediment between her and Nemo brightened unexpectedly. Turning, Cassie saw lights coming towards her, bright enough to almost over-whelm her suit's sensors. After a moment, they recalibrated to show the distinctive outline of a mini-sub moving towards her at speed.

A scream stalled halfway up Cassie's throat. Somehow Braemar had guessed at her ruse. Most likely, Cassie realized in a daze, Braemar had used infrared to detect her heat signature next to the reactor.

In all her panic, she'd forgotten about that possibility. But really, there were a hundred different ways Braemar could have figured it out.

And Braemar, Cassie knew by now, was paranoid enough

to anticipate every eventuality. Especially down here, without Holland to back her up.

Cassie turned and ran under the station, desperately seeking the shelter of one of the anchored legs. Her silhouetted outline started out long, but rapidly grew shorter, the water churning around her.

Instinct drove Cassie to throw herself flat just as the sub caught up with her. Servos whined in protest and more alarms flashed up in her HUD as the sub went sailing over her and missed her by scant millimetres.

Ten minutes of air left. Less, if she had to keep running and dodging. Even the slightest damage to her suit could kill her in a microsecond.

Somehow, Cassie found the willpower to push herself back upright. The clouds of silt cleared enough for her to see the sub veering wildly as Braemar struggled to avoid colliding with one of the station's legs.

Then, with an effort of will she hadn't been sure she could summon up, Cassie got moving again, no longer caring whether or not Braemar saw her. With her time running out so fast, all that was left to do was make a break for it.

Instinct drove her back towards the reactor. Braemar's sub meanwhile veered around the far side of the station, clearly intent on circling back around for her.

Cassie checked her remaining air and power and then wished she hadn't.

Light flared from far away. Off in the distance, Cassie saw the lights of the other sub—*her* sub, the one Marcus had used in an attempt to lure Braemar far from the station—as it rose back up from the abyss.

The lights came closer, and closer, and Cassie realized Marcus must be pushing it as fast as he could. Braemar's sub, meanwhile, had halted in its progress, meaning she was aware of the second sub's approach.

Marcus came straight towards her at near-ramming speed.

Silt boiled up around Braemar's sub as she slammed it into reverse, seeking the shelter of the station's legs.

Marcus swept past her—missing, it looked to Cassie, by only a metre or two.

Move. Cassie had come to a halt halfway to the reactor. Now she turned back, seeing she had a clear, if temporary, route back to the cradle.

As soon as she reached it, she backed into the cradle until the magnetic locks engaged with her suit, then hit the switch to carry her back up to the airlocks.

Nothing happened.

A wild keening pushed up from deep inside Cassie's throat. She punched the switch again. And again.

A sub reappeared from out of the clouded waters and drove straight towards her. Cassie struggled loose of the magnetic restraints and took a few steps forward before, again, throwing herself flat.

More alerts flared in her HUD. But where was Marcus? What—?

For now, she could see the lights of only one submersible. Which one, she had no way of telling.

The light from the sub moved through the great clouds of silt that now obscured much of the undersea base. Staring up at the great bulk of the station, her HUD crowded with flashing warnings, Cassie came to a sudden realisation.

I'm not going to make it.

The light found her.

Some part of Cassie knew that whether she stood or ran made no difference: her tanks were as close to empty as they could be. If she stood still, and Braemar was genuinely crazy enough to ram her, it might kill them both. If she could take Braemar with her…

But instinct was a powerful thing. And almost before she knew it, Cassie was running. Not towards, but away from the station.

Brian has this insane idea how to keep us alive.

An idea had been running through the back of her mind ever since she'd watched the video of Chastain, and especially since she'd seen the bodies by the hydrothermal vent. Something that seemed too outrageous to possibly be true.

Light illuminated the seabed all around her, and Cassie knew Braemar was coming for her for the last time. Up ahead, she saw the edge of the shelf, and beyond that—a thirty kilometre drop straight down.

There was barely enough power left for Cassie to power up her suit's jets, briefly putting distance between her and the pursuing submersible. Suddenly, the edge of the shelf was much closer.

Something slammed into Cassie just as she reached the point where the rock gave way to an abyss of water, and she flailed, a guttural bellow working its way up from deep inside her throat.

Suddenly there was nothing beneath her boots: nothing around her but a void, and the light of the pursuing sub.

Her jets sputtered and gave out. Cassie sank. After several tries, she got just enough juice into the jets to push herself closer to the cliff beneath the shelf. Its surface was uneven and ragged and offered multiple opportunities to hide.

The air tasted warm and close in Cassie's lungs as her suit slammed into the cliff. Reaching out, she grabbed at the rock face, her microphones picking up the faint drumming of debris and gravel sliding past and over her suit. Her boots somehow found purchase.

She turned and looked behind her to see the sub's lights flare brightly as they found her. Not that it mattered anymore —the only thing left to do was to die.

Oh, she'd had a half-assed idea she could try to climb back up, except for the unfortunate fact she'd asphyxiate long before she could walk back to Station Nemo—not forgetting the minor matter of her being locked out.

You win, she thought, staring back at the sub, which hovered motionless in the water. *Go ahead and gloat, you fucking bitch.*

And yet, there was something else out there, beyond the submersible. Something Cassie couldn't quite see, but which was showing up on her thermal imaging.

One very large something, she realized, with just a touch of awe. Big enough, it could only mean her sensors were damaged.

Either that, or she was seeing something impossible.

It first showed up as a radiant blob easily a hundred metres across. Cassie craned her head around inside her helmet, but could see nothing directly.

The sub yawed slightly, perhaps struck by an upwelling of warm water from the vents far below. Cassie could now see a kind of sparkle in the water that seemed familiar.

Then she remembered: the first expedition had seen that same curious sparkle, when they'd witnessed a gigantic jelly-fish spontaneously assemble itself in seconds.

She was seeing the same thing now, with her own two eyes, but on a far, *far* larger scale.

Cassie tried uselessly to press herself deeper into the shallow cleft where she'd taken shelter as the creature became more solid—and more real. Her readouts showed a sudden and temporary increase in pressure. The image on the thermal readout was now a single mass of throbbing orange and yellow, long tentacles reaching out from its centre.

Reaching towards Braemar's sub.

It was getting harder for Cassie to stay awake. A persistent throbbing in her skull made it difficult for her to focus, even with something so incredible for her to witness. She watched as the creature—for it had by now fully assembled itself—wrap Braemar's sub in untold thousands of fine, filament-like tentacles.

It all happened in seconds. Cassie gaped as the sub

suddenly surged forward, as if trying to ram the very spot where Cassie was hiding.

No, she realized: Braemar wasn't trying to kill her—she was attempting to pull the sub free of the creature.

The great bell of the newly formed benthocodon pulsed softly, lit almost from within by the sub's searchlights. The vessel skewed from side to side, suggesting Braemar was still trying to get free.

Then Cassie's microphones picked up a terrible, tortuous sound; a deep, almost animal-like groan.

One of the sub's lights suddenly went out, and she realized she was hearing the submersible's hull being placed under extreme pressure.

And then the sub imploded.

It happened with such speed that Cassie didn't at first realize what had happened. First Braemar's sub was there, just metres away, and then came an explosion of bubbles and a crashing boom that punched Cassie further into the narrow crevice where she hid.

And then, where the sub had been, she saw only a wrecked and flattened thing spinning down into the depths. A trail of bubbles came rushing up and past her.

Already, the creature that had destroyed the submarine had become blurred around its edges. Its bell pulsed gently, then faded, coming apart as the individual organisms that made up the whole went their separate ways.

Cassie's lungs snatched at air that contained little oxygen.

And yet she lived.

By any rights—if her DNA had been unmodified—she would already be dead. Counting her heartbeats, she found they were down to barely a dozen a minute: the benefit of gene sequences derived from South Asian divers able to hold their breath for tens of minutes without surfacing.

She remembered, then, scaring the shit out of Tingshao by staying at the bottom of a municipal pool for over fifteen minutes. While his own DNA had been optimized just us much as hers, it hadn't been graced with *that* particular tweak.

With an effort, Cassie tried to move, but her suit was out of juice. And with no power, she'd be trying to move a suit that weighed nearly a quarter of a ton back on Earth.

So this really is it, she realized. Something must have happened to Marcus. Either the sub he'd been piloting had been damaged, or it—and he, along with it—had been destroyed. And while he didn't need to breathe, neither was his makeshift robot body designed for such enormous pressures.

And Evan Harrow? Dead, surely, at Braemar's hands.

And that meant she was all alone down here.

She almost laughed when the surrounding rocks brightened. Wasn't this what it was supposed to be like when you died? A tunnel of light—or maybe it was nothing more than the circuitry in her brain blowing as oxygen deprivation took its toll.

Or—

Wait. She wasn't imagining it.

There really was light coming from above.

Marcus. It had to be him.

A yearning, urgent need to live overtook Cassie. Why had she been so stupid as to treat him like he wasn't alive? Like he wasn't anything more than a machine?

No, he still wasn't the same Marcus she'd been engaged to —that man was long gone—but this other Marcus, the one that shared his memories and instincts, was as real as she was.

Her chest heaved as her lungs tried to draw in air that was no longer there.

The lights came closer, and at last she saw they had an unexpected source. Not Marcus, but another behemoth—the same one that had led her a merry dance through forests of kelp. It gripped the cliff face next to her, and she watched as whoever was inside found themselves a foothold next to her.

The behemoth looked as if it had been wandering the depths of Europa's oceans for a thousand years. Rust and grime streaked its outer shell, which appeared as battered and scarred as some long-drowned warship.

It also had a cable looped around one heavily armoured shoulder. She recognized it as the same type she'd used to reconnect Nemo's nuclear generator.

The rogue behemoth slid the cable from around its shoulder and looped it under and around the armpits and crotch of Cassie's suit. Once she understood what it was doing, Cassie fought to stay awake. She gripped a rock outcropping and turned, so her rescuer could knot the cable behind her back, then carefully loop the other end around its gloves and arms.

This done, the rogue wrapped its metal-shod arms around Cassie's behemoth, and she gasped as she was suddenly yanked upwards. Mud and ancient dirt billowed up from the other behemoth's jets.

They span wildly as they ascended. Cassie had one brief glimpse of Station Nemo before her thoughts were swallowed up by a black tide as wide and deep as all the seas of Europa.

CHAPTER 30

THE INCIDENT

Again, Cassie dreamed.

She floated at the bottom of an abyss, balanced between eternal heat and unending ice, her head tipped back to stare up into infinite blackness.

But she was not alone: there were others like her, and close by. She sensed rather than saw them, as they, in turn, sensed her.

Together they dreamed without end: of other worlds, other stars, other beings. Most of these creatures were themselves now only memories, their bodies and homes long since turned to dust. Dust that, one day, would become fuel for other, newer stars.

She and the others who floated there at the bottom of the abyss had once had names. Whatever hers had been was long forgotten. Names meant nothing when you could reach out through the synapses and sinews of the world, and into the cold divide between stars to touch the long-dead memories of distant worlds.

Then she sensed one mind in particular, separate from all the rest. And with it, for the first time in a seeming aeon, a name.

Chris.

And with that name came another memory: of clutching a dinosaur backpack tightly against her chest, while she squeezed her tiny, frail body into the space between a desk and an art supplies cupboard.

Bright light spilled in through a classroom window. A tree outside, next to the playground, cast shadows against a wall poster explaining what a genetic sequence was.

Through the forest of desks and chair legs, Cassie saw Mrs Appleton, her math teacher, lying on the floor of the corridor outside the classroom. She lay curled up, as if she had simply decided to lie down then and there and go to sleep.

Blood pooled beneath Mrs Appleton's body, the scent iron and sickly. From further down the corridor came the sound of screams and the occasional gunshot.

An eternity passed, filled only with the thud of Cassie's heart as she tried not to breathe.

Then someone stepped in through the classroom door, wearing camouflage. Cassie could see only their legs from where she hid. Their boots were paint-spattered, like they'd been in the middle of doing some home decoration.

The legs stopped, then took another step, and when she lowered her head a little, Cassie could see their owner: a man carrying a rifle, his hair shorn tight against his skull. Odd, geometric tattoos on his cheeks and neck glistened beneath the overhead lights.

The gunman swung his rifle first one way, and then the other, and then he saw Cassie in her hiding place.

As if drawn towards her by some arcane magic, the barrel of his rifle swung towards her.

"Hey! Cocksucker! Come out here, you fucking asshole!"

Chris. Cassie would know her brother's voice anywhere. Her heart froze in her chest: he sounded like he was right outside the classroom.

The gunman turned away, immediately forgetting about Cassie and stepping back into the corridor. Then came a sound like all the thunderclaps Cassie had ever heard, but squeezed together into one, thunderous boom: a sound that somehow became a scream, one she realized only later had come from her own throat.

"I said over here, asshole!" Chris shouted. He sounded a little further away now. "C'mon, come and get me!"

His voice diminished further, as if he were running back down the corridor and around the corner towards the front entrance of the school.

The gunman's boots retreated from the classroom as he gave chase. Cassie remained where she was, paralysed, not caring about the pins and needles from staying so still for so very long.

Then a shadow bent low over her, and she gasped in fright before she saw who it was.

"You're okay?" Chris asked, reaching down to help Cassie stand.

She stood with difficulty, her legs cramped and her heart still pumping furiously. Except...

Something was different. The Chris who stood before her was older now. In fact, he was the same age he'd been—

For a moment, she had to squeeze her eyes shut against the onslaught of memories. This was Chris, as he'd been the week before going into pre-launch quarantine. Not the teenager who'd saved her life from an Opt-hating madman.

"Where is he?" she asked, almost tumbling over her own words. She wasn't small any more: not a child. They stood face to face, his hands clutching her upper arms, and she remembered the warm, close smell of the inside of her behemoth. "Is he—?"

"He ran straight past me," Chris reassured her. "Didn't even see me."

But of course, she remembered now: he'd told her this story himself, in the days following the shooting. There had been seven dead, including two teachers.

Very nearly eight, if not for Chris.

"I'm sorry," she said, then shook her head. This was confusing. All terribly confusing. The school furniture looked so small, it made her feel like a giant.

Chris cocked his head, his expression quizzical. The school was oddly silent; gone was the whoop of police sirens, along with the shouts and screams of students and arriving parents.

"Sorry for what?"

"I thought I could save you." She realized tears were cascading down her face. "I know it's stupid, but I thought somehow if I could get here on time, and then I saw the video of someone on the ice and I thought maybe you were still alive…"

"It's okay." Her brother pulled her closer until her face was pressed into her chest. "I'm right here."

Then she had a flash of him tangled in kelp-like growths at the bottom of an abyssal ocean. His eyes, empty as they were, somehow still saw her. His fingers, blue-white and encrusted with lichens, reached out to touch her cheek.

Then she was swimming through deep green waters. Shafts of moonlight pierced the waves. She had a long, undulating body like that of an eel. Overhead, just visible through the ocean waves, she saw the great spiral of a galaxy filling half the sky.

Alive.

She knew it without a flicker of doubt. Europa was *alive*.

Then she woke to a harsh chemical stench, and hard, unyielding metal beneath her cheek.

Her lungs felt bruised and raw, her every ragged breath full of pain.

She was inside a secondary airlock, the interior of her behemoth visible through an open hatch. Somehow, she'd got herself back to the winch and inside Station Nemo—not that she remembered a damn thing about it.

Or had she? It was all so confusing.

"Cassie? Are you all right? Will you please respond?"

Marcus.

His voice came through a comms panel mounted on the airlock wall. Cassie thumped a button on the panel with her fist.

"I'm here," she gasped, then fell into a coughing fit for most of a minute before she could continue. "What happened out there?"

"Braemar rammed me with her sub," Marcus said hurriedly. "Disabled one of my engines, then went chasing after you. The sub started yelling I had to return immediately to the station, but I didn't want to. I was afraid that maybe—"

"Marcus," she said, her voice soft and ragged. "Shut up."

He fell silent for a moment. Then: "What you were saying before. What did you mean?"

Saying before?

"I don't understand."

"You kept saying it was alive. What was?"

It came back to her then: the ancient, scarred behemoth, the cable wrapped under her arms as it dragged her back up to safety. It must have carried her the whole way back.

Instead of answering, she reached up and hit the airlock release. There were some things she wasn't ready to talk about. Not yet, anyway.

The inner airlock door swung open, bringing with it the scent of blood mixed with the odour of sweat.

Not good, she thought, steadying herself against the rim of the door with one hand. *Not good at all.*

Evan Harrow lay on the floor next to a chair, Marcus squatting next to him on ungainly and spindly legs. He was clumsily wielding a knife with a couple of manipulators and trying to sever a computer cord that had been looped and knotted around the oceanologist's wrists. Harrow's face was a mask of blood.

And yet, Cassie felt relieved to see the rise and fall of his chest.

"Move," said Cassie, yanking the knife from the machine's grasp and hurriedly slicing through the cable.

Harrow groaned, and she saw how badly bruised and cut his face was. What the hell had Braemar *done* to him?

When she tried to help him upright, Harrow first drew in a sharp breath, then turned away and vomited noisily onto the floor.

"Braemar?" he managed to mumble.

"Dead," Cassie replied without elaboration. All that could come later.

He nodded and coughed. "Good. Med kit?"

"Over here," said Marcus.

Cassie saw the kit on the floor where Marcus had dropped it. She snatched it up and pulled it open.

"Going to have to clean you up first," she told Harrow. "I'm just glad you're alive."

He gave her the faintest of nods. "Said she wasn't done with me." His voice sounded odd, soft around the edges, almost like a lisp.

"Hey," said Cassie. "You don't need to talk right—"

"No," he said, his voice a little stronger now. "I can talk." His hand reached out tentatively to hers. "About Braemar: she looked like she'd been in a fight. A bad one."

Cassie nodded, not daring to hope Lebed or Haunani might still be alive. "What about Holland?"

"I overheard Evan asking where Holland was," said Marcus, sparing the injured oceanologist the effort of speaking. "She said he was a problem she'd taken care of."

Huh. "And she didn't elaborate?"

"The way she said it, it sounded like she meant he was dead. Then she—"

Harrow coughed and then grimaced, exposing his teeth. Cassie drew in a sharp breath when she saw them: Braemar must have worked him over with a pair of pliers.

"We need to get you back up to the Veles," she said, a chill spreading through her guts at the sight of his ruined mouth. "You need real medical attention." She turned to look at Marcus. "We need to prep the sub for the return journey. Is that possible?"

He probably needed surgery, assuming Doctor Haunani was still alive—which, judging by the evidence so far, seemed doubtful.

"I'm not sure it is," said Marcus. "Not after the way it got slammed about. I got more than a few integrity warnings."

Fuck. "How long to fix it?"

The machine was silent long enough that Cassie felt a growing sense of dread.

"I don't know," it said at last. "I can engineer parts here using the equipment printers, but it could take weeks. And we'd have to go out in suits to do a lot of the work on the hull. It's not like we have a dry dock down here."

The bottom fell out of Cassie's stomach at this news. Working repairs on a sub at this depth was about as hard and desperate as it got.

"If that's the good news," she said, "I don't want to hear the bad."

"What about Braemar's sub?" Marcus asked. "What happened to it?"

"It was destroyed," Cassie said automatically. "By…something."

"…something?"

She tried her best to explain what she'd seen: a monstrously huge benthocodon, forming out of nothing and attacking Braemar's submersible. Then the sudden appearance of the rogue behemoth suit, and how it had dragged her back to the station.

"That's…quite a story," Marcus said at last.

"I know I must sound like I've completely lost my mind."

"No," Marcus said thoughtfully. "No, what strikes me is that these two things happened at the same time. Braemar being attacked by this creature, and you being rescued by whomever was inside the behemoth." He shifted slightly on his spidery legs. "As if they were connected, somehow."

She regarded Marcus—far more than just a machine to her now—with tired eyes. In truth, the same thought had occurred to her.

"What are you suggesting?" she asked.

"Honestly," Marcus replied, "I'm not sure." After a pause, he added: "Then there's the question of who brought you back here."

"Risuke," she said immediately. "It can't be anyone else."

Marcus' cameras whined faintly as they changed focus, zooming in on her. "You sound very sure."

"The only thing I'm really sure of," she said, "is that it wasn't Chris. Or anyone else from the first Europa Deep expedition."

"Did you…find him?"

She knew he meant whether she had discovered his body near the hydrothermal vents. "Kind of," she said after a moment.

"'Kind of'?"

How to even try to explain?

Instead of trying, Cassie knelt down to grasp Harrow under his shoulders, seeing he'd passed out. "We need to move him," she said. "We can put him in one of the cots."

"Is he conscious?"

Cassie shook her head. "I think he's gone into shock."

———

OVER THE NEXT FEW DAYS, Cassie kept Harrow pumped full of the few sedatives she'd been able to dredge up from the station's meagre medical supplies.

After getting him comfortable, she had slept for nearly sixteen hours while Marcus watched over the injured oceanologist. It seemed a mercy that she did not dream.

It was not until late on the second night that Marcus awoke her with the news that another mini-sub—the same one, she presumed, she had chased around the vents—had docked with the station.

"It's him," the AI announced with unbridled enthusiasm. "It's Hayashi Risuke—he's requesting permission to board!"

Still befuddled from lack of sleep, Cassie quickly checked on Harrow and found him mumbling quietly as he slumbered. Then she swallowed down half a mug of thick and tarry instant coffee. It left her tongue and the back of her throat feeling like they were coated in gravel.

When the airlock door swung open to reveal the empty interior of the newly arrived sub, it smelled dusty and not a little mouldy.

Making her way through and inside the sub on hands and knees, Cassie saw that the sub's secondary airlock was green, indicating that a behemoth suit was mounted to its hull. And crouched on the pilot's seat was something that looked not unlike an avant garde sculpture of a crab built from scrap metal and plastic. It even had pincers.

Its cameras swivelled to regard her.

"Miss White," the AI said to her with a distinct Okinawan accent. "A delight to meet you. My name is—"

"Hayashi Risuke," she said. "Marcus told me all about you."

It waved a pincer-thing at the primary airlock door behind her, and beyond which lay Station Nemo. "May I?"

Cassie nodded wordlessly. The AI dropped out of the pilot's seat and lumbered past her towards the airlock.

"Wait," she said, as Risuke prepared to enter the station. "How did you know my name?"

It paused, its cameras again swivelling towards her.

"Why," it said, "your brother told me."

CHAPTER 31
HAYASHI RISUKE

"Eat this," Cassie said a short while later, handing Harrow a bowl of tepid chicken soup with a straw sticking out of it.

It had been several hours since Risuke's arrival. It was touch and go whether Harrow could even eat in his current state, but Cassie didn't know what else to do for him while the two machines bickered over their preparations aboard Risuke's sub.

Harrow looked like he might argue, then begrudgingly did as she asked. He coughed hard after the first sip, but then ate more than she had expected him to.

"Christ," he said, letting his head fall back onto the pillow. "Tastes disgusting."

It was still hard for him to talk with so many broken teeth, and his words slurred as he spoke, but it was getting easier for her to interpret his halting, broken speech.

"It's been down here for years. Of course it tastes disgusting." She pushed the bowl onto a nearby shelf. "How do you feel?"

"Like I got hit by a train." He shifted slightly and winced. "Several trains."

"Try not to move too much," she suggested.

"I'll have to move anyway when we leave," he said, then

looked as if something had just occurred to him. "We can't all fit inside the sub, can we…?"

Cassie shook her head. "We'll strap you into the pilot's seat. Risuke will pilot us up. I'd do it myself, but he's made a lot of modifications I don't understand. I'll ride up inside the behemoth instead, attached to the hull."

She saw his surprise. "Is it safe for you to do that?"

"It's not recommended, no." She shrugged. "But these aren't normal circumstances."

Harrow glanced at the soup bowl on the shelf where she'd left it and grimaced. "So when do we leave?"

———

WHEN CASSIE WENT in search of the two AIs, she found they had returned from the sub and were now convened at a table close by the kitchenette. Dropping heavily into a chair across from them, she let her head and arms fall back, the rear of the chair pressing into the back of her lower neck.

"How is he?" Marcus asked.

"I gave him a sedative for the pain," she said, slowly bringing her head back up. "It'll help him sleep. But…"

"But?" Risuke's cameras whirred faintly.

Cassie sat up more straight, smoothing her hands across her face and through her hair. "I think he'll probably have to spend the entire trip home in cryo."

"I thought it might come to that," said Marcus.

Cassie focused on him. "I could hear the two of you arguing inside the sub, you know that?"

"We weren't arguing," Risuke countered. "But my submersible hasn't had to carry passengers in years."

"Which is why," said Marcus, "I wanted to run extra checks. Anyway, we're ready to go if you can help get Evan inside."

Cassie nodded, then tapped a finger on the table, thinking. "There's something I need to know first, Hayashi."

"About your brother?"

Her next words seemed to fail her, so she just nodded instead.

"He's close by," Risuke confirmed. "I...avoided you at first, not knowing precisely who you were. That was to protect both him and the others."

She leaned forward, both arms on the table. "All of them are down there? The rest of the crew, as well as Chris?"

"There is much to discuss, Miss White," the machine said with care. "But rest assured, your every question will be answered when the time comes."

———

HALF A DAY LATER, having docked with the borehole station back up on the surface, they soon found signs of violence. There were streaks of dried blood in the cockpit of their crawler, and when they drove it back out onto the surface of Europa, they found Lebed, wearing nothing more than his mission jumpsuit, sprawled on the ice immediately outside the station's primary airlock.

His flash-frozen expression registered disbelief, a single, thin trail of blood reaching down from one ear. His wrists had been secured behind his back with plastic ties.

"I suppose," Risuke said into the silence that followed, "it's not hard to guess what happened here."

Cassie nodded, not wanting to say anything. She sat behind the controls of the crawler and looked out at the pilot's crumpled body, her stomach twisted into a tight, sour knot.

From behind her, she heard Harrow mumble something. They'd stretched him out on the crawler's rear deck, but it was almost impossible to get him really comfortable. Ever since they'd loaded him into the sub, he'd been slipping in and out of consciousness.

She found herself wishing she could have seen Braemar's face in those last few seconds of her life, when she must have known she was about to die.

"Why not kill him back at Station Verne?" asked Marcus. "Why bring him all the way out here?"

"Leverage," said Cassie.

"Come again?"

She glanced at the AI—at him. "If she'd found us at the borehole station, she'd have used Lebed to force us to do whatever she wanted. When she found we'd already gone down, she decided it was easier to kill him rather than take him with her."

The answer was that simple, and that monstrous. She tried hard not to think what his last seconds must have been like, trapped inside that airlock and waiting for the doors to open.

Swallowing back a surge of bile, she looked away, the blood drumming in both temples.

And there was still the question of what, precisely, had occurred between Braemar and Holland.

————

THE WHOLE LONG trip back across the ice to Station Verne, Cassie could feel the dread building up inside her like dark clouds on a distant horizon. The dread lessened only slightly when they picked up an ident signal from their own lander, revealing it had landed close to Verne.

And that meant they could get back to the Veles.

Once they docked with Station Verne, Cassie volunteered to be first through the airlock. While she waited for the light to change, she stood before the door with a wrench grasped tight in one hand.

Except Holland wasn't waiting for her. Instead, there were more streaks of blood on the inner airlock's control panel.

Moving with extreme caution, the wrench held out before her, Cassie made her way into the station's main living area.

Empty.

Behind her, she heard the faint, metallic clatter of the two AIs as they followed her inside, peering around with their cameras.

"Did you notice," said Marcus, "that one of the emergency spacesuits is missing?"

Frowning, Cassie stepped back through, seeing an empty space on the rack next to the airlock. The suits were for emergencies like blowouts—not surviving out on the surface of Europa. That required a behemoth suit at a minimum.

He couldn't possibly have gone out there. Could he?

There wasn't time to think further on this: first, she had to move Harrow out of the crawler and into one of the station's cots. He looked even paler than before, his skin clammy and cold to the touch. He seemed barely aware of where he was.

Cassie couldn't remember ever feeling so helpless as she did just then. Whatever damage Braemar had done to the oceanologist, it was far outside of her ability to treat it. They needed Doctor Haunani, but he, she now felt sure, was dead.

She went looking for Marcus. "Are any of the behemoth suits missing?" she asked.

"They're all present," the AI replied. "But someone did a very good job of junking them. Their heuristic routines are scrambled beyond recognition."

Braemar probably had the skills for something like that, Cassie figured. It took a certain kind of mind, she thought, to be quite so thorough.

"You thought maybe Holland took one of them?" Marcus asked.

She nodded and sat on the edge of a couch. "Let's think this through," she said. "The two of them landed here, then had some kind of disagreement. Holland came out of it worse. But why leave him alive?"

"Maybe she only thought he was dead," Marcus suggested. "But he survived."

"How do you figure that?" she asked.

"Because it's the only thing I can think of that makes sense."

"Fine," said Cassie. "So say, for the sake of argument, that he and Braemar, for whatever reason, tried to kill each other. Once she was gone, he took one of the spacesuits and tried to make his way back to the lander."

"No way," said Marcus. "He couldn't possibly survive the radiation out there in a standard suit."

She did some mental calculations. "Not for long, no, but don't be so sure about his chances. The surface radiation isn't constant. It gets much lower when Europa passes through Jupiter's magnetotail, which happens every couple of days."

Marcus' cameras whirred. "And he'd have known that?"

Cassie shrugged. "Maybe."

She could tell from his voice he didn't believe it was at all possible. And, in truth, she was far from sure it was. Certainly, nobody had been crazy enough to try.

She stood, feeling a sudden urgency.

Marcus' cameras moved to follow her. "Where are you going?"

"If the only place he could be going is the lander," she said, "we need to go out there and make sure it's safe."

"But it's still there," Marcus pointed out. "If he'd reached it, he'd be long gone by now."

"Let's not take any chances," she said, and made her way back through to the crawler.

———

FOR ALL HER WORRY, Cassie wasn't surprised when she spotted a figure in a spacesuit slumped on the ice midway between Verne and the lander.

Marcus remained at the crawler's controls while Cassie used Risuke's behemoth suit to investigate. Holland's head lifted slightly as she approached, but she didn't feel in any danger. She already had a pretty good idea of what she would find.

Holland's face was invisible behind his visor. How many hours had he been out here, she wondered? How many sieverts of radiation had his body absorbed by now?

Cassie glanced up, imagining she could see the high-energy ions that constantly rained down on Europa.

The servos inside Cassie's suit whined faintly as she lifted Holland in both arms, like a mother scooping up a child. By the time she returned to the crawler, Marcus had already opened the rear cargo airlock so she could lift him inside.

Once she'd cycled back inside the crawler, she placed Holland on a fold-down seat and removed his helmet. He looked even worse than she'd imagined. His skin was ashen and patterned with discoloured blotches, like raw meat left out in the sun for days, his cheeks coated with a damp sheen of perspiration.

His eyes opened into thin slits, and he looked at her.

"You're alive," he said in a thin croak. His eyes moved like he couldn't quite focus on her.

To Cassie's surprise, he paid no attention to the robotic AI beside her, its camera lenses whining faintly as they focused on him.

"No thanks to you," said Cassie. "What were you doing out here?"

"Trying to get to the lander," he said, and chuckled. "Almost made it." His gaze registered alarm. "Alex?"

Cassie frowned. "Who?"

"Sorry," said Holland. "I meant Sally. Did you kill her?"

Cassie nodded, declining to elaborate. She had little desire to explain how Braemar had met her end.

Holland took this news with no visible reaction. He slumped on one side, and she had to reach out and catch him before he slid off the fold-down seat.

"What happened between you and Sally, Jeff?" *Or whatever your real first name is.*

Pain flickered across Holland's face. "She left me for dead."

"Why?"

Holland summoned what little strength remained in his body to bring his head back up. "Playing both sides."

Cassie exchanged a look with Marcus.

"I think he means like a double agent," he said quietly.

"And you?" Cassie asked Holland. "Who were you working for?"

The look he gave her implied this was the dumbest question she could possibly ask. "No idea," he said.

Unable to hide her confusion, Cassie's mouth worked for a moment. "Then why—?"

"It's business." He made a sound that might have been a gasp of pain or a chuckle. "You never get told, you never ask." He swallowed. "A better question is, who were *you* working for? Because you sure as hell weren't supposed to be on the Veles."

She thought about this for a moment. "Right now," she said at last, "I'm just working for myself."

Holland held her gaze for a moment longer, then leaned his head back and closed his eyes.

"Your doctor's still alive," he said. "Locked himself inside the radiation shelter."

If she hadn't already been sitting down next to Holland at that moment, Cassie might have collapsed with relief. "All this was for what?" she demanded, her anger rising. "Why—?"

Holland didn't answer. His head tipped slowly forward until his chin rested against his chest.

"Is he dead?" Marcus asked.

"I don't think so." Cassie touched the side of the man's neck. "There's still a pulse."

"So what do we do with him?"

Shove him back out the airlock, she almost said, knowing that no matter how much she wanted to, she never could.

"No idea," she muttered. "How long do you think he'll last?"

One of Marcus' legs twitched in his version of a shrug. "If Haunani was here, he could—"

Marcus halted, his cameras swivelling towards the front of the crawler.

"Look," he said.

At first, Cassie didn't know what he meant. Then she saw it through the windscreen: a single bright point of light dropping towards the ice of Europa.

CHAPTER 32
THE TIANJIN

The Tianjin's lander touched down seven klicks south-east of Station Verne. Cassie watched it descend the entire way before disappearing behind tall daggers of ice. It was, she knew, only a matter of time before whoever was inside came calling.

In the meantime, Cassie and Marcus drove the rest of the way to the Europa Lander with Holland slumped, comatose, in the rear. Once there, Cassie went through the laborious process of getting back inside the behemoth and docking with the lander. Once inside, she was able to confirm the lander was operational and had sufficient fuel to reach orbit.

They got back to Station Verne before the delegation from the Tianjin arrived, but only barely. Soon, an unfamiliar crawler with the flag of the New Chinese Republic emblazoned on either side arrived, requesting permission to come inside.

Cassie had already known Tingshao was part of the Tianjin's crew. But she hadn't guessed he would be the one in charge.

———

"I JUST SPOKE to our medics up on the Tianjin," Tingshao told her most of a day later. "They've stabilized both Holland and Harrow. Harrow seems to have the better chance, though they agree his recovery is likely to take some time."

Cassie stared blearily at the man with whom she had last spoken while sitting in a kid's play park in Taipei. They sat facing each other next to the kitchenette's counter. Two of Tingshao's companions, a short, stout man with a haggard expression and a bright-eyed woman with a strong Beijing accent, were meanwhile in deep conversation with Risuke, the man occasionally gesturing at an image on a console next to them.

"Just how bad is he?" she asked. "Evan, I mean."

"They tell me he's badly concussed, with a possible intracranial haemorrhage. Any more than that I can't say, because I'm not a doctor. But you're welcome to talk to one of our medical staff over our comms."

Cassie let out a long, slow breath. "All I really need to know is if he'll recover." She'd watched with a heavy heart as two of the Tianjin's medics had sealed both injured men inside coffin-like medevac units for transportation to the Tianjin.

"Our medical bay is equipped with the best possible medical technology," he assured her. "I'd say his chances are excellent, but again, it's going to take time. I've been given to understand Doctor Haunani was quite impressed by our facilities."

Albert had been freed from his self-imposed confinement on board the Veles and was currently on board the Tianjin at the invitation of its rebel crew. He'd sounded a little worse for wear when Cassie had spoken to him over the comms, but in decent spirits.

"Anyway," said Tingshao, folding his hands on his lap and looking directly at Cassie. "I suppose you want to know more about the other thing."

"Seizing the Tianjin and killing your command crew—was that all part of a plan?"

Tingshao's mouth twisted up in distaste. "We didn't want to kill anybody. Commander Hu and his two lieutenants, unfortunately, forced our hand when they pushed one of us out of the airlock."

"But how long were you planning all this? This...rebellion, or whatever it is?"

"Ever since myself and certain of my fellow Opts in the NCR learned the Tianjin was to be sent to Jupiter." He smiled at the look on her face. "Yes, long before you were approached to join the crew of the Veles."

"You should have told me," she said, a touch of bitterness in her voice.

"The less you knew, Cassie, the better." He shifted in his seat. "It's getting very bad for people like us back there," he added. "For a while we were accepted in the NCR, but not anymore."

"Right after the UN banned Opts from working in space, you told me you'd been offered a chance to work in the NCR's space agency. Do you remember what I said to you at the time?"

She'd never told him how deeply his decision had hurt her, so soon after their relationship had ended. Even when she and Marcus began dating a few months later, the pain had lingered for a long time.

"You told me it was a mistake." He smiled sadly. "You were right, of course. Then again, if I hadn't left for Beijing, I wouldn't have found my way out here." He leaned towards her. "There are detention camps for Opts now. They don't call them that. But that's what they are. And there are rumours of forced sterilisation programs."

"If it's that bad, how come the Tianjin had a mostly Opt crew?"

"Propaganda." He looked tired, she saw—worn-out. "Our

presence here is supposed to be proof that nobody back home is being suppressed. The truth is, they see us as disposable."

Risuke came towards them, his crab-like body low to the ground. Gripping the leg of a chair with one pincer-like limb, he raised himself up into a semi-standing position on his other limbs, then, using a second pincer, pulled himself up and onto the seat. The chair wobbled slightly as he found his balance.

"I'm sure," said Risuke, "the two of you have had a lot to discuss."

"Actually," said Cassie, "the thing I really want to know is how the hell you know each other."

As soon as Tingshao had stepped inside Station Verne, Risuke had greeted him as if they were old friends. Cassie had just stared at them both, speechless.

"Well," said Risuke, "you know I'd been planning an exodus for the likes of myself and Marcus for a long time. But even I was taken by surprise when the tide turned so swiftly against the Optimized. Eventually I came to believe Opts and revenant AIs could work together to our mutual aid." He waved one titanium and carbon pincer at Tingshao. "Strength in numbers, you see. But also, strength in common purpose."

Cassie shifted her gaze back towards Tingshao. "And that common purpose is?"

"People like us," said Tingshao, gesturing to show he meant Cassie, himself and the AI, "are far better equipped for survival in extreme environments than baseline humans. Our future belongs out here. Back there, we face only extinction."

"I can sense your objections," Risuke said to Cassie. "It will be hard, yes. Extraordinarily so, if not impossible. Jovian space is one of the harshest imaginable environments. But Europa, along with several other moons both here and at Saturn, offer resources and building materials that are otherwise unavailable to us."

"Hard doesn't even begin to cut it," she said. "None of you would ever see a blue sky again."

"The real choice," said Risuke, "is between life and imprisonment, if not death. A blue sky is less enticing when only occasionally glimpsed through the bars of a prison cell."

Unable to find a response, Cassie shook her head. "I feel like I've blundered into a situation where I'm the only one who didn't know what was going on the whole time."

Tingshao and Risuke glanced at each other.

"Then we did our job well," said Risuke. "If not for Marcus revealing himself to you, you might never have known."

"On a related subject," said Tingshao, "we should speak further about Mr Holland. He's offered us quite a lot of information since arriving at the Tianjin."

Cassie looked at him with surprise. "He has?"

"He knows his time is limited. We can keep him comfortable, but he has a few days, perhaps a few weeks at most, given the dose he took. However, what he's given us is more than enough to incriminate David Ketteridge."

Cassie stared at him. "Come again?"

"Holland suspected all along you were working for Ketteridge. According to him, prior to recruiting you, Ketteridge had an arrangement with a privately owned bioweapons think tank based out of Moscow. Through some arcane financial sleight of hand, it seems a significant chunk of the funding for the second Europa Deep expedition came from that think tank."

It took a moment for Cassie to absorb this. "According to Marcus, malware supplied to me by Ketteridge was designed to wipe out any evidence of bioweapons research being carried out by members of the first expedition. I came here thinking he wanted me to find that evidence, not destroy it. Why would he do that?"

"My assumption," said Risuke, "is that this think tank had

originally financed Medina and Wojtowicz's illegal research. They would have faced very intensive scrutiny if their involvement were to be uncovered, particularly from the NCR. I believe that you, Cassie, were intended to be the unwitting means by which they would destroy that evidence."

"Holland," Tingshao added, "was sent by parties unknown to retrieve that same information, most likely so it could be used to continue the development of more biological weapons."

"It does seem," said Risuke, seeing Cassie's appalled expression, "as if nobody comes out of this well."

"I don't want to hear any more," Cassie said tiredly. She looked at Risuke. "If we're going to do this, maybe now is the best time."

Risuke's lenses shifted and whirred. "You still wish to go back down?"

"One last time, yes." She found she had unconsciously folded her hands into fists on her lap. "You said you know where I can find him."

"There are," said Risuke, "some other matters I would like to discuss with you. Perhaps we should do so on the way?"

CHAPTER 33

FINAL DESCENT

Adjusting her seat, Cassie spoke quietly to the mini-sub's onboard computer. She felt a slight lurch as it detached from Station Nemo. One of the two AIs crouched on the floor of the sub directly behind her stumbled before righting itself.

Marcus had insisted on joining her and Risuke on the not unreasonable grounds that, after having come this far, he ought to have the opportunity to see Europa's ocean. After all, he had further explained, given what they had so far learned from Risuke, this was not so much a visit to a grave-yard as it was a first contact situation.

"And you really think more people will come here?" Cassie asked over her shoulder. "I mean, other than Opts?"

"I have no doubt," Risuke stated with certainty. "Europa is a treasure beyond imagining. And one that would be exploited, were there no one here to guard it. How much do you know about Brian Hall's research?"

"I told Cassie about his Medusa Net theory," Marcus offered.

"Ah yes," said Risuke. "Much more than mere speculation, of course."

Something about the AI's words made Cassie's skin prickle.

"Since I first arrived at Europa and discovered the fate of the previous expedition, I have been endeavouring to continue Hall's research," Risuke continued. "I collected space-borne extremophiles from Europa's surface and made a close study of them. Their chitinous shells, once in vacuum, flatten out to form a primitive solar sail. This allows them to navigate the solar wind during journeys that last aeons."

"And they carry—" Cassie struggled to get her next words out, given how ridiculous it sounded, "—what?"

"Encoded race memories," said Risuke. "Dreams, if you will. I came to believe that modified DNA, extracted from these extremophiles, can trigger intense and even incapacitating hallucinations in humans."

Cassie drew in a sharp breath, her hands damp where they gripped the sub's controls.

But she needed to know more. *Had* to know more.

"You're talking about the Whispers," she said. She remembered Marcus suggesting the same thing, but she had dismissed it out of hand.

"Indeed. Ice worlds such as Europa are likely to be extremely common throughout the universe. It was Hall's conjecture—and, I believe, a correct one—that throughout the lifespan of the universe these worlds have acted as repositories for the memories of long-vanished races who, having visited those worlds, became infected by the same highly adaptive microorganisms found in Europa's ocean. By now, Cassie, you surely carry a number of such organisms within your body—as did the members of the first expedition. As do, thanks to the Whispers, many millions back on Earth. Enough, perhaps, for fragments of human race memory to have already been absorbed by Europa's gestalt mind."

The sonar reflectors left by the first expedition showed up on Cassie's sonar screen. *Not long to go now.*

"But you don't really believe Europa's somehow alive, do you?"

"Why not?" Risuke countered. "You've been talking to it for years."

"What?" It was getting harder to hide her disbelief.

A rattling sound that might have been laughter emerged from the machine's speakers. "You dream of your brother, do you not? That is how Europa speaks to you. Through him."

"You talk like he's alive," she said. "But I saw the others. They were—"

Dead. Why couldn't she just say it? Why was it so hard?

"Life and death," said Risuke, "are such crude binary terms. Europa, Cassie, challenges everything. Not just science, but our very understanding of what life and death mean. This, I believe, is why Hall deliberately drowned Wojtowicz and Medina following their betrayal. To see if, even after their apparent death, they could still communicate with each other through the Europan microorganisms now infecting all of their bodies. I sense that you have trouble accepting these ideas, and that is only natural. Some things take time to absorb. But consider the evidence of your senses, and of the visions Europa has so far granted you."

Cassie couldn't find an answer, so she remained silent as they dropped closer to the hydrothermal vent, now appearing on the infrared monitors as a patch of brilliant red, yellow, and white.

Then, at last, their sub settled onto the ocean floor, a short distance from the two boulder fields where she'd discovered Medina and all the rest.

"We're at the coordinates you gave me," she said, unbuckling herself. Turning, she looked at the two AIs crouched behind her. "Now show me where he is, Hayashi."

———

CASSIE MAINTAINED communication with the two machines via a cable, trailing out behind her suit once she disengaged from the sub.

"Almost there," Risuke said over the comms. "Another hundred metres."

Behind her, the sub lifted again and moved up behind her before dropping back down. Risuke was at its controls. Cassie waited until it had settled before moving on, checking the cable every minute to make sure it hadn't become snagged on anything.

"I meant to ask you," she said. "The rest of the crew of the Yatagarasu. Where are they?"

"They opted to continue on to Saturn, and then Titan, while I remained here. There, they have ready access to hydrocarbons and pools of liquid water and ice necessary for survival, beneath the surface. They have enough resources to build and maintain a simple colony—and, eventually, defences."

"Defences? Against what?"

"More like us will come. First, a trickle of the very few Opts and revenant AIs able to make the journey. Eventually, more. And we will need to be ready to defend our new home against those who sent the Tianjin and others like them."

Cassie navigated a sudden dip in the terrain, her suit's lights picking out a cluster of kelp just ahead.

"You really think they'll come here again?"

"The Tianjin's purpose was not merely to lay claim to Europa," the AI explained. "Some of my compatriots were captured, and this led to some powerful and dangerous people learning about my survival and, worse, of my intentions. An outer system colony for Opts and AIs represents a challenge not only to the NCR's plans for the solar system, but the plans of other nations as well. And some corporations that are nearly as powerful."

Trudging on, Cassie came to a crevice choked with kelp.

She shone her lights into it, seeing it went down perhaps twelve metres.

"Down there, Miss White," said Risuke. "Be careful as you go."

She used her jets to descend beneath the floor of the ocean, the lights of her bulky armoured suit revealing the base of the crevice another twenty metres down. The kelp made it hard going.

For once, however, she wasn't afraid of what she would find.

Chris and the two remaining members of Europa Deep's crew were gathered close together, their opened behemoth suits wreathed in kelp. They had bypassed the safety limits on their suits so that the helmets came off, despite the terrible pressure.

Time and the ocean had made a ruin of Chris' once delicate features. Without thinking, she reached out to him, forgetting that her hand was encased within a heavy armoured glove.

To touch him—*really* touch him—she would have to join him in death.

You saved me, she thought, salt stinging her eyes. *But I couldn't save you.*

She waited for a sign, any sign, that there was someone alive in there, that Risuke wasn't just some addled old mystic.

Around her, the kelp drifted lazily in the abyssal ocean.

———

TWO DAYS LATER, the Tianjin's lander returned to orbit, then returned within hours with Doctor Haunani on board. Tingshao had remained at Verne with a team of engineers, while Risuke took the sub back down under the ice to continue his research as well as tending to his strange garden.

When he emerged from Station Verne's airlock, Haunani

had one arm in a sling, and a vivid bruise covering one half of his face. Marcus, she learned, had returned to the Veles to assess the damage.

At first, the doctor's expression was grim. Then his mouth twisted up into a grin, and suddenly they were hugging each other like long-lost friends.

"I'm sorry about Anton," he said at last. "And I'm not at all sorry Braemar is dead."

Cassie led him over to a low couch where she had been eating as well as catching up on news and messages from home.

"We shouldn't delay talking about the future," said Tingshao, who joined them from one of the other domes once he learned the crawler had arrived. "About where we go from here."

Cassie nodded, smoothing the skin over her knuckles in a nervous gesture. "I've been thinking about that too," she said. "I'm not going home."

Haunani glanced at Tingshao, then back at Cassie, his expression perplexed. "You want to stay on Europa?"

She shrugged and looked at Tingshao. "Either here or Titan, if you want me. Although, to be honest, I don't know how much use I'd be."

Tingshao's eyes narrowed. "I don't understand."

Her expression was hopeless when she looked at Haunani. "Those treatments you were giving me? They weren't working."

Haunani gave her a concerned look. "I'm pretty sure they were."

"Look," she said, her voice trembling slightly, "I should have told you this before, but I... I was still having tremors. I used to get them before I'd black out."

To her shock—and consternation—Haunani rolled his eyes and laughed.

"Those tremors," said Haunani, "have nothing to do with your treatments or your genetic predisposition to blackouts."

At first, Cassie wasn't sure she'd heard him right. "They don't?"

"You're right," he said, his tone admonishing. "You *should* have told me. But the tremors you're talking about are a known side effect of remaining in cryo for too long."

She stared at him, open-mouthed. "Are you saying there's nothing wrong with me?"

He shrugged amiably. "Give it another couple of months, and they should go away altogether."

A pressure Cassie hadn't even known was there, lifted from her shoulders. She felt almost giddy with relief.

"As for me," said Haunani, "I am sure as shit going back." He nodded at Tingshao. "I'm hitching a ride on the NCR's cargo transport. I'm taking Ernest and Daphne with me, so I can keep an eye on them."

"Why not the Veles?" Cassie asked.

"Actually," said Tingshao, "this might be a good time to tell you that the Veles has already left orbit around Europa under Marcus' command."

Cassie couldn't hide her dismay. "Why didn't he tell me?"

"It seems," Tingshao continued, "that while we were all on our way to Jupiter, a cadre of revenant AIs conspired to get themselves shipped into orbit aboard a decommissioned cargo launcher, then put themselves into a solar orbit. Marcus hopes to rendezvous with the launcher three years from now, but to do so, he had to leave immediately. He's left a message on your wristcomm, I understand." He paused briefly. "And he sends his apologies for not speaking to you personally before he left."

Cassie took the news harder than she'd expected. It felt oddly like losing him all over again.

"I'll read it later," she said, then moved to clean away the detritus of her meal.

"There's something else," said Tingshao, and she paused. "Forgive me, Cassie, but I believe it would be best if you were to return to Earth, along with Doctor Haunani." He offered her a pained smile. "For a little while, at least."

Some heat came into her voice when she next spoke. "Come again?"

"Few back home on Earth really understand what we're doing out here, and why," Tingshao continued, his tone apologetic. "We have no one to advocate for us, or to explain our intentions."

"Advocate?" she repeated.

"If any of us were to go back," Tingshao continued, "we'd face arrest by our own government. Even if we sought asylum with other nations, we could equally be treated as agents of an enemy state. You, by contrast, Cassie, are a neutral party. You can speak for us and explain what we mean to do out here."

They locked gazes long enough for Cassie to realize he was serious.

"But...what would I do or say?" She felt off balance, as if the station and the ice beneath it were gently rocking from side to side. "I'm not remotely qualified to be any kind of spokesperson, Ting."

"It won't be just you," Tingshao explained. "We're going to broadcast our message as well. Tell people what we're doing here at the same time you're back there, to give hope to other Opts."

"They'll hate you," said Cassie. "Not just the NCR. All of them. I can talk all you like, but they'll still see you as an enemy."

"We have no choice," Tingshao insisted. "Once Marcus has made his rendezvous, he intends to return to Earth orbit and, if possible, return here with however many Opts and AIs might wish to join us.'

"But the Veles could only carry a tiny number of them,"

she protested. "My God, Tingshao! Do you know how many Opts there are?"

"Over seven hundred thousand," he agreed. "But I know of a few wealthy Opts working to buy or build their own private space fleets. You can speak to them as well. Get their help on Earth and make sure they don't forget about us out here."

He really means it, she realized. And with that, a sudden, terrifying thought struck her: that there were people back home whose fate might hang on her decision.

But there was, she knew, only one possible answer she could give him.

CHAPTER 34
TWENTY THOUSAND
A.D.

The Explorer's guide was nominally human in their bilateral structure, but their eyes were made from some hard, crystalline material precisely calibrated to Europa's harsh surface conditions. They spoke with the Explorer in a combination of radio and emitted light suitable for the airless environment, guiding him through a forest of bone-white tree-like growths that rose up from the ice.

"What are these?" the Explorer asked, his translucent body pulsing with light as he gestured at the growths. "Do they have some cultural or artistic significance? Because they are quite remarkable."

The guide seemed taken aback, its exterior flashing purple with embarrassment. "I apologise," they said. "I had been told you had previously journeyed here. Perhaps I was misinformed?"

"No," said the Explorer, rotating his machine-body back towards his guide. "I think it's that so much has changed since I *was* last here."

"Oh." The guide thought for a moment, then grew even more perplexed. "But this forest has been here since at least the end of the Interregnum, slightly more than—"

"Seven thousand years ago, yes," the Explorer agreed.

"My last visit here was before all that." *By quite a few millennia, in fact.*

Although the guide had a face, it was nearly impossible to read their emotions. But the way they stood very still and quiet for several seconds suggested they were either taken aback or simply didn't believe him.

"I am old," the Explorer added by way of emphasis. "Very old."

"This place we call Tanis," the guide replied, stumbling slightly over their words, then gestured ahead. "If you would care to follow me?"

They continued on until they reached the end of the pale white forest. Beyond lay a settlement of crystalline buildings separated by narrow, shadowed streets. Jupiter was mostly out of sight on the far side of the tidally locked moon.

Soon they passed through the streets of the town, and the Explorer saw the buildings were, in fact, carved directly out of the ice. Those few others they encountered on the streets, like the guide, mostly walked unclothed. Their alabaster skin was oddly wrinkled and mottled—some adaptive feature, he assumed, necessary to protect them from the intense radiation.

Only once or twice did he spy figures wearing spacesuits or protected by shimmer fields, all clearly visitors from the less-developed inner worlds.

"Might I ask," the guide enquired hesitantly, "what brought you here? I don't mean to pry," they added quickly. "It's just that we get so few visitors of your, well, stature. And when they do visit, it's usually because they have friends or family in the Necropolis. Perhaps…?"

Necropolis. City of the dead. A fitting name. "You surmise correctly. I'm here to visit someone. But before we continue," he added, "I would like to incarnate, if I may."

"Of course." The guide gestured ahead. "We have a facility just over here."

———

IT TOOK ALMOST a full day for the Explorer to incarnate in biological form—enough time for him to reflect on old memories. Once it was done, he opened his eyes to find himself lying inside a tank that still carried the powerful reek of chemicals and flushed nanobots.

He looked down at hands that had the same mottled and wrinkled flesh as the native Europans. His machine body sat quiescent behind a containment field on the other side of the room. He would retrieve it later, once he was done with this temporary body.

Standing, the Explorer—although now he was back in flesh and blood, it felt more appropriate to once again take the name Marcus Junger—flexed his new muscles. Then he stepped outside, his bare feet crunching across ice streaked with sediment, and found the guide waiting for him.

The guide nodded their approval at seeing him. "Much better." They gestured up at the black sky. "I was wondering. Is that your ship up there?"

Marcus tipped his head back to see a tiny, brilliant star pass across the Europan sky. "It is, yes."

"Amazing." The guide brought their head back down. "You must have visited so many worlds."

"A few," Marcus agreed.

The primary borehole to which the guide led him measured half a kilometre in width. Other pilgrims stood near its edge, watching as a platform rose from within its inky depths.

The platform descended the moment they had all stepped onto it. A long-forgotten memory resurfaced in Marcus's mind: the time he'd ridden the New York subway a thousand lifetimes ago, and the lights inside the train carriage had briefly failed. He had that same sense of rushing darkness and closeness.

More than a thousand seconds passed before the platform hit the ocean and kept going, the water flowing up and around the platform's containment field. Down they went: down, down, down, bright haloes of light ringing the platform flashing by in an instant.

Time passed, and sooner than he had expected, the lights of Deep Europa revealed themselves far below. Europans of the gilled variety swam up to meet the visitors as the platform finally came to a halt amidst a vast collection of domes and pressurized structures that stretched as far as he could see.

A curious tension gripped Marcus just then. So much had changed. The Europa he'd known so briefly was ancient history to these people.

Then they were off again, Marcus and his guide boarding an open submersible that carried them past a towering monument to the architects of Deep Europa.

They soon left the city behind, and then came to the Necropolis: a world of drowned graveyards.

"If you'd rather," the guide said, bringing the submersible to a slow halt, "you can go ahead alone. Or I could—?"

"I'll be fine on my own," said Marcus. "It's not my first visit to such places."

"Of course. It's been my pleasure to guide you."

"And to be guided," Marcus responded.

The tension returned, and with it a hollow sensation in the pit of his newly grown body.

It was a long time to wait, to visit an old friend.

The Necropolis' attendees moved here and there through forests of kelp that wreathed info-pillars and other markers designed to help visitors find their way. Marcus allowed one such attendant to lead him to an ancient hydrothermal vent, still, even after so many millennia, disgorging super-heated ash into the surrounding ocean.

And then, at last, he was alone, traversing the narrow

pathways made between tumbled boulders. Here and there, info-pillars displayed images from the earliest centuries of colonisation and the wars that shaped the destiny of the moons of Jupiter.

Much of it, unfortunately, almost hilariously inaccurate. More had been forgotten than he could have anticipated. Perhaps, before he departed, he would donate some of his memories to Europa's archives. As he had told the guide, after all, he went back a long way.

Then, at last, he came to them: the strands of kelp that held each in place had been tended to with care. Each body was further protected by a framework of spun diamond strands shaped into tapering helices. A faint dusting of light around each further betrayed the presence of nanoscale machine attendants.

Chris White and his sister had been placed side by side, Marcus saw. Even after tens of millennia, he had no trouble recognising her.

Cassie.

The one he'd wanted to see the most for this one last time.

Soon, he and his travelling companions would head into the Great Reach, a thousand light-years distant. They did not expect to return.

Reaching out, Marcus—known to some as the Explorer—let his hand slip between the glistening threads of diamond to touch Cassie's.

Then he closed his eyes and heard her call his name from the depths of Medusa. And for a while, they swam together through an ocean in a world that had been reduced to ash and memories aeons before.

What, after all, thought Marcus, is a million years between friends?

ACKNOWLEDGMENTS

The road to completing Europa Deep was a long and arduous one. It passed through three major drafts, each new draft bearing little, if any, resemblance to the one previous.

Thank you to my Patreon supporters, some of whom read and commented on Europa Deep in its earlier drafts: in particular, I'd like to mention John Root, John Woodhouse, Bradley Leu, and Pedro Moura Pinheiro.

Thanks also to Dafydd McKimm and Jeffrey Sloop of the Taipei Science Fiction Writer's Workshop, who provided comments and suggestions during the final stages of writing.

It's inevitable when a book takes this much research that errors creep in. Any such errors are, of course, the fault of the author.

If you enjoyed this book (or even if you didn't) and have time to spare, please take a few moments to write a review. Reviews go a long way to helping other readers find a book they might enjoy. Thank you!

ABOUT THE AUTHOR

Since 2004, Gary Gibson has written seventeen books, mostly for Pan Macmillan. A number have been translated and published around the world, including Russia, Brazil, Germany, and France.

A native of Scotland, he currently lives in Taipei.

Visit www.garygibson.net and sign up for a monthly newsletter with reviews, news and details of upcoming releases, or visit www.patreon.com/garygibson for an advance look at up-and-coming novels, plus articles and essays on publishing and writing.

ALSO BY GARY GIBSON

Made in the USA
Middletown, DE
04 October 2023